ROSIE, THE NOT-SO-FRIENDLY GHOST . . .

I backed up a step. "Stop right there. I am not buying into this."

"Buying into what?"

"You, the T-shirt, this whole thing. You're obviously an illusion."

"You think you're imagining me?"

"Yes, although I can't for the life of me come up with a single reason why."

Rosie propped her butt on the railing and smiled. "Good old Sammy. Still as thick as a plank. It's nice to know some things don't change."

I gave my head a shake, even laughed a little. "Enough is enough," I said, and closed my eyes, honestly expecting her to be gone when I opened them again, forced back into thin air by my refusal to believe. But there she was, sitting on the railing, swinging those damn shoes back and forth, back and forth.

"I don't believe in you," I said. "I don't believe you're here."

"I don't believe *you're* here, either, but that doesn't change a thing, does it." She slid off the railing, sank into a Muskoka chair, and took a sip of my iced tea. "To be honest, I was surprised when I first realized you could see me. You hear about that kind of thing now and then, but I never took it seriously. Then all of a sudden, there you were, mouth open, staring at me like you'd seen a ghost. It's kind of fun, don't you think?"

GETTING RID OF *Rosie*

LYNDA SIMMONS

BERKLEY BOOKS, NEW YORK

THE BERKLEY PUBLISHING GROUP
Published by the Penguin Group
Penguin Group (USA) Inc.
375 Hudson Street, New York, New York 10014, USA
Penguin Group (Canada), 90 Eglinton Avenue East, Suite 700, Toronto, Ontario M4P 2Y3, Canada
(a division of Pearson Penguin Canada Inc.)
Penguin Books Ltd., 80 Strand, London WC2R 0RL, England
Penguin Group Ireland, 25 St. Stephen's Green, Dublin 2, Ireland (a division of Penguin Books Ltd.)
Penguin Group (Australia), 250 Camberwell Road, Camberwell, Victoria 3124, Australia
(a division of Pearson Australia Group Pty. Ltd.)
Penguin Books India Pvt. Ltd., 11 Community Centre, Panchsheel Park, New Delhi—110 017, India
Penguin Group (NZ), 67 Apollo Drive, Rosedale, North Shore 0632, New Zealand
(a division of Pearson New Zealand Ltd.)
Penguin Books (South Africa) (Pty.) Ltd., 24 Sturdee Avenue, Rosebank, Johannesburg 2196,
South Africa

Penguin Books Ltd., Registered Offices: 80 Strand, London WC2R 0RL, England

This book is an original publication of The Berkley Publishing Group.

Cover photograph by Floresco Productions/Getty.
Cover design by Rita Frangie.
Interior text design by Kristin del Rosario.

PRINTING HISTORY
Berkley trade paperback edition / August 2009

Library of Congress Cataloging-in-Publication Data

Simmons, Lynda, 1954–
Getting rid of Rosie / Lynda Simmons. — Berkley trade paperback ed.
p. cm.
ISBN 978-0-425-22792-3
I. Title.
PR9199.4.S547G48 2009
813'.6—dc22
2009013767

PRINTED IN THE UNITED STATES OF AMERICA

10 9 8 7 6 5 4 3 2 1

To girlfriends.
Where would we be without them?

acknowledgments

With special thanks to Shannon, who went to work so I didn't have to; Lindsay, who walked with me uphill both ways to make sure I got it right; and Hedy, who hid out with me until the end—cracking the whip as only she can. And, of course, Sylvia, Cathy, and the fabulous Hamilton bunch: I'm lucky to call you my friends. And as always, love to Lorne, who still believes.

ONE

Picture Michael. Six foot two, dark hair, blue eyes—a classic Irish rogue right down to that sexy half smile I never could resist. It has been a while since I last saw him, eight years to be exact, so I had to look twice to be sure it was indeed Michael Hughes and a buddy checking out the menu in my window. After all, it was Friday morning on the Danforth. The sun was shining, the weekend was coming, and that could have been anyone standing out there, thinking about lunch. Two guys from the bank, a gay couple out shopping, even restaurant critics for one of those Toronto lifestyle magazines. But as much as I might have liked it to be someone else, there was no doubting the way that mouth curved when he spoke to the man beside him, or the way my heart jumped when he raised his head and looked straight at me. Or rather through me. The bugger didn't even notice me standing there behind the bar with a towel on my shoulder and Guinness running all over my hand.

"Damn," I muttered, pushing the draft tap up and trying to maneuver the glass of froth to the sink without making the mess worse.

"Taps are working again, I see."

That was my chef, Eva MacRae—six feet tall, shaved head, and matching dragons tattooed on her upper arms. A big woman, the kind they used to call statuesque before starvation became a look. She grew up in New Germany, Nova Scotia, studied culinary arts in New York and rides a bike to work. A Harley Hugger. "Loud enough for a man, but made for a woman," she always says.

She showed up at the front door of the Silver Swan one night when I was still in the middle of renovations, a refugee from the bistro across the street. "Heard you're looking for someone," she said, then made herself comfortable on my drop sheet and laid out The Rules According to Eva.

One. The wine and beer list would be limited and local, with the exception of Guinness, of course, her nod to the fact that the Silver Swan was an Irish pub.

Two. The menu would be simple and the specials would change daily, based on whatever was fresh at the market that morning.

And three. We would not be limited to Irish cuisine, but neither would we follow trends. And above all, we would never use the words *fusion food* in her presence.

Then she handed me a résumé, pointed out that she came complete with her own knives, herb garden, and intimate knowledge of the best vendors at the St. Lawrence Market, and said that if I didn't hire her on the spot, she was catching the next bus to Calgary.

After six years in finance, I am well aware that the key to running a successful business is knowing when to hold on to power and when to gracefully delegate.

"Welcome aboard," I said and handed her a paint roller.

After only eight weeks of operation, I'm pleased to report that the Swan has been mentioned by one radio talk-show host and in two daily newspapers, one going so far as to label us "the spot to watch on the Danforth." While the reviews have yet to translate into crowds, Eva's Friday chowders have already developed a following, and her former boss at the bistro still doesn't speak to me. I take that as a good sign because the guy couldn't resist dropping by almost daily before that, just to give me a condescending "atta girl" and smile at my definition of a pub. Just because he's never seen a pub without a big screen TV or ten-cent wing night means nothing. A classy pub is not an oxymoron. And this city is ready for one. I'm sure of it. Most of the time, anyway.

Eva never did say why she left that job, and I don't care enough to push. We aren't girlfriends, after all, just co-workers, and I have always believed that secrets should stay that way on the job. Which is why I wasn't about to tell her anything about the man at the window, despite the fact that she was standing there with a lemon cheesecake in one hand, a chocolate mousse in the other, and something close to a smile on her face, which is not at all her usual prelunch expression.

"It's the damn draft line again," I said. "A little gas in the tube and the stuff goes everywhere. I should put a couple of foam protectors on the kegs."

"Yes indeed. Nothing like a foam protector to stop a girl from noticing a couple of hot guys at the window."

Not only is Eva a fabulous chef, she's also a brutally honest one, making her a pain to work with much of the time.

"The one on the right's not bad at all," she said and glanced over at me. "What do you think?"

Michael was, of course, the one on the right.

"I hadn't noticed," I said, telling myself to stop being an idiot and just breathe, something I might have managed had he and his friend not stepped back from the window and approached the front door.

"Want me to wave them in?" Eva asked.

"No," I said too quickly, adding, "we're not ready yet," when her smile broadened.

"Suit yourself," she said, and mercifully continued on with her cakes to the dessert case at the end of the bar.

Like everything connected to the kitchen, the dessert case is strictly Eva's territory, ensuring proper cheesecake alignment at all times. Apparently, above the pies but below the tortes makes for maximum impact. I trust her on this. Studies have been done, after all.

Michael hesitated at my front door, and for a moment I thought he might walk back into my life as smoothly as he'd walked out. But he was only slowing down to pull a cell phone from his pocket. He didn't even glance inside, just kept right on walking after he answered it, which wasn't surprising. Good reviews aside, the Silver Swan is still just another hole in the wall on the Danforth, the kind of place that's easy to dismiss unless you're trapped by one of us waving you in, or you saw that bit in the paper or heard about us from the friend of a friend of a friend. The odds of a person stopping to read the menu and then deciding to come through the door are twenty to one. I know because I counted one day last week, when we were sitting around with twelve empty tables and four trays of magnificent beef pies congealing in the kitchen.

Truth is, no one understands why I left a great job in finance to open a restaurant, and there are plenty of days when I don't either. Starting the Swan was a huge risk, taking every cent I had and leaving me deeper in debt than I had been after graduation. But six months ago, with my thirtieth birthday looming, it seemed like it was time for a change.

When I walked through that front door, I knew the renovations would cost a fortune, there would never be room for more than a dozen tables, and Irish fiddle music is not the reason people come to Greek Town. But somehow the space was right for me, exactly the kind of place I'd dreamed of owning since the summer Michael took me to Ireland to meet his granny.

We spent three weeks there that year, exploring narrow country roads by day, each other by night. We were young and in love, and it was there in a squeaky bed at the Castleknock Inn in Killarney that we decided to open a place of our own in Toronto. A small, comfortable pub like the one at the inn, serving local beer and great grub to a cast of regulars who wouldn't miss a night to save their souls.

Sam's Place, Michael wanted to call it, after me, Samantha Marcello, the fool who believed it really could happen. Just like I believed we were going to stand up in church later that same summer and say *I do* to spending the rest of our lives together.

Michael and his friend disappeared from view and I went back to rinsing the beer glass, telling myself it was better this way. A reunion could only be awkward at best. Still, it might have been interesting to see him up close. Find out if he was going bald in the back, putting on a little weight around the middle, all the things that make seeing an old flame worthwhile.

Finished with her cakes, Eva opened the front door and propped it with a rock she picked up that morning. "Nothing says, *come in* like an open door," she said.

While I hadn't included door positioning in my original business plan, I was willing to play along as the sounds of the street drifted in on a delicate swirl of dust. The Danforth had been coming to life when I arrived at six that morning, and now traffic was humming and the temperature was climbing, inviting me to come outside, take a break before the lunch hour started. Maybe find out where Michael finally stopped, discover what kind of food he was eating these days.

"Is the sandwich board ready to go outside?" I called to Eva.

"Ask Johnny. Last I saw, he was trying to figure out how to shorten *Wilde Boar Terrine with Red Onion Marmalade on Bed of*

Rocket Salad down to something snappier. I told him to forget it, but you know our Johnny."

Our Johnny is cute, twenty-one, and an actor in waiting. He dreams of playing Hamlet and Macbeth in Stratford one day, and he made it clear when I hired him that when his big break comes, he'll be gone faster than you can say *To thine own self be true*. While I would never wish him ill, I'm glad the big break hasn't come yet because he's good with the customers, he keeps the daily specials straight, and I have yet to meet a man who looks better in a fitted white shirt and tight black pants than our Johnny.

"He should leave well enough alone," Eva said on her way to the ladies' room. "And quit leaving roses in my fridge."

Our Johnny also has an unfortunate crush on Eva, one that is destined to leave him heartbroken. His attempts at courtship are both interesting and embarrassing to watch, but he's a smart kid and I have every confidence that youthful optimism will give way to adult cynicism any day now. It's part of growing up, and despite those big brown eyes, our Johnny isn't a little boy anymore.

"Tell him to quit farting around and get that sign out there," Eva said and slammed the bathroom door shut behind her just as Johnny came out of the kitchen with the sandwich board.

He grinned and held it up for me. "*Wild Pig in a Rocket*. What do you think?"

"I think Eva will kill you. Give me the chalk."

He let the swinging door close behind him and relinquished the stick with a sigh. "She's a hard woman," he said and wandered off to finish setting tables.

"He may be starting to lose interest," I whispered when Eva came out of the ladies' room.

"It's about time. I can't take any more love poems on my windshield."

I followed her into the kitchen. "He leaves you love poems?"

She lifted the lid on her Friday chowder. "Twice in the last week. The boy is hopeless. And this needs salt."

Personally, I'd found her soup perfect when I helped myself to a sample earlier, but unlike Johnny, I knew enough to keep my opinions to myself. Besides, her soup keeps bringing people back for more, so what do I know?

Taking advantage of her preoccupation with the salt, I went back out to the dining room and changed *Wild Pig in a Rocket* to Eva's more precise, if long-winded version. Johnny moved slowly among the tables, sighing and dropping silver onto the placemats, his face dark with the pain of thwarted creativity and unrequited love.

I thought about telling him to stop putting his faith in old-fashioned romantic gestures, clue him in to the fact that poetry and roses won't work on a woman like Eva, but I didn't know how to tell him without letting on that we'd been talking about him. So I left him to take out his frustrations on the silverware and hauled the sandwich board out to the street myself.

It was only early June, but already the sun was warm on my skin and the air sweet with the first real promise of summer, which meant only one thing: Patio time was on the way. Soon, the Danforth would blossom with brightly colored umbrellas and plastic tables and chairs. The pace would slow and night would fall softly. People would linger over glasses of wine and mugs of draft, laughing and talking and searching for love while music floated from every open doorway: bouzoukis, violins, and good Irish ballads all blending together, creating something new and fleeting, heard only in the summer.

I forgot all about looking for Michael and was busy calculating the cost of my own patio when I saw them coming back toward me—Michael Hughes and friend, deep in conversation, completely mindless of the woman not ten feet away. They stopped in front of the Swan, and his friend went inside. Michael finally glanced my way, nodded absently, and turned to follow his buddy through the door, but he didn't make it that far. He paused and slowly looked back over his shoulder.

"Sam?" he said.

"None other." I smiled and automatically lifted a hand to my hair, hating that it mattered how I looked and certain that *frazzle*d was the best I could hope for, since I'd last checked a mirror at six that morning.

Naturally, he looked even better close up. Trendy without trying too hard in blue jeans and a leather jacket. A little thinner than I remembered, with features more angular than they used to be. Sadly, the pretty boy had grown into a handsome man. No bald spot, no paunch, nothing rewarding at all.

He came toward me. "It's great to see you."

He sounded genuine enough, as though he really was glad to see me. "You too," I said, wondering why I couldn't be as genuine. "What brings you here?"

"My brother."

So that's who the friend was. His older brother, Donald. Or was it Darrin?

"Derek has it on good advice that we have to try this place."

Derek, that was it. He had been away at school most of the time while Michael and I were dating. I saw him three, maybe four times, but he was a nice guy as I recalled, and smart too. Planned to be an engineer of some kind.

"Do you work here?" Michael asked.

"It's my place," I told him and watched his smile widen.

He shook his head with what I swear was a look of admiration. "You did it then. That's fabulous, Sam. Really fabulous."

We stood there smiling at each other for a few agonizingly long seconds. There seemed to be nothing to say because there was too much to say. I was dying to ask about his life, his work, and whether he was as miserable as I'd always imagined. But mostly I wanted to ask about his wife, about Rosie. The woman who used to be my best friend.

How is the bitch? I wanted to say. *Still conniving and manipulative? And is she fat yet?*

God I hoped so, and I hoped she had a dozen kids too, all of them clinging to her sweatpants and wiping their noses on her knees. Of course, it would have been rude to ask, so I settled for, "Will you be joining your brother?" to which Michael said, "Yes, of course," and let me precede him into the pub. Ever the gentleman.

Derek waved from the table by the window, then smiled and got to his feet. "Samantha Marcello? I don't believe it."

And I didn't believe he remembered me, considering how little we had seen of each other. He was shorter than Michael, stockier too, but their coloring was the same. He also sported jeans, but without the leather jacket, opting instead for a McGill sweatshirt that had seen better days. Neither trendy nor trying. Just going for comfort, I'd say. While he had never been as good looking as Michael, he did have a nice smile, now that I took the time to notice.

"Good to see you, Derek," I said, accepting the light hug he gave me.

"This is Sam's place," Michael told him. "And I'm hoping she'll join us for a moment."

"I really shouldn't . . ."

"Of course you should," Derek said. "It's not often we get to sit with the owner of a hot new restaurant."

I laughed. "Hot, according to whom?"

"The old man at the fruit market," Derek said. "He's the reason we came back. He stopped us on our way by and asked why we were wasting our time checking out menus. 'You don't read about food, you experience it,' he said. Then he swore you had the best fish chowder in town, but only on Friday. If we didn't try it today, we'd have to wait another week for the chance, so here we are. He's very persuasive. Has he been on your payroll awhile?"

I laughed again. "About two weeks. I pay him in soup."

"He's worth every drop. How long have you been open?"

"Eight weeks tomorrow."

"An eternity in the food business. You must be doing something right." Derek motioned to his chair. "Here, take my seat. I'll grab a beer at the bar and give you two a little time to catch up."

I shook my head. "I don't know."

"Please, Sam," Michael said softly, and that was my undoing.

I sat. I smiled. I even told Johnny to bring coffee. I just didn't know why. There was nothing to catch up on, nothing to talk about except the obvious. So I figured fine, get it over with, and I jumped in. "How's Rosie?" I asked.

"Rosie's dead," Michael said.

My hand stilled on the way to the sugar. "What?"

"A car accident, two years ago."

That hand found its way to his all on its own, I swear. "Oh Michael, I'm sorry."

"It was a shock." He looked down at my fingers covering his, but made no move to pull away. "We're getting on with it though, Julie and me."

My fingers curled back. "Julie?"

"My daughter."

Of course. How could I have been so dense?

He reached into his jacket pocket and pulled out his wallet. "She's seven now. Looks just like her mother."

"Lucky girl," I said, taking the picture he offered.

She did look like Rosie, with the same blond hair and delicate features that had taken her mother anywhere she wanted to go, but she was younger than Rosie had been the first time I saw her.

I'll never forget watching her walk into Sister Teresa's sixth grade class at Our Lady of Victories Elementary School. Rosemary Louise Fisk, with all the wrong clothes and hair so short she looked like a boy. The kind of girl who should have instantly become the new target and made my life easier. But there was something about the way she moved, with her chin lifted and her shoulders back, looking each one of us straight in the eye as she passed, that held the giggles in check and made the boys move their feet out of her way. She could have sat anywhere, could have picked anyone to be her friend, but for some reason she took the desk next to mine.

We were nothing alike, Rosie and I, yet we ended up being inseparable all the way through high school. When I went away to university, we talked on the phone at least once a week, and Rosie's was always the first number I called when I came home. Which is why I wasn't surprised to find out she'd been calling since five A.M. on the day Michael and I were expected back from Ireland. Seemed she had something to tell me. Something big.

I didn't think twice. Just dropped everything and told her to come right over. Rosie was blubbering all over the place when I opened the front door. She managed to choke out the word *pregnant;* then she started weeping so hard, I couldn't make out a thing she was saying.

"Rosie, calm down. Who did you say the father was?"

"Michael," she whispered.

I drew my head back. "The guy at your uncle's hardware store? Jesus, Rosie, he has to be fifty at least."

"Not *that* Michael. *Your* Michael. Michael Hughes."

I stared at her, speechless. That will happen when you stop breathing. But instead of thumping me on the back or calling 911, she took my silence as a sign to continue.

"Believe me, Marcello, I'm as surprised as you," she said and sat back with the cup of tea I'd made her, more her usual self now that the tough part was out of the way. "We still haven't decided what to do yet."

We? I thought, still trying to suck in a breath.

She wiped her nose on a napkin and picked up one of the shortbreads I'd set out for her. "He wants to do the honorable thing, of course, which is so like him it makes me laugh. I haven't told anyone at home yet. I can only imagine how that will go over."

My breath came back in a rush. "Hold on. What do you mean, honorable? Honorable, how?"

She blinked her stupid cow eyes at me. "Honorable as in marrying me. What did you think?"

"Oh, I don't know. Maybe that he's my fiancé? That I'm the one with the ring."

I held up my hand in case she needed reminding, and the diamond sparkled for emphasis. Such a lovely thing it was too. A quarter-carat solitaire presented to me on Valentine's Day in the revolving restaurant at the top of the CN Tower. Like our Johnny, Michael was also a born romantic. Champagne, candlelight, a single rose by my plate, he didn't miss a trick. And as soon as the waiter had cleared away the main course, the love of my life got down on one knee and took my left hand in his.

When I said yes, the whole place exploded with applause. The waiter brought strawberries dipped in chocolate and all around us people kept saying "Congratulations" and "Good luck." I even cried, which surprised both of us because I have never been a crier. Except at that movie with the two dogs and the cat who find their way home. That one works every time.

But I didn't cry when Rosie told me the big news. Or while she sat there on my grandmother's floral couch, going on and on about being sorry, and how things had just happened, and couldn't we still be friends? I didn't even cry later when Michael admitted to sleeping with her.

"It was just the once," he told me. "I had a bad week at work, you changed your mind about coming home for the weekend—"

"I had exams."

"I didn't say it was your fault. It was just a moment of—"

"Of what, Michael? Lust? Passion?"

"Weakness. It was a moment of weakness."

I laughed a little. "And now she's pregnant. What are the odds?" Then I smacked him, hard, right across the face. "You are such an idiot."

He nodded and rubbed his cheek, looking sad and bewildered and lost enough to make me feel sorry for him. It had been just the once, after all. And anyone could make a mistake. Hadn't I kissed that guy at school last year? Ryan, who was studying to be a doctor but was good-looking enough to be on TV. I kissed him on the last day of the semester, went home to Michael, and never said a word about it to anyone. That was kind of the same, wasn't it? Only neither of us had been naked, so I guess it wasn't even close. Nevertheless, I was ready to forgive Michael, to work things out, to find a way because love conquers all, right?

I took his hand, held it in both of mine. "What do we do now?"

"There's only one thing I *can* do."

I nodded in sympathy. "How much do you think she'll want?"

"Who?"

"Rosie, of course. You don't earn much now, but who knows what you're capable of in the future." That was when my business training kicked in, running full speed ahead, taking us to the only clear, the only logical conclusion possible. "You should nail down an agreement now," I said. "One that spells everything out clearly. Support payments, regular increases, education allowances. And make sure she has independent legal advice. We don't need this cropping up to bite us on the ass in five years. Will you want visitation rights? Wait, forget that. Of course you will, so it's better to hammer those out too before the baby is born." I smiled and held his hand tighter. "Do you have a good lawyer, honey?"

"Sam," he said softly, "I don't want visitation rights."

I tried not to look relieved. "I understand completely."

"No, I don't think you do." He paused and all I could hear was Rosie's voice inside my head. *He wants to do the honorable thing, of course.*

I'd assumed it was wishful thinking, pipe dreaming, the kind of thing every single pregnant woman thinks about. I never believed for a moment that he would squeeze my hand, look me in the eye and say:

"I have no choice. I have to marry Rosie."

"What are you talking about? This isn't the nineteenth century. You don't have to marry anybody, even if she does have friends who work for questionable people. There are laws to protect you—"

"Samantha, I don't want to be protected. I want to be a father to my child. A real father."

I had to stand up, walk around. "You don't have to marry Rosie to be a father to your child."

"If I want to be there every day for him I do."

I realized then that the concept of an Honorable Man was highly overrated.

"Sam, believe me, you're the one I love," Michael said.

Yet Rosie was the one he married six weeks later at city hall. I'd heard they had a daughter, but had never known her name until now. Julie, who looked just like her mother.

My fingers were tingling when I handed him back the picture. "I don't know what to say. I'm so sorry."

"Me too." He ran a thumb over the snapshot, then slid it back inside his wallet. "Let's talk about you, instead. How did you come to own this place?"

We talked for a few minutes longer, about the career in finance that I'd left behind, the challenges of the restaurant business these days. Nothing of any consequence, nothing that mattered. How could anything I had to say possibly match the news he had dropped on me? Rosie dead and Michael a single father. It was too much to take in.

"What are you up to now, then?" I asked, tired of talking about myself.

"Derek wants me to move back to the city. Leave my contracting business behind and join his. He does custom homes, renovations, the same kind of work I do. He's restoring one of those old semi-detached houses over on Fenwick near McConnell for himself right now, and Julie and I stay with him whenever we're in the city. It always was a great neighborhood and we did take a look at a couple properties in the area, but I'm still not convinced that moving is a good idea."

"It's not a good idea," Derek called. "It's a great one. Especially since he's currently living way up north in the middle of nowhere."

Michael laughed. "Huntsville is hardly the middle of nowhere. Sam knows how great it is up there, don't you, Sam?"

He probably thought so, considering the number of summers Rosie and I spent at church camp up on Little Doe Lake when we were kids. Lumpy mashed potatoes, tabernacle twice a day, and mosquitoes so thick you had to breathe through your teeth when you ran to the outhouse. Had I never told him how much I hated the place? That I only went because of Rosie?

"Sorry, Michael," I said, "but I'm not the person to ask. I haven't been north of Barrie in years."

"Then you don't know what you're missing. Huntsville has really grown. We have everything the Danforth has now. Shops, pubs, even a literary festival. Plus there's a lake you can actually swim in and plenty of open countryside." He looked over at Derek. "How could I ever duplicate what I have up there on a fifty-foot lot in the city?"

"Thirty-foot," Derek said, dragging over a chair from a neighboring table and joining us at last. "And you don't try to duplicate anything. You keep the place up north and you find something modern and compact here where Julie can have cable TV, and high-speed Internet, and all the other things kids need." He turned to me. "You tell him."

"I never could tell him anything."

Michael laid a hand on mine. "Only because I wasn't ready to listen. But things change."

His fingers were warm and strong, his smile wide and bright. And for the first time in years, I found myself thinking about second chances. Wondering if all the hurt and the pain could simply melt away and we could start over again, fresh and new. Michael and Sam, Sam and Michael, the golden couple with everything ahead of them.

Then that warm spring breeze swept through the Swan again, picking up all of my silly romantic notions and carrying them back out to the street where they belonged. As my Nona Marcello always says, life doesn't go backward. And going forward with Michael wasn't something I'd wanted for a very long time.

"Welcome to the Swan," I heard Johnny say. "Table for three?"

I pushed back the chair. "I should get back to work."

Michael rose with me, then drew a business card from his jacket pocket. "I'd like to see you again, Sam. A drink, maybe dinner. Whatever you're up for." He pressed the card into my hand. "I've thought about you a lot over the years. Wondered where you were, what you were doing. I'd love a chance to really sit and talk for a while, but if you decide to throw that card away and never speak to me again, I'll certainly understand."

He caught me off guard. A date with Michael was the last thing I'd expected, the last thing I needed, yet I had no snappy comeback, no comeback at all because the only thought in my head was *Why*? Why had I been on his mind all these years? Why should it matter now? And why was I starting to sweat?

The room was suddenly too warm, too close. I needed the bar, the kitchen, things that were familiar and predictable. Things that wouldn't shift and sway and fall out from under me when I least expected it. "I'll think about it," I said, shoving the card into my shirt pocket.

"I'll wait to hear from you."

I nodded and turned to Derek. "Good luck getting him to move."

He rose and stood beside Michael, an odd expression on his face, as though he were trying to figure something out. "I'm feeling optimistic."

The breeze blew another couple into the Swan, with four guys following close behind. I pointed to the kitchen. "Lunch hour. Gotta run." I backed away, bumping into a chair and jostling a couple of tables before finally turning and walking back to the bar on shaky legs. On safe ground again, I took a deep breath, put on my apron, and tried not to fumble with the strings.

Johnny grinned and pulled a couple of beers. "Well, look who's all pink and fluttery."

"I am never fluttery." I willed my fingers to tie something resembling a bow, then calmly blew the hair out of my face and took my rightful place behind the taps. "What do you need?"

"Six Guinness." He got down two more glasses. "Who are those guys anyway?"

"Just an old flame and his brother. You should find out what they're having."

"Unfortunately we're leaving," Derek said. He stood on the other side of the bar, watching me with that same odd look on his face. "Michael got an emergency call." He jerked his thumb toward the front door. Michael was outside, pacing back and forth, and talking on his cell phone. "The local kids have the day off from school," Derek continued. "Julie was playing with the next-door neighbor's daughter and apparently there was an accident with the swings in the yard."

I handed the glass of beer off to Johnny. "Nothing serious, I hope."

"She fell and the swing bopped her on the head. She's fine but shaken up a little, and I know he's going to want to go and pick her up."

"Understandable. I'm only sorry you didn't get to try the food. Maybe we'll see you in here again soon."

"I'm hoping you'll see Michael very soon. Like tonight, for instance."

"I beg your pardon?"

Derek glanced at the door, then leaned closer and spoke quickly. "I know this must seem strange to you, and I know it's sudden, but I haven't seen my brother this happy, this animated since Rosie died. And I'm convinced it's because he found you again. If you'll just agree to go out with him—"

"Wait a minute—"

"Sam, I've been waiting two years as it is. Ever since Rosie died I've been watching him close himself off further and further from friends and family. He doesn't go out, doesn't meet people, and he's only dated a few women in all that time. That's why I want him to move down here, join me in the business, start living again. I've only got him for a few days, but I honestly think you can help turn him around."

I held up my hands. "Sorry, Derek, but I see no point in revisiting the past."

Johnny nudged me. "You might want to reconsider. Sometimes love works out better the second time around."

I turned on him. "Don't you have an order to deliver?"

"She's worried because he left her at the altar," Derek said.

Johnny's eyes widened. "Are you serious?"

"He did not leave me at the altar—"

"You were engaged?" Eva asked.

"It was a long time ago. What are you doing out here anyway?"

She held up a quart of orange juice. "Experimenting." She turned to Derek. "How come he dumped her?"

"He got her best friend pregnant and had to marry her."

"You mean the Rosie person you were talking about? The one who's dead now?" Johnny had obviously been eavesdropping, something I appreciated when the target wasn't me. His mouth opened wide. He covered it with a hand. "Oh my God, she was your friend?"

"This is none of your business," I said to him, then looked back at Derek. "Will you stop?"

Eva squinted at Michael through the window. "Funny. I wouldn't have taken him for a jerk."

"He's not," Derek said. "He's a nice guy. Just stupid sometimes."

"What guy isn't?" Johnny asked.

"Can we get back to work here?" I said.

Eva headed back to the kitchen. "That whole altar thing must have been a bitch, but it explains a lot."

"Explains what?" I asked. "What are you talking about?"

"The fact that you're not getting any."

"What? Why would you think such a thing?"

She paused at the swinging door and looked back at me. "Because you're always here working and no men ever come to see you or pick you up or anything at all. Ergo, you're a practicing celibate."

"Ergo, you're jumping to conclusions. I simply prefer to keep my private life private."

Eva glanced over at Derek. "She's not getting any."

"Neither is he," Derek said.

Johnny sighed. "It's all so sad."

"Okay, that's it. Everybody back to work."

I waited until Eva and Johnny were safely in the kitchen, then leaned over the counter and whispered to Derek, "Why are you doing this?"

"Doing what?"

"Being so obnoxious."

"I was just telling the truth. And I'm sure your waiter would love to hear about the way you got the ring back to him."

"Don't you dare."

He put a hand over his heart. "Sam, I promise I'll take it to the grave if you just go out with Michael. We're not talking a commitment here, just a drink, a chance to talk. Think of it as your good deed for the day."

"I don't have time for good deeds," I said, but couldn't stop myself from turning to watch Michael through the window. Was it empathy that drew me around? A natural response to a cry for help? Or was it something else? Something deeper, something pathetic that would need months of therapy to work through?

Empathy, I decided, because not only was it easier and cheaper, it also explained the very real tug of sadness I felt in seeing him out there, still pacing back and forth, phone pressed to his ear, trying to comfort his little girl, little Julie. He was probably a wonderful father. Patient, devoted. The kind who would knock himself out day after day trying to be both mother and father, and would end up spoiling the kid rotten if he didn't let go of the sadness, didn't start living again. Maybe Derek had a point. Maybe a good deed was exactly what was needed. Besides, what harm could it do to have a drink with an old flame? Might even be fun to catch up, talk about old times and all that. It wasn't like there was anyone around to be jealous, anyone that either of us had to call and talk to first.

While I hadn't spent the past eight years mooning over Michael, I hadn't had a serious long-term relationship either. I'd meet a man and things would go well for a while, but then a few months into it, the restlessness would start again. I'd find myself looking around, checking out alternatives, and eventually moving on. I hadn't bothered to analyze the *whys* or the *hows* because frankly I didn't care. I was enjoying myself, although I have to admit this last year had seen a definite drop in numbers. Ever since I started planning the Swan, come to think of it. Got lost in the work, I guess. Forgot how to have fun. But I wouldn't call myself a practicing celibate. An unintentional one, perhaps, which was completely different. Not that sex would be part of my good deed. My duties would end at the bar.

I turned back to Derek. "Fine, I'll have a drink with him."

"And maybe dinner?"

"And maybe dinner."

"And a movie afterward?"

"Don't push it."

"Sorry." Derek lifted a takeout menu from the holder and laid it on the bar in front of me with a pen. "Write down your number, your cell phone number. That way he'll know you're serious when you take it out to him."

I scribbled my number beneath the Swan's. "But he's still on the phone."

"He'll be off soon." Derek picked up the menu and hustled me toward the door.

I hesitated on the threshold and glanced back at him. "I feel ridiculous."

"You look beautiful." He smiled when I raised an eyebrow. "You really do. Better than ever, in fact."

"Thanks. You're looking pretty good yourself."

"It comes of living wrong." He handed me the menu. "You really are doing a good thing, Samantha."

"I hope you're right."

The frown left Michael's forehead when he spotted me coming toward him, and I tried not to smile, not be ridiculously pleased. Then again, if a good deed feeds the soul, then mine was simply getting to the buffet early, an overachiever as usual.

"I have to go now, honey," he said, "but I'll be there soon. Love you too. Bye-bye." He tucked the BlackBerry back into his pocket. "That was Julie. I'm afraid—"

"Derek told me. I'm just glad she's all right." We stood there again, staring awkwardly at each other, and I would have chickened out if Derek hadn't come through the door.

"You want to get going?" he asked Michael.

"Yes, thanks."

"See you again, Sam," Derek said, giving me a quick wink behind Michael's back.

"I hope so," Michael said, and the menu weighed heavy in my hand.

I held it out to him. "Actually, I wanted to give you this. My cell phone number is on it." I took a quick breath and smiled with renewed purpose. Who knew philanthropy could be this difficult? "I'd love to have dinner with you."

Michael's face lit up with the same brightness I'd seen earlier. "Tonight?" he asked.

I laughed. "Sure."

He glanced down at the menu. "I'll call you then. To arrange a time."

"Sounds good."

He laughed and tucked the menu into his pocket with the phone. "Till tonight, then."

"You coming?" Derek called from the passenger side of a brand-new black Lexus parked at the curb. Home building in Huntsville had obviously been good to Michael. "I'll walk with you," I said, pleased with myself and my decision. He did look happy, and I didn't care that I couldn't wipe the smile from my own face either.

I waited while he started the car and pulled away from the curb. Derek gave me a thumbs-up. I raised my hand to wave and noticed someone sitting up in the backseat. A woman with blond hair and a narrow face.

My hand stilled midwave. It couldn't be.

I blinked and checked again. There was no denying it .

That could only be Rosie in the backseat, smiling broadly and giving me the finger.

TWO

I was still standing by the curb long after Michael's car had been swallowed up by the traffic, trying to make sense of what I'd seen. Granted, Rosie and I had been horror fans for years. Lining up to see all the latest monster flicks and trying to persuade those around us that Amityville would be the perfect spot for a family vacation. But even back then I never lost any sleep wondering if the stories were real.

By the tender age of ten, I'd figured out that if the dead really did roam the earth looking to suck the blood of the living or take back their golden arms or anything else they'd left behind, there would have been ghoul squads out in force every night and my grandmother would have put garlic and a wooden stake under my pillow, just to be sure. The fact is, no matter how much I loved those stories, there was simply no good reason to believe that any of them were real.

So how then was a lifelong skeptic, an unrepentant nonbeliever in the paranormal, supposed to explain Rosie in the backseat? A mirage perhaps? A trick of light and shadow? Or was she something more sinister, something my own mind had conjured up out of some long-buried need for revenge? Then again, if I created her, why would I have her give me the finger? How much better would it have been to see her looking terrified, scared to death to discover that Samantha Marcello was back on the scene. But could someone already dead look scared to death?

There were too many questions and not enough answers. The only thing I knew for certain was that I had seen Rosie in that car. Or a woman who looked like Rosie. Could have been someone else. Come to think of it, Rosie did have a younger sister, Marcie, who also had blond hair and had been just as comfortable in the backseats of cars as her big sister. If Marcie had lost about fifty pounds over the last eight years, then that very well could have been her waiting for Michael and Derek to come back. But why would they have left her there? Seemed awfully cruel to go for lunch and leave the former fat girl alone in the car. Not at all the behavior of an Honorable Man.

Or was the sighting something else entirely? Did Rosie represent the onset of some rare and undoubtedly incurable neurological disorder brought on by years of drinking city water, inhaling exhaust fumes, eating junk food and—

"We have a lunch hour going on in here, in case you're interested."

I turned to see Eva waiting in the doorway of the Swan, arms crossed, dragons twitching. I jogged back to the pub. "Sorry, I got distracted."

She made no move to let me pass. "Are you going out with him?"

Rosie aside, I couldn't stop that smile from coming back, and I realized I was genuinely pleased with the idea of seeing Michael again. *Just feeding the soul*, I told myself, but to Eva I said, "We're getting together later tonight."

"Good," she said, the dragons relaxing when she lowered her arms.

"I guess." She turned to go back inside but I checked the street before following her, wondering if talking about Michael had conjured Rosie up again. Brought her back as a meter maid or a teller at the bank, or the driver of that blue SUV. The one that was moving too slowly, almost coming to a stop right outside the Swan. But the face wasn't hers, and neither were any of the others. Maybe Rosie had been an isolated hallucination, a momentary lapse. Or maybe it had been Marcie after all.

"Sam?" Eva asked.

"Hm?"

"Are you nervous?"

I shrugged. "Maybe a little, why?"

"Because you look pale, like something's got you spooked."

Spooked? That was one way of putting it. Although if Rosie hadn't been a hallucination, and I really had seen Marcie in that car, then maybe I had nothing to worry about at all. Maybe I was fine. Maybe—

"Sam, for God's sake, what's wrong with you?"

I shook my head. "Nothing. I just hope it was Marcie, that's all."

"Who's Marcie?"

I hesitated. Should I tell Eva what I'd seen? Talk it over with someone instead of driving myself crazy, wondering if I was crazy? "You won't believe this," I said and laughed a little, to prove that I didn't take any of what I was about to say seriously. "I saw the strangest thing in Michael's car."

Johnny stuck his head over Eva's shoulder. "It can't possibly be any stranger than what's going on in here. Why, just moments ago I saw a waiter dishing up his own order because the chef had left her post. Buggered off in the middle of lunch hour. It was positively frightening."

"I've been gone five minutes," Eva said.

He gave her a sultry look. "Six, but if you're very good, I'm prepared to forgive you later. Right now, however, I need another order of Wild Pig pronto."

"It's boar, much like yourself."

"Sweet talker," he said and was gone.

Eva watched him walk back to the bar. "I should jump that kid's bones next time he's in the kitchen. Just to show him what he's up against."

"Later," I said and nudged her into the pub. "Right now, I need him in one piece."

Eva went back to the kitchen and I drew in a deep breath, glad that I hadn't told her about Rosie after all. She would have had questions; I wouldn't have had answers. It could only have been messy. Better to wait until I had more time to think about it.

Stepping into the Swan, I took a quick look around. When had all the people arrived? The place was almost full, with the ladies at table three waving an empty wine bottle at Johnny while the guys at table six called for another pitcher. Who knew Wild Pig would draw a crowd? Or maybe it was the old man at the fruit market again, drumming up business for the nice Italian girl. Either way, Eva hadn't been kidding. We were definitely having a lunch hour.

Three more men came through the door. The one in the lead pointed to the table still calling for another pitcher. "We're with that bunch over there."

I handed them menus. "Looks like a party."

He smiled. "We signed our biggest single contract an hour ago. We eat again."

I knew that feeling well. "Congratulations. The next pitcher is on me."

Hurrying to the bar, I grinned at Johnny and reached for a jug. "This has to be a record crowd."

"It's about time." He banged two old-fashioned glasses down on the bar, dropped in some ice, and poured shots from the bottle of Canadian Club. "So are you going out with Michael?"

I glanced over at him, wondering how my personal life had gone from private to public in a matter of minutes.

"We're having dinner," I said, the smile creeping back and settling into place like it belonged there. "It's my good deed for the day."

"Okay, we'll call it that," he said, "But right now there are three things you need to know about this lunch hour. First, we're running low on Wild Pig. Second, bangers and mash need a push. And three, your grandmother has landed again." He slid the old-fashioned glasses toward me. "I need ginger ale for these and two glasses of white."

I went to the fridge for the wine. "Loretta's here?"

"You didn't notice a change in the music?"

I hadn't, but then again, I'd been thinking about Michael and ghosts and a shortage of Wild Pig. Now that I listened, I wondered how I could have missed the distinctive sound of Frank Sinatra singing "That Old Black Magic."

"You really should start locking the back door again," Johnny said.

"It *was* locked." I poured the wine and took another quick look around while I shot ginger ale into two carafes. "Where is she?"

"In the kitchen."

I froze. "Eva just went in there."

At sixty-eight, my Nona Marcello, who insists on being called Loretta because it makes her feel younger, still grows her own vegetables, bench-presses one hundred pounds, and can run farther than anyone else I know.

"A real Clydesdale," her marathon trainer calls her, meaning a big, strong woman built for the long haul. The kind who doesn't know how or when to quit, which is why she can't stay away from the Swan. For all that she likes to think of herself as progressive, Loretta will never understand why a nice Italian girl needs an Irish pub. A cozy pasta place, a chic Italian bistro, even an upscale pizza parlor. But an Irish pub?

She figures I'm suffering some sort of identity crisis, so she keeps a candle burning at St. Catherine's, leaves cannoli on my doorstep, and tries to bring me back to my roots by sneaking Old Blue Eyes and Dean Martin into my CD player as often as possible. And as long as she's at my stupid restaurant anyway, she might as well make a few suggestions in the kitchen, right? Even an Irish pub needs standards, after all.

Every time she comes, she leaves behind a recipe for something: minestrone, chicken cacciatore, anything Italian. She loves me and she means well, so I keep the recipes in a binder under the bar, but I never push Eva to look at them, and I try to make sure Loretta stays out of the kitchen when Eva's working.

I pushed Eject on the CD player and plugged in the Irish Rovers. "I'll get her out of there now."

"Don't worry about it," Johnny said. "Eva put her to work doing dishes or something."

"Eva encouraged her to stay?"

Johnny shrugged and hoisted the tray. "She needed help and Loretta was there. It made sense at the time. Just think positively. Everything's going to be fine. We don't have time for it to be anything else."

He had a point. The guys at table six were getting impatient for their beer, another couple was at the door, and three more ladies were reading the menu in the window. An extra body in the kitchen right now could only be a good thing, right?

Hoping for the best, I delivered beer and wine, seated our new guests, and was back at the bar pouring drinks when my grandmother came through the swinging door from the kitchen, all sweaty and beaming, obviously having a hell of a good time.

"*Ciao, bella.*" She brushed a kiss on my cheek and scooped up a handful of olives from the condiment tray into a saucer. "It's crazy busy in there. And the bald girl's in a bad mood like always."

"Her name is Eva, and you can only stay if you're helping."

"I'm helping, I'm helping." She bounced the olives on the saucer. "Her Wild Pig thing needs perking up. I'm thinking olives."

"Loretta, I'm warning you—"

She popped a couple into her mouth. "I'm kidding. Relax, okay?"

Eva passed her on her way through the swinging door. Neither woman spoke. Not a good sign. But the fact that Eva silently pulled herself a beer was worse.

"I'll make Loretta come out here," I said. "Get her to help Johnny with the orders."

"Don't you dare," Johnny said.

Eva shook her head. "It's okay. We need someone on dishes. But I'd change the locks on the back door if I were you. I think she has a key."

Why was I not surprised?

A bell in the kitchen rang.

Eva spun around.

Johnny handed me a couple of glasses. "Two Cokes, table one, pronto."

The two of them raced into the kitchen while I delivered the drinks to table one and yet another basket of bread to the couple by the window. Johnny came back with three plates of Wild Pig garnished with what looked suspiciously like olives. I was on my way to the kitchen when the couple by the window decided they wanted to order. I told them about the chowder, gave the bangers and mash a push, and prayed they would hurry while Dean Martin sang *When the moon hits your eye* . . . I stared at the speakers. How had she done that?

By the time the couple made up their minds, the bell in the kitchen was ringing again. But instead of waiting for Johnny or me to come pick up the order, Loretta brought the plates out to the bar and sprinkled olives on top of the boar.

"The bald girl doesn't know good advice when she hears it." She waved me away. "Take these. It'll be better now."

"Loretta, you can't," I called after her, but she was gone, returning through the swinging doors with a swagger.

Johnny was running between tables, and people were starting to check their watches. There was no time to argue with Loretta and no way to get those olives out of Eva's delicate sauce without a lot of messy digging. All I could do was deliver the order and try to make light of the rising voices coming from the kitchen. While I couldn't make out everything, phrases like "pushy bitch" and "*porca miseria*" helped point us all in the right direction while the bell rang yet again.

"Keep it down," I said when I went in for the order. "We can hear you out there."

"Tell it to your grandmother." Eva dumped green beans onto a plate, downed the rest of her beer, and smacked the empty on the bell. "Two bangers and mash up. And if she puts one fucking olive on them—"

"She won't, I promise." I picked up the plates and made a point of stopping by Loretta's post at the dishwasher on my way out. "Do not mess with the food," I told her.

"I only wanted to help."

"Then do what Eva says. And keep the noise down."

"Don't worry, *bella*," she said softly. "The bald girl and I will be real quiet. Isn't that right?"

Eva only grunted, which I hoped was a sign of goodwill, but the plates hadn't hit the table before the shouting started again.

Something about worn-out ways of thinking and hitting yourself in the head with shit, if I was translating it right. Thankful that no one else seemed to understand Italian, I made the rounds with the coffeepot and prayed that people would pass on dessert. But Eva had done a fine job with the display, and the lemon cheesecake was proving a popular choice.

The kitchen fell quiet at last, but I hurried with the bills and a few last slices of cake, just in case. People finally started to leave and Johnny and I had just exchanged a hopeful thumbs-up when Loretta suddenly hollered "*Sporcacciona*!" and something big smashed in the kitchen.

All eyes went to the swinging door, then came back to me. "I'll check for bodies," I said and made a dash for the kitchen.

Both women froze when I came sliding through. Eva was still at the grill, Loretta by the dishwasher, and on the floor between them lay what used to be a stack of dinner plates.

"*Bella*, I'm sorry," Loretta said. "They slipped."

"Slipped, my ass." Eva banged a saucepan into the sink. "Because she's your grandmother, I decided to ignore the olives, give her another chance. I was even talking nice to her, telling her what's been going on here today when all of a sudden she calls me a lying bitch and we're into it. That woman is seriously nuts."

Loretta shook her head. "Not nuts, just worried. The bald girl says you let a rat in here earlier."

"A rat?"

Another pot landed hard in the sink. "She means your ex."

Of course. Michael the rat.

Loretta was at home the day I found out about Michael and Rosie, and she was the one who helped me come up with a creative way to return the ring. There's an old Italian saying that revenge is a season in hell, but with Loretta, it can also be a lot of fun.

I should have told Eva to keep my date with Michael to herself, but it never occurred to me that she might try to chat with my grandmother. Eva didn't make small talk, couldn't see the point in discussing the weather or award shows or who was dating who in Hollywood. I'd counted on aloofness and got Miss Congeniality instead. Who would have guessed?

Loretta took a broom from the hook on the wall and started sweeping up what was left of my plates. "I was mad you even let him in. But when she said you were going out with him, I knew she was lying. You're too smart to go out with a rat. Especially a married one."

"He's not married anymore," Eva said. "Rosie's dead."

Loretta closed her eyes and crossed herself. "May she rest in peace, the bitch. You still shouldn't go out with him."

I backed toward the dining room. "We'll talk about this later."

She followed me to the door. "Just tell me what you're hoping for, *bella*. An apology? An act of contrition? A chance to tell the bastard off once and for all?"

I lowered my voice. "I'm not hoping for anything. I'm going because he's lonely. Rosie's been dead for two years and he's having trouble moving on."

"And it's your job to help him with that?"

"Of course not. I felt sorry for him, that's all."

But was it? Sympathy didn't explain the rush of excitement when he asked me out, and it certainly didn't account for the nonstop smile when I told Eva and Johnny. Philanthropy aside, maybe Loretta was on to something. Was I hoping for more? Expecting something and keeping it a secret from myself?

"Why should you feel anything for him?" Loretta asked. "Have you forgotten what he did to you, what he put you through, because I haven't. I remember everything, including you and me sitting outside Old City Hall, eating hot dogs and waiting for those two to arrive. Remember that?"

I did. Just like it was yesterday. I'd heard through the grapevine that they were getting married at city hall and I couldn't stop thinking about it, couldn't stop wondering if he'd really go through with it. Every day I stayed home, expecting the phone to ring, to hear his voice telling me it was all a mistake, that he wasn't going to marry Rosie after all. On the appointed day, Loretta couldn't stand it anymore. She dragged me downtown, found us a spot on the grass in front of Old City Hall, and we waited. Just when I thought they might not come, that I'd been right all along, there they were at the top of the stairs, the deed already done.

"Remember the way he held her hand when they came down the stairs?" Loretta asked. "How they smiled for the pictures? And when he kissed her, he didn't look like a boy being forced into anything, to me. He looked like a boy in love, remember?"

How could I forget? Michael wore a black suit and Rosie wore the blue maid-of-honor dress we had picked for my wedding. The one we'd shopped for forever, searching the stores for something that wasn't too fancy, something she could wear again. She looked great in it too. Slim and lovely. A beautiful bride laughing and running down the stairs with her groom. That's when I started to cry, while his mother took pictures and threw fucking confetti, like there was something to celebrate. Like the world wasn't crumbling around me.

Loretta had pulled me away, taken me to the Second Cup across the road, bought me a biscotti and a latte. I puked it up on the way home. Her car stunk for weeks.

I looked down at the plates on the floor. "We're just having dinner together."

"Just dinner," Loretta repeated. "*Bella*, listen to me. Why do you think he ended up here today?"

"Because he's in town visiting his brother."

"And of all the gin joints in all the world—"

"I know what you're getting at, but he had no idea this was my place. He stood at the window and didn't even notice me. Looked right through me, in fact."

"You're sure about that?"

"Yes. No. All right, I don't know for sure. But why wouldn't he say he'd seen me? What good would it do?"

"To make you think it was coincidence. Suck you in like before."

"You're being ridiculous."

"Am I?" She took my hands in hers, her knobby fingers holding on tight, like she might never let go. "There's an old saying, *Fidarsi è bene, non fidarsi è megio*. 'To trust is good, not to trust is better.' Do not trust Michael Hughes. That's all I'm going to say."

"If only we could believe that," Eva said.

Loretta pointed a finger. "You shut up. You know nothing about this."

Eva banged more pots into the sink. "I know what I saw. And I also know that people sometimes do really stupid things. They screw up the good things in their lives and spend years paying for it. Judging by what I saw, I'd say this Michael of yours has paid plenty." She stopped banging pots and came toward me. "But this isn't about what either of *us* wants or thinks. It's about what *you* want. What do you want, Sam?"

I didn't know, couldn't think. Loretta had a point. Once a bastard, always a bastard, isn't that the rule? Then again, Eva was right too. Everyone screws up now and then. Lord knows I've spent years torturing myself, wondering if I gave up too easily. Imagining how things might have turned out if I'd been inside city hall that afternoon, hunting them down instead of sitting outside. Banging open doors, searching offices, ready to shout *I do* when the judge asked if anyone knew just cause why those two shouldn't be wed.

If I went out with Michael now, what did that mean? Was I merely doing a good deed, or was I screwing up again? Becoming one of those women you see on talk shows, the ones who choose the wrong men over and over again because they can't find a way to break the cycle. I had no idea. All I knew was that I needed time to think.

I shook off Loretta's death grip. "I have to get back to work."

I hit the door with my hip and strolled into the dining room as though everything were fine. But Loretta wasn't ready to let go.

"I'm gonna light another candle and pray you come to your senses," she called after me. "That man is no good and deep down, you know it."

Thank God there weren't many people left in the dining room.

"Just my grandmother trying to save me from myself." I smiled and headed straight for the bar. "How's everybody doing?"

Heads nodded. Murmurs of "Just fine" and "Really great" followed me. "Perfect," I said and kept my back to them; loading the glass washer, slicing lemons, anything to keep the customers from seeing my red face or my goddamn watery eyes.

"Come again," Johnny said, filling the space I should have occupied. "And keep watching the sandwich board for more specials."

Would any of them come back? I didn't care. All I wanted was the place to myself and a chance to think.

The door closed behind the last of them, and Johnny plunked himself on a stool at the bar. "That was amazing. Wild Pig is officially a hit."

I handed him a beer. "Thanks for jumping in. I appreciate it."

"No problem. You okay?"

"Never better."

"Whatever you say. Loretta still here?"

"I hope not."

Johnny downed half the glass and sat back. "Why do you let her get to you?"

"Because she's wise and good, and maybe she's right. Maybe I'm nuts to trust Michael. I can't even say for sure why I agreed to go out with him."

"Maybe you're looking for closure."

"And maybe you're spouting psychobabble." Eva dropped onto the stool next to Johnny and eyed his glass. "Get me one of those."

I pulled a beer and slid it across the bar, then took a bottle of red from under the counter, poured it into a small rocks glass, and polished it off in one shot. I may own an Irish pub, but I still drink Italian. I refilled the glass and took it slower this time. "Where's Loretta?"

"Went out the back door muttering something about Santa Maria and stupid women, and I didn't catch the rest. But don't you worry. She's got her head up her ass on this. There's nothing wrong with wanting to see your ex again."

"Well, part of me must agree with her because I swore I saw Rosie when I was outside."

The two of them froze, beers halfway to their mouths.

"You're joking, right?" Johnny said.

I grabbed a cloth from the sink. "Forget it. Let's get this place cleaned up."

Eva slapped a hand down on the cloth. "You can't just throw out something like that and then say, forget it. Where exactly was she?"

Johnny laughed. "More important, what were you smoking before you saw her?"

Eva turned to face him. "You don't believe in ghosts?"

He was instantly serious. "Why? Do you?"

She sighed. "Only a fool doubts the existence of that which he cannot see."

Johnny looked over at me. I shrugged, understanding his confusion. Of all the people I had ever met, Eva MacRae was the last one I would have pointed to as a believer.

"All right, then," Johnny said. "Where did you say this ghost was?"

They were both looking at me, waiting for an answer. I hadn't meant to say anything, but now that my sanity was formally up for discussion I was relieved, happy to drag them into my nightmare.

I knocked back the rest of the wine and reached for the bottle again. "She was sitting in the backseat of Michael's car, giving me the finger as they drove off."

"*Madre de Dio*, it's a sign," Loretta called from the kitchen door.

Eva slumped forward. "Sweet Jesus, it's back."

Loretta ignored her and shook a finger at me instead. "That was God saying, 'Don't get in that car.' " She set her backpack down, raised her face to the ceiling, and crossed herself. "*Madre de Dio*, help my *bella* in her time of need."

Eva banged her head on the table. "Someone make it stop."

"Loretta, knock it off." I shoved a hand under Eva's forehead and lowered my voice. "But what if she's right? Not about God sending me messages, but rather that I'm sending messages to myself. I've been trying to convince myself that if I saw anything in that car, then it must have been Rosie's sister, Marcie. But maybe it was my own subconscious telling me not to go there. Maybe I saw Rosie because I wanted to."

Eva lifted her head. "You saw her because she was there. She exists whether you like it or not."

Loretta threw up her hands. "That's it, we need a priest. Maybe two."

"What we need is to turn our backs on superstition and fear," Eva said, "and move forward into understanding."

Johnny leaned back. "You are so deep."

"And you are such a fool." She looked over at me again. "Evidence of Rosie was in front of us all along, but you're the only one who saw the physical proof."

"What exactly was in front of us?" I asked.

"Michael, of course. Derek told us he's lonely and miserable, yet he can't move on. Why do you think that is?"

"Depression and guilt are good places to start."

"Rosie's a better place," Eva said.

She sat there watching me, a tattooed biker chick chugging beer and acting as though her theory made perfect sense. Odd how you think you know someone and with one turn of events, you realize you have no idea who she really is.

"Who sold you this crap?" I asked.

"Nobody sold me anything. My mother's a psychic. Tells fortunes over in Kensington Market. She says most people don't believe in spirits because it's easier to think your mind is playing tricks on you, making you see what isn't there rather than trusting your own senses. Believing throws everything you've been taught into question. You have to accept the possibility that there are things beyond your understanding, beyond science, even beyond the church's teaching, and that's too hard for most people."

I held up a hand. "I don't know whether you're right or not, but either way, Loretta has a point. There's nothing good for me in that car."

Loretta clasped her hands together. "*Grazie*, Maria. Finally, she shows some sense."

Eva slouched over her beer again. "How do you keep from choking her?"

Ignoring them both, I dug Michael's card out of my apron. "I'm going to call him now and cancel."

The phone rang before I could pick it up.

Johnny smiled. "Maybe it's Rosie. Calling from beyond the grave."

Eva glanced over at him. "That's the first thing you've said that makes sense."

Loretta's eyes widened. "*Bella*, don't you dare touch that phone."

The hairs on my arms rose when it rang again.

"Aren't you going to answer it?" Johnny asked.

"Yes," I said, letting it ring a third time.

"Fine, I'll get it." Johnny picked up the receiver. "Silver Swan, how can I help you. Sure, hold on." He held the phone out to me. "It's Derek."

"Proof that Rosie is at it again," Eva said.

Loretta hugged her backpack to her chest. "This is too much. I'll be at the church if you need me. If you're smart, you'll come too."

I watched Loretta march out the front door, head held high, while Eva calmly finished her beer, and I envied them both. Neither doubted that I'd seen Rosie; they simply disagreed on the reasons. I wished I could be as sure myself.

I took the phone from Johnny. "Derek? What's up?"

"Michael's going to call you. He's going to cancel."

"What?"

Eva nudged Johnny. "Rosie got to him."

"How do you know?"

"Look at her face."

I turned my back on them. "Why would he do that?"

"Because it's what he does." I heard exasperation in Derek's voice, impatience in the rustling of paper, the slamming of a drawer. "We shouldn't have given him time to think. We should have just packed the two of you off somewhere and let things unfold."

"I don't know what to say."

"Say no, of course. When he calls, don't let him cancel."

"I don't know, Derek. If he doesn't want to see me—"

"He definitely wants to go out with you," Derek said. "It was all he talked about when we got in the car. How great it was to see your place, how good you looked, how easy it had been to talk to you. We weren't two blocks from your pub when it started. He went quiet, stared out the window. I tried to bring him back into the conversation but he was gone, brooding again like always. I thought I could take his mind off it once we were back at the house, but he just told me a minute ago that he can't do it. Said it's not right, he's still in mourning, the same crap all over again. I tried arguing with him, but he blew me off, picked up his BlackBerry and went outside. I can see him out there by the car, walking up and down with that damn phone in his hand. He doesn't want to cancel, but he will, I know it."

I looked over at Eva and all I could think was *Rosie got to him.*

"You're jumping to conclusions," I said out loud.

"What?" Derek asked.

"Nothing. Listen, Derek, thanks for calling but it's no problem if Michael's having second thoughts. I was having doubts myself. In fact, it's probably better all around if we call this thing off."

"Coward," Eva said.

Derek sighed. "Sam, please, don't do this. If it was anyone else I'd say forget it. But I honestly think you can talk him around, get him to go out the door. Promise me you'll try."

"I can't promise anything. But I'll think about it. And if he calls, I'll deal with it then."

It wasn't what Derek wanted to hear, but what choice did he have? What choice did any of us have? We hung up and I went for the wine again.

"So the date's off," Eva said. "It figures."

"Do you really believe Rosie got to him?" Johnny asked her.

"No," I said before Eva could answer. "He simply had second thoughts. Just like me."

"You only had second thoughts because of Loretta," Eva said. "I don't know why you listen to her."

"Because she's the voice of reason."

"She's the voice of superstition. I can't believe you fell for her crap."

"*Her* crap? What about you and the whole ghost thing?"

"All right, we'll leave the ghost out of this for the moment.

Answer one question. How do you feel about canceling your date with Michael?"

"Relieved."

"Be honest."

"Okay, I'm confused. Maybe a little disappointed. And definitely pissed off that he wants out."

"Not as happy as you were earlier, then?" I nodded and Eva smiled, really smiled, for the second time that afternoon. "Then with or without Rosie, the choice you're making is wrong."

"She has a point," Johnny said. "Could be you need to stop analyzing this so much, and just do what you want."

Eva glanced over at him. "Keep that up, and I'll start thinking there's intelligent life in there after all."

"So you'll have dinner with me?"

"Dream on."

I sat down next to Eva and dragged my glass over. "I wish I knew what to do."

"You do. You're just second guessing yourself, which surprises me."

I closed my eyes, pressed the glass to my eyelids. "You don't know me well enough to be surprised by anything."

"I don't have to know you to be sure that plenty of people tried to scare you off when you decided to open this place. *Restaurants are high risk. Don't quit your day job*. Am I right?"

I nodded and moved the glass to my forehead.

"But you didn't listen to them. You knew what you wanted and you went for it. But the second Michael is involved, you turn all wishy-washy, let yourself be turned around in a matter of seconds. Why is that?"

"Because I've been known to screw up."

"That was a long time ago, and you didn't screw up, he did." She lowered the glass from my forehead and waited until I opened my eyes. "Why don't you just say what you want and be done with it?"

I swirled the wine, watched it go round and round. "I want to see Michael."

"Then see him. Don't let Rosie win again."

The phone rang.

"That'll be Michael," Eva said.

I'm not usually the intuitive type, but for some reason I could picture him standing by his car with the BlackBerry pressed to his ear and Rosie sitting on the fender, doing her nails.

The phone rang again. Johnny shifted in his seat. "Will you answer the damn thing?"

I felt myself shaking my head. "No," I said, and my feet moved on their own, taking me to the door. I managed to grab my purse along the way, throw my apron on a chair, and turn off my cell phone, just in case. "Tell him I'm not here," I said. "Tell him I'm on my way over."

THREE

The moment the door clicked shut, I realized I was being hasty. I should have fixed my hair, put on some fresh lipstick, at least brushed my teeth. Then again, the afternoon was slowly slipping away, heading relentlessly toward the dinner hour rush, leaving me with a little over two hours to do this. The walk to Fenwick and McConnell would take at least ten minutes, and then I still had to find Derek's house. Should be easy enough to spot a semi under construction, but even so I'd lose too much time if I went back inside now. Besides, Eva had already locked the door and was watching me through the glass, arms crossed, dragons daring me to go for my keys.

"What?" I said, then shrugged my shoulders as if I had no idea what her problem was and struck out with renewed purpose, heading east along the Danforth toward Fenwick and Michael, consciously resisting the urge to check my reflection in the windows along the way. I got as far as the fruit market when it hit me: Eva had done me a favor by locking that door. I didn't need a brush or a lipstick or anything else. Not when I had the sun to put a little color in my cheeks and the breeze to explain my hair. If I picked up a pack of gum along the way, I'd arrive not only minty fresh, but pink and glowing as well, something Michael was bound to appreciate, being a man of the north these days. A man with a preference for fresh-faced, natural women. The outdoor type who wouldn't know tapas from tap shoes, but could spot the difference between an elk and a deer track at fifty paces, and pee in the bush without getting it all over her shoes.

Rosie had always been good at that. While I came to prefer mild dehydration to squatting in the woods, Rosie would drop her drawers anywhere and not mind using leaves when she was done. She grew up in a hunting camp north of Chapleau and came south only because her mother's new boyfriend put his foot down. Said he couldn't live with two goddamned kids in the house, girls at that. Naturally, Rosie's mother kept Marcie, the younger one, and sent Rosie to live with her Aunt Barb in Toronto, a lapsed Catholic who sent Rosie to Our Lady of Victories Elementary during the week, but secretly took her to the Church of the Nazarene on Sunday mornings. Rosie went along with the scheme because her mother would be pissed off when she found out, and that girl must have been born again three or four times before Barb finally figured out that her niece was a confirmed atheist. Had been ever since the day God ignored her prayers and let the boyfriend put her on a bus bound for Toronto.

But the Nazarenes must not have suspected anything because as long as Rosie showed up on Sundays and took those weepy walks to the altar every now and then, Pastor Llewellyn was happy to let her attend their heavily subsidized camp on Little Doe Lake every summer. And if she kept bringing along a friend who needed saving, so much the better.

The first time Rosie asked me to go with her, I wasn't surprised when my mother shook her head and said, "What are you? Nuts?"

Ours wasn't a family that took advantage of day camps or soccer leagues or anything else designed to keep kids busy in the summer. My parents didn't live with Loretta because they liked it; they lived with her to save money. Loretta owned the four-bedroom house we lived in, the one with the blue and white painted bricks, the kitchen in the basement, and crops in the backyard, and she never missed an opportunity to remind my parents of this fact. She oversaw their finances, refereed their fights, and looked after the children so they could each work two jobs and get the hell out of there before they killed her. Little wonder neither of them saw the value in spending money on summer camp, especially one put on by heathens.

Of course, Aunt Barb took on the cause and sat them down with a brochure outlining the benefits of three weeks of sun, fun, and fellowship for a city child, while Rosie pointed out that every Canadian kid was duty bound to learn to canoe. I didn't care much about canoes or anything that called itself fellowship, but I cared deeply about losing Rosie for three whole weeks.

It was mid-July, for God's sake. Far too late to try wheedling my way into some other group of girls. Tagging along with my sister would only lead to abandonment on the subway again and my brother wasn't worth thinking about, which left canning vegetables in the downstairs kitchen with Loretta as my only option. And the whole time I was down there boiling jars and being miserable, I would know that Rosie was out in the wilds of northern Ontario, tracking animals and drawing new friends the way some people draw mosquitoes.

I could lose her to some girl who already knew how to hold a paddle. Some girl who would come down to the city on weekends, sleep in her bed, and become a treasured pen pal or worse. My mind was made up. One way or another, I was going to camp.

That night before bed, I promised my mother I would tune out everything I heard in their Protestant tabernacle, say the rosary three times a day, and help her and the altar ladies when I got home if she'd just let me go. Next morning, she bought me a sleeping bag, sewed name tags into my underwear, and told my father to shut up when he questioned her. What did he know about being Canadian anyway? His mother still kept chickens in the shed.

I was the only one who knew that her decision had nothing to do with my being more Canadian. She let me go for the sake of poor motherless Rosie, who had come to her secretly on the night of my promises, begging her to let me go because she was afraid to be at camp by herself.

The night had been hot, the air heavy and hard to breathe, and all the windows in the house were open in the hope of catching a breeze. Lying there in the dark, sweating and listening to Rosie's voice at the back door, I felt pride and relief swelling together inside my chest. She told my mother I was her best friend. Said it right out loud for anyone to hear. Too bad my mother and I were the only ones within earshot.

It took me three days to figure out how to sleep in a bag and two more to believe it was okay to breathe in the outhouse. If only I'd been as quick to figure out that Rosie had been playing my mother, telling her whatever she wanted to hear in order to get what she wanted, the same way she played Pastor Llewellyn every year after that so we could continue going to that damn camp.

For four summers in a row I swam with the leeches, cursed the outhouse, and hiked the woods with Rosie, watching her follow tracks and poke around in animal shit while I swatted deerflies and tried not to drink anything so I wouldn't have to pee. She loved Little Doe Lake in a way I never could, mostly because it reminded her of life back in Chapleau. Maybe that's the real reason I hated the place, because it made her want to run away, leave

Toronto for good. And as much as I wanted her to, I couldn't imagine her stopping by my house in the middle of the night, begging my mother to let me get on that bus with her.

Fortunately, things changed the year the pastor's nephew came to give the campers a little wilderness training. Because it was an all-girls camp, boys were in short supply. One grass cutter, two dishwashers, some nameless unfortunate who cleaned the outhouses, and now Bobby Llewellyn. Tall and tanned, Bobby was the best of the bunch and competition was fierce, but Rosie had him where she wanted him by the end of the first day.

"I've never met a girl who appreciates what a fountain of information animal skat can be," he'd said.

Then again, he'd never met a girl like Rosie, and contrary to what the Nazarenes tried to tell her later, we both knew God had nothing whatsoever to do with her being caught in the tabernacle with her pants down and the pastor's nephew grunting above her. That was pure spite on the part of pimply-faced Denise Brooks, who slept in the bunk across from us. Although I did say a prayer of thanks when the pastor banned Rosie from camp for life and loaded the two of us onto a bus bound for Toronto.

After that, I didn't have to worry about her making friends at camp anymore. And when her mother called her a disappointment and a bad influence, and said she couldn't even entertain the thought of bringing her home now, having her around poor little Marcie, Rosie stopped talking about Chapleau altogether, and never mentioned running away again, which made me want to send Bobby Llewellyn a thank-you card.

But for all that she didn't talk about it anymore, I knew she had always missed the north, and it didn't surprise me in the least that she'd dragged Michael up to Huntsville after the wedding. I could picture her teaching her daughter about bird calls and animal tracks and how best to wipe with a leaf. The only thing I couldn't picture was Michael being happy there.

When I reached the corner, I dashed into the convenience store, grabbed a pack of Chiclets, and popped four into my mouth, just to be sure. Then I crossed the road and left the Danforth, heading south on Fenwick where the pace slowed and the mood shifted. Scrawny maples in concrete containers gave way to towering oaks and birch. Joggers nodded on their way by. Dog walkers smiled as they passed. Toddlers and seniors said hello as they played in the dirt amid wildflowers, gnomes, and found art. It was a different world here among the tidy rowhouses and Victorian painted ladies. And in the middle of it all stood Michael, laughing and talking with a knot of people gathered around a lawn mower.

He was animated, chatting easily with kids and old folks alike, obviously enjoying himself. And why not? He was home again, surrounded by people in the city he had loved as much as I did.

Whenever Michael and I had spoken of the future, we had never imagined ourselves anywhere else. We were city dwellers, happy to ride the subway, shop at Kensington Market, and stand in line at Honest Ed's when the door-crasher specials were worth it. On those rare occasions when we wanted nature, we would hop a ferry to the Island or take ourselves hiking in the valley. But usually you could find us at a movie, or a club, or in our favorite booth at the Flamingo, hunkered down with a couple of peameal bacon sandwiches, making a million plans together.

I stopped several houses from where he stood, watching him squat down with the owner of the lawn mower to examine the machine more closely, remembering those bacon sandwiches and the talks that went on late into the night. Rosie used to scoff and call him a cheap bastard, ask why he didn't take me somewhere else once in a while, but I never paid any attention. She didn't know him, and didn't care to. Had in fact hated him from the first night he walked into the Flamingo.

Rosie and I had been sitting in a back booth, sharing a plate of fries and studying the latest edition of *Cosmo*, committing to memory the Ten Things a Man Wants You to Do and discussing the possibility that number four might be a joke, when he walked in with some guys from school. We'd known the bunch he was with for years, but Michael was new and Rosie was instantly alert, her shoulders pulling back, her mouth softening into that pouty half-smile I always admired.

Outside, the first snow of the season was falling and the new guy stood at the door, stamping his feet and shaking heavy wet flakes from his jacket before following his friends to a table.

He scanned the room as he sat down, taking in the posters of Greece, the jukeboxes on the tables, the red vinyl stools at the counter, and me. He smiled and I turned away, my face suddenly hot and my pulse racing. This was not the way things usually went. Boys always noticed Rosie first, but when I glanced back, he was still looking at me. He smiled again, only turning away when one of his buddies elbowed him and passed him a menu.

He ordered a peameal bacon sandwich and then came over to the table to introduce himself. He nodded at Rosie, but sat down beside me. I couldn't believe it and neither could she. That pouty smile had never failed before. She left the table, went over to talk to his friends instead, and Michael and I started to chat about everything and nothing. Some people were born to make small talk, and then there was me. But with Michael, things were different. I was different.

I watched him now, laughing with the owner of the lawn mower and patting the guy's golden retriever, and suddenly every plan we'd made came rolling back, threatening to crush me under the weight of a house on Fenwick and the life we had dreamed about with our pub, our dog, and our kids.

He glanced over his shoulder and I ducked behind a tree, my heart beating as fast as it had that night at the Flamingo. I should have planned this better, given some thought to an opening line.

Something witty yet sincere to explain why I was there. Another piece of gum wouldn't hurt either. And neither would one quick check in a mirror. There had to be one in my purse somewhere.

"Sam?"

I jumped and peeked out from behind the tree. Michael had left the group and was standing on the sidewalk about twenty feet from my hiding spot, looking confused. "What are you doing here?" he asked.

Hadn't Johnny answered the phone? Hadn't he told Michael to expect me? Hadn't I known in my heart that this couldn't possibly go well?

"I was just in the neighborhood," I said and wished I hadn't, but my mouth was already in gear and my brain couldn't catch up fast enough. "Out for a walk. Afternoon constitutional, that sort of thing."

Shut up, shut up. But there was no stopping this train until I said, "Fancy meeting you here," and finally came to a grinding halt.

Afternoon constitutional? Fancy meeting you here? He was going to regret ever asking to see me again, I could see it in his face. Or was that a smile? My God, it was. Maybe he hadn't heard me. Maybe I was far enough away.

"Fancy meeting you too," he said.

Or not.

We stood there, smiling at each other, both awkward again while a kid went by on a skateboard and a dog yapped. The sprinkler came on in the garden beside me, turning in a lazy circle large enough to reach the pink peony bush, the gnome under the birdbath, and the toes of my shoes.

I looked down at my shoes, wondering why I'd ever believed this was a good idea, when Michael said, "I'm glad you're here," and suddenly I couldn't remember why I hadn't run all the way.

"Why?" I asked, taking the hand he offered and stepping onto dry pavement.

He shrugged and released my hand, but he kept looking at me, straight into my eyes, as though he couldn't believe I was really there. "Because I was about to make a huge mistake," he said at last. "Only now I can't remember why. Come on, I'll fix you an iced tea."

I walked beside him, past the house where Lawn Mower Appreciation Day was still in full swing, to a two-story semi in the throes of renovation, half a block down. A Dumpster took up most of the driveway, and a load of lumber was killing both the front lawn and the few tulips left in the garden. But even with the gingerbread trim only half-finished and the new windows still wearing tape, it was easy to see that the place was destined to become a neighborhood showpiece.

"This is the house you're sharing with Derek?" I asked.

"For now," Michael said, leading me up the stairs to the veranda. "He lives in this half, and Julie and I are camping out in the other."

"Derek owns both sides of the house?"

"He's doing well," Michael said. "He plans to stay on in this side and sell the other, if Julie and I decide to stay in Huntsville."

I nodded and looked up at the house again. The veranda was new, stretching the length of the house, but there was no divider separating the two halves, and three Muskoka chairs sat squarely in the middle—a sure sign that Derek was still optimistic about persuading his brother to stay.

"Is Derek here?" I asked.

"He's around the side, building a mantel. I'm supposed to be inside, getting the fireplace ready for installation, but it feels like break time to me."

"I should go and say hello."

"No, don't," Michael said and gave me a sheepish grin. "I'm not ready to share you yet."

I was ridiculously pleased and couldn't help smiling back. "I'll wait here then."

"And I'll get the iced tea." We walked up the steps to the veranda, and he motioned to the Muskoka chairs under the window. "Make yourself comfortable," he said on his way into the house, letting the screen door slam shut behind him.

Too nervous to sit, I wandered instead, inspecting the new posts, running a hand over the railing, and peering into the front windows, curious about the rest of the renovations. But all I saw in the glass was my own reflection with trees, houses, and Michael's car in the background.

I jerked around. The Lexus was parked across the road, as real as any other car on the street. I hadn't imagined it. But how could I have missed it when we arrived?

I walked closer to the stairs, half-expecting to see Rosie and her finger in the backseat again. Logic told me I was being silly. There was no good reason to believe she had been there in the first place, but what if she was?

I couldn't resist. With a quick glance at the front door, I went down the stairs, slowly I admit, but steadily nonetheless. About twenty feet from the passenger door, I still couldn't see her. Maybe she was lying down, catching a nap. Did ghosts sleep? Who knew? I kept going, determined to find out.

About five feet from the car I stopped again, suddenly conscious of the hairs on my arms and a shortage of air in my lungs. I rubbed at the goose bumps, made myself draw in a few slow, deep breaths, and asked myself the obvious: Even if she was in there, what could she do? Attack me? In broad daylight? Not likely. Ghosts are night creatures, after all. And chances were good that she couldn't leave the car even if she wanted to. After all, weren't ghosts tied to one spot? Doomed to haunt a single dwelling or area for eternity? Because Rosie had died in a car accident, the car was probably her home now. While I would have preferred to think of her tied to the actual wreck, hanging around a scrap yard for all time, I suppose she could have found her way to Michael's car instead. It made as much sense as anything else I could think of.

An SUV approached, forcing me to decide. Move closer to the Lexus, or back off and return to the veranda. I inched closer to the Lexus and peered into the backseat. Nothing. Not even a box of Kleenex. Michael had the cleanest backseat I'd ever seen. The front seat was equally neat, with no sign of Rosie there either. I bent closer, cupping my hands on the glass, making sure she wasn't crouching on the floor. Again, nothing. I laughed and strolled around the car, feeling cocky and lighter than I had in hours. Ding-dong, the witch is dead. And she wasn't coming back anytime soon.

"Sure is a great car," a man called.

I jumped, my hand on my heart when I turned to see Derek coming across the road, looking every bit the builder with his steel-toed boots and a tool belt slung low on his hips.

"Sure is," I said. "And don't ever do that again."

He smiled. "I called your name a couple of times, but you were really wrapped up in the Lexus. You thinking of buying one?"

"One of these?" I laughed. "No, I was just curious. This is Michael's car, isn't it?"

"Brand new. Hasn't had it a week."

"That explains the unnaturally clean backseat."

"Another week should put things right."

I laughed again and motioned to the house. "I love what you're doing with the place. It's going to be fabulous."

"Thanks," he said, and we walked back across the road together. "I'm pleased with the way things are going." We stopped on the sidewalk, facing the house instead of each other. "I want to thank you for coming so quickly," he said. "I really appreciate it."

"I appreciated the heads-up. Michael seems genuinely happy to see me."

"I knew he would be. The guy was miserable as hell while he was trying to reach you. Snapping at me, impatient with Julie. He was being an ass, and I hoped you'd get here in time, but just in case, I took out a little insurance." He pulled Michael's BlackBerry from his tool belt. "I stole it when he went inside for a coffee."

I stared at the phone. "Didn't he miss it?"

"He got sidetracked by a lawn mower." Derek smiled. "But now that you're here, I'm sure he'll forget all about canceling."

"Iced tea's ready," Michael called as he pushed open the screen door. He stopped when he saw Derek and gave him that same sheepish grin. "We're just about to take a break. Care to join us?"

Derek shook his head. "You go ahead. I'm on my way to the hardware store." He nodded to me as he jogged toward his truck. "Nice to see you again, Sam."

"You too," I sang and had to stop myself from skipping up the stairs.

I took a glass from Michael and sat down in one of the Muskoka chairs. "So where would you like to have dinner tonight?" I asked.

"I have no idea." He sat down beside me. "Where's your favorite place these days? Other than the Swan, of course."

He seemed more relaxed, easier, the way he used to be with me, and I found myself relaxing too, happy to settle into the deep comfort of a Muskoka chair with the glass dripping water on my skirt. One sip told me the iced tea was instant, which was not his fault considering he'd gone into Derek's kitchen, but I was disappointed that he seemed to be enjoying the stuff. I put it down to years of living with Rosie and looked forward to reintroducing him to real iced tea, decent food, and anything else he might have forgotten.

"There's a great Thai place," I said, but was interrupted by a sudden, piercing screech and the sound of running feet.

Michael jumped up as a little girl came around the side of the house. She was skinny with short brown hair, a tear-stained face, and a mud-caked Barbie dangling from her fingers.

"My mother is going to be so mad," she yelled and kept coming, stopping only when she reached the porch stairs. "And it's all Julie's fault."

"Neighbor's kid," Michael whispered to me, then hurried over to the stairs. "Megan, what's wrong?"

She shook the doll at him. "She ruined my brand-new Barbie, that's what."

"Julie did that?" Michael went down the stairs and took the doll from Megan. He held the thing at arm's length and gave it a shake, splattering mud on himself and the little girl. "How did this happen?" he asked.

Megan sniffed loudly. "She said it was a game."

I stood up and walked to the stairs, my eyes on the naked, dripping doll. I had seen Barbies like that before. Barbies with mud caked so thickly in their hair that it would never be the same again, and permanent-marker tattoos on their backs, arms, and legs. I thought this Barbie might have escaped the tattoos, but with that much mud, it was hard to tell.

"It was kind of fun," Megan continued, "until she got the hose. When she put it in the sand pile, I told her to stop, but she turned on the water and then she spun around and around, splashing mud all over, and before I could stop her, she dropped my doll into the muck and yelled—"

"Barbie in the Slime Pit."

I hadn't meant to say it out loud, and I winced when Megan nodded, her face crumpling anew. "How did you know?" she wailed.

"Lucky guess," I said, those hairs on my arms rising again.

"Julie," Michael called. "Come out here, right now." He went around the side of the house, Barbie in hand and Megan following close behind. "Julie, where are you?"

On the other side of the veranda, a small blond head peeked around the corner.

Even if I hadn't seen her picture earlier, I would have known she was Rosie's daughter. Same hair, same fine bones, same comfort crawling around in the mud.

I walked quietly across the porch and leaned over the railing. "Your dad is looking for you."

Julie jerked her head up. Her clothes and face were splattered with mud, her blue eyes round and frightened.

"Don't worry," I whispered. "I won't tell him you're here. But things will go easier if you turn yourself in. You can't hide forever."

Michael's voice again, calling from the backyard. "Julie? Where are you?"

"What happened back there?" I asked gently.

She rose up on her knees, peering at me through the railings. "After I fell off the swing, Megan's mother told us to take her new Barbie and go and play quietly. We were doing that, but it was getting boring, you know? Then I saw the hose and thought we could give her a bath. And then we saw the pile of sand and suddenly playing with Barbie was a whole lot more fun."

"I can understand that. But did Megan tell you to stop?"

Julie shook her head. "She was laughing and having a good time until her stupid cell phone rang."

"She has a cell phone?"

"It's pink and she can only call home, and I think it has a GPS in it so her mother always knows where she is. Anyway, as soon as her mother called, Megan got all worried and started to yell and said it was all my fault, but it wasn't." She sighed and sat back on her heels. "We were just having fun."

"Julie, answer me," Michael shouted.

She closed her eyes. "He's going to kill me."

"No, he's not."

"You're right about that," a voice said, and I couldn't move.

Rosie smiled at me as she climbed the stairs to the veranda. "Boo," she said and started to laugh.

FOUR

As hallucinations go, Rosie had to be one of the best. No deathly pallor, no chains, not a hint of rot anywhere. If anything, she looked better than ever in tight blue jeans and a white T-shirt with *Wild Rose* emblazoned across her chest in sparkly letters. Surely Michael hadn't buried her in that. Surely he'd chosen something conservative, somber even, for her last public appearance. Then again, somber had never been Rosie's style. She had a thing for bright colors, sparkly jewelry, and sequins. I swear nothing was ever too tacky for Rosie. In fact, if I hadn't put my foot down when we were choosing that maid-of-honor dress, I'd have ended up with a Las Vegas showgirl walking down the aisle in front of me instead of the simple elegance I had in mind. Not that it mattered. Might have been better, in fact, considering where that simply elegant dress ended up. But now, watching her strut across the veranda in her bare feet, faux-diamond bangles shimmering on one hand, a pair of silver stilettos dangling from the other, it occurred to me that the outfit was perfect. That subtle blend of excess and tastelessness that she had perfected years ago, and I understood why Michael had sent her off in her Saturday night best.

"Wow," she said and stopped in front of me, giving me a quick once-over. "You look like shit, Marcello."

I backed up a step. "Stop right there. I am not buying into this."

"Buying into what?"

"You, the T-shirt, this whole thing. You're obviously an illusion."

"You think you're imagining me?"

"Yes, although I can't for the life of me come up with a reason why."

Rosie propped her butt on the railing and smiled. "Good old Sammy. Still as thick as a plank. It's nice to know some things don't change."

I gave my head a shake, even laughed a little. "Enough is enough," I said, and closed my eyes, honestly expecting her to be gone when I opened them again, forced back into thin air by my refusal to believe. But there she was, sitting on the railing, swinging those damn shoes back and forth, back and forth.

"I don't believe in you," I said. "I don't believe you're here."

"I don't believe *you're* here, either, but that doesn't change a thing, does it." She slid off the railing, sank into a Muskoka chair, and took a sip of my iced tea. "To be honest, I was surprised when I first realized you could see me. You hear about that kind of thing now and then, but I never took it seriously. Then all of a sudden, there you were, mouth open, staring at me like you'd seen a ghost. It's kind of fun, don't you think?" She stuck a finger in the tea and swirled the ice around. "So tell me, what brings you to my neck of the woods anyway?"

Mere minutes in her company and already my face was growing hot, my skin prickly. I walked over and snatched the glass out of her hand. "*Your* neck?" I said. "How does this get to be *your* neck?"

"Who are you talking to?" Julie asked, and suddenly the air around me filled with the sounds of the street. Lawn mowers, cars, a leaf blower roaring two doors down. I turned, spilling iced tea all over my hand. How had I missed the bloody leaf blower?

"Julie, I'm getting angry now," Michael called from the backyard.

Had he been hollering for her all that time too? And was the kid still crawling around in the dirt? I peeked over the railing. Sure enough, there she was, crouching in what was left of the tulips and looking up at me like I was the crazy woman everyone warns their kids about.

"Are you okay?" she asked.

"Isn't she a nice girl?" Rosie whispered in my ear, making me jump again. "Compassionate, friendly—"

"No thanks to you, I'm sure."

"What?" Julie asked.

"Nothing," I said and waved a hand, trying to keep things light while I walked the length of the railing, away from her mother. "Just out of curiosity, do you see anything up here? Besides me?"

Julie's eyes widened and she sank even lower, as though trying to disappear completely. "Why? What do you see? What's up there?"

"What do you think is up here?"

"Leave the kid alone," Rosie said. "She can't see me. You're the only one with that privilege."

"But why?" I moved farther along the railing. "Why me?"

"Why you, what?" Julie asked, her tone turning whiny, frustrated. "Who are you anyway?"

"I'm a friend of your dad's," I said and was selfishly grateful when Michael called, "Okay, Julie, that's it. You're in big trouble now."

"That man can be such a horse's ass sometimes," Rosie said. She leaned over the railing, hollering at the backyard, "It's a stupid doll, for Chrissakes. Lighten up."

I ignored her and focused on her daughter instead. "Why don't you just talk to him?"

"Yeah right." Julie wrapped her arms around herself, her eyes fixed on the tulips in front of her. "What am I supposed to say?"

"How about the truth?"

Rosie turned me around, shoved a finger in my face. "Back off, Marcello. That is my kid and Michael is my husband. I'll thank you to stay out of my business."

I consciously lowered my voice. "What business? You don't have business. You're dead."

"Just keep your distance." Rosie slipped her feet into her silver shoes and headed down the stairs. "Don't worry, sweetie," she called to Julie. "Mommy will take care of everything."

She blew the girl a kiss, then dashed off, heading for the backyard. I watched Julie closely, hoping for a reaction. A turn of the head, a loosening of the shoulders, anything at all to indicate that she had heard her mother, perhaps seen her too. But the girl didn't move. Just sat there in the tulips, waiting.

"This is nuts," I muttered, wondering what it all meant. Could I be close to death myself? Was Rosie my escort to the other side? What kind of sick cosmic joke would that be? But if that wasn't the reason, then how come I was the only one who could see her?

It made no sense that I should be the chosen one. I didn't even like her. In fact, it wasn't so long ago that I actively hated her, wished her the worst at regular intervals. If you want the truth, when Michael told me she was dead, I had to fight back a smile. Horrible, isn't it, to be pleased with the news of someone's death, but we're talking about Rosie Fisk, the woman who ruined my life. What else should I have been expected to feel?

Perhaps that was why I could see her. Maybe this was the universe punishing me for all the ill feeling I bore her. But wouldn't I have to be the sort of person who believed in universal interference or divine punishments in order for that to work? Wasn't it like voodoo in that way?

"There you are," Michael said, coming around the veranda with the Barbie and Megan at his side. He had obviously tried to help by rinsing off the mud, thus matting the doll's hair even more and pushing Megan from tears to righteous wrath. Watching that little girl, I hoped Julie had other friends on the block because I wouldn't have bet on her keeping this one.

"Get up," I said, so only Julie would hear. She looked up at me. "You can't let her see you like that. Now get up," I repeated and felt my own shoulders relax slightly when she scrambled to her feet, meeting her father and Megan with some semblance of pride.

Michael held up the doll. "All right, young lady. How do you explain this?"

Julie stared at the Barbie. "We were just playing—"

"I wasn't playing," Megan cut in. "I told her to stop."

Julie's back stiffened. "You did not. You said it was the most fun you ever had with a Barbie."

"She's lying." Megan snatched the doll from Michael's hand. "She made me give her the doll and then she ruined it because she's jealous. And now you owe me a new Tatiana Barbie. You said so."

"I promise, you'll get a new doll," Michael said.

Megan pointed the doll at Julie. "And you can't get her one too. That's not fair."

"I don't even want a stupid Barbie," Julie yelled. "They suck, just like you."

"Julie, that's enough," Michael said.

She looked at Michael, her lower lip starting to tremble. "But she's lying, Daddy. I didn't make her do anything."

"Maybe you should take this inside," I suggested. "Talk to Julie in private."

Michael nodded and held a hand out to his daughter. "Come on, Jules. We'll talk inside."

Rosie came around the corner of the veranda. "I thought I told you to stay out of this, Marcello."

"I was only trying to help."

Michael gave me an odd look. "And we appreciate it, don't we, Julie?"

I shook my head. "No, no, I didn't mean you."

"Now look what you've done," Rosie said. "You've got her running from that little toad."

"She's not running," I said and wished I hadn't when Julie also turned to look at me, and the little toad started to smile.

"Who *is* this person anyway?" Megan asked.

Julie shrugged. "I don't know."

"Exactly," Rosie said. "So why don't you shut the hell up and let me handle this."

"I'm sorry," Michael said. "Julie, this is Sam, my—"

"Hey, what about my new doll?" Megan demanded.

"We'll get back to you," Michael said.

But that wasn't good enough for the toad. "I don't believe you. I'm going to get my mom. And I am never playing with you again, Julie Hughes. And I'm going to tell everyone else not to play with you either."

"I've had enough of this," Rosie said, then knelt down and spoke softly in Julie's ear. "Who cares? Everyone here is so boring it hurts."

I watched, amazed, as Julie's face relaxed for the first time and she spoke the line word for word.

Then Rosie whispered, "I only played with you because I felt sorry for you," and my legs went rubbery when Julie repeated exactly what her mother had said.

"What do you think you're doing?" I asked.

"I don't know, but I'm as appalled as you are," Michael said. "Young lady, I want you to apologize to Megan this instant."

"Michael, no," I said. "You don't understand. I didn't mean for Julie to stop."

He stared at me. "Then what did you mean?"

"It's hard to explain," I started, but stopped myself in time.

How could I tell him what was going on? Just follow the advice I'd given Julie and jump right in with the truth? *Hey, Michael, good news. Your wife has returned from the dead.*

Something more subtle, perhaps? *Michael, you'll never guess who's back in town.*

How about a little humor? *So three ghosts walk into a bar.*

He would never believe me. I hardly believed myself and I could see her clearly right there in front of me, impatiently tapping her stiletto-clad toes.

Michael's face softened. "Sam, look. I know you don't have children, and what I'm doing may seem harsh, but it's my job to ensure that Julie learns right from wrong."

"Here we go again," Rosie said. "The man is such an idiot lately."

I shook my head. "You're perfect, I suppose."

"Far from it," Michael said. "But I believe children need to learn responsibility."

I smiled brightly. "Of course you do. And no one else should have any input whatsoever. You're the one in charge now, after all."

Rosie came toward me. "Back off, Marcello."

"You're doing a splendid job too," I continued. "Not like some parents."

"Thank you," he said and turned to Julie again. "Now what do you say to Megan?"

"Forget it," Megan said. "I don't care if she ever apologizes. I'm never coming back, anyway. She's a geek, just like *her*."

Megan thrust a hand out at me and Julie frowned. "You take that back, Megan Jarvis."

The girl smiled. "Why? Because the black cat will get me if I don't?"

I looked around. "What cat?"

"Shut up," Rosie said. "There is no cat."

"What cat?" I asked Michael.

"I'll explain later."

"It's a big black cat," Megan said, inching closer. "One that only Julie can see."

"Stop it right now," Julie said.

"It's a ghost cat, isn't that right, Julie? With its head half off and all covered with blood. And it follows her all the time—"

"Megan, that's enough," Michael said, but the kid was in control and not about to give up yet.

"Where's the cat now, Julie?" she taunted. "Is it over here? Maybe it's over there." She put a hand to her mouth. "Oh no, it's right behind you. Look out."

"Don't you dare look," Rosie yelled at Julie. "Don't you dare."

Julie's face had drained of color, but she didn't turn, didn't look. Just stood frozen with her eyes fixed on the ground in front of her, obeying her mother.

"This is nuts," I muttered.

"So's Julie," Megan said. "Everyone thinks she's crazy. Even my mom thinks she's crazy."

"I'm not crazy," Julie hollered, and Michael had to grab her before she got her hands on Megan.

"Both of you stop right now," Michael shouted.

Megan laughed and backed away, chanting, "Crazy Julie, crazy Julie."

"You asked for it, you little toad," Rosie muttered, and put her lips to Julie's ear again. "At least I don't smell," she whispered.

Not this again.

I shook my head at Julie. She hesitated a moment, then lifted her chin and delivered the line perfectly.

Megan stopped and her mouth clamped shut. A vast improvement, I thought, but it didn't last long. "I do not smell," the toad said.

"Yes you do," Rosie whispered. "And your mother gives out dental floss at Halloween."

"Julie, don't," I said softly, but she was already playing her part, head tipped to one side the way Rosie's was, speaking the words in the same tone, pausing in the same places.

Megan punched her bony little fists into her waist. "Flossing is an important part of dental hygiene." She turned to me. "You can never have too much floss."

"This has got to stop," I said to Rosie.

"I couldn't agree more," Michael said and knelt down beside his daughter. "Julie, what's going on here?"

Julie shook her head, blinked her eyes. "Can we go inside now?"

"Of course," he said softly and turned to Megan. "Tell your mother I'll be in touch."

Rosie strolled around Julie, knelt down beside Michael, and whispered in his ear. "And when she gets home, perhaps she should tell her mother it was *her* idea to give Barbie a mud bath."

My whole body went cold when he turned to Megan and said, "Did *you* put the doll in the mud?"

"I don't have to answer that," Megan sniffed and headed off across the driveway to the house next door. "You're all crazy. I'm telling my mom."

Rosie started after her. "That toad needs to be taught a lesson," she said but was blown off course when Julie said, "I'm sorry, Daddy," and started to cry.

Rosie came back and knelt beside her daughter. "Don't cry, baby. She's not worth it."

But Julie's tears were flowing and somehow I didn't think they were all for Megan.

"We were just going to bath the Barbie," Julie continued. "And then we saw the sand, and we thought it would be fun to make mud instead. And it was."

Rosie looked over at me. "Barbie in the Slime Pit," she said and started to laugh. "Such a great game, remember?"

I did, and it was. With the right Barbies. And the right friend.

You bitch, I mouthed. "You put her up to it."

Rosie applauded my technique. "Congratulations. I was beginning to think you'd never figure that out. But rest assured, the girls thought it up all by themselves. I was proud of them, so I passed on the name."

"I really am sorry, Daddy," Julie said again.

Michael gathered her in his arms and held her tight. "I know, sweetheart. I know."

Rosie looked over at me. "Isn't that touching?"

"You can't keep doing this," I mouthed.

"You think not? Watch this." She leaned in to whisper in Michael's ear again. "The poor thing is completely overwrought. She needs some quiet time, don't you think?"

Michael rose, taking Julie with him. "I think you need some quiet time."

"Lemonade would be good too," Rosie said.

He brushed the tears from his daughter's cheeks. "Why don't we go and see if Uncle Derek has some lemonade hidden in that fridge of his."

Rosie looped an arm through his. "Sam should probably leave now."

He looked over at me. "I'm sorry, Sam, but Julie needs my attention. I'll call you."

"No he won't," Rosie said.

"I'll look forward to hearing from you," I said. "And if I don't, I'll phone you. Make sure we have that dinner date."

He smiled as he climbed the stairs with Julie. "That would be great, thanks."

Rosie released his arm when they reached the screen door, waited until Julie and Michael went inside, and then came back down to where I stood. "Just out of idle curiosity, what exactly do you think you're doing here?"

I took a look around before answering, making sure no one was within earshot before crouching down in front of the garden, pretending to deadhead the tulips in case anyone was watching. "I'm making a date with an old friend," I told her. "How about you? What are you doing?"

"Taking care of my family."

"That's ridiculous."

"Why? Because I'm dead? You think just because some drunk ran me off the road that I should suddenly go away? Walk off into the white light with my long-lost granny? Forget it, Marcello. While you're at it, forget everything you've been told about the hereafter. There's no white light and no granny, no heaven and no hell. It's just me and a bunch of others wandering around with a long stretch of eternity staring us in the face." She gazed out at the street. "You can't see them, but they're everywhere. Making sure the lawns get cut, the weeds pulled, the kids fed and dressed. Honestly, if not for us, nothing would get done."

I tossed a bright red tulip head to one side. "You always did have an exaggerated sense of your own importance."

"I'm only telling you the truth. Doesn't matter if you like it or not."

Didn't matter if I believed it or not either, because I still found myself turning, checking out the street, wondering if I was seeing real neighbors or something else entirely.

She laughed and crouched down beside me. "Forget it, Marcello. You're not that privileged. Consider yourself lucky to be seeing me."

Like I said, an exaggerated sense of her own importance. I turned back to the tulips and tossed a dried yellow head to one side. "You're all stuck here then, is that it?"

"We're not stuck anywhere. We can go wherever the hell we like. Hong Kong, Sydney, even Venus if we feel like it." She plucked a red tulip and held it to her nose. "I stay because Michael and Julie want me here. They need me."

"They need to move on."

Rosie tossed the tulip aside. "Define *moving on*."

"Moving on means going forward, being happy. Living again."

"In that case, they're fine. Have a listen."

From out of nowhere, the low rumble of a male voice drifted toward me on a breeze scented with lemons and touched with the high, sweet giggle of a little girl. Ice clinked into glasses, liquid poured, and a satisfied sigh followed a moment of silence.

"How did you do that?" I asked.

"Just a cheap trick. I like to avoid them if I can."

From behind the screen door came another swell of laughter, followed by the sound of running feet. "Gotcha," Michael growled, and Julie laughed harder.

"Mommy was the best runner, wasn't she, Daddy," she said between giggles.

"She was indeed," Michael said.

"No one could catch her," Julie said, and I watched the lines around Rosie's mouth soften, relaxing into the kind of smile that clearly said *Mom*.

"That," she said quietly, "is the sound of a happy family. And it's my job to keep it that way. To take care of them."

"Do you honestly believe you were taking care of Julie today?"

"She got the best of the little toad, didn't she?"

"Only by being meaner."

"Whatever works." Rosie got to her feet and dusted grass from her knees. "Julie needs to toughen up. There's only so much I can do to help her, so she has to learn to protect herself."

"But she can't protect herself from the black cat, can she? Can't bluff her way out of that one."

Rosie's hands stilled, but she didn't look at me, and I knew I'd hit the right spot. "I told you, there is no cat."

I got to my feet, took a step toward her. "That's not what Megan thinks. And judging by Julie's reaction, I'd say she doesn't either." I smiled and took another step closer. "What's the cat about, Rosie? What are you hiding?"

"I'm not hiding anything. And the goddamn cat is gone for good." She turned and headed for the stairs. "Now get lost. Like I said, I have work to do."

I surprised both of us by racing ahead and blocking the way. "I'm not going anywhere."

She looked me up and down, then simply walked around me. "Suit yourself, but we'll be turning on the sprinkler soon, so be warned."

"Rosie," I said and she stopped dead, as though speaking her name held some power over her. So I said, "Rosie, Rosie," and held my breath, hoping she'd disappear, melt away, maybe get sucked back into the earth—anything at all that would get rid of her. But she merely laughed and started up the stairs.

"Forget that too, Marcello. There are no magical incantations. It's just been a while since anyone has called my name." She paused on the top step and looked back. "You know what else doesn't work? Séances. They just piss us off. See you 'round, Sammy."

I followed her up to the veranda. "Just so you understand, you're not going to win this time. I'm not giving up on Michael again."

Rosie stopped at the door, but she didn't say anything. Just stood there, tapping her fingernails on the knob and watching me as though taking my measure, figuring out what kind of threat I posed. When she spoke again, I recognized the soft tone, the even delivery, and I couldn't stop a shiver from moving through me.

"Right now, you probably think that's true," she said, "and I have to admire your confidence. Comes from your new life, I guess, and that fabulous new pub you own. The Silver Swan, isn't it? Irish diner deluxe with a gas fireplace and a picture of Queen Victoria over the mantel. Don't look so surprised. I may not have been inside, but you and that pub were all they talked about on the way over here. Doesn't Sam look fabulous? Isn't her place great? Blah, blah, blah. It was enough to make me puke, but the car's still new so I held on. The only interesting bit was the way you threw yourself at Michael so quickly. What's the deal, Marcello? No love life of your own?"

Heat moved up my throat and into my face. I hated knowing that Rosie would see my red cheeks and think she had me pegged. "I did not throw myself at Michael. I didn't even know you were dead, for God's sake."

"But you jumped all over the chance when you found out, didn't you? Couldn't even wait till I was cold in the ground."

"It's been two years. How long do you think you can hold on to him?"

"Forever," she said, her tone so reasonable it was hard to equate it with the absurdity of the words.

I heard singing coming from the other side of the screen door. *You are my sunshine, my only sunshine*, in two-part harmony. Another cheap trick, or simple coincidence? It didn't matter. The effect was the same and she knew it.

Rosie came toward me, her steps slow, measured. "Never forget, Marcello, that Michael is mine. And I will do everything in my power to keep you away from my family."

She stopped in front of me, standing close enough that I could see the fine spray of freckles across her nose, the golden flecks in her eyes, but I didn't back up, didn't give her an inch. "Then I guess we've reached an impasse," I said. "Because this time, I'm not running away."

Rosie put a hand on my shoulder, gripped harder when I tried to shake her off. "You want to think long and hard about this, Sam."

I pried her fingers from my shirt. "Are you threatening me?"

She laughed in that low throaty way I used to envy and walked back to the door, opened it, and went inside. Didn't slide through the screen or vanish into the air. Just walked into the house like any other woman might. Any woman who was alive.

"This isn't over," I called after her.

She smiled and closed the heavy inside door, locked it, and twiddled her fingers at me through the sidelight before sauntering away, cutting me off from Michael as easily and cleanly as she had eight years ago.

"Bitch," I muttered and swung back the screen, pounced a fist on the inside door. "Michael? Can you hear me?"

Another chorus of "You Are My Sunshine" drifted around me. Three voices this time. *You'll never know, dear, how much I love you.*

I kicked the door. "Michael Hughes, where are you?"

The singing finally stopped, followed by the sound of a little girl giggling and begging, "Again, Daddy! Again!"

"Oh, give me a break." I let the screen door slam and grabbed my purse from the Muskoka chair as Derek's truck pulled up to the curb across the street.

He climbed out and grinned at me. "Hey, how'd it go?"

"Swimmingly," I said, brushing grass from my skirt and digging dirt out from under my fingernails. Stupid really, mucking around in the garden so the neighbors wouldn't see me talking to Rosie. They weren't even my neighbors. What did I care if they thought I was crazy? And now I was going to be late for the dinner shift at the Swan.

Derek's grin faded when I met him at the top of the stairs. "Where are you going? What's wrong? Where's Michael?"

"Everything's wrong, and Michael's inside." I consciously unclenched my fists and kept on marching, down the stairs to the walkway, along the walkway to the street. "And you were right to be worried about him," I called over my shoulder. "That man is in deep trouble."

Derek caught up with me in front of the next-door neighbor's driveway. "What are you talking about? What trouble?"

I kept my head down, and my feet moving. "It's hard to explain."

Hard? It was bloody impossible. How exactly was I supposed to tell Derek that his brother was being haunted without putting him on guard against me? He didn't know me well enough to know I didn't believe in any of this. That I was still having trouble accepting the fact that Rosie was real, even though I'd seen her in action. Had talked to her, for God's sake.

Derek touched my arm. "Sam, please. I need to know what's wrong with Michael."

I stopped and faced him. "Nothing's wrong with Michael, exactly. It's more the situation that's the problem. The circumstances he finds himself in."

Derek shook his head. "I don't understand."

"I don't either," I said honestly, but knew I had to come up with something believable, something Derek would accept. Right now, Rosie was in charge, the battle lines had been drawn, and I desperately needed him in my camp. Derek could be my man on the inside, my ace in the hole, and I couldn't afford to alienate him with the truth.

"What I'm trying to say is that Michael has been grieving for so long now, it's become a pattern, one he won't be able to break without a push. A shove, really."

"Are you willing to shove?"

"Absolutely," I said, meaning it. "But I can't be sure I'm shoving the right way unless I know what I'm up against."

He shrugged and folded his arms. "Tell me what you need."

A psychiatrist, probably, but I didn't think it would help to let that slip right now, so I said, "Information," instead, and pressed ahead even as his eyes began to narrow.

"I need to know about Michael's life since Rosie's death. Where he goes, what he does, that sort of thing. Once I get a feel for the patterns that are holding him back, I'm sure I can come up with a way to break them." I paused and moistened my lips. "Does that make sense to you?"

It wasn't making much sense to me, but he must have been just as desperate to have someone in his camp because he shrugged again and said, "I suppose it does. There's just not much to tell."

I gave him an encouraging smile. "Anything at all would be helpful." And hopefully I'd figure out what to do with it later.

But he didn't smile back. In fact, he looked away, focused on the house as though there were answers to be found in the shingles, the chimney, the gingerbread trim. I could see how hard this was for him. I was still a stranger, after all, just some woman he barely knew asking him to betray family secrets. It was a leap from setting up a date to telling all, and I wasn't sure he was going to make the jump until he sighed and turned back to me.

"It's been rough, okay?" he said at last. "Michael works and he goes home, that's his life. As for Julie . . ." He paused, keeping his eyes on the house. "The kid's been through hell since her mother died. Nightmares every time she closes her eyes and hallucinations when they're open."

"Hallucinations? You mean the black cat?"

He turned back to me. "You know about that?"

"Megan was going on about it earlier. Being really nasty too."

"I'm not surprised." Derek sighed and looked away again. "Truth is, Julie can't get away from the damn thing. Sees it all the time now, no matter where she goes."

"She told Megan this?"

"Didn't have to. She slept over there last night."

"And she saw the cat?"

"In the middle of the night she started screaming that the cat was in bed with them. Woke the whole house up, of course, and couldn't be calmed. Michael had to go and get her."

"Poor little thing," I said, hoping Rosie was right, hoping the cat really was gone for good. "But why does she see a black cat?" I asked. "Why not a brown dog or a blond hamster?"

He took a few steps along the sidewalk. "Because some idiot told her a black cat was killed in the same accident that took her mother."

I drew up beside him again. "Rosie hit a cat?"

"No, the cat was in the car with her. Julie had been bugging Rosie and Mike to get her a kitten for months. Not another barn cat, but one she could keep in the house as a pet."

"But Rosie's allergic to cats. *Was* allergic to cats."

"Which is why they always said no. But for some reason, she picked up a cat on her way home that day. There was no receipt, nothing at all to indicate where she got it, so we still have no idea where it came from. Unfortunately, when Julie found out about the cat, she decided the accident was her fault, because if Rosie hadn't stopped to get the damn thing, she would have been home before the storm started."

"And now Julie sees a ghost cat."

Derek nodded and rubbed a hand over his face. "The therapist says her guilt is so profound it has taken on a concrete form, manifesting itself as what she imagines the injured cat would look like."

"I see," I said, but knew the therapist had it all wrong. Rosie had sort of admitted the cat existed. And if I could see Rosie, why couldn't Julie see the cat?

"The therapist had her draw the cat for him once," Derek continued. "You wouldn't believe what that girl sees. No wonder she has nightmares."

That was the only part that didn't make sense. Rosie had been in the same accident, yet I didn't see her injuries at all. What was different about the cat? Why did Julie see her that way? And how far would some therapist go to stop the hallucination?

"What are they doing for Julie?" I asked.

"MRIs, CAT scans, drugs, hypnotism. You name it, they've tried it. That's part of the reason they're here. Some specialist Mike's been trying to get Julie in to see called with an opening next Monday. Naturally Michael grabbed it, and I told them to come down early, spend a few days with me. I thought that being in a different place with different things to do and different kids around might help her put that cat on hold for a while. But it doesn't look like it worked."

I tried for an encouraging smile. "You never know. Maybe today is the beginning of a change. Maybe she won't see it anymore."

Who knew? Maybe Rosie had actually done something good. Stranger things had happened.

"So does it help?" Derek asked.

"Does what help?"

"Knowing about the cat. Does it help you figure out a way to push Michael out of this holding pattern?"

"I think so," I said, and started walking again, wishing I had a plan, a strategy, even a vague idea of what to do next. The only thing I knew for certain was that I wasn't willing to give up, which meant I needed to see Michael again, and soon. Somewhere different. Somewhere safe. Somewhere Rosie had never been.

That's when the light went on.

I stopped abruptly. "Michael needs to come to the Swan."

"We could come for dinner tonight."

I shook my head, started to pace. "It has to be more than that. He's only in town for a few days. I need him with me all the time. I need his full attention as long as he's here."

Derek smiled. "You really care about him, don't you?"

The question took me aback. "Yeah. I guess I do. So how do we get him to the Swan?"

"It's too bad all your renovations are done. He could have helped with that."

I snapped my fingers and pointed one at him. "The patio."

"What patio?"

I turned and jogged back to the house. "An outdoor one at the Swan. I have all the permits and approvals. I was holding back because of the money, but what the heck. You only live once, right?"

At least that's what I had always believed.

I pulled up short at the bottom of the stairs, smoothed my hands over my hair and my skirt while I waited for Derek to catch up. "I'll do the talking, you just back me up, okay? Then can you drive me back to the pub? I'm late as it is."

"Done," he said, following me up to the veranda.

I knocked on the front door. "He *can* build a patio, can't he?"

"Of course, but it would have to be wood. He doesn't do wrought iron."

"I prefer wood. Wood is perfect."

I knocked again, louder this time. "Michael, are you in there?"

Derek reached around me and opened the door. "It's okay. I live here."

"I knew that," I said and led us both inside.

The interior layout was typical of houses built in the thirties: a tiny foyer with a set of stairs on the left, a hallway leading to a small kitchen straight ahead and a door on the right that opened into the living room. The overall feeling would have been dark and cramped if not for the skylight Derek had installed at the top of the stairs. Already his renovations were making a difference.

"Don't mind the mess," he said, taking me past a stack of ceramic tile boxes to the living room. "I know there's a couch in here somewhere."

The living room gave on to a dining room, both of which were in the throes of renovations. Apart from the fireplace waiting patiently for a mantel, the living room offered a leather couch with matching ottoman, a big-screen television, a DVD player with a stack of movies, and, of course, a rolling rack of TV trays beside the couch. Enough for any single man to get by on for a while.

"Have a seat," Derek said. "I'll go find Michael."

I couldn't have sat still if I wanted to, so I wandered over to the television to check out Derek's movie collection. Not a great selection. Some kid stuff for Julie, some car chases for him, the big-eyed Disney heroines mixing easily with the *Die Hards*, *Lethal Weapons*, and *Terminators*. Nothing out of the ordinary, nothing unexpected, except for one old VHS tape at the bottom of the pile. *The Odd Couple*, with Jack Lemmon and Walter Matthau, my favorite movie. I smiled. So Derek Hughes was an *Odd Couple* fan. Who would have guessed?

"Back already?" Rosie said, lounging in the dining room doorway with a glass of white wine. "You really are a sad case."

She was right. Sad, desperate, clutching at straws, any of those probably described me perfectly right now, but I wasn't about to stop. Things had gone Rosie's way long enough. It was my turn for a change.

"Sammy?" Michael said, stepping around her. "What are you doing here?"

"I need a patio." I watched Rosie loop her arm through his and snuggle in closer, clearly marking her territory. "Nothing fancy," I continued. "But wood, definitely wood." I stopped talking. Tried a smile. Even took a breath. "I need you to build it for me."

"Why you?" Rosie asked.

"Why me?" Michael repeated.

"Because Derek said you're the best, and I want the best."

Michael laughed and walked toward me. Naturally Rosie came with him.

"What kind of patio are we talking about?" he asked.

I pushed my shoulders back and smiled up at him. "I was hoping you could give me some ideas."

He smiled back. "There's nothing I'd like better."

Rosie ran a finger up and down his arm. "This all sounds like a lot of fun, but what about your commitment to Derek? He's counting on you to help with the wiring tomorrow. You gave your word."

Michael sighed; his smile drooped. "Of course, I can't do anything until we've finished the wiring tomorrow."

"What are you talking about?" Derek walked in from the front hall and stood beside me. "The wiring can wait; her patio can't. Not if she wants to catch the summer season. Business before pleasure, isn't that what you always say?"

Michael nodded, Rosie frowned, and I could have kissed Derek for knowing the right note to hit.

"Then why not come back with me now?" I added for harmony. "Have a look at the site, take some measurements, that sort of thing."

"I can't tonight," Michael said. "I have to go Barbie shopping. But I can come by tomorrow morning. Early."

"The earlier the better," I said, then lowered my voice along with my lashes. "And when you're finished with the patio, you and I can have that supper we were planning."

"Give it up, Marcello," Rosie said. "You never could do sexy." She put her lips to Michael's ear and went for the gold. "What about Julie?" she whispered. "You promised tomorrow would be pizza and a movie night."

"Derek can take Julie for pizza night," I said before Michael could open his mouth. "What do you say, Derek?"

He looked from me to Michael and back again. "Sure. Of course. I'll take her to Gino's, then we'll come back here with a movie. We'll have such a good time she won't even know you're gone."

"We wouldn't have to be late," Michael said. "In fact, we could come back here for the movie after dinner."

I had no intention of ever coming back here, but this was not the time to argue.

"Sounds wonderful," I said and took a chance. Moved in on Michael's other side and pressed my breasts against his arm. "See you in the morning, then?"

His eyes widened, but he couldn't speak, and it was all I could do not to stick my tongue out at Rosie.

"Sounds like a plan," Derek said for him. "I know Sam's in a hurry, so I'll drive her back to the restaurant now."

"Great," Michael said, softly at first and then louder, with conviction. "This is so great."

"Daddy?" Julie called from somewhere upstairs.

I realized Rosie was gone but couldn't remember seeing her leave, which figured. And I wasn't a bit surprised that she'd already called in the reinforcements.

"Coming, sweetheart," Michael called to Julie before turning to me. "I'll see you in the morning."

"Count on it," I whispered and slowly released his arm, letting my fingers linger on his skin a moment longer than necessary.

"Till tomorrow, then," he said, still smiling as he walked backward into the hall.

"Daddy," Julie called, more insistent this time.

I waved and Michael laughed. Then he headed off, bounding up the stairs to see to his daughter.

"Let's get this show on the road," Derek said, giving me a high five on his way to the front door.

"Amen to that," I said, but when I tried to follow him outside, Rosie appeared in front of me, blocking the way.

"Another cheap trick?" I asked.

"Sometimes you need them." She leaned back against the frame. "Just remember, Marcello. I'll be right behind you."

I smiled and pushed past her. "Only if you can keep up, bitch. Only if you can keep up."

FIVE

The Danforth is never the place to be at rush hour on a Friday afternoon, and the warm weather had added even more drivers to the mix. A long line of cars lurched from light to light, honking at delivery trucks, fighting for parking spots, and narrowly missing those brave, stupid souls on bicycles, all of which was turning what should have been a two-minute drive into a fifteen-minute ordeal. Granted, I could have said good-bye to Derek and started walking at the first sign of trouble, but to be honest, I wasn't in as big a hurry to get to the Swan as I should have been.

While I wanted to believe that everything was fine, that Michael would indeed show up in the morning as planned, I couldn't help looking back toward Fenwick every time we started moving, wondering if I'd made a tactical error in leaving.

"What if he doesn't come tomorrow?" I finally asked Derek. "What if he changes his mind again?"

"You worry too much. Besides, you saw how happy he was. What could possibly change his mind?"

A delivery truck pulled in behind us, filling the window and cutting off my view of Fenwick, and I realized with sudden, jarring clarity that this was a sign. If I wanted to keep Michael in my sights, I shouldn't be in the pickup, I should be at the mall, shopping for Barbies.

"Take me back," I said. "I need to be with Michael."

"Okay, if that's what you want. But you might want to find out who that is blocking the front door of the Swan first."

I snapped around and squinted into the sun. As opposed to the road, traffic on the sidewalks was orderly and courteous, with the unwritten rules of rush hour allowing those eager to get to the subway to set the pace in the outside lane, leaving the inside clear for browsers and shoppers, and those blessed few trying to read menus. Fortunately, the height of Derek's pickup gave me a clear view over all of them, and I started to sweat when I realized the woman in the white jacket and black cap blocking my front door could only be Eva.

She scanned the street, checked her watch, and was about to go back inside when something across the road caught her attention. I followed her gaze, saw the line outside the bistro, and quickly looked back at her, hoping this wasn't the beginning of a reverse defection.

"Who is it?" Derek asked.

"My chef."

"She doesn't look happy."

"That's because I'm late." I checked the clock on the dash. "Really late."

I wiped my palms on my skirt and took a deep, calming breath. Tried not to panic when Eva flipped open her cell phone and punched in a number, her eyes still on the bistro. If she left now, I'd be in deep trouble, and it would be my own fault. Correction.

It would be Rosie's fault, but I'd be the one cleaning up the mess, again.

"Shall I take you back to the house, or are you going in?"

"I'm going in," I said and unbuckled my seat belt. "Wish me luck."

"Always."

He threw open his door and jogged around to open my side.

"You didn't have to do that," I said, but was grateful for the hand he offered because it was a long way to the sidewalk, and my skirt was not made for the journey.

"Thanks for everything," I said. "And I'm sorry about the traffic."

He gave me a *What can you do?* kind of shrug and handed me a business card. "Call my cell if you need backup."

"I'll be fine," I said, tucking the card into my shirt pocket just in case.

He raced back around the truck and climbed in. Shifted into drive and advanced the six feet he'd missed by helping me out, then put an imaginary phone to his ear. "Call me," he mouthed.

I laughed and joined the wave of pedestrians, sticking to the curb lane for speed and taking an odd comfort in the fact that Derek would pass the Swan about the same time I arrived.

Eva scanned the street one more time. I waved to let her know I was almost there, but she didn't see me. Her attention was focused on the bistro again. I glanced over, knowing envy is a sin, a deadly one at that, but feeling it nonetheless. What must it be like to have a line at your door? Especially when your former chef is watching?

I looked back at Eva, wondering if she'd ever regretted leaving and why I'd never thought to ask. But this didn't seem like the best time to pose the question, so I smiled broadly when I finally made it to the Swan and said, "Sorry I'm late. Are we busy?" instead.

"Some of us are." She finally took her eyes off the bistro and gave me a cursory once-over. "I'm curious. Are you planning to stick around for a while, or are you going to bugger off again?"

"Of course I'm staying. And don't look at me like that. You're the one who told me to leave in the first place."

"I told you to go and visit, not camp out for the day." She held up her cell phone. "I've been calling for over an hour. Why didn't you answer your phone?"

"My phone?" I pulled it out of my pocket and stared at the darkened screen, remembering.

I'd turned it off so Michael couldn't call and cancel, but had forgotten to turn it back on again, which was strange because I never forget to turn on my phone. It's my number one work rule—always be available. Yet I hadn't been, thanks to Rosie.

"It's on now," I said, holding the phone up for Eva to see, but she merely grunted, cast one last glance at the bistro, and walked into the Swan.

I've never been able to grunt with that kind of authority, so I looked across the road, raised my chin slightly, and flicked it with my fingers the way Loretta had taught me. Then I turned and followed Eva, hoping the guy at the bistro had seen me.

I hurried to catch up with her, smiling and nodding at customers along the way. The place wasn't as crowded as it had been at lunch, but there were definitely more tables than she and Johnny could handle alone. No wonder she was ticked.

"I'm sorry I took so long," I said when we reached the bar. "But it wasn't easy to leave."

She stopped and rounded on me. "You saw Rosie again, didn't you."

It wasn't the response I'd expected, but I nodded and leaned in closer, pleased to have someone to tell. "I even spoke to her this time. You have no idea how weird that was."

"I'll bet I do, but we'll talk later. And you have to tell me everything, understand? You have to be careful with ghosts."

I watched her go through the swinging door into the kitchen, wondering just how careful one had to be, and what happened to those who weren't. But there wasn't time to think too long about Eva or Rosie or anything else. Not when four more people were at the door and Johnny was rushing past with salads, shouting, "Thank God you're here. Take two Cosmopolitans, one strawberry daiquiri, and a Guinness to table three. And mineral water to four."

I delivered the water, hurried back to the bar, and pulled on my apron. Four hours later, I finally took it off again and fell into a stool beside Johnny, who was happily counting his tips for the night.

"Did I imagine things," I said, "or did we have both a lunch *and* a dinner rush on the same day?"

"You didn't imagine a thing." He kissed the stack of bills and shoved them deep into his pocket. "A few more nights like this, and I might make the rent on time."

He wiggled his eyebrows at me and went into the kitchen, passing Eva on her way out. She'd traded her chef's jacket and pants for jeans and a leather jacket.

"This had to be a record day," I said.

She grunted again and went around to pull herself a beer. "Tell me everything about Rosie. Leave nothing out."

"So much for niceties."

She slid the beer across the bar. "You want niceties, talk to Johnny. You want help, talk to me."

"What help?" Johnny asked, coming into the dining room with his jacket slung over his shoulder. "What are we talking about?"

Eva sat down beside me and dragged her beer toward her. "Her afternoon with Rosie."

"You saw her again?" He chuckled and sat down on my other side, still the skeptic. "How was it?"

I didn't know where to start, so I simply jumped in, telling them what Rosie had said about there being no heaven or hell, no white light and no granny. I told them how she whispered to Michael and Julie, making them say and do whatever she wanted. I even told them about her thinly veiled threat when I refused to stay away from Michael. Everything, in fact, except the black cat, a detail I wasn't ready to share until I understood more about it myself.

By the time I finished, Johnny's smile was gone and his face had grown pale. A believer at last, just like me.

"Hang on a minute," he said. "If there's no granny and no white light, does that mean there's no God and no devil? No higher power at all? Just us, running around with ghosts whispering in our ears, making us do all kinds of things?"

"It doesn't work like that," Eva said, but Johnny was already on his feet, backing toward the wall.

"Kind of makes you wonder who's whispering in your own ear, doesn't it?" he said. "I mean, if Rosie can make Michael and Julie jump through hoops, how many other people are being led around by ghosts? The prime minister perhaps? Or how about the president?" He pointed out the window at the street. "Who's in charge out there anyway?"

He flinched when Eva put a hand on his arm, only relaxing when she said, "Trust me. No one is whispering in your ear."

Johnny blinked at her. "You're sure?"

"Absolutely."

He laid his head on her shoulder. "Will you whisper in my ear?"

She shoved him away. "I swear one day, I will knock you flat."

"I'll bet you say that to all the boys," he said and tried to smile, but his face was still pale and he kept his back pressed to the wall. "So Rosie isn't here now, right?"

"That's right," I said.

"At least she's not where Sam can see her," Eva said.

Johnny's eyes widened. "You think she's in the kitchen?"

"She's not in the kitchen." I turned to Eva. "What are you doing?"

"Just being honest." She sat down again and picked up her beer. "You're the one who pissed off a ghost, not me. Now, anything can happen."

"Like what?" Johnny asked.

I sighed and propped my chin in my hands. "Like more cheap tricks."

"Or worse," Eva said. "Which is why you need to stay away from Michael for the time being."

"I can't."

"Why not?"

"Because Rosie's with him all the time. If I back off, she'll win again, and I can't let that happen."

"For a smart woman, you can be pretty dumb sometimes." Eva drained her glass and stood up. "I'm starving. Why don't we take this to the Indian place down the street? We can argue while we eat."

"I love to argue while I eat," Johnny said, picking up his jacket.

Eva pointed a finger at him. "You can only come if you promise not to talk to me."

"We're starting the argument here then, are we?" he asked.

"This is not an argument, it's a rule. Don't talk to me." She turned back to me. "You ready?"

I rose and carried her empty glass around the bar to the sink. "You guys go ahead. It's been a long day, and Michael's coming early tomorrow . . ."

"Unless Rosie changes his mind," Eva said.

I looked over at her. "Are you always this much fun?"

"Are you always this annoying?" She took a step toward me. "Sam, you should come with us. You need to eat, and you need to listen to reason."

"Reason? We're talking about a ghost here. How much reason can there be?"

Luckily, the cell phone in my pocket started to ring before she could answer. At least it seemed lucky until I saw Loretta's name and number on the screen. "Oh Christ," I muttered.

"It's the witch," Eva told Johnny.

"Then don't answer it," he said.

I shrugged. "She'll just call back."

"Then turn the damn thing off," Eva said.

"I can't," I said and pressed Talk, putting the phone to my ear before Eva could object. "Hi, Loretta, what's new?"

"I don't know why I bother," Eva muttered and headed for the door.

"*Ciao, bella*. Are you with the rat?"

"No, I'm at the Swan."

Eva paused and looked back at me.

"My date with Michael fell through," I continued.

"Hah!" Loretta said. "That's the power of prayer for you."

Or the power of Rosie, but I wasn't about to argue the point.

"Listen, Loretta, as much as I'd love to chat, I'm just finishing up here—"

"Why don't you tell her about the ghost?" Eva called.

"Is that the bald girl?" Loretta asked. "What's she doing there?"

"Nothing," I said, and should have known better than to send Eva anything resembling a warning look. It only made her smile and walk toward me, stalking me in my own pub.

"Ask her about the ghost," she called, louder this time.

"Did she say ghost? *Madre de Dio*, is it there?"

"It's not here," I said, taking a few steps backward.

"But she saw it again," Eva yelled, still advancing, closing the gap.

Loretta gasped. "You saw it again?"

"Nona, she's kidding," I said, and kept moving, knocking into chairs as I went.

"I don't think the bald girl kids. Tell me the truth, *bella*. Did you see the ghost again?"

"No, I didn't see it."

Eva raised her voice even more. "She's lying."

"Okay, yes, I saw it."

"Not again," Loretta said and started to pray, "*Ave Maria, piena di grazia*. Say it with me, *bella*."

"Maybe later." I slapped my hand over the phone. "Now she's praying. Are you satisfied?"

"Almost." Eva lifted my hand. "Why don't you tell her about the way Rosie threatened you?"

I snatched my hand back. "Are you trying to make my life hell?"

She tilted her head. "Are you?"

"I hate it when you do that." I put the phone to my ear again. "Loretta, I have to go."

"*Bella*, it's not safe for you to be alone. You'll spend the night at my house."

I heard the jingle of Loretta's car keys, the slamming of a drawer. "Nona, stop. I'll be fine at my place."

Eva smiled. "If only you hadn't answered the phone."

"If only you'd kept your mouth shut."

"I'm leaving now," Loretta said. "I just have to find my purse."

"No, please." I turned to the window, half expecting her to be there already. And damned if a car wasn't pulling up in front of the Swan.

A black Lexus. Very new. Very shiny.

"Don't worry, *bella*," Loretta said. "That stupid purse is here somewhere."

"Loretta, it's fine," I said, my heart beating faster as I moved closer to the window. The car was double parked, blocking traffic, yet a man was getting out anyway. A good-looking man. Six foot two, dark hair, blue eyes.

"What's he doing here?" Johnny asked.

"Making things worse," Eva said.

"You want worse?" I pressed Speaker on the cell.

"*Maria*, please," Loretta said for all to hear. "Watch over my Sammy till I get there. And help me find my goddamn purse."

I turned off the speaker. "*That*," I said, "is worse."

Eva glanced out at Michael. "Not if he brought Rosie with him."

"Why would he do that?" Johnny asked, creeping closer to her.

"He wouldn't have a choice," Eva said.

Michael switched on his four-way flashers, gave the guy behind him the *One minute* sign, shrugged when the guy leaned on the horn, and slammed the door. "Sammy, I'm gonna call you back," Loretta said. "Sammy? Did you hear me?"

"What? Yes, of course." I turned away from the window. "But honestly, Loretta, everything's fine."

"You think so, eh?"

"I do," I said, watching Michael walk around the car, oblivious to the honking and the shouting in his wake. A man on a mission. Determined, reckless, with only one thought on his mind.

"You want me to stay here, then," Loretta said.

"Might as well." I pointed a finger at Johnny and whispered, "Unlock the door."

"Sammy?" Loretta snapped. "What's going on?"

"Nothing. I'll talk to you tomorrow."

"Okay, whatever you say." I heard her keys drop, heard her rifling through papers. "Just promise you'll take a taxi home."

"I promise."

"*Ciao, bella.*"

She hung up and I stared at the phone. "That was too easy."

"Is she out there?" Eva asked.

"She said she wasn't coming."

"I meant Rosie."

I stared at Eva. Of course, Rosie. How could I have forgotten?

Stashing the phone in my pocket, I walked closer to the window, searching for a blonde in the backseat, or maybe on the sidewalk. Or how about two cars down? I couldn't see her anywhere. Had Michael escaped without her, or was this another cheap trick? Was she in here already, planning to leap up from behind the bar, or dart around the corner, or pop out of the bathroom? I jerked around. Had that door always been open?

I jumped when Michael threw open the front door, and only relaxed when he stepped inside, bringing with him nothing more than the warm night air. And a small paper bag.

"Michael," I said. "What are you doing here?"

A wonderful boyish grin lit his face. "I know this is silly and I can't stay long, but I had to bring you this." He held up the bag. "Midnight doughnuts."

"It's only ten-thirty," Eva said and held out a hand when he looked over at her. "I'm Eva, this is Johnny, and you're the Michael we've been hearing so much about."

"Guilty," he said, shaking hands with both of them. "And I know it's only ten-thirty, but I originally made the trip for my daughter, and she can't stay up past eleven." He turned back to me. "But when I got to Tim Horton's, I couldn't stop thinking about you, and the Bluffs, and midnight doughnuts." He held out the bag. "Remember?"

"I remember. And it's not silly at all. It's perfect."

"It's a doughnut," Eva said.

"Doughnuts are fun," Johnny offered.

"They can be." I took the bag and slowly unrolled the top. "If they're sour cream glazed."

Michael nodded, serious again. "I hope that's still your favorite."

"She doesn't eat doughnuts," Eva said and frowned when Johnny jabbed her in the ribs. "What? Go ahead and ask her. Sam, do you eat doughnuts?"

"I used to," I said and looked up at Michael, saw him smile again, and for a moment, I was back in my bedroom at Loretta's house, hearing him toss pebbles at my window in the middle of the night. Begging me to come outside so we could make our escape.

It was early summer the first time he showed up at my window, a night just like this when the air was warm and the sky clear and bright. "You're crazy," I whispered through the screen, and he laughed and said, "Crazy for you. Now get down here."

We hadn't been dating long and I hesitated, torn between taking time to dress and making a clean getaway. Not trusting Loretta to sleep through the opening of drawers, I crept down the stairs in my pajamas and stifled a giggle when he picked me up and carried me along the street to his car. We drove to the Bluffs in his old Duster, where we sipped coffee and ate doughnuts, listened to the waves, and talked about the future. For a while, anyway.

I felt my face warm, remembering how I lay awake in the dark the rest of that summer, listening and waiting. My heart lifting on those rare, sweet nights when Michael was out there again, tossing pebbles from my grandmother's flower beds.

"I always loved midnight doughnuts," I said softly.

"Me too," he whispered and lifted a hand to touch my cheek.

"So, did you come here alone?" Eva asked.

We both turned and she gestured to the door. "I mean, you've left your car out there double parked and unattended. Or is someone watching it for you?"

"No one's watching it." I smiled out the window. "No one at all."

"But she's right," Michael said. "I should be going. Julie's waiting for her apple fritter and Derek's got something lined up. They'll be wondering where I am."

"They're not the only ones," Eva said.

He looked confused, so I took his arm and said, "I'll see you in the morning."

He grinned at me. "Bright and early."

I opened the door and we stepped outside, the paper bag still in my hand.

The guy with the horn had given up and driven off, and the rest of the traffic was finding its way around his car. Confident that Michael was safe for the moment, I took his arm and we strolled across the sidewalk to the curb. Up and down the block, tiny white lights twinkled in the trees, music floated from the pubs and bars, and Rosie was nowhere to be seen. The power of prayer, or just a lucky break? What did it matter? We were here, and she wasn't, making everything just about perfect. Too bad about the tow truck slowly making its way toward the Lexus.

"Talk about timing," Michael said, kissing me quickly, lightly on the cheek. A kiss that was chaste and sweet and filled with promise, just as that first midnight doughnut had been. "Till tomorrow," he said, and ran back to his car, arriving at the same moment the tow truck did.

"What a beautiful night," a voice said, and I turned, gooseflesh rising on my skin.

Rosie laughed and walked toward me out of the shadows. "Ah, Marcello, you should see your face. You look like you've seen a ghost." She nodded at the tow truck. "What do you think? Will he catch a break or not?"

The truck was parked now and the driver was out, talking to Michael.

"He'll be fine," I said quietly. "How long have you been here?"

"Here? Only a few minutes." She motioned to the bistro across the street. "I was over there for the most part. Great spot. A menu to die for. Have you tried their tapas? Oh, wait, doughnuts are more your style, aren't they?" She touched the bag in my hand. "Did you enjoy yours?"

I snatched it away. "Not yet."

She turned to watch Michael and the driver. "Well, I wouldn't wait much longer. That kind of thing grows stale so quickly. But as long as you had a little fun that's what matters most."

"What exactly is that supposed to mean?"

"Nothing. I just thought you'd enjoy a trip down memory lane, that's all. I did get it right, didn't I? Sour cream glazed is what he used to bring you. He's hopeless with details."

My fingers tightened on the bag. "You're telling me the doughnut was your idea?"

She looked hurt. "Not just the doughnut, Marcello, the whole thing. Michael had a movie going and a couple of beers in the fridge. Believe me, he was in for the night, but I couldn't help thinking about you, feeling badly about the way things ended this afternoon. So I thought, why not do something nice for her? Leave her with a lovely memory of her visit with Michael. I started with Julie, who immediately decided she wanted something salty. But you didn't have midnight chips, did you, so I had to convince her that she wanted sugar instead. Took a while, let me tell you. That girl can be so determined when she wants to be. Reminds me of myself, when I was her age."

"I don't believe you."

"Oh she is. I mean just look at—"

"Shut up, Rosie. You know what I'm talking about. I don't believe you set this up."

She gave me a small, patronizing smile. "Of course you don't. And I would never have said a word if you hadn't gone all soft and moony on me. I guess I should have thought it through better.

After all, that was the spot where you lost your virginity, wasn't it? High on a cliff in the back of a beat-up old Duster." She laughed. "I will never forget *that* phone call."

My stomach tightened. "You bitch."

She pouted and put a hand to her heart. "Marcello, why so mean? I was only thinking of you. I didn't want you to get your hopes up and end up being hurt all over again."

She glanced over at the tow truck and gave her head a little shake. "Poor Michael. Looks like he's losing the battle." She stepped off the curb and twiddled her fingers at me over her shoulder. "See you in the morning, Marcello. Bright and early."

"I don't believe this," I said, watching Rosie smile at the tow truck driver and lay a hand on his shoulder. He kept talking and she leaned in close, whispered something in his ear. The driver stopped talking and drew his head back. She whispered again, and this time he smiled at Michael, even shook his hand, and headed back to his truck, whistling.

Michael grinned at me. "That was close."

Rosie took his arm and smiled up at him. "Wasn't it, though?"

"He'd have been fine," I muttered around my smile, thinking about presidents and prime ministers and hoping Eva was right.

Michael waved and opened the car door. Rosie climbed in ahead of him and settled herself in the passenger seat. He tooted the horn as he pulled away. Rosie gave me a royal wave, and the midnight doughnut weighed heavy in my hand.

Eva and Johnny came outside, carrying my purse and my jacket.

"You don't look happy," Eva said, handing both to me when I came back to the step. "What happened?"

"Rosie. She was at the bistro the whole time."

Johnny hesitated with his key in the lock. "Is she still here?"

"She went home with Michael." I held the bag out to him. "You like doughnuts?"

"Love them. But don't you want it?"

"Not anymore." I shoved the bag into his hands and turned my back on it. "Seems the visit was Rosie's idea, not Michael's."

"She told you that?" Eva asked. I nodded and she came to stand beside me. "And you believed her."

"You think I shouldn't?"

"I didn't say that. I just wouldn't be so quick to trust a ghost."

Johnny drew up on my other side. "Are you going to cool things with Michael now?"

I shook my head. "Not a chance."

Eva sighed. "Then at least come and eat with us."

I sighed, torn, then raised my chin and backed up a step. "Maybe another time."

"Suit yourself," Eva said. "But your grandmother's right. You might not want to be on your own tonight."

As if on cue, my cell phone started to ring. Loretta again. This time, however, I took Eva's advice and ignored it.

"You'll pay for that," Eva said.

"For years," I said, and started walking, heading home alone.

SIX

My house is small. Two bedrooms, one bathroom. A dollhouse if you compare it to my sister's suburban starter mansion, which Loretta does all the time, but I like the place. Sure, a main-floor laundry would be nice, as would a table in the kitchen, and I admit that Angie's walk-in closet can make my heart hurt, but I console myself with the knowledge that I can walk to the butcher instead. And the fruit market, and the subway, and most importantly, the Swan.

Loretta thinks I'm crazy to walk home at night, always wants me to take a taxi, so I always lie and tell her I will. Truth is, I look forward to those twice-a-day strolls. That's my time to think, to plan, to dream now and then. And I can honestly say that I've never once been afraid, until Rosie.

All the way home, I kept looking over my shoulder and hesitating before passing bushes, unable to shake the idea that Rosie was behind me, or in front of me, biding her time, preparing her next strike. By the time I made it to my front walk, I was sweating, my heart was racing, and I couldn't make it up the stairs fast enough. I fumbled with the keys, rammed the front door open with my shoulder, and slammed it shut behind me—bolting it, chaining it, snapping every extra lock Loretta had insisted on installing into place. Also for the first time.

Walking away from that door, I knew I was being ridiculous. If she was anywhere, she was with Michael, whispering in his ear, turning his head, keeping him right where she wanted him, the bitch. But who really knew what Rosie would do next, or where? And any ideas of sleep I might have had evaporated in a night spent on the couch with all the lights on, the Food Network turned up, and a poker on the floor beside me. I can't say what good I thought it might do, but at two A.M. it seemed like a great idea.

I finally sprawled across my bed at five and switched off the alarm. Who'd need it, after all? I was only going to close my eyes for a few minutes, just long enough to stop the burning. The next thing I knew, my cell phone was ringing somewhere off in the distance—the first lines of "Pomp and Circumstance" playing softly, coming to a close, then starting again. I jerked upright, blinked at the clock. Nine thirteen. How could it be nine thirteen?

Stumbling out of bed, I stood in the doorway a moment, hanging onto the frame and trying to focus while I listened for the phone. The tune started again, the sound muffled, but definitely there. If only I could remember where I'd left the phone. My purse? A pocket?

I pushed off and headed for the kitchen. Either way, the phone was in that direction.

I found it in my purse, saw that Johnny was calling, and pressed Talk. "I slept in," I said, flicking the switch on the kettle on my way to the stove for the teapot. "I'll be there soon."

"You better be. Your grandmother's here. And it's bad."

The teapot clattered to the floor. I gripped the phone tighter.

"Oh my God, poor Michael. I should have warned him. I should have been there—"

"Sam, slow down. Michael's not even here."

I zipped into the bathroom and turned on the shower. "Not there? Where is he?"

"How should I know? Just get over here."

Running back through the living room to my bedroom, I grabbed my robe off the dresser and took it with me to the bathroom. "Has she done something to Eva? Tell me the truth."

"Eva's at the market."

I tossed the robe on the counter and tested the water, adjusted the taps. "Then how bad can it be? Just keep her out of the kitchen until I get there."

"The kitchen would be easy," Johnny said.

"What?"

"Never mind. Just hurry. Derek's on his way over to get you."

I pulled my hand out of the stream of water. "Derek? What's he doing there?"

"He's not here. And I have to go."

"Johnny?" But he had already ended the call, leaving me staring at the phone, wondering where Michael was, why Derek was coming to get me, and how long I had before Eva made it back to the Swan and found Loretta there.

"Another wonderful day," I muttered, dropping the phone on the counter and dashing back to the living room to open all the bloody locks on the front door so Derek could let himself in. Then I hurried back to the bathroom, kicked off my pajamas, and was showered and pulling on a white blouse and black skirt when the doorbell rang.

"Come in," I shouted, grabbing a brush and going at my hair.

I heard the front door open, heard Derek's voice calling, "You ready?"

"Almost," I called back, but naturally curly does not take well to being rushed. I fluffed and tugged and finally resorted to an elastic band. Tying it all up on top of my head, I avoided the mirror and hurried out to the living room, promising myself I'd put on makeup when I got to the Swan.

Derek stood at the front door, evidence of my campout on the couch spread before him.

"Sleep well?" he asked.

"No, and thanks for asking." I picked up my keys from the coffee table, hung the poker back in the rack by the fireplace, grabbed my purse and cell phone and followed him out the door. "How come you're here?" I asked when we reached his truck. "Where's Michael?"

"Mike got a call from the new therapist this morning. Apparently they had a cancellation and wanted him to bring Julie down right away. Can you believe that?"

"Definitely," I said, certain that Rosie had something to do with Michael's sudden stroke of luck. I took the hand Derek offered and climbed into the pickup. "When will he be back?"

"It's probably just a paperwork appointment, so he shouldn't be long. But it's best he's delayed anyway right now." Derek gave me a sympathetic smile. "According to Johnny, you're going to be busy for a while."

I slumped back in the seat. "I may have to kill my grandmother."

"I'm sure she means well," Derek said, then closed the door and hurried around to the driver's side.

"Any idea what she was doing?"

"Not a clue," Derek said as he started the truck. "Michael asked me to call the Swan and tell you he'd be late. Johnny answered, but he wasn't making much sense. Said something about having trouble with your grandmother, gave me your address, and asked me to pick you up right away."

"I'm sorry he dragged you into this. My grandmother just scares him. In fact, she scares most people."

Derek laughed. "I remember some of Mike's stories. She's an interesting woman."

We turned left onto the Danforth and joined the line of cars waiting for the light. We were still a block from the Swan, but with the bird's-eye view from the pickup, I could see a small group gathered on the sidewalk outside the pub.

I sat up straighter. "Can you make out what's going on up there?"

"Looks like a protest group, unless you offer Seniors Day specials."

"Not a chance. Loretta is all I can handle."

The light changed and we moved forward. As we drew closer, a taxi pulled up in front of the pub and more old women got out. There were now twelve in total. Some carried tin foil–wrapped plates, others cups of takeout coffee, and all of them were being herded into a circle by Loretta.

Derek pulled into the first available parking spot and shut off the engine. "Any idea what she's doing?"

"Nope." I grabbed my purse and let him swing me down from the truck. "But whatever it is, I'm sure it will be interesting."

"Do you know any of them?" he asked, pushing loonies into the machine for a parking ticket.

"A few," I said, taking the ticket from him and setting it on the dashboard.

Even at this distance, I recognized Mrs. Volpe, Mrs. Delvecchio, and crotchety old Mrs. Moon. All women I'd known since childhood, but hadn't seen since my sister's wedding, the last time I set foot inside St. Catherine's Church. The rest were strangers to me, but not to Loretta, who was obviously in charge and having a hell of a time.

Another taxi pulled up in front of the Swan. Four more old ladies got out, and she waved them over. "We should hurry," I said, and we started walking, dodging strollers, bundle buggies, and those damn bicycles locked to the racks lining the curb.

"Maybe you're being hasty," Derek said when we circled a man with a toddler on his shoulders. "Maybe she's just bringing customers."

"She would never do that. Besides, look over there." I paused in front of the fruit market, discreetly pointing to the bistro across from the Swan. The owner was standing at the curb with a few of his staff, watching Loretta and her cronies. When he spotted me, he smiled and waved—the first time he had acknowledged my existence since the day Eva defected.

"Friend of yours?" Derek asked.

"He hates me," I said, smiling and waving back. "Which means something is horribly wrong."

"Then let's go," Derek said.

I laid a hand on his arm, holding him back. "That's not a good idea. Loretta might remember that you're Michael's brother, and she's not fond of Michael these days."

"I imagine she'd like to kill him. I would if I were her." The surprise I felt must have shown on my face because Derek smiled a little and said, "Sam, I'm Michael's brother, not his lawyer. I don't have to defend what he did to you. As far as I'm concerned he was an idiot, and if you refused to talk to him ever again, he'd have it coming. But you *are* talking to him, and more important, you're giving him a chance to feel normal again, to realize what he's been missing by holing himself up in that house for two years. How can I let you walk into that crowd alone? You never know what can happen when old ladies get ugly." He started walking again. "Besides, I can probably run faster than your grandmother and I'm curious as hell now. I want to know what they're up to."

I hesitated, not at all sure *I* wanted to find out.

But when another taxi pulled up in front of the Swan I picked up the pace, stopping short of a full-out run that would have delighted the guy across the street. By the time I reached the florist, there were a dozen candles in red hurricane glasses circling my sandwich board. By the hardware store, I realized those were rosaries in the ladies' hands. When I reached the edge of my own pub, I could finally read the writing on the sandwich board. *Resist the Devil and He Will Flee You.*

That's when it came together. Loretta was trying to exorcise my ghost with her prayer group.

"I'll kill her," I said, and it was only Derek's hand on my arm that kept me from charging into the circle.

"*Bella*, you're here," Loretta called, and all heads turned. "This is my Samantha. The one cursed with the evil eye." The ladies crossed themselves, Derek raised an eyebrow, and I tried to laugh it off.

"She's exaggerating," I told him quietly.

"Exaggerating?" Loretta said. "Then how come you see ghosts?"

"You see ghosts?" Derek asked.

"Only one," I said, quickly adding, "It's a long story," before moving away from him and into the circle. "Mrs. Delvecchio, nice to see you too. And you brought biscotti, how thoughtful. But really there's no problem. Mrs. Moon, yes, it has been a long time. No, I'm not going to cut my hair, but thanks for the tip. Mrs. Volpe, how are you? I understand, but honestly my grandmother is making mountains out of molehills. And who the hell painted my front door red?"

"That was me," Loretta said. "It's supposed to keep away ghosts, but it's an Irish thing, so who can tell. I only did it because I thought it would make you happy. But everything else is gonna work, guaranteed. Ready, girls?"

The women nodded and closed the circle around me. My brain was nudging me to pay attention, to do something, but I couldn't move, couldn't do anything except stare at my fire-engine-red front door. High gloss at that. "When did you do this?" I asked.

"A little while ago, so be careful, it's still sticky," Loretta said. "The bald girl tried to stop me, of course, but she's the devil's spawn and you should fire her."

I snapped my head around, searching the windows. "How long has she been here?"

"Ten, fifteen minutes. But I finished painting anyway, so now she won't let us in. But who cares? We'll do this outside. Right here, right now. Who wants to start?"

Mrs. Delvecchio held up a hand, made the sign of the cross, then smiled at me. "*Nel nome del Padre, e del Figlio, e dello Spirito Santo*," she said, and the rest joined in for the first round of the rosary.

I shook my head, held up my hands. "Ladies, please. You can't do this here."

Naturally, they ignored me and I turned to Derek for help, but he was busy directing traffic around the circle, trying to keep people from joining in. "Please, sir, if you could just move along. No, ma'am, we're not collecting money."

The prayer chugged on, more gawkers paused to watch, and my cell phone rang at the same time someone started tapping on glass. I followed the sound and saw Johnny and Eva at the window, Eva with a cell phone pressed to her ear while Johnny rapped on the glass with a penny. She slapped his hand away. "Answer your phone," she mouthed, then made a rude gesture at Loretta, who replied with a sign I have never associated with prayer.

Backing out of the circle, I handed off the biscotti to Derek and fumbled inside my purse for the phone. "What the hell is going on?" I asked when Eva answered.

"I'm sorry about the door," she said. "I was at the market and Johnny was in the back prepping vegetables. He had no idea she was out front. When he finally went into the dining room, she already had half the door painted. Since an all-red door is better than a half-red door, we figured we'd let her finish."

"Why didn't he call me sooner?" I asked.

"He called us both as soon as he saw her. What difference would it have made anyway? What could you have done?"

I pointed to the candles. "I could have stopped this."

"You think so? Go ahead and try. Johnny and I tried putting them out as fast as she lit them, but then a taxi pulled up and we were under attack."

Johnny pointed to a bruise on his right shoulder and another on his left forearm, proving what every Italian child knows from a very young age: Nona is tougher than she looks. Mess with her at your own risk.

"We couldn't stop them," Eva continued. "So we went back inside and locked the door. It was all I could think of."

"*O Gesù, perdona le nostre colpe*," the ladies chanted and started to spread out, making the circle larger and slowing traffic even more.

Somebody hollered from a car, someone else swore on the way by, and the guy at the bistro called, "You go, girls."

"This is bad," I said to Eva. "Very bad."

"What do you want me to do?"

"Unlock the door."

She frowned at me through the glass. "You can't be serious."

The ladies launched into the first mystery, their voices blending together, their fingers working the beads. Anywhere else, it might have been a moving experience. But out here in front of my pub, it was just plain embarrassing.

"Join us," Loretta called to passing pedestrians. "Help us clear this place of evil."

"They got ghosts," Mrs. Moon added and pointed inside.

"Just one," Derek said, still encouraging stragglers to move along. "It's a long story."

"Thank you," I mouthed.

He nodded while gently herding the prayer group back toward

the window. Then he folded up the sandwich board and leaned it against the wall, but I could tell by the way he kept looking back at me that he was going to want answers later. Answers I couldn't afford to give.

"Eva, unlock the door," I said. "I have to get these women off the street before I get rapped for holding an unlawful demonstration or some other ridiculous thing."

"Fine," she said. "Just tell me one thing. Have you seen Rosie this morning?"

I glanced over at Derek and lowered my voice. "No, but you won't believe what she did to keep Michael away. Don't worry, I'll tell you everything later, but right now I have to get these ladies off the street."

"Be sure to call me if she shows up."

"I know, I have to be careful around ghosts. Now open the damn door," I said and pushed End before she could argue.

Johnny unlocked the door and swung it open.

"Okay, ladies," Derek said. "Let's take this inside."

They paused in their round of the rosary, looking to Loretta for confirmation. She grinned at the sky. "*Grazie*, *Maria*, *grazie*. Grab the candles. Everybody inside."

Mrs. Volpe took back her biscotti, Mrs. Delvecchio started picking up candles, and Mrs. Moon was the first in line at the door. "Mind the paint," Johnny said as they filed past. "Yes, ma'am, I'm sure it will come out with mineral spirits. Mind the paint."

Loretta hung back while the others shuffled into the pub. "We need to talk," she said to me.

"No kidding." I took her by the elbow and led her to one side. "What do you think you're doing?"

"Taking care of you. I know I should have asked your permission first, but there was no time to argue, and we both know you would have argued, right?" She waited for me to nod. "See. I know you, *bella*. But him I don't know." She pointed at Derek. "Who's this guy?"

She didn't recognize him. Something had finally gone right.

"I'm the contractor," Derek said, extending a hand. "Pleased to meet you."

She ignored the gesture. "What contractor? Why are you here?

"I'm putting in an outdoor patio," I told her. "Derek is here to give me a price."

"Patio?" She shrugged and took his hand. "Whatever helps. Nice to meet you." She switched back to me. "Okay, turn around."

"What?"

"Sammy, don't argue all the time." She looked over at Derek. "She always argues. Makes me crazy."

I sighed and turned around, felt her put something around my neck and clip it beneath my ponytail. "That will keep you safe. Wear it all the time, okay?"

"What is it?" I asked, stretching out the chain, peering down my nose. My grandmother's Miraculous Medallion gleamed in the sunlight. Crafted in Italy more than sixty years ago, the necklace was eighteen-karat gold with a chain fifteen inches long and a charm the size of a quarter. In the middle of the charm stood St. Mary and the inscription around the outside translated as: "Oh Mary, conceived without sin, pray for us who have recourse with thee." Loretta had worn the medallion for as long as I could remember and swore it had been blessed by the pope himself when she was a little girl. An impressive thing, if you believed it helped.

"Loretta," I started, but she held up a hand.

"Don't thank me. I do this because I love you. And I know you have to get back to work. We'll be thirty minutes, tops. Okay?" She cupped a hand on my cheek and her voice softened. "Everything will be fine, *bella*, I promise. Thirty minutes, tops."

She gave me a thumbs-up and hurried into the pub. The moment she disappeared inside, Eva appeared outside, stepping through the door carefully, minding the paint. She stood in front of me with her hands on her hips, blocking my view and scowling. "I can't believe you let her take over."

"Didn't look like she had a lot of choice," Derek said. "Those women had their minds made up."

"Exactly," I said, grateful for an ally. "If I'd stopped her out here, she'd have taken the show across the road, or up on the roof, or God knows where else. At least this way, she's contained and it will all be over in thirty minutes."

Eva laughed. "You think so?"

"She promised."

"And you trust her?"

"I'd like to." I leaned left, then right, trying to see around her, but Eva wasn't budging. So I walked over to the window, cupped my hands on the glass, and peered inside. The group had lined up the candles on the mantel, pushed a couple of tables together, and seated themselves in front of the fireplace, sipping coffee and passing biscotti. I could see Johnny putting on another pot while Mrs. Moon poked through the bottles at the bar. It certainly didn't look like anyone was in a hurry. Still, I was prepared to give Loretta the benefit of the doubt. What choice did I have?

Stepping away from the window, I turned to Eva. "Go back inside and lower the blinds. We're officially closed until this is over."

"I don't mean to sound pessimistic," Derek said, "but isn't there someone you can call for backup in case they go into overtime? A brother, a sister—"

"She has a sister in Oakville," Eva said.

I shook my head. "Nothing doing."

"Wouldn't she want to help?" Derek asked.

"You don't know my sister."

I left them there by the step and peered through the window again, watching the ladies dither over coffee and cookies, and wondering why people always assumed my family was close simply because we're Italian. As though we're born with some kind of bonding gene that automatically makes us embrace big weddings and dinners for forty. If that's true, then the Marcello family must have missed out, because the five of us have been going our own ways for as long as I can remember.

Loretta blames my mother, of course, and never misses a chance to remind my father that life would have been so much better if he'd married a real Italian girl instead of one born in Ottawa. Personally, I think living with Loretta for too many years was the real problem. How much weight can one family be expected to bear?

But whatever the reason, my parents are now happy to spend six months of the year in Florida, my brother has been out west since he left high school, and I've seen my sister, Angie, once since Christmas, and only because Loretta threatened to cut her out of the will if she didn't get her lazy butt into the city and help me at the Swan.

Naturally, Angie drove in from Oakville the following Saturday with her husband and their three kids in tow, more to see how badly I was screwing up than to help. I was at the pub wallpapering the ladies' room when they arrived with a cup of coffee from Timmy's—double cream, double sugar, just the way Angie likes it—and a sprinkle doughnut with a small bite taken out of the bottom.

She hung around long enough to drink the coffee and pass judgment on the décor while her husband ate the doughnut. Then she handed me an article listing the number of restaurant failures in the city last year and left me with a kiss on the cheek and a toilet that wouldn't flush for two days.

The plumber never did figure out what those kids had stuffed down there, and Angie never did acknowledge the message I left on her machine. I would have been more surprised if she had, but it would be a long time before I ever dialed her number again.

The funny thing is that I used to wish we were closer, more like Rosie and her sister, Marcie. When Rosie first arrived, they used to talk to each other on the phone at least once a week and they wrote all the time, united in their belief that Rosie would be going home soon. I used to try to imagine Angie writing to me, or talking to me in anything except insults, but always came up empty and jealous. And I remember having to bite down hard on my cheeks to keep from smiling when Rosie discovered that her sister had changed her mind, that Marcie didn't want her to come marching home after all. But who could blame her? As my mother explained later, there were benefits to being an only child. Benefits I'd have jumped at too, given half a chance. Rosie was devastated, of course, having lost her only ally at home, but it was one of the happiest days of my life.

At last, Loretta held up her rosary and the prayer began again. *Thirty minutes, tops,* I told myself and went back to face Eva and Derek by the step.

"So what are we doing?" she asked.

"I'm waiting out here. You're going inside to lower the blinds."

"You're the boss," she said, but was no longer looking *at* me, she was looking over me.

I turned around. The guy at the bistro across the street was leaning against the parking machine, motioning to Eva to come on over. He saw me watching and had the grace to lower his arm. "Are you thinking about it?" I asked her.

"Not yet," she said and went back inside to take care of the blinds.

Derek leaned closer. "What's their story?"

The guy waved and I turned my back. "She used to work for him."

"Dose he want her back?"

"Apparently."

Inside the Swan, the first blind came down with a thud. The second one stuck halfway, as though fighting back. I sighed, knowing the guy at the bistro must really be enjoying this. "Is he still out there?" I asked Derek.

"Yup. You want me to go over there and beat him up?"

"Maybe later."

I watched Eva yank the cord again and again. The bloody blind wouldn't give up.

Derek put an arm around my shoulder and walked me away from the window, but I couldn't stop myself from checking the other side of the street. The guy waved again and I quickly turned away. "This is going to come back to haunt me, isn't it?"

"Like the ghost?" Derek asked. "Probably."

We stopped in front of the bargain bin at the hardware store, nodded to the girl standing guard at the door, and started sifting through socket wrenches, drill bits, coffee warmers, Christmas coasters, and a bottle opener shaped like a moose that played the "Hockey Night in Canada" theme. Derek picked it up, pressed the button, and smiled at the familiar anthem. "Are you going to tell me about the ghost, or should I come up with something myself?"

"It's nothing." I took the opener from him and pressed the button again, letting the anthem fill the silence. "I should have one of these at the bar. See if you can find another one."

"Sam," Derek said softly.

"Honestly, it's nothing," I said and kept pawing through the bin so I wouldn't have to look him in the eye. "Just Loretta overreacting to something she heard in the pub earlier. Strange noises, that sort of thing. Now she's convinced we're haunted, but why wouldn't we be? These buildings are old. Probably full of spirits. Did you know they found a body under the concrete floor of a basement near here? The thing had been there for over fifty years. Who knows what's buried in any of these basements?" I pointed the bottle opener at him. "If I was smart, I'd start a ghost tour of the neighborhood. Dress up in 1940s costume and take people around. I'd make a fortune."

"Maybe. But your acting would have to improve because right now you're not convincing me of anything." He took the opener from my hand and set it back in the bin. "Whatever is going on at the Swan is your business. But if you ever want to talk about it, you know where to find me. Right now, however, I'm going to take some measurements so you and Michael can start planning that patio."

"He's not even here yet."

Derek pointed past me. "He will be in about one minute."

I spun around. Sure enough, Michael was less than a block away and closing fast, cutting a path through the traffic with Julie on one side and Rosie on the other.

SEVEN

My breath caught. My stomach lurched. I grabbed Derek's arm. "You have to head them off. Tell them there's a burst pipe or a kitchen fire, anything at all, just keep them away until I can get Loretta out of here."

"No problem. Call my cell phone when it's safe to come back," he said, then dashed off to intercept Michael.

He reached the threesome in front of Marilu's, three doors down. Marilu is really Mario and Luigi, two gay Italians giving the Greeks a run for their money with some of the best souvlaki on the block. Loretta has been a regular at their side counter since they opened a month ago, and I often wonder if she ever gives them a lecture about abandoning their roots while spooning tzatziki onto her pita.

Derek pointed to me. I smiled and waved. Michael smiled and waved. Julie didn't acknowledge me at all. Simply shrugged a backpack from her shoulders and dropped it on the ground. Of course, none of them saw Rosie blow me a kiss, or stretch in the sunshine, or run a hand over Julie's hair while Derek explained what was going on at the Swan. I was the only one with that privilege.

Rosie burst out laughing when Derek finished. "A prayer meeting?" she yelled. "That is perfect."

I stared at Derek. He told them the truth? What in God's name was he thinking?

Rosie was still laughing but I ignored her, focusing instead on Michael, who was looking at me curiously, as though waiting for me to confirm Derek's story. I shrugged in a *What can you do?* way.

He motioned to the souvlaki shop.

I nodded and held up my phone to confirm that I'd let him know when it was safe to come over.

Michael led Julie into Marilu's, with Derek following close behind, but Rosie didn't go with them. She sauntered down to where I stood, stilettos clicking on the sidewalk, a wide smile on her face. "I have always loved Loretta," she said. "Especially since that episode with the ring."

"Loretta didn't do anything."

"Come on, Marcello, it was your grandmother's handiwork and we both know it. You're just not devious enough to have come up with that on your own. To be honest, I always wondered where she found that woman, but I didn't think she'd take my call, under the circumstances. You should tell her that everyone at the shop where Michael worked talked about it for weeks afterward. They're probably still talking about it, for all I know." She glanced over at the pub and shook her head in admiration. "I have to say, that red door is her best work yet. Where is the old bat anyway? Inside? How about I just pop in and say hello."

I resisted the temptation to speak, to give her the satisfaction of knowing she had any effect on me at all. Instead I turned and walked the other way, hoping she'd follow, hoping to lead her far away from my pub and my grandmother, and breathed a quiet sigh of relief when she fell into step beside me.

"You really are getting the hang of this, Marcello," she said. "Talking to ghosts in public probably isn't the smartest thing you could do right now. Especially after Loretta's little prayer circle. God, I wish I'd seen that. Where are we going, anyway?"

I didn't answer, just kept moving.

"Fine, be that way. But I hope you don't mind me tagging along because I really do want to thank you for coming by yesterday, and I hope you enjoyed the doughnut."

"I didn't eat it."

"Too bad, because it might have given you exactly the kind of boost you gave me."

I glanced over at her. "It's true," she said. "Michael and I have been such homebodies for the last two years, I think we've both forgotten what fun it can be to get out and about. So after our little get-together last night, I thought, what the hell? Why not spend a little time seeing the sights, visiting the old neighborhood. Not that I recognize a thing. It's all so different now. So nearly gentrified. So upscale billiard hall. No wonder you fit right in."

"I'm not listening," I muttered, keeping my lips still, like a ventriloquist.

"Really, Marcello. You can't bullshit a bullshitter. Oh my God, will you look at that?"

Rosie grabbed my arm, slowing me down outside a shoe store. "You know what I miss most about the city? Great shoes. Like those pink espadrilles. I would die for a pair like that."

I started walking again. She sighed and joined me. "Honestly, Marcello, you've lost all sense of humor."

"I just don't find you funny."

"That's too bad, since we're going to be spending so much time together." She took my arm again. "Is that a jewelry store?"

To avoid a scene, I allowed myself to be led to the jewelry store window, then discreetly withdrew my arm and kept my voice low. "What exactly do you think you're doing?"

"Just a little window shopping. Do you like that necklace? It's not as blatantly Christian as the one you're wearing, but it does have a nice sparkle." She touched a finger to Loretta's medallion. "Cute, but I wouldn't have thought it was your style."

I jerked away from her, smiled at a woman coming out of the store, and leaned in closer to the window, pretending to search for price tags on watches. "You've made your point, okay? Why don't you save us both the aggravation and go back and sit with Michael?"

"Because I'd much rather spend time with you. It's nice having a conversation for a change instead of doing all the talking. Gets boring after a while, believe me." She turned and leaned her back against the glass. "But if having me around bothers you so much, why not put a stop to it right now?"

"I'd like nothing better."

"All you have to do is tell Michael to go home, and you and I will never have to see each other again."

I smiled at her. "Do I detect a note of desperation? Could it be that you've finally realized you can't make him do whatever you want? That I might actually win this time?"

"Don't embarrass yourself, Marcello. There's no way you can win. Michael's life is in Huntsville, and that's where he and Julie will be heading in a few days. You're just a momentary distraction. A whim, like all the rest."

"What are you talking about?"

"Michael and other women, sweet cheeks. Do you think you're the first one to come sniffing around, looking for a way in? Don't be naïve. He's a good-looking man. They're lining up back home, honey. And the selection ain't half bad."

"But Derek said . . ."

"Derek doesn't know everything. How can he when he lives so

far away?" She swung an arm around my shoulder, tried to turn me toward the pub. "Why don't you save yourself any more humiliation and tell Michael to take his daughter home? The poor kid needs to be in her own room with her own things."

I slipped out of her grasp and walked back to face the window. "If you ask me, I'd say that's half the problem. Too much time alone, or with you. She needs friends her own age. A little fun without her mother poking her nose into it."

"You're just like Derek, both thinking you know what's best for my family when you know nothing about us at all. Julie's a happy girl and Michael is not the boy you remember. We're country people now, Marcello. We have an old farmhouse with acres of land around us. We grow our own vegetables, we raise cows and chickens. It's a good life, one you can't possibly understand. And whatever it is you think you're doing with Michael can only hurt Julie."

"No more than what you're doing."

"You're such an ass."

"Really? Then how come you helped move up the appointment with the therapist? You wouldn't have done it if you didn't think she needs help."

Rosie waved a hand. "The only problem Julie has right now is that she doesn't want to live in the city. While *I'm* not worried that Michael will pack up and move, the kid doesn't know that. You and Derek are putting her under all kinds of unnecessary stress. And Lord knows she has enough stress as it is."

"Because of the black cat?'

"Will you forget the cat? I took care of the stupid thing."

"Then you admit there is one."

"*Was* one. Trust me, Marcello, that sucker won't be back any time soon. So here's my offer. You leave my family alone, and I'll leave you alone. Do we have a deal?"

"Forget it."

My cell phone rang. I flipped it open, grateful for a reason to turn away, to avoid seeing her face, hearing her voice. "Eva? Tell me they're gone."

"No such luck," she answered. "In fact, they're talking about taking this thing outside again. Something about doing a sweep of the neighborhood."

"Keep the door locked. I'm on my way."

"We're going back to the pub? Wonderful." Rosie kicked off her stilettos and picked them up. "I can't wait to see the place."

"Stay out of my pub," I whispered.

"Then stay away from my husband."

"Not a chance."

"Have it your way, but in case you think you scored any brownie points with Julie yesterday, you can think again. We had a long talk. She officially hates you."

"Then I have nothing to lose." I dropped the phone into my pocket and headed back to the Swan, keeping my head down and my eyes on the sidewalk. Counting cracks, humming the *Hockey Night in Canada* theme, anything to avoid being sucked into another conversation with Rosie.

Loretta was stepping outside when I reached the pub, her eyes bright, her smile triumphant. "Good news, *bella*. We're finished, and I know for a fact there are no ghosts in there now."

"She's looking good," Rosie said. "Healthy, feisty. Just the way I remember." She leaned in to give Loretta a kiss on the cheek. "*Ciao*, Nona," she whispered in her ear. "It's wonderful to see you again."

Loretta frowned and rubbed at her ear, then pulled a mason jar from her purse. "We even sprinkled this everywhere." She took off the lid and grinned at me. "Holy water. I stole it from the church. They'll never miss it." She stuck a finger into the water and tried to make a cross on my forehead.

"Loretta, stop," I said, batting her hand away and ducking the blessing.

"You shouldn't be so ungrateful," Rosie said. "This stuff is great." She stuck her own finger into the holy water, dabbed some behind both her ears. "What? You think this hurts me?" She laughed lightly and dipped into the jar again. "I'm not a demon, Marcello. I'm a ghost. There's a world of difference." She sucked the water off her finger, then nodded at Loretta. "Tell her I'll pop by for a visit later. She still at the same address?"

"Stay away from her." I said out loud and watched Loretta's smile fade.

"*Bella*, what's wrong? Is the ghost still here?" She narrowed her eyes and looked around. "We need the priest," she announced and hurried back into the Swan. "Party's over," she called to the ladies. "Leave the candles. We're getting the priest."

"No, Loretta, please," I said, but she was already rounding up the troops, preparing to storm the church and bring back the priest by force if necessary, I was sure of it.

Eva pushed past Loretta in the doorway and stood in front of me, arms crossed, dragons snarling. "This is nuts. You have *got* to call your sister. She owes you."

"Oh my God," Rosie said. "What is *this*?" She walked around Eva, looking her up and down. "No makeup. White jacket. Five o'clock shadow on the head." She stopped and faced me. "Tell me she's not your chef. Oh, Jesus, she is, isn't she. Shit, Marcello, you must have been scraping the bottom of the barrel for this one."

"Shut up. Not you, Eva."

"It's Rosie, isn't it." She glanced around, then lowered her chin and planted her feet a little wider apart. Like a sentry holding her post. "Why didn't you call me?"

"Call her?" Rosie looked over at me. "You told her about us? Marcello, I'm shocked."

"I didn't tell her about *us*. I told her about *you*." I rolled my eyes at Eva. "She's surprised I told you."

Eva grunted. "She needs to know we're not afraid of her."

Rosie stuck her head over Eva's shoulder. "You always did have a thing for tough girls, didn't you?"

"Call your sister," Eva said. "Get Loretta out of here. Then we can take care of the ghost."

Rosie came around to stand beside me. "Allies are always a good idea. I know a few vampires myself . . ."

"Shut up," I yelled. "Just shut the hell up."

Naturally, Loretta and her friends chose that moment to come out of the pub. They huddled together watching me, their lips moving in constant prayer.

"It's okay, ladies. Really," I said, but they merely smiled and nodded, then shuffled into a circle, discussing the situation and deciding Loretta was absolutely right. They needed the priest.

"I'll meet you at the church," Loretta told them, and the group struck out without her, heading east along the Danforth. Twenty old women on a quest. God help me.

Loretta looked over at me, her eyes full of sympathy. "Don't you worry, *bella*. They'll be back with the priest, real soon." She gripped her bottle of holy water tighter and went back into the pub, holding it in front of her like a shield.

"This is all just too good," Rosie said. "I'm so glad I came." She started following the prayer group. "Don't you worry, *bella*, I'll be back too. And give some thought to what I said about Michael. He's just looking to get laid."

"Bitch," I muttered while she moved up the line of women, fingering their rosaries, touching their arms, making a few of them shudder.

"I am having so much fun," she called back. "I can't wait to meet the priest."

"Is she gone?" Eva asked.

"Is who gone?" Johnny asked, pushing in between us.

"Rosie," Eva said.

His eyes widened and his face paled. "She was here?"

"And she'll keep coming back unless Sam backs off," Eva said.

"Then we'll have to get used to having her around," I said, "because I'm not giving in."

"Where is she now?" Johnny asked.

I pointed up the street. "On her way to the church with the prayer group."

"Which gives us a few minutes without her." Eva seized my arm and walked me backward to the window. "Tell me everything she said and everything's that happened since you left here last night. Leave out the sleepless night. I can see that for myself."

"Thanks," I said, hoping there was some concealer in my makeup bag,

"I'm going in the kitchen now," Loretta called from the doorway. "I've got just enough water left."

She gave me the A-OK sign and headed off again. It was hard not to admire that kind of blind faith. Just hard to understand how anyone could have it.

Eva shoved Johnny toward the door. "Get in there and make sure she doesn't put any of that stuff in my food."

He saluted her and was gone, calling for Loretta to let him help.

Eva folded her arms again. "Are you going to call your sister and get your grandmother out of here or what?"

"I'm calling," I said because I couldn't think of anything else to do.

Eva didn't gloat, didn't say anything in fact. Just waited while I took out my cell phone, making sure I didn't change my mind.

I searched my directory for Angie's number. Surprisingly enough, it was still there, along with Loretta and my parents. I could have sworn I deleted her number after the toilet incident, but I must have changed my mind in a weak moment.

I hit speed dial and stood on my toes to check the prayer group's progress while the line connected. They had only made it as far as the fruit market, their speed hampered by the few who were too old to move quickly and had to pause now and then to catch their breath. But Rosie hadn't lost interest. She was still with them, tormenting Mrs. Moon and giving me a moment of guilty pleasure.

The phone signaled that the connection had been made and I put the cell to my ear. I had no idea what I was going to say, but the moment the line was answered, the words found their own way out. "Angie, it's Sam. You have to call Loretta and tell her to come out to Oakville right now. . . . Angie, you owe me this. Your last visit cost me two hundred dollars and you know it."

I waited while my sister listed all the reasons she couldn't possibly have Loretta out to her house. Soccer games. Meetings. A standing appointment with the manicurist.

"Have it your way," I said. "I'll just tell Nona you refused to help me. Again. And this time, I'll drive her to the lawyer's office myself. I'll make sure she signs that codicil to her will and . . . what was that?" I smiled and gave Eva the thumbs-up. "I'm glad we had a chance to talk too, Ange. Call her on my cell. Make sure she knows she has to get on the next train. And Angie, you have to keep her there for three days, understand? Three days."

I hung up and stared at the phone. "She won't call back." But she did, within seconds. Amazing what a little estate terrorism can do.

I dashed into the pub, found Loretta in the kitchen, and held out the phone. "It's Angie for you." I shrugged when she frowned. "I don't know. It's some kind of emergency." She took the phone at last, and I hoped I didn't look too relieved. "I'll wait outside. Give you some privacy."

I went through the swinging door and waited on the other side, holding my breath while Loretta said, "Yes. No. Yes. No. Of course. I'll leave right now."

I couldn't believe it. She was going to Oakville.

I dashed outside, struck a casual pose beside Eva, and tried not to smile when Loretta came outside with her purse and her mason jar, looking scattered and flushed, and more pleased than I would have expected. "*Bella*, I have to go," she said. "Angie needs me."

"What's wrong?" I asked.

"The oldest girl, Maria, photocopied her sister's diary and handed out copies on the street. Now Theresa's threatening to throw herself off the roof. It's like the two of you all over again, I swear."

"Your sister did that?" Eva whispered.

"When I was ten, only I was threatening to throw *her* off the roof when Loretta came home."

"And I almost let you," Loretta said, then handed me the cell phone, opened the sandwich board, and set it by the door again. "I'll have to catch up to the ladies first. Tell them to keep the vigil going here until I get back. It shouldn't take more than a day or two. They can take shifts." She smiled at me. "We'll beat this thing, *bella*. I promise."

Inside the pub, Johnny took down the Closed sign and opened the blinds one by one. Any minute now, we'd be back in business.

Loretta shoved her purse under her arm, took a couple of breaths, and dashed off to catch the prayer group.

"Flag down a cab," I said to Eva and sprinted after my grandmother. "Nona." I gasped as I jogged beside her. "Why not let me take care of the ladies? The trains leave Union at twenty to the hour. You can make the next one if you leave right now." She stopped running and looked at me, so I gulped more air and added, "Theresa needs you. Who knows what might happen if you take too long?"

"You're right." She turned abruptly and headed back to the pub. "Promise you won't tell the ladies why I'm going to Oakville.

They don't need to know our business. Just say Angie's sick or something. Cancer's always a good one."

"You can tell them whatever you like when you get back." I bundled her into the waiting taxi and kissed her cheek. "Give Angie my best. Tell her I hope everything goes well." I looked at the driver. "Union Station."

And just like that, Loretta was gone, heading for Union Station and Oakville with no one in her prayer group the wiser, including Rosie.

"Okay, let's get started," Eva said.

"On what?"

"A plan." She picked up the sandwich board and took it inside with her.

I stood on the sidewalk a moment longer, watching the prayer group's progress. They were at the corner now, waiting for the lights to change, with Rosie still tagging along. The church was only two blocks away. Even at their pace, it would take another fifteen minutes at most, and once Rosie saw the priest, how long would she stay? Long enough to hear the ladies' argument? To find out the priest's decision? Probably not. The trek was just a lark, a way to show me she could do anything she damn well pleased. But knowing Rosie, she'd tire of the game once she'd had some fun with the priest, and then she'd head back here, which meant I had about twenty minutes left. Less if she didn't take the conventional way back. Twenty minutes I could spend planning with Eva, or talking to Michael.

I glanced over at Marilu's. That twenty minutes might be all the time I'd have alone with him today. Once Michael started working on the patio, Rosie would park herself at the pub for the day, and God only knew what she'd do to amuse herself. But if I put the patio on hold for a while, if I took him somewhere else right now, then maybe Rosie wouldn't find us. Maybe Michael and I could have an uninterrupted lunch together. Linger over coffee, go for a walk, find out what we were trying to do here.

Then again, it was Saturday. The pub was ready to open, and with any luck at all, today's lunch hour would at least be as busy as yesterday's.

Then again, I had years to devote to the pub. Years to work too many hours and have too little fun. But I only had a few days to make things right with Michael.

I checked the prayer group's progress again. They had crossed the road. The church was only another block. My heart beat faster.

Eva came back outside. "You coming?" she called.

I shook my head and thought of Michael. Already picturing the two of us at some quiet little pub, sipping wine, laughing and talking while Rosie sat at home, furious because she couldn't find us. How could I resist?

"You're in charge," I called to Eva. "I'll be back shortly."

"Are you joking? Where are you going?"

I grinned at her. "Somewhere with Michael, I hope. Wish me luck."

"You'll need more than that when Rosie gets back."

"I'm not worried," I lied, and ran all the way to the souvlaki shop.

EIGHT

I couldn't tell Michael the real reason I wanted him to leave Marilu's with me, so naturally I blamed Loretta. Told him she held the prayer meeting because she heard he was back in town and had been spotted at my pub.

"She's still ticked off?" he asked. "Even after that woman and the ring?"

"She's Italian," I said, and he nodded sadly.

Derek didn't say a word, didn't even blink. Just played along, nodding with Michael and looking concerned, bless his conspiratorial little heart.

I went on to explain to Michael that Loretta was planning to bring the prayer group down for souvlaki and I didn't want to think about what might happen if she found him there. Not surprisingly, he was happy to leave his gyros special and follow me anywhere. Derek picked up on my plan and offered to stay with Julie, and that was where everything stalled.

She was drawing on a paper placemat, her territory defined by a neat line of markers, a glass of iced tea, and an untouched plate of fries and gravy. She didn't look up once while I was explaining the situation to Michael, just kept her head bent over her artwork and one arm wrapped protectively around the page. I figured she was trying to keep me from seeing, but even upside down, I could tell she was drawing a farmhouse. White with black trim and matching cows in the background. She was obviously a detail-oriented child, some might even say obsessive, because she'd added flower boxes on the porch railings, a playhouse, and even a firepit on the front lawn, surrounded by three chairs. The focal point, however, was a touching portrayal of herself and Michael in front of the wraparound porch, holding hands and smiling under a bright yellow sun. An interesting ploy and a clear message: *I hate Toronto. Take me home.*

Rosie couldn't have played it better herself.

"Can't I come with you?" she asked when Michael stood up.

"Wouldn't you rather go to the movie with me?" Derek asked.

"It's too nice to stay inside." She turned a sad face to Michael. "Unless you don't want me to come with you."

"Of course I want you with me," he said quickly. "But we have to leave now. Pack up your markers and let's go."

Instead, she uncapped the yellow marker and started adding a chicken to the picture. "But *where* will we go?"

"Anywhere you like," Michael said, giving me a *What can you do?* look while taking the marker from her hand. He stuffed the marker into the empty box and held it out to her. "Now put the rest away, because we're leaving."

I glanced at the clock over the cash register. Unless Rosie tired of playing Find the Priest sooner than expected, another minute or two should be okay. But I couldn't see Julie giving in that easily. Not when she was drawing again, adding apples to a tree.

"Julie, that's one," Michael warned.

She drew a happy face on the sun.

"And that's two," he said.

"Okay, okay," she said, and I couldn't help wondering what happened on three.

While Michael took care of the bill at the front counter, Julie took a moment to tuck her hair behind her ears, take a sip of iced tea, and check to make sure her backpack was still by her feet before finally capping the red marker and sliding it into the box. The very picture of innocence, the very soul of defiance. It was like being back in Sister Teresa's class with Rosie.

She rolled the green marker slowly toward her, and I was tempted to say "three" just for the hell of it. But I don't know much about kids or parenting skills, and what I've learned from my sister and her brood has only made me less curious. Maybe Michael knew what he was doing. Maybe endless patience paid off in the end. But I have to admit, I was this close to packing up those markers myself.

"Let me help you," Derek said, picking up the markers and shoving them into the box in one deft movement.

I gave him a quick smile of thanks and went to join Michael at the counter, confident that we would soon be on our way.

"I don't know what's gotten into her," Michael said. "She's not usually this ornery."

"She just wants to be with you," I said, in case he thought I didn't like kids, but there was no real mystery afoot. Rosie had simply done a good job of turning the girl against me. "I'm sure she'll be okay once we're on our way," I told him, and glanced back at the table.

With Derek busy packing the markers in her backpack and Michael safely occupied at the checkout, Julie cast a quick glance my way, her slightly raised chin clearly saying, *If you think we're leaving any time soon, you can forget it.* The battle lines had been drawn, the gauntlet dropped with a flair I had to admire.

She picked up a fork and pushed the fries around on her plate. "But where would we go if we left?" she asked Derek.

"We could go for a walk," I said, and strolled back to the table. "And Mario could wrap those fries for you, if you like."

She set her fork down, dropped her napkin on the plate. "I don't think so, thank you. And I don't want to go for a walk either."

"Then how about the park?" I suggested. "Withrow is close by. They have swings and slides."

"*Baby* swings, and *baby* slides. It's boring there."

"Boring?" Mario called. "Not when you have a genuine Marilu's Super Gyros Frisbee." Julie looked over, and he held up a white Frisbee with Marilu's Super Gyros written across the front in bright gold letters. "Pretty nice, eh?"

Julie slid back her chair and got to her feet. Just like her mother, she couldn't resist a shiny object.

I smiled a thank-you at Mario when she waved the Frisbee high over her head and called, "Who wants to throw it with me?"

"I do," Derek said. "We'll fight it out for the Frisbee championship of the world."

"The park it is," I said and checked the clock one more time. Maybe it was just a pipe dream believing Rosie couldn't find us if we got out of there quickly. She was a ghost, after all. Maybe there were more cheap tricks at her disposal. Maybe she could see all and know all in an instant. But if that was so, then why wasn't she back already? And why was I wasting time wondering?

"Mario," I called. "Is it okay if we use your back door?"

"Be my guest."

I handed Julie her backpack, ruffled her hair, and smiled when she tried to bat my hand away. This could be fun after all. I gestured to the kitchen. "Shall we go?"

Derek went first, followed by Michael, but of course, Julie hung back.

"Thank you for the Frisbee," she said to Mario. "And could you wrap my fries, please?"

"Be sure to include the napkin," I told him and smiled sweetly when the kid frowned at me.

Mario wrapped the wad of fries plus the napkin in tin foil, fashioning a swan that took another few seconds but made her smile, and we finally left, waving to Luigi as we walked single file through his kitchen and out to the alley.

Our alley is not one of the city's hidden treasures. No funky doors, no art masquerading as graffiti, nothing at all that might one day win us a spot on the Back Alley Bike Tour. Our alley is strictly functional. A place to keep the garbage, receive deliveries, and catch a quick smoke on a break. Its only charm lay in the fact that we could avoid both the Danforth and Rosie by following it out to the street.

I took the lead at a quick march, hoping Michael would follow suit, but Julie wasn't in the mood to hurry and Michael wasn't about to leave her behind. Thinking she might be more inclined to hurry if I weren't around, I called, "We'll meet you by the statue on the corner," and Derek and I went on without them.

"Sorry I couldn't help you out in there," he said. "I was sure she'd go for the movie. But I'll do what I can at the park. Try to give you two some time alone."

"Thanks, although I'm not holding my breath. She seems determined to keep her dad close by."

"She is, but don't take what she did in the restaurant personally." He laughed when I raised my eyebrows. "Honestly, it wasn't you. She's just had enough of therapists, and the surprise appointment this morning did nothing to change her mind."

With no way to hurry Julie, I figured this was as good a time as any to find out more about Michael and his daughter. So I slowed down, setting a leisurely, more conversational pace. "Did Michael say how the appointment went?"

"Julie hates the guy, of course, which is nothing new. But apparently he takes a more homeopathic approach to things, so Mike's pleased. And if he finds a way to get rid of that damn cat, then I'll be happy too."

I glanced back at Julie, feeling badly about the whole fries/napkin thing until I spotted the foil swan abandoned beside a Dumpster. There was no doubt about it, that girl was going to grow up to be a horror, but right now she looked like any other kid, laughing and smiling while she and Michael took turns kicking a can and chasing it.

I turned back to Derek. "Has she seen the cat today?"

"Not that I know of, which makes it more than thirty-six straight hours. A record, if you can believe it."

"Maybe that's a good sign," I said, wanting to believe it was true, that the cat really was gone for good. I didn't have to like the kid to hope her mother had done something right for a change.

We reached the end of the alley and I paused, checking the street before stepping out into the open in case Rosie was there, waiting. The square at Logan Avenue is always filled with people stopping to watch the fountain or sit under the trees or have their picture taken beside the bust of Alexander the Great. This is normally my favorite spot on the Danforth, the place I like to linger with a coffee or an iced cappuccino on afternoons like this one. But today it was simply a checkpoint on the path to freedom, and I was grateful for the extra coverage of trees and people.

"Do you honestly think she's looking for you?" Derek asked.

"No question about it," I said and started walking. Past the statue to the tree. Past the tree to the fountain.

"She must really be worried about you," Derek said.

"What?" I looked back at him. "Oh, you mean Loretta. Yes, she is. Come on."

I was about to make a break for the lights when I realized

Michael and Julie still hadn't emerged from the alley. I checked my watch, tapped a foot, checked my watch again. "What's taking them so long?"

He smiled. "Maybe Loretta got him."

I pointed a finger. "You should be careful. One word from me, and you'll end up on her hit list too."

He laughed. "Does your grandmother really believe the ghost at the pub is real?"

"She sent for the priest, so she must."

"What about you? Do you think it's real?"

"Not a chance," I said, afraid of where the conversation might lead, questions I wouldn't be able to answer. Still, I couldn't help asking, "Why? Do you believe in ghosts?"

"Can't say that I do." He glanced over at the fountain pulled a few coins from his pocket, and handed me a quarter. "Here, make a wish."

I laughed. "You don't believe in ghosts, but you make wishes in fountains?"

His smile widened. "I just like to see if I can get one into the spray."

He flipped the quarter high into the air, sending it spinning over the heads of the couple by the water and landing it neatly in the center of the spray.

"Perfect shot, and no wish to go with it," I said. "How sad."

He leaned close to my ear. "Don't believe everything people tell you. I know I don't."

I turned quickly but he was already walking away, heading for the lights at the corner. He stopped at the curb, glanced back at me, and smiled. What was his wish, I wondered, and almost missed Michael and Julie dashing past, playing a game of Gotcha Last.

"See you at the park," Michael called back to me.

"After you cross the road, take the next alley," I hollered after him. "It's faster."

He nodded to let me know he understood and called instructions to Julie.

Julie bolted ahead and turned left into the alley. She'd done what I asked. A miracle. I glanced over at Derek. Or maybe a wish come true.

"I thought you were in a hurry," he called.

"I am." I glanced down at the quarter in my hand, darted over to the fountain, and dropped the coin straight into the water. "Why take unnecessary chances?" I said to the couple seated there and ran to catch up with Derek on the other side of the street.

We followed Michael and Julie through the network of alleys leading to McConnell Avenue and Withrow Park, where summer had come early. Frisbees were flying, dogs were barking, and kids were running everywhere, all determined to make the most of a day that was too warm, too soon. Folks not brave enough to buy street meat from the hot dog lady were spreading out blankets and picnics brought from home. Cold meats and deli salads, fried chicken and scotch baps. And if you forgot to bring dessert, the boy ringing the bells over by the clubhouse would be happy to sell you something cold and sweet from his cart.

We walked past the baby swings and the clubhouse to the slope leading down into the bowl at the center of the park. Here was the skating rink in winter, the tennis courts in summer, and plenty of room to throw a Frisbee any time of the year. Julie dropped her backpack at the top of the slope, grabbed her Marilu's Super Gyros Frisbee from Michael, and raced ahead, calling, "Come on, Uncle Derek."

"You're up now," he whispered to me, then shouted, "For the championship of the world!" and followed her down into the bowl to claim a piece of ground for their own.

"Watch us, Daddy!" Julie called over her shoulder.

"Always," Michael answered.

Figuring we were there for the duration, I sat down on the

grass to watch Derek throw the Frisbee straight into Julie's outstretched hands, and Julie send it soaring back, high over Derek's head. It was hard to say who would be the champion of the world, but if total distance run was calculated into the score, I'd have put money on Derek.

I shielded my eyes with a hand and looked up at Michael. "He's good with her."

"He spoils her. But I definitely owe him one today."

"For what?"

"For keeping Julie occupied so I can finally spend some time with you." He turned to me at last. "When do you have to go back to work?"

Right now, if I was smart. Lunch hour was definitely upon us, and Eva and Johnny must be cursing me back there. If the priest did show up, I'd be lucky not to find letters of resignation taped to the door. But so far this had not been a day for reason. Why change things now?

"I've got about an hour," I said, and hoped I didn't come to regret it in two.

"Then let's make the most of it." He motioned to the clubhouse. "You think there's any chance that kid's got some Honey and Spice in that ice cream cart?"

Honey and Spice. Rich vanilla ice cream with a touch of honey and cinnamon, tucked into a waffle cone. The perfect sweet on a warm Killarney night.

Strolling down to the ice cream parlor after dinner with his granny became a ritual that summer in Ireland, a kind of foreplay. We'd stand in line with everyone else, arms around each other, thumbs latched into belt loops, fingers grazing bare skin. Tickling, teasing, making ourselves crazy while the girl behind the counter pushed double scoops into cones and wished us a nice evening.

Eating the ice cream slowly was a must, a deliberate holding back, a prelude to what we both knew lay ahead in the back of his granny's caravan, the only place we could be sure she wouldn't find us. I couldn't remember the last time I'd ordered a double scoop of anything, but that summer in Ireland, I couldn't get enough Honey and Spice.

The ice cream bells beckoned. I got to my feet. "If he has it, I am stealing that cart."

Michael swung Julie's backpack over his shoulder. "Not if I get there first."

"Dream on," I said, then hiked up my skirt, clutched my purse like a football, and ran.

He didn't follow, and I almost stopped. What was I thinking? What was I doing? I must look like a fool.

Then I heard him holler, "I promise to save you some," and I knew I wasn't running alone anymore.

I glanced back, saw him coming toward me and closing fast. I whooped with joy and shot forward, weaving through kids and dogs and picnic tables, racing him across the field to the clubhouse. It was like running backward in time. Back to the days when we chased each other across fields and beaches. Played Gotcha Last along roads and footpaths, or round and round Loretta's dining room table, laughing and screeching and hoping to be caught.

He'd always been fast, and soon he was running backward in front of me, smiling and asking, "Do you want me to order you something when I get there?"

"You wish," I said and lunged forward, taking him off guard, making him leap out of the way. Holding that lead for almost a full second before he was out in front again, high-stepping it this time and singing, "Knees up, Mother Brown," until I gave up and collapsed on the grass, laughing and gasping for breath.

He fell beside me, laughing and holding his side and declaring himself too old for this nonsense. I'd forgotten what it was like to run like that, without a pedometer or proper shoes or an iPod plugged into my ears. Just running for the sake of running, with no thought to cellulite or calories or anything else beyond fun.

He closed his eyes and folded his hands on his chest. "You still want ice cream?"

"Absolutely." I rolled over to face him but made no move to get up. I was too comfortable with the sun warming my face and the grass tickling my fingers. It was probably sticking to my skirt too, and my white blouse wasn't going to be fresh enough for work when I went back, but I didn't care. There was always another change of clothes in the office, but not nearly enough time spent lying in the grass with a good-looking man.

He seemed equally content to stay where we were for a while longer, so I took advantage of the moment, looking at him closely for the first time since he'd stepped back into my life. Taking in the fine lines that came with age and the shadows that hinted at sleepless nights. Tempted to run my fingertips over cheekbones that were more prominent now and wondering at the grave and serious set to his mouth. All the while secretly enjoying the way my blood warmed and my body grew restless, the way it always had whenever Michael Hughes was lying close by.

It wasn't that there hadn't been men since the summer he married Rosie. On the contrary, at one time there had been far too many. A time when I'd get all dressed up and pound back doubles at the best hotels in the city while deciding which man was going to take me up to his room. Didn't matter if they were married or single, and I never wanted a last name or a phone number when I was done. I wasn't looking for a relationship, after all.

We'd have sex the way I wanted it and I'd put another notch in my bedpost when I got home, using the pocketknife Rosie gave me one summer at camp. About halfway down the first post, the big hotels stopped letting me in. They thought I was a hooker. A high-class one, I hoped, and went elsewhere. The entertainment district. Queen West. Even a few jaunts down Yonge Street. It didn't matter anymore. I could get drunk anywhere.

Six months after Michael's wedding, my mother threatened to kick me out, and Loretta started spending the night in the hall outside my room, sleeping on the rug surrounded by flickering candles. I'd sneak out the window to avoid my mother, and sneak back in to avoid Loretta. Bungalows are made for drinkers. One year to the day after Michael's wedding, some guy dropped me off on the front lawn. I had no idea where I'd been or who I'd been with or how he knew where I lived. I staggered in the front door because I couldn't find the window. Loretta met me in the foyer, called me a slut, and laid me out flat. The time had come to move on or move out.

So I sobered up, got myself an HIV test, and cried when it came back negative. I'd been lucky. Only one fat lip and one sprained ankle in a year of living stupidly. I tore up my secret picture of Michael, the one I'd kept hidden from Loretta, and went back to finish my degree at Queen's. Since then, I've dated a few men and lived with one. We lasted eight months, mostly because he didn't believe in marriage, and neither did I. He did, however, believe in children and had no difficulty moving on when I told him I wasn't sure. I got an invitation to his wedding a few months ago. I went, of course. Threw confetti, gave the bouquet a miss, and left early to finish putting up pictures at the Swan.

Yet despite my best efforts to tell myself it was fine, that I was happy working alone, every blow of the hammer echoed through the empty rooms of the pub, making me wish someone were with me. Someone to argue that the pictures weren't straight, or that Queen Victoria had no place in an Irish pub. That night, I finally admitted to Victoria that I was lonely, and wondered if I was missing more than bouquets.

Michael opened his eyes and caught me watching. "What are you thinking?" he asked softly.

That I was crazy to be there, lying in the sun, thinking about going backward when I'd spent the last seven years going forward. Wasn't that what we were supposed to do after all? Wasn't that exactly what I'd told Rosie to do? To move on, go forward. Forget the past and think about the future. But what if the future was tied to the past? What if this really was the second chance I'd wished for all those years ago?

"I was thinking you're in great shape," I said and rolled over on my back, needing time to think, to sort things out. "Something to be said for the country life after all, I guess."

"More to be said for having a seven-year-old around, if you want the truth. And I swear, if you hadn't stopped running, I'd have passed out in about three more steps."

I turned my head to look at him. "Do you like farm life?" I asked. He looked at me curiously, and I realized he hadn't told me about a farm. Rosie had done that. So I shrugged and went back to watching clouds. "I just gathered from Julie's picture that you live on a farm now."

"Not a real farm." He reached out and brushed the hair from my forehead, that brief touch enough to make my skin tingle and my heart beat faster. "It's just ten acres and an old, drafty house. We have a few cows in the summer, some chickens year round."

"And you grow vegetables." I looked over. Smiled again. "I mean, doesn't everyone grow their own vegetables up there?"

"Most everyone, yes." He stroked a finger along my cheek. "It's a good place for kids."

I took his hand and held it away from me. "But is it a good place for you?" I asked, because I needed to know. "Do you like it there?"

He didn't answer right away. Simply drew his hand back and kept looking at me, as though trying to see me clearly too, figure out who I was now. "I used to," he said at last. "But I'm not so sure anymore."

Then he was rolling away, getting to his feet, and holding out his hand to me again. Letting me know the subject was closed. For now.

He pulled me up and I brushed the grass from my skirt, my blouse, tried to shake it from my hair. We didn't speak, but he kept looking at me, watching every flick of the wrist, every turn of my head. I couldn't read his expression, couldn't tell if he found me frumpy or beautiful, graceful or awkward, and I was suddenly self-conscious, aware of every movement, every imperfect curve and angle.

The bells on the ice cream cart started tinkling again. The boy was leaving, pedaling furiously across the grass to the street, taking the past and the possibility of Honey and Spice with him.

"I should get going," I said and picked up my purse, checked my watch, anxious to get away, to put my feet on familiar ground again. "The pub is waiting, and Julie must be wondering where you are." I swung the purse strap over my shoulder and turned to the street so I didn't have to look at him. "I guess we won't have lunch after all."

Michael took my hand, waited until I turned to look at him. "Then we'll do dinner instead. How does that sound?"

"It would have to be after nine."

"Nine it is. And for now, I'll walk with you as far as the street and you can fill me in on what you'd like to see in a patio. That way, I can think about it before I come over to take measurements." He linked his fingers with mine as though to anchor me, to keep me from running away while he bent to pick up Julie's backpack.

We started walking, past the clubhouse and along the path toward McConnell Avenue. "What kind of patio do you have in mind?"

I shrugged. "Something cheap, but not tacky."

"How about three horizontal rails? It's fast and easy."

"Too much like a barnyard fence."

"You prefer picket fences?"

"Doesn't everyone?"

We reached the street, as far as he could go. But he didn't let go of my hand, just dropped the backpack on the grass at the edge of the park and stood in front of me. "White pickets?"

"I'd have to say red, to match my new front door." In keeping with the business discussion we had established, I pulled my purse between us and started to open it. "Do you want a pen to take notes?"

"Not yet." He slid the purse strap down my arm, drew the purse from my fingers, and dropped it beside the backpack. "Colonial style or classic?" he asked, as though my patio really were the only thing on his mind. But something in the way he was looking at me, in the way his eyes lingered on my mouth, my throat, the curve of my cheek, made me wonder. Made me blush.

"Classic?" I said, although I had no clue what the difference was.

"Classic is good," he said and reached out, resting his hands lightly on my hips. "You're certain about the red?"

I wasn't certain of anything beyond the tingling in my skin where he touched me, and the fact that my feet were moving of their own accord, taking me that one critical step closer to him. "I like red," I said softly, standing near enough now to breathe in the scent of him, feel the heat of his skin against my breasts. If one of us leaned in slightly, we'd be touching. "Or maybe white. What do you think?"

He didn't answer, and didn't pretend to be listening anymore. If my guess was right, he didn't look like a man who wanted to talk business either. He looked like a man who wanted to kiss me.

"Red it is," I said, and laid my hands on his chest.

If I was wrong about the kiss, then he could back away, let us both out gracefully. But I felt his arms move around me, saw his eyes close a moment before he bent to me, and I let myself lean into him, certain I'd got it right this time.

He pressed his lips to my throat, my cheek, the lobe of my ear. I tipped my head to the side, giving him room and drifting on sensation and wondering when he'd get around to my mouth, when through the haze I saw people walking by hand in hand, arm in arm. Seeing them for the first time as more than potential customers, more than just the target market made flesh. They were couples. Lovers. And when Michael put his mouth on mine at last, I sighed and opened my lips, realizing how much I had missed being one of them. How much I had missed being in love.

Michael raised his head, his eyes searching mine, making sure he was reading me right. I wrapped my arms around his neck, whispered his name, and we were off again, his hands moving over my back, pulling me closer, holding me harder while we went on kissing and kissing, neither of us caring about the yappy little dog off to the right or the kids going "Eww, yuck" to our left, or even the old couple muttering "Get a room," as they went by. We were too busy fanning a fire that hadn't died, stoking flames that were still as hot, as powerful as they had ever been.

He dragged his mouth from mine, whispered something about dinner, then came back for more, as though kissing me were his right, as though I were still his. My mind charged ahead to tonight, trying to remember when I'd last changed the sheets, and whether I'd cleaned the bathroom recently, and did I have anything in the fridge for breakfast?

And that was where the thinking stopped. Crashed straight into reality. He wouldn't be there for breakfast because he had a child to think about. A child who wanted to go back to Huntsville and a life without me.

What if Rosie was right? What if I was nothing more than a distraction? A chance to get laid?

"Michael, stop," I said.

"Soon," he said, kissing my throat and making my blood warm even as I pushed him away.

"I want you to stop now," I said and stepped back, needing room to breathe, to think, to get Rosie's warning out of my head.

He blew out a breath, ran a hand over the back of his neck. "Did I just screw up here? Because if I did, I am so sorry."

"You didn't screw up. I just need to know what we're doing."

He shook his head. "Doing?"

"Yes. You and me. I'm not trying to pressure you, I just need to know what's on your mind, what you're thinking. What we're *doing*."

"How should I know? It's only been a day, Sam."

He snatched up Julie's backpack and swung it over one shoulder. I knew I'd surprised him, probably shocked the hell out of him if I was honest. But I needed to know if Rosie was right. I needed to know what was on his mind.

"Look," he said. "I didn't plan on seeing you. Didn't think I'd even want to if I had the chance. But when I saw you outside the pub, it was like everything fell into place. Derek buying that house on Fenwick, Julie getting an appointment with a new doctor in the city. It all made sense. Like I was meant to be there, to see you again."

He looked sincere enough, as though he believed what he was saying, but I'd never put much stock in fate. Mind you, I'd never put much stock in ghosts either, so what did I know? "If you believe there's a reason we met, then what is it? Why are we here together?"

He shrugged. "I haven't had time to figure that out."

"Yet you kissed me anyway."

"And you kissed me back."

"That's not the point." I picked up my purse and started walking, heading back into the park because he couldn't go farther and I couldn't stand still. "I need to understand what you want from me, Michael. Am I just another roll in the hay, another notch on the bedpost?"

He grabbed my arm and made me face him. "Is that what you think of me?"

I shook him loose. "I don't know what to think of you anymore. I haven't since the day I found out you were going to marry Rosie."

He sighed and looked at the ground. "Sam, this is an old issue."

"Not for me it isn't. I need to know where I stand, what you want from me. And why you slept with Rosie in the first place."

"What?"

The question surprised me too. I hadn't even known it was there until I asked it. But now I was curious, and not about to let go until I had an answer.

"You heard me. And don't give me that line about 'weak moments' either. I want the truth this time. I want to understand what went wrong. Why you thought it was okay to fuck my best friend." I laid my hands on his chest and shoved him hard. "I need to know what the hell you were thinking."

I started walking again, faster this time. If I'd been hoping to lose him, it didn't work. He was beside me before I'd covered more than a few feet. "I wasn't thinking at all," he said. "I was pissed off. Frustrated that you said you'd marry me, took the ring, and then buggered off to Kingston without me."

"I went back to school, remember?"

"So what? I could have found a job there. We could have shared an apartment. But you didn't want me around."

"That's not true."

He took hold of my arm, spun me around to face him. "No? Then tell me why you never wanted me to visit. Why we went months without seeing each other when I would have been there every weekend if you'd only let me."

"Is that why you slept with her? Because we didn't see each other every weekend?"

He let me go, almost pushed me away. "Don't change the subject, Sam."

"No, you answer the question. Is that why you slept with Rosie?'

He threw his hands up and turned away. "I don't believe this. You're acting as though I planned it, which is ridiculous. Rosie and I didn't even like each other."

"Yet somehow you ended up in bed together. Isn't that some kind of romantic cliché? Enemies falling in love, living happily ever after? Tell me, Michael, did it happen slowly, or did it hit you all at once? Like lightning. Bam. You were in love with Rosie Fisk."

"I wasn't in love with her, and I didn't plan on seeing her, either. I just kept running into her at the Flamingo."

I could picture that easily enough. Rosie waiting at a booth, watching the door, playing coy when he came in. *Fancy meeting you here. You alone?* It was one of her best acts. One I had always enjoyed. I just never imagined she'd play it for Michael.

"Honestly, she was the only familiar face in a place where I used to know everybody. We started having coffee, taking in a movie now and then. I never kept that a secret from you."

And neither did Rosie. *I'm keeping an eye on him for you, Marcello*, she'd say, and I swallowed every word because she was my best friend, and that was what best friends did for each other. Yes indeed. I was blessed.

"If you're interested," Michael said, "all we ever talked about was you. About how well you were doing, how bright your future was. How much she missed you."

So much she had to sleep with my fiancé. That sounded like Rosie's logic.

I smiled and folded my arms across my chest. "And were you talking about me while you had sex with her?"

"Yes," he said and looked away. "At least we had been. We were at her apartment, deciding what movie we wanted to see. She said she'd been talking to you. Said you were going to the Dominican for spring break with friends from school."

"*Girl*friends, you idiot."

He glanced back. "Does it matter? The point is, I told her she must have heard wrong. You were staying at school to study. That was what you told me, remember?"

"I was. The trip came up suddenly. One of those last-minute deals. I had to make a decision."

"And you decided not to tell me."

"I did tell you."

"Only because I called you from Rosie's apartment."

"I didn't want to fight with you about it, okay? I just wanted to go."

"I figured that one out for myself."

"So you slept with Rosie to make yourself feel better." I turned my back on him and looked out over the bowl in the center of the park, watching the tennis balls in the court fly back and forth, back and forth. Going over the same ground again and again, getting nowhere—just like the two of us. I sighed and checked my watch. "You were right, this is old news. I should be going."

He came around in front of me, blocked my escape. "Not until you hear me out. You have no idea how much you hurt me, Sam."

"I didn't mean to."

"You were running away, for Chrissakes."

"It was just a holiday."

"A holiday without me. And as much as you don't want to hear it, sleeping with Rosie *was* a weak moment. I was pissed off when I hung up. Hurt, betrayed, the whole ball of wax. And when she put her arms around me, I didn't fight it. In fact, I pushed it further. You want the truth, I did it because I figured it would get back to you. I wanted you to find out. I wanted to hurt you the way you'd hurt me."

I slapped him hard across the face, taking us both off guard.

"I'm sorry," I said. "I shouldn't have—"

"Yes you should. I deserved it." He sighed and rubbed his cheek. "What I did was stupid and wrong, but you have to believe that I didn't plan any of it. Especially the pregnancy. Rosie said she was on the pill and I believed her. We were the statistical one in one hundred."

"And I was the jerk at the altar."

"Sam, be reasonable. I couldn't just walk away once I knew. I wanted that baby as much as Rosie did."

"And there we have it. I should go."

I turned to leave but he stopped me, holding my hands at my sides so I wouldn't hit him again. "Sam, listen to me. Julie is my pride and joy. I love that little girl. But I tell you now and I'll stand by it forever, I was not in love with Rosie when I slept with her and she knew it. In fact, it was the only thing we fought about in all the years we were together. She was convinced I was still in love with you. That if you ever showed up at the door, I'd leave with you."

"And would you?" I asked. "Would you have left?"

"It was never an issue, was it? Because you never came looking." He sighed and let me go. "From the very beginning, you never once came looking." He turned away and stared down into the bowl of the park. "You should get back to work. I'll call you later about the patio."

He shielded his eyes with a hand, searching for Derek and Julie, expecting me to walk away, to give up on him again. Instead, I walked around in front of him, smiled when he raised an eyebrow. I laid my hands on his chest and closed my fingers on the fabric of his shirt, drawing him to me. Making it clear that this time, I wasn't letting go. This time, I was coming for him.

NINE

Michael didn't react at first. Made no move to hold me, to let me know he wanted this as much as I did. Was it already too late? Had dredging up the past sharpened the edge on those old hurts, made them harder to forget, impossible to forgive? I loosened my fingers and was about to step away when suddenly he tossed the backpack aside and threw his arms around me. Lifted me up and swung me around, his mouth finding mine amid the laughter and the screaming. Filling my head with wild ideas of love and regular sex and living happily ever after until a single sigh froze those thoughts solid. And five words nailed my feet to the ground:

"Poor Marcello. So goddamned predictable."

I held absolutely still, hoping I'd heard wrong.

Michael cocked his head, looked at me curiously. "Is something wrong?"

"No." He started to talk, and I slapped a hand over his mouth so I could hear better. Tried to laugh it off when he pulled it away. "Trust me, everything's fine."

"I don't know about you," Rosie said, "but I don't think he's buying it."

I pushed him back and spun around.

"Sam, what the hell is going on?" he demanded.

That's when I saw her. Sitting on a blanket about ten feet away, watching a well-groomed family spread out their picnic supper. A mom, a dad, a toddler, and a ghost. What could be more normal?

"Come on, Marcello, don't look so surprised," Rosie said. "Did you really think I wouldn't find you?" She wrinkled her nose at something in a bowl. "Now I ask you, what kind of mother brings zucchini to a picnic?"

"Sam, talk to me," Michael said.

The mother looked over at me. Smiled. Waited a beat, and finally asked, "Can I help you with something?"

I shook my head.

"She's just a little tongue tied," Rosie told the mother, then pointed to a bowl of dip. "Now that looks good." She scooped some up on her finger and stuck it in her mouth. "Could use a little salt," she said, but dipped again anyway before turning back to me. "And you could use some smarts, Marcello. Honestly, it hurts me to think you're dumb enough to believe this thing with Michael has a future."

How long had she been there? More important, how much had she heard?

Michael came around in front of me, blocking my view. "Will you please tell me what's wrong?"

"Better yet," Rosie said, "tell him good-bye before you embarrass yourself any more than you already have."

"Forget it," I said, and grabbed him by the neck, pulling his mouth down to mine and kissing him hard. He resisted a moment, obviously confused, then I felt him relax and join in, willing to follow wherever I was planning to lead. I winked at Rosie over his shoulder, as I ran my fingers through his hair.

"There is something seriously wrong with that woman," the mother on the blanket whispered to her husband, then raised her voice to add, "carrying on like that when little eyes are watching."

Rosie frowned at her. "What's your problem? It's only a kiss. Not even a good one at that." She stuck her finger in the dip one more time and got to her feet. "Really, honey, you need to lighten up. Get the pickle out of your ass."

Michael raised his head and smiled at me. "We should probably take this somewhere else."

"You read my mind," I whispered, running my hands up and down his back and laying my head on his chest when he chuckled and drew me to him again. All the while making sure I kept Rosie in sight.

But she wasn't watching me. She was watching the mother, obviously waiting for something. If I could have warned the woman, I would have, but how do you tell someone to watch out, a ghost is planning an attack? When the woman turned away to open another container, Rosie nabbed the pickle off the toddler's plate. The little boy stared at the spot where the pickle had been, looked over at his father, then back at his plate and began to cry.

"Baby, what's wrong?" the mother asked.

"Picko," the kid said between sobs.

The woman checked the boy's plate and the blanket around it. She turned to the bewildered father. "Did you take his pickle?" The poor guy shook his head. "Are you sure?" she asked

That pickle was right beside her, dangling from Rosie's fingers, but no one else could see it. Otherwise, the father would have pointed and said *Hey, look at the floating pickle*. People walking by would have done a double take, and all the dogs would have gone for it. But nothing like that happened. As far as the rest of the world was concerned, the pickle was gone.

Rosie chuckled and glanced over at me. "I tell you, Marcello, this is the only good thing about being dead. People never know what happened to their shit. It's there one minute, then poof. It's gone. Amuses me for hours."

The father put down his fork. "Why do you always blame me?"

"Because she's clearly a bitch," Rosie said, then slipped the pickle under the edge of the mother's plate and grinned at me. "And poof, your shit reappears."

The kid spotted the pickle first. His mouth fell open in shock. He pointed to his mother's plate. "Picko," he wailed.

"Ha," the father shouted in triumph. "*You* took it."

The woman blinked at the incriminating evidence beside her plate. "Someone put that there."

"Sure they did," the father said, and handed the boy the pickle from his own plate. "Here you go, sweetie. Have mine."

Rosie laughed. "And it's one for dad, zero for the tight-ass. Didn't I tell you this was fun?"

Michael stroked a hand over my hair. "Are you still up for our dinner later?"

"Use your head, Marcello," Rosie warned. "He's letting his dick do his thinking again."

"What do you say?" he asked.

Rosie strolled over to where we stood and picked a blade of grass from his shirt. "Not that you wouldn't enjoy it, of course. He got awfully good under my guidance. But don't take my word for it. Let me give you a list of references. Phone numbers of all the women who've tried to help him get over me."

Michael frowned. "Sam?"

"You should start with Joanne Pritchard," Rosie said. "Then call Audrey Moore and Nancy Wilkins. And how could I forget Katherine Murphy? Just don't call her Kathy. She hates it. Michael found *that* out at a very delicate moment. You'd have laughed, Marcello. I know I did."

I moistened my lips, told myself she was making it up. Using any means possible to scare me away.

"What's wrong now?" Michael asked and took a step back, still holding my hands but putting distance between us nonetheless.

"Then there were the Vidovic twins," Rosie said. "Luba and Milka, followed by Laura from the bookstore, and Monica the checkout girl . . ."

I squeezed my eyes shut so I wouldn't have to watch her counting off names on her fingers.

". . . Megan the hygenist, some blonde at the bank, and a redhead who followed him home from a party. She was wild, that one."

"Sam, are you all right?" Michael asked.

I nodded but kept my eyes closed.

Rosie nudged me with her elbow. "And be sure to call Kirsten Clancy. She'll tell you exactly what to expect from Michael Hughes. Nothing. That's what. No phone calls, no notes. Nothing. And she doesn't live two hundred miles away. If you don't believe me, go ahead and ask him. Ask him to tell you about Kirsten Clancy. I dare you."

Michael took hold of my upper arms, almost shaking me. "Sam, what is it?"

"It's nothing," I said and opened my eyes, resisting the urge to call her bluff, to ask him about Kirsten what's-her-name, just to satisfy myself that Rosie was lying.

"But you're acting so strange," he said.

"Strange?" the woman on the blanket whispered to her husband. "She's downright scary."

"You stay out of this," Rosie warned her.

Michael stroked a finger down my cheek. "Sam, please. Tell me what's on your mind."

"I know exactly what's on her mind," Rosie said. "She's thinking she's in over her head, that she can't do this. And she's right. She can't."

Really? I flicked her a glance, then pulled my shoulders back and smiled up at him. "I'm sorry. I guess I'm just having a hard time taking all of this in." I lowered my gaze and let my smile fade just a little. "It's silly, I know, but I needed to reassure myself that this is real. That you're real." I paused for effect, lifted only my eyes to his. "I needed to prove to myself that you'd still be there when I opened my eyes."

Rosie laughed. "Wow, Marcello, that was really lame. Even for you."

But Michael didn't seem to think so. In fact, his smile widened. "Then we're still getting together later?"

Rosie leaned closer, pretending to hold a microphone. "This is it, folks. The moment of truth. Will Marcello be next in a long line of suckers, or will she tell him to shove his dick somewhere else?"

I took a deep breath. Focused on the tenderness in Michael's eyes and the telltale beads of sweat on Rosie's upper lip. She'd always hated that about herself, the way her face would sweat when she was nervous. The first time I noticed it was the summer her Aunt Barb said we could build a tree house in her backyard. We knew it was a ploy to keep Rosie where Barb could see her, but because Rosie liked power tools almost as much as she liked tracking animal shit, she was happy to set to work, and I was happy to help her.

After a full week of hauling wood and hammering nails, we were getting ready to put on the final touch—a secret trapdoor—when I tripped over a power cord and fell out of the damn tree. Fifteen feet straight down onto Barb's freshly mown lawn.

I lay there, hot white lights going off in my head and struggling to draw in a breath. I couldn't move, but every part of my body hurt, so I took that as a good sign and worked harder at trying to breathe. Barb wasn't much help, just kept pacing up and down beside me, wailing and praying while Rosie ran and got Loretta. They came back together and Rosie sat down beside me while we waited for the ambulance, stroking my hair and telling jokes so I wouldn't fall asleep.

"What do you call a woman with no arms or legs sitting outside your tent? Peg."

"What do you call her on top of the fence? Barb."

But my eyes were heavy and my head hurt. I started to drift.

"Come on, Marcello, wake up," she said and tapped my cheek, shook my shoulder. "Sammy, for God's sake, wake up."

I remember opening my eyes and seeing her face only inches above mine, her hair falling on my cheeks, her freckles standing out against her white, white skin, and that telltale line of sweat on her upper lip. "Don't you die, Marcello," she whispered. "Don't you fucking die."

I had a broken arm, a concussion, and more bruises than I could count, but death was not imminent. While I recuperated in front of the television, Rosie finished the trapdoor alone. And when we came back from camp, we spent the rest of the summer up in that tree house, reading dirty books we stole from Barb's cedar chest and making a pact in blood never to let any boy touch us "down there," even if his name was Wulfgar and he rode a black horse and had the steeliest manroot of all time.

I felt myself smile. We must have been twelve years old. Our last summer without boys.

"Sam?" Michael asked.

"We're waiting," Rosie whispered, and wiped away that line of sweat in one casual, practiced motion, but it was too late. I already knew she was every bit as afraid right now as she'd been that afternoon I fell out of the tree. Only back then, she'd been afraid of losing me. Today, she was afraid of having me around.

So I put a fingertip on one of Michael's shirt buttons. Ran it around in a teasing little circle, and said, "Pick me up at nine. I know a little Indian place that has a fabulous late-night menu. We can go back to my place for a nightcap afterward."

"And she fumbles," Rosie said. "Sets herself up for another heartbreak." She dropped her imaginary microphone and shook her head. "Like I said, Marcello. You are so predictable."

Michael started to speak, but whatever he was going to say was lost when Julie suddenly hurled herself at him, knocking him sideways and landing both of us on the ground.

"I hate you," Julie yelled at him, but cut her tantrum short and started backing away before her father was even on his feet again.

"Julie, listen to me," he tried, but she kept backing away, her eyes locked on something behind us. Something that had drained the color from her face.

"The cat," she whispered.

Rosie looked behind me, genuinely confused. "Why, you bloody bastard. How did you get back here?"

Of course I turned around to have a look, which was silly when you think about it. What did I expect to see? Certainly not a half-dead cat lying on the kid's backpack, trying to lick its paws.

My throat tightened and my hand went to my mouth. I could see the damn cat as clearly as Julie could, lying right there, trying to get a paw up high enough to clean its face. The thing was hideous. Head drooping to one side, fur matted, and a gash on its throat that was open and red. No wonder the kid was backing away. I wanted to get away from it too, and I wasn't the one the cat was after.

"It's okay, honey," Michael said, holding out a hand to Julie. "Come on back. I promise the cat won't hurt you."

"Here kitty, kitty," Rosie said, but the cat was already on its feet, limping toward a picnic table and driving Julie back even farther. "Oh no you don't," Rosie muttered, and dove under the table, trying to grab the thing.

"Julie, stand still," Michael said, and she hesitated, making me think she might do as she was told, when suddenly the cat darted out from under the table and ran straight for her, brushing my foot as it went past. I screamed and everyone turned around, including Michael.

That was when Julie bolted, heading across the field to the clubhouse.

"Julie, come back," I called.

Rosie and Michael both spun around.

"This is your fault, Michael Hughes," Rosie shouted at him.

"My fault," Michael whispered and started to run after his daughter.

"I've got her," Derek called, already on an intercept course.

Michael nodded his thanks and jumped when I tried to take his arm.

"Michael, listen to me," I said. "This isn't your fault."

"Bullshit." Rosie wedged herself in between us, stuck her nose in his face. "Julie is your responsibility now. You can't just palm her off on Derek whenever you feel like it."

He shook his head, started backing away from me the same way his daughter had backed away from him. "I have to get Julie home."

"You didn't do anything wrong," I said, but it was too late. Rosie knew the targets and I still had a lot to learn.

"Tell Marcello it's over," she said and muttered a curse when he looked at me curiously. "I mean Sam," she corrected herself. "Tell Sam it's over."

He probably would have if Derek hadn't turned up at his side. Alone.

Michael looked around. "Where's Julie?"

"In the Eco Centre, next to the clubhouse," Derek said. "I didn't even know it was there. She's getting pretty good at the dodge and weave. Had me thinking she was going right, then she ducked left and pushed through the door."

"Why didn't you bring her out?" Michael asked.

"Because she's shut herself up in the staff bathroom. The staff unlocked the door, of course, but they couldn't open it. She's barricaded herself in somehow."

"At least we know where she is." Michael bent to pick up her backpack. "Let's go."

"What are you going to do?" I asked.

"First I'm going to get Julie out of that bathroom. Then I'm going to take her back to Derek's and call that new doctor. Insist that he sees her again on Monday. One way or another, this has got to stop."

"You and your goddamn doctors," Rosie said. "I told you, I'll take care of it."

I followed Rosie's gaze. The cat had gone as far as the blanket and collapsed beside the mother's plate.

Rosie sprinted past me to the blanket and snatched up the cat. "Now I've got you," she said, holding the thing at arm's length but supporting its head like a baby.

Michael handed the backpack to Derek. "Can you take this home for me?"

Derek nodded and swung the backpack over his shoulder. "I'll take the measurements for the patio too. Save you some time."

"Will you forget the goddamn patio?" Rosie muttered. "We've got more important things to think about."

The cat tried to squirm out of her grasp. "No, you don't," she said and tightened her hold.

The cat stopped struggling, but its ears were back and I could see its claws working, trying to latch onto a section of exposed skin. Rosie never had been good with cats, probably because of her allergies. And I couldn't believe it when she started to sneeze.

She sniffed and glared at me. "Don't look so amused, Marcello. You'll be ruing ragweed season for eternity."

"I have to go," Michael said and started walking toward the clubhouse.

Derek nudged me. "Go with him," he whispered.

I shook my head. "I should get back to the Swan. Find out what's going on."

"That reminds me," Rosie said, still clutching the cat and sneezing. "The priest couldn't make it today, but he'll come by the pub after mass tomorrow. Personally, I'm looking forward to seeing the old guy in action." She sneezed again and sighed. "Could you get Derek to put the backpack down? I could really use it about now."

"Why don't you call the pub?" Derek suggested. "See if they need you yet."

"I don't know—"

He held out his cell phone. "Just call. Find out what's going on."

"I can assure you it's not much," Rosie said. "The bald bitch was sitting on the front step reading a book when I went by. And no one was trying to squeeze past her to get to a table, believe me." She smiled and wiped her nose on her sleeve. "You really should be getting back."

Instead I took the phone and started to dial. I hated it when Rosie was right.

The line rang six times and finally the answering machine kicked in. "You have reached the Silver Swan."

I pushed End. "There's no answer. I have to go."

"How sad," Rosie said, giving up on the backpack and carrying the cat over to the family having the picnic instead.

"Look," Derek said, "I have to go back that way for my truck anyway. Why don't I stop in at the pub and have them call you, tell you what's going on."

"I don't know," I said again.

The father and the little boy were tucking into dessert now, and the mother was packing up the rest of the food. A bright orange thermal bag, a cooler, sat open and waiting behind her.

"Can you believe she gives them grapes for dessert?" Rosie called back to me. "Where are the cookies? The Twinkies? The homemade Rice Krispie squares?" She shook her head in disgust. "This isn't a picnic, it's a goddamn shame."

The father and the little boy started tossing grapes up in the air and catching them in their mouths. The mother got to her feet. "Stop that right now," she said and Rosie moved in. Grabbed the orange thermal bag, stuffed the cat inside, and zipped it up.

"Perfect." She swung the bag over her shoulder and strolled back to where we stood. "Now we'll see who has the last laugh."

"I mean, if they have everything under control at the pub," Derek said to me, "then what's the point in hurrying back?"

The mother sat down again and felt around behind her for the cooler. She turned her head and stared at the empty spot. "Where's the bag?" she asked. The husband shrugged. She folded her arms. "I suppose it just got up and walked away. Like the pickle."

The father stopped eating and took a slow look around. "It has to be here somewhere."

Rosie laughed. "Don't count on it." She wiggled her fingers at me. "See you later, Marcello," she said, but didn't leave.

"Did you hear what I said?" Derek asked.

I turned to him. "I'm sorry, what?"

"I said, it will only take me ten minutes to walk over there. You'll have a full report in fifteen." He smiled. "What do you think?"

Rosie pursed her lips. "Sounds irresponsible to me."

"Sounds great to me. Have them call." I handed Derek his phone, faced the clubhouse, and hoisted my purse higher on my arm. "Wish me luck."

"Good luck," he said and started to leave.

I laid a hand on his arm. "Derek, wait. Just tell me one thing. Has Michael been seeing a lot of women since Rosie died?"

"There was only one that I know of. Krissie something. Or Kristen—"

"Kirsten?"

"Yeah, that's it. As far as I know, she made a few dinners for him and Julie, but that was it. Why, did Michael mention her?"

"Just in passing."

"I can't say for sure, but I don't think he's seen her in quite a while." He headed off toward the street. "They'll phone as soon as I get there."

"I'll be waiting." I smiled at Rosie. "Seems there weren't quite so many women after all."

"I've already told you not to count on Derek for information. He only knows bits and pieces."

"He knows enough." I smoothed a hand over my skirt and dusted off my shirt.

"You're about to make a grave tactical error," Rosie said. "The last thing my daughter needs right now is to see you with her father."

I lifted my chin. "No, the last thing she needs is to hear that cat hissing."

The thing was moving around inside the bag, making first one side bulge, then the other. Not only was it hissing, it was making that low, threatening sound cats make when they're about to fight. "I thought you said you got rid of it."

She gave the bag a shake and the cat settled down. "I did. The goddamn thing just keeps coming back."

"You've tried to get rid of it before?"

"What do you think? The bastard is haunting my daughter; I can't just ignore it."

"But what does it want with Julie?"

Rosie shrugged. "How should I know? They don't give you a handbook when you die, and getting an appointment with God is impossible. Takes years, I'm told."

"But why is the cat so banged up?" I asked. "Why isn't it whole, like you?"

"I don't know and I don't care. The only thing that matters is keeping it away from Julie."

"What are you going to do with it this time?"

She smiled. "Take it to your pub. Give it a good home."

"Excuse me," a man said.

I turned, nearly bumping into the father from the picnic. He looked around to see who I'd been talking to, then gave me a small, uneasy smile. "I'm sorry to bother you, but have you seen an orange thermal bag? One of those collapsible coolers?"

I glanced at Rosie then shook my head. "I'm sorry, no."

He nodded and headed toward a group of teenagers sitting under a tree. "Excuse me," he said.

The cat made that low warning sound again. Rosie thumped the bag. "I wish I had never seen this goddamn cat."

"Where did you get it?"

"Huntsville," she said and gave the bag another thump. "But this time, I guarantee the bugger is not coming back." She started walking, heading for McConnell Avenue. "Just be sure to ask Michael about Kirsten. You'll find his reaction interesting."

I watched her go, the bag thumping and bouncing beside her, then turned and started walking toward the clubhouse. I had no idea what I was going to do once I got there, and no intention of ever asking him about Kirsten Clancy. Or Audrey or Nancy or Katherine who hated to be called Kathy. Even if they existed, even if he had slept with every one of them, so what? They were in the past, just like Rosie. All that mattered now was going forward, moving ahead. And taking Michael with me.

"Excuse me." A tap on my shoulder drew me around. The picnic mother smiled at me. "Did you happen to see anyone with an orange thermal bag?"

TEN

The Eco Centre is a recent addition to the park—a small, tidy nook beside the clubhouse with a single counter, racks of recycling brochures, and corkboards with posters of trees and wildlife lined up in precise rows. No doubt a reflection of the director, a no-nonsense woman with a long face and short hair who greeted me at the door. "I'm sorry," she said, "but the center is closed at the moment."

"It's okay." I pointed past her to Michael. "I'm with him."

He was on the other side of the room, talking to what I assumed was the bathroom door, indicating that no progress had been made. Julie was still in there.

The director moved back so I could step inside, then she locked the door and took up a position on Michael's right. Her assistant stood to his left, wringing his hands and biting his lower lip, an obvious asset in a time of crisis.

"Julie, honey," Michael said. "If you unlock the door, I promise I won't be mad."

"Only if you promise not to see that Sam person anymore," she called back.

Michael sighed when he saw me. "What are you doing here?"

I shrugged. "Helping?"

"Is that her?" Julie asked. "Tell her I hate her and I want her to leave."

"Ma'am," the director said, "perhaps it would be best—"

"No," Michael said, then turned back to the closed door. "I will not be bullied, young lady."

"Then I'm never coming out."

"Sir," the director said. "It's nearly closing time."

"I know. I'm sorry."

I gave the door a quick once-over. It was nothing special, just a typical wooden door, probably hollow, with a sign reading Staff Only and a map indicating where the public bathrooms could be found.

"I guess you've tried pushing your way in," I said. All three nodded. "How about taking it off the hinges?"

"They're on her side," the director pointed out. "I assure you, we've tried everything short of smoking her out."

"And there's no smoking in the clubhouse," the assistant said.

Michael banged his head lightly on the door. Something had to give soon.

"Look," I said, "I'm no expert, but it strikes me that Julie's enjoying the attention. If everyone leaves, then maybe she'll come out."

"Don't listen to her," Julie said. "She's a horrible person who hates me and wants me to die in here."

I smiled at the faces around me. "That's not true. I don't want her to die."

"Anything's worth a try," the director said.

"Daddy, don't go," Julie wailed.

Michael hesitated. I gave him my most understanding smile.

"It's up to you, of course, but if you stay, you're just giving her what she wants."

"Fine, go," Julie said. "But I might come out if Sam stays and talks to me."

"What?" I looked back at the door. "Why me?"

"Maybe you should stay," Michael said.

I didn't believe for a minute that the kid was going to open that door for me. This was nothing more than a way of regaining control, a power play worthy of her mother. But the rest of them seemed eager to trust her. Even Michael. "What do we have to lose?" he asked.

I sighed. "Okay, I'll stay."

The little group filed out through the main door, closed it behind them, and stood watching me through the glass. I turned and faced the bathroom. I felt my shoulders slump. "Okay, they're gone. You can come out now."

I heard shuffling around, saw the knob turn and the door open a crack.

"Julie?"

No answer. I crept closer. "Julie?"

Still no answer.

I took another step. "I don't know what your game is, but I'm willing to talk." I put my hand on the doorknob. "Julie, are you coming out now?"

The door swung back and I stumbled in, landing hard against the wall. Julie slammed the door and dropped to the floor with her back flat against it and her legs braced against the garbage bin on the other side. That was how she'd done it. Kept them all at bay with a garbage can.

I heard the outside gang coming inside, all of them talking at once until Michael banged on the bathroom door. "Julie," he yelled. "What do you think you're doing? Open this door."

She didn't answer, and she didn't get out of the way. Just folded her arms and stared at me, a look so like her mother's it took my breath away. But Rosie wasn't in the bathroom. Neither was the cat. It was just the two of us and a large stack of printer paper Julie had been coloring on with highlighters.

"Where'd you get the drawing material?" I asked.

She jerked her head toward a metal cabinet in the corner. "In there." She held up a yellow highlighter. "They're not the greatest, but they'll do."

Being reserved for staff use, the bathroom also doubled as a utility room with the metal cabinet holding office and cleaning supplies. The cabinet appeared to have been locked at one time, but now the doors hung open and Michael was going to owe them for paper, highlighters, and a visit from a locksmith.

"Sam?" Michael called. "What's going on?"

"I'm not sure. Give us a minute."

Julie was still watching me, so I put the lid down on the toilet and sat. I even smiled. "Well, now that you have a hostage, what are your terms for release?"

The kid's eyes never once left my face. "I know who you are," she said.

"Really?" I folded my arms and stared right back at her. "Okay, who am I?"

"You're the one my daddy almost married. But then he met my mom and married her instead."

"Who told you that?"

"Who do you think?"

"Could be any number of people. Your dad, your uncle." *Your mom*, but I didn't think it wise to confuse the issue.

"My Uncle Derek told me. He's the only one who ever tells me anything."

And he had obviously turned the story into one she could live with, which made sense. The kid was only seven, after all. How horrible to learn at that age that your mother was a lying, conniving bitch. She'd have to be at least sixteen before she'd appreciate having that bit of truth.

"He said you want us to stay in the city too," she continued. "But I don't want to stay here. I hate the city, I hate your stupid pub, and I hate you."

"Fair enough. But if you hate it here, why have you locked yourself in the bathroom? Why not just tell your dad you want to go back to Huntsville?"

"Because I have another stupid appointment with that stupid doctor, and my dad has to build you a stupid patio." She shook her head and reached for a fresh sheet of paper. "He's such a horse's ass sometimes."

That wasn't Julie talking. That was Rosie. But after two years of whispering, there was bound to be some spillover now and then.

The floor looked clean enough, so I slid off the seat and sat down across from her. She didn't seem bothered by my action. Simply selected a blue highlighter from the box and started coloring a sky, leaving white for clouds here and there. "It's not going to work, you know," she said. "I've been to therapists. I'm used to the whole silent waiting routine. And you're not very good at it."

"Ma'am, we're closing in ten minutes," the director said.

"No, you're not," I told her.

Julie went on coloring, leaving me to make a choice: move her by force or wait her out. I wasn't ready to opt for force just yet, but neither was I ready to play by her rules. If we were waiting, we were talking. And I was under no obligation to be polite.

"Are you in here because you saw the cat?" I asked.

She picked up a green highlighter and started adding grass to her picture. I took the highlighter away from her, held it out of reach. "I saw it, you know."

"Saw what?"

"The cat. Outside, earlier. On your backpack."

She took a pink highlighter from the pack and started drawing flowers instead. "You're a liar."

"I wish I was." I reached over and plucked a few drawings from her stack.

She dropped the highlighter and held out a hand. "Give me those."

I ignored her and went through the drawings one by one. Most were pictures of the cat in action. Licking its paws, catching a butterfly, batting a ball of wool. In every one, the cat was whole and well. As though she were in here trying to cure it by sheer force of will.

"She can't do any of these things, can she?" I said. "Can't play, or jump. Can't even clean her ears, poor thing."

"She can do it sometimes," Julie said. "She's getting better."

"No she's not," I said softly. "The blood is still matted on her fur and the wound is still open and red. She must be exactly the same now as she was two years ago." I handed her back the pages. "I know because I saw her, Julie. I saw the cat."

She shook her head and clenched her teeth. Pressed the marker down hard on the page, coloring the same spot over and over again until she made a hole in the paper. She stared at the hole and I watched her jaw soften, heard her sniff back tears. She looked small and tired huddled there against the door. Less like Rosie now, and more like a little girl who had locked herself in a bathroom with a stranger and didn't know how to get herself out.

"Julie, I know how frightening it must be when no one else believes you. Not even your dad."

She recovered quickly, scrubbing a fist over her eyes and raising her chin. Still her mother's daughter, I thought, picturing Rosie on the roof of her Aunt Barb's house with a pack on her back and that same look on her face, getting ready to jump, to run away. Heading back to Chapleau even though she still had the bruises her mother's boyfriend had given her the last time she ran home.

"You were talking to yourself on the veranda yesterday," Julie said. "How do I know you're not as crazy as they think I am?"

"You don't. But I'm not going to tell anyone else I saw the cat, because then they really will think I'm nuts."

She considered this a moment, then used the highlighter to draw huge glasses on the sun. "I didn't mean to tell Megan about the cat. I never tell anyone anymore. But the fucking thing . . ."

"Enough of that."

She shrugged in that offhand, adult way. "The *stupid* thing came to her house, and I had to go home in the middle of the night." She tossed the marker across the room. "I shouldn't have played with her the next day. I should have stayed inside. But I like playing with Megan. She's snooty but she has neat stuff. And I didn't mean to put her stupid Barbie in the mud. It just happened."

"I believe you."

"You're just trying to get on my good side to make my dad happy."

"That's partly true. I would like you to like me, but even if you never do, I still believe that you didn't mean to play Barbie in the Slime Pit. Sometimes things happen, and we don't know why. We're just stuck in the middle of it."

"I don't want to be stuck anymore. I want to go home." She dropped the marker, and the drawing slipped off her lap, slid out of reach. "I know Megan's going to tell everybody on the street about the cat. And then they'll all start calling me names and no one else will play with me. It's not like it hasn't happened before."

I thought about what Derek had said. How Julie's life had been since her mother's death. I could see it in her face, in the way she colored and the way she was worrying a piece of thread on the cuff of her jeans, twisting it round and round until it finally snapped. From the look of her, I'd say she was ready to snap too, and Rosie wasn't helping her at all.

"Sometimes people are mean," I said, because I couldn't think of anything better, anything less lame.

But she didn't roll her eyes the way Rosie would have. Didn't say, *Jesus, Marcello, you're a dork*. The kid just sighed and said, "Yeah, but friends are supposed to be different."

"Sometimes they're worse. My best friend did something really mean a long time ago. Hurt me a lot."

She looked over at me. "Did you ever forgive her?"

I shook my head and got to my feet "Nope."

Julie nodded. "I wouldn't either. My mom always said you can't trust girls."

"She would know," I said, and my cell phone started to ring.

"What is going on with you?" Eva demanded when I answered. "Lunch was over hours ago, and dinner is about to start."

"I'll be there soon, I promise."

"You'd better," she said, and I was only a little surprised when she hung up without saying good-bye. I shoved the phone in my pocket and held out a hand to Julie. "You're going to have to move now. I have to go to work."

She hesitated, looking me up and down, trying to figure out if I was the kind of person who would follow through or fall apart. I must have taken the right tone because she took my hand and let me pull her up. I slid the garbage pail out of the way and opened the door, keeping a firm grip on it until she was all the way out of the bathroom.

Michael picked her up and held her tightly. "I thought you'd be in there till morning."

"She was just looking for a quiet place to color," I said.

The director hurried into the bathroom. "The lock on the cabinet is broken. There's paper everywhere." She poked her head out. "Someone has to pay for this."

"I'll take care of it," Michael said.

"Can we go now?" Julie asked.

"Yes." He set her down. "But first you owe these people an apology."

I had no desire to witness Julie's punishment and went outside, heading back along the walkway to the street, wondering where Rosie had taken the cat, hoping I wouldn't find it at the pub.

"Sam," Michael called. I turned and he waved. "I'll see you later," he called.

"Count on it," I said, but behind his back, Julie was shaking her head at me.

So much for winning over the kid.

ELEVEN

I made it back to the pub in less than ten minutes, a personal record for both sweat and speed. Through the open front door I could see Loretta's red hurricane glasses still lined up on the mantel, and four tables of customers. Three were already tucking into appetizers, Johnny was delivering main courses to the fourth, and Derek was behind the bar, whirring something in a blender. Who let him back there? I wondered as I jogged down the street to Marilu's. I didn't need a mirror to know I wasn't fit to be seen in the dining room yet. The grass stains on my shirt alone would have been enough.

I sprinted through Marilu's, calling hello to Luigi and thanking Mario again for the Frisbee on my way to the back door. I didn't slow down when I hit the alley, just kept on running, hoping Eva wasn't up to her neck in orders so I could tell her about the cat while I cleaned up for work. As luck would have it, she wasn't busy at all. In fact, she wasn't even at the grill. She was standing outside my back door, talking to the guy from the bistro across the street.

Her back was to the wall and he was standing in front of her. Right in front of her. Almost touching her. Yet it didn't look like a shakedown. She was smiling up at him, her expression soft and open. If I had to describe what was going on, I'd have to say she was flirting, which wasn't a word I would ever have used in the same sentence with Eva.

She straightened when she spotted me, pushed him back a little. "Sam, you've met Leo from the bistro. Leo, you remember Samantha."

Leo. That was his name. He was around my age, tall and dark with deep-set brown eyes, a full mouth, and a slight but indiscernible accent I'd found intriguing the day he came over to introduce himself. At the time, I'd been slightly disappointed to see he was wearing a wedding ring.

"Of course I remember Sam." He held out a hand. "It has been too long since we last spoke."

"Twelve weeks, to be exact." I smiled and took his hand. "Ever since Eva came over to our side."

He laughed. "That is water under the bridge now."

"Really?" I drew my hand back, turned my smile to Eva. "Since when?"

"I should get back to work," Leo said, and looked back at her. "We will talk later."

I waited for her to deny it, to tell him they had nothing to talk about, but she didn't. She merely nodded and slipped back into the kitchen.

Once she was gone, Leo tipped an imaginary hat to me. "Nice to see you again, Samantha," he said and sauntered off down the alley, whistling like he didn't have a care in the world.

"Cocky bugger," I muttered and went after her.

Eva was already at the grill when I stepped into the kitchen, suddenly very busy flipping chicken breasts with one hand and whisking sauce with the other.

"Take those salads to table five," she said, nodding at three plates on the counter.

"No." I waited until she turned to face me. "What was that all about? What did he want?"

"To talk to me."

"I figured that out for myself."

She turned away and drizzled more sauce on the chicken. "Then why did you ask?"

"Because I assume he wanted to talk to you about coming back to the bistro." I went to the sink and washed my hands, giving her a chance to elaborate, to fill me in on the details, but she kept her eyes on the chicken and her back turned, leaving the discussion up to me. "Is that what he wanted?" I finally asked.

"Yes."

"And you told him . . . ?"

She shrugged and flipped. "I told him I'd have to think about it."

I went around to her side of the counter. "You can't be serious. When you came here, you said you hated that place. You'd never go back."

"Things change." She motioned to the cutting board. "If you're on this side, you're chopping parsley."

She was trying to get rid of me, hoping I'd let the issue drop rather than pick up a knife, because in Eva's kitchen, no one chopped without first donning an apron and a fetching hairnet. I wouldn't have minded a snappy little baker's cap or even one of those poor-boy chef's hats I'd seen in the restaurant magazines, but Eva was adamant. Chef's hats were for chefs only. The rest of us wore hairnets.

Usually that was enough to send me back around to my side of the counter, but if it meant finding out more about Leo, I'd wear two of the damn things and fishnet stockings to match, just to spite her.

I pulled an apron from the hook and one of those godawful nets from the box above the sink. "You're doing this because you're ticked at me, aren't you?" I said, stretching the thing over my head and stuffing my hair inside. "You're mad because I left you and Johnny alone again."

"Lunch was hard with only two of us. We ended up turning people away. And you have hair sticking out the back."

"So you *are* mad at me," I said and stuffed harder, trying not to think about people being turned away, and what they might have ordered, and what the profit might have been.

"I'm not mad. I'm just grateful Derek was able to pitch in with dinner."

And I was grateful there were no mirrors in the kitchen. I patted the net down, picked up a paring knife, and went at the parsley. "If you're not ticked off, then why would you think about going back to the bistro?"

"Not everything is about you, Sam. You're using the wrong knife."

"I like this one." I scraped the parsley into a bowl and wiped my hands on a towel. "Just tell me I'm not going to lose my chef to a crush."

She pulled a baguette from the bunk and slapped it down on the counter. "I don't know what you're talking about, and those onions need chopping too."

"Come off it, Eva." I pulled an onion from the basket and started peeling the skin. "I saw the way you looked at him. You've obviously got a crush on the guy, which is understandable. But it's not a good reason to go running back. Workplace romances never work. Besides, I think he's married."

"He is married. To me."

My knife slipped on the onion, cutting into my finger. I dropped the knife, shoved my finger in my mouth, and talked around it as best I could. "What do you mean he's married to you?"

"What do you think it means? Leo is my husband. Has been for almost a year. He came over because he misses me." She hauled the first-aid kit out from under the counter. "I told you it was the wrong knife. Now take that out of your mouth and go wash it. There are Band-Aids in the box."

"Just like that, he misses you." I shoved my finger under the tap and watched the blood swirl around the pots and down the drain. "When exactly did this revelation hit him?"

She shrugged and sliced the baguette in half lengthwise. "Today, I guess."

"In other words, as soon as he saw the prayer group outside the Swan."

She looked over at me. "What are you trying to say?"

"Nothing. But don't you find it strange that he picked today to come over and declare himself?"

"No stranger than your ex suddenly rolling into town and declaring himself to you."

"That's different." My finger was going numb under the cold water, but the blood was still flowing. "I think I'm going to need stitches."

"You are such a baby." Eva took my hand out from under the tap and wrapped a paper towel tightly around my finger. "And why is my situation with Leo any different from yours with Michael? Is it so hard for you to believe that the man missed me? That after twelve weeks, he was finally ready to swallow his pride and walk across the road to talk to me?"

"I didn't say that."

"You didn't have to, I can see it in your eyes. A man as good looking as Leo couldn't seriously want a bald bitch. He must be after a chef, which means this whole thing is about you after all." She handed my wrapped finger to me. "Hold this while I get a Band-Aid. Hold it tight."

I held tight. "Eva, I'm sorry. I didn't mean that at all."

"Didn't you?" She ripped the paper off the Band-Aid and took the toweling off my finger. "I know what people think when they look at me. They see the tattoos, the bike, and the bald head and they think, *Freak*. Don't tell me you didn't think that when I first walked through your door, because I know you did. Your face doesn't serve you well sometimes, Sam. Especially when you're trying to hide something."

"All right, I admit I was taken aback. No one ever said the chef at the bistro was bald."

"That's because I wasn't."

"What happened?"

"It's complicated." She held my finger still, wrapped the Band-Aid around it securely, then went back to the grill and flipped the chicken breasts one last time. She drizzled sauce on them, divided them between two plates, and then added rice and crisp, buttery green beans to each before hitting the bell to let Johnny know his order was up.

"No parsley?" I asked.

She banged the plates down on the serving shelf. "You didn't chop it fine enough."

"Eva," I said softly. "What happened at the bistro?"

"Why do you care?"

"Because I consider you a friend."

"Bullshit." She hit the bell again, harder this time, then brushed oil and garlic over the baguette and shoved the two halves under the broiler. "In all the time I've worked here we have never once gone for a drink or to a movie after work, and we never talk about anything that isn't related to the restaurant. You've made it crystal clear that we work together and that's all. Our personal lives are not up for discussion, which is okay by me, but you can't suddenly change the rules to suit yourself."

"I'm not changing the rules. And what I've been doing is called keeping a professional distance because it's good for business. Things don't get messy that way. Although they certainly got messy over the last couple of days, didn't they? Thanks to Derek, you and Johnny know all about Michael and Rosie, even the fact that I was left at the goddamn altar. It doesn't get much more personal than that, does it?"

Eva smacked the bell again. "Come on, Sam. That only happened because Michael showed up. If he hadn't, you wouldn't have said diddly about him or anyone else you've ever dated, and we both know it."

I picked up Johnny's order and carried it to the door. "Okay, you're right, but now that you do know, you have to give me something back. To even out the playing field so I don't end up feeling like a complete goof."

"Talking about your personal life makes you feel like a goof?"

"Sometimes. But like you said, this isn't about me." I pushed open the door with a hip and hung back, signaling Johnny to come get his order. He walked with small, mincing steps toward the kitchen.

"You're back at last," he said. "And looking lovely, I might add. No one wears a hairnet like you." He nodded at my finger. "Industrial accident or a run-in with the ghost?"

"Industrial accident." I nodded at his feet. "What about you?"

"Ghost," he said. "Eva put match heads in my shoes to keep it away. Something about them hating the smell of sulfur. Anyway, I saved you some. They're a bit crunchy underfoot at first. Kind of like having little stones in your shoes, but you'll get used to them. They're in my pocket if you want them."

"Maybe later, thanks." I saw Derek turn my way and quickly pulled my head back into the kitchen. "What's he doing here?" I whispered to Johnny.

He winced and shifted from one foot to the other. "Not much. Just dishes, prep, serving, tending bar—"

"I get the picture." I risked a quick peek at the bar, but he wasn't there. He was circulating among the tables, serving drinks and refilling water glasses. Not only did he have a nice smile, he was also proving handy to have around. And as long as he was out there, I could stay in the kitchen and find out what was going on with Eva. "Tell him I appreciate the help," I told Johnny. "Ask if he can stay awhile longer."

"You're planning to spend the evening in the kitchen, then?"

"Someone needs to man the dish pit."

He looked at me curiously. "Whatever you say. But as long as you're in there, tell Eva I need two orders of grilled tiger shrimp. And find out what's keeping my bruschetta."

"It's on the way," she called. "Shrimp will be up in fifteen."

I let the door swing closed and went back to the grill. "Are you going to tell me what happened to you and Leo?"

"Like I said, it's complicated." She took the baguette from the oven, spread her secret bruschetta mix on both halves, then cut the loaf into slices and slid them onto a board.

"I've got time."

I carried the bread to the door, handed it off to Johnny, and let the door swing shut when Derek turned my way again. The man had called me beautiful only yesterday. Why spring a hairnet on him this soon?

Hoping he stayed behind the bar awhile yet, I went back to the grill, and the grilling.

"We'll start with the assumption that Leo is a jerk," I said. "But what *kind* of jerk is the issue. A sloppy one? An adulterous one? A cross-dressing one?"

"Cross-dressing would have been easier." She handed me two wooden skewers. "I need five shrimps on each one."

I took the skewers with me to the fridge. "Then what kind of jerk is he?"

"I'd have to say a cultural one."

"Meaning?"

"Meaning he's European and I'm East Coast. He's Conservative and I'm NDP. And to top it all off, he's old money and I'm . . ."

"New debt?"

She sighed. "Unfortunately."

"An interesting match."

"You could call it that."

The shrimp had been marinating in garlic and oregano since early that morning. When I lifted the lid, the aroma was pungent, to say the least. But Eva's recipes have never failed yet, so I scooped ten green tiger shrimps into a bowl and took them back to the prep counter with the skewers. "I assume the two of you were fine for a while?"

"I thought so. We worked well together and we liked all the same things, including motorcycles. That's how we met, at a bike show. We started talking, went for a drink, ended up at an all-night tattoo parlor. Got matching dragons. Then we went back to my place and he never left."

"Are we talking love at first sight here?"

"Are you making fun of me here?"

"Certainly not. Okay, maybe. But I'm cynical by nature. Pay no attention." I handed the skewered shrimps to her and stood back while she lined them up on the grill. "He went home with you and never left. Then what?"

"Then we started working together. He wanted to open a restaurant, I wanted to move up in the cooking world. It was great. We got married on a boat, cruised the harbor for our reception, then went back to the bistro and had a perfect life."

"Until?"

"Until I found out he has a family and a life I knew nothing about."

"Leo has another wife?"

"No, he has parents, two brothers, and a sister living in Belgium."

Belgium. That explained the accent at least, but not the problem. "What's wrong with having relatives in Belgium?"

"Nothing, unless they're fabulously wealthy and descended from minor royalty."

"Leo is royalty?"

"He is one thousand and something in line for some European throne, and the black sheep of the family. He came over here to go skiing in Whistler and decided to stay. He hadn't been home, hadn't even spoken to any of them in ages, and then his favorite uncle died and everything changed. Get me the mango salad."

I hurried to the fridge, brought back the bowl, and didn't have to be told that plates would be needed next. "What made him decide to finally tell you all this?"

"He didn't tell me. I found out because I picked up the extension phone when he was in the middle of a call." She frowned when I scowled. "It's not like I do it all the time. I didn't know he was on the line. Normally, I would have hung up the moment I heard voices, but there was a woman on the other end calling him *Leo sweetheart*, so naturally I hung on."

"Makes sense. Who was she?"

"His mother. She went on and on about how much she missed him and how happy she was that they were talking again, and the next thing I know she's telling him she's booked a flight for him to come home. Couldn't wait to see him. And she had the most fabulous young woman she wanted him to meet. Alyson somebody, a little on the chubby side at size eight, but a truly lovely girl. She met everyone at the uncle's funeral and they all agreed she was perfect for Leo."

"His mother didn't know he was already married?"

"Apparently not. And instead of coming clean, he said he'd be happy to come home and meet this girl."

I stared at her. "You're kidding."

"If only." She flipped the shrimp twice more, arranged them on a bed of rice next to the mango salad, and rang the bell. I headed Johnny off at the door and exchanged the shrimps for a stack of dirty dishes.

"I need three green salads," he said. "Raspberry vinaigrette on the side."

"I'll bring them right out," I promised. "How's it going out there?"

"Fabulously." He tried to see past me. "Why can't I come in? What's going on?"

"Nothing." I let the door close on his questions and loaded the dishes into the dishwasher. "What did Leo say when you asked him about the call?"

Eva arranged greens on the plates, added chopped vegetables, then ladled dressing into little white ramekins and slapped the bell again. "He didn't lie, I'll give him that much. In fact, he told me his mother had tracked him down a month earlier, when his uncle took sick. He'd already spoken to her a few times since that call, and he admitted he should have told her about me right away. But their estrangement had hurt his mother enough. He couldn't bring himself to tell her he hadn't invited her to his wedding. He said she caught him off guard with the whole 'perfect girl' thing and he knew he couldn't wait any longer. He had to do something."

"Smart man," I said, racing to the door with the salads and shaking my head when Johnny opened his mouth to speak.

"I thought so, too." Eva picked up the scraper and went at the grill. "Especially when he promised he'd call his mother right away, tell her the truth then and there. But he never finished dialing. Said it was too late to start a conversation of such importance. But he told me not to worry, said he loved me and he would straighten everything out in the morning. We went back to bed. Had the most fabulous sex you can imagine."

"I don't want to know. Did he call her in the morning?"

Eva kept her head bent and went on scraping. "He said he tried, but for weeks afterward she was never available whenever he phoned. Eventually, it became the only thing I could think about, our only topic of conversation. Did you try today? Do you want to try now? I even offered to make the call for him."

"I don't imagine he took you up on the offer."

She gave a short, bitter laugh. "It only made things worse. We started fighting all the time until one day I *did* dial the number myself. Got his mother on the line and introduced myself as her daughter-in-law. Then I handed the phone to Leo. He had no choice. I was sitting right there. He finally told her everything. She cried and asked to speak to me again. She was very nice and wanted to make arrangements to bring the family here instead, to see his bistro and meet his little bride."

"Little bride?"

"He left out a few details when he was describing me, but that was okay. I was happy, and we started planning the party. Had I known what was coming, I would have stayed home. At least I'd still have hair."

"You had hair?"

"Down to my ass. Thick and wavy. Absolutely gorgeous."

"But you shaved it off?'

"It seemed like a good idea at the time." She tossed the scraper into the sink and turned her attention to the onion I'd abandoned earlier. "Leo loved my hair. Swore it would break his heart if I ever cut if off."

"You did it to spite him?"

She shrugged and wrapped the onion in plastic wrap. "We

threw the party at the bistro and everyone came. His family, our friends, the banker, suppliers."

"Alyson?"

"She stayed in Belgium. He was a married man, after all. We hired kitchen staff, I bought a new dress, got my hair done, even painted my fingernails. I felt great and I liked his family. They wanted to know all about me, wanted to ride the Harley and see the tattoos. I was having a great time, dancing, chatting, drinking martinis. I went out to the alley to cool down for a minute and discovered Leo and his brothers out there already, laughing and talking, really yukking it up about something. I almost called out to him when I heard Leo say my name, and for some reason I kept quiet."

"You hung on and listened."

She tore off another length of plastic wrap and laid it over the mango salad. "I know I should have turned around and gone back inside, but I couldn't resist. I had to know what they were laughing about."

"And?"

She sighed and carried the salad bowl to the fridge. "And they were laughing about me. Talking about what a joke I was, a real freak with my Harley and my tattoos. And huge? My God, none of them could believe they made women that big."

I felt my stomach twist, my heart beat faster. "What did Leo do?"

"He agreed with them. Said that seeing all of them again made him realize that I'd been his rebellion, a way of thumbing his nose at his family and all the demands they tried to make on him. He said he cared for me, the way a person cares for an ugly mutt, but he'd really like to meet Alyson because it was probably time to stop slumming and go home."

"Jesus, Eva," I said, because I couldn't think of anything else.

She smiled and opened the fridge. "Don't worry, I got my own back."

"By shaving your head?"

"Should I have cried and played the pathetic wife instead? The one everyone pities and laughs at behind her back? Not on your goddamned life. Going into that room bald was the perfect way of saying *Fuck you, Leo* without once opening my mouth."

She nodded with what might have passed for smug satisfaction had she been breathing a little less deeply, shoving the salad into the fridge a little more patiently.

"Definitely caused a stir at the party," she continued. "The whole room went quiet for a full ten seconds. Then Leo started yelling, called me a freak and told me to get my giant ass out of his restaurant. I gave him the finger and walked over here."

"So I only have you because your husband was a jerk, and now I'm in danger of losing you because he came over and made nice."

She kept her head bent over the bowl, still trying to jam it into a spot that was too small, determined to make it fit. "I didn't say I was going back."

"But you're thinking about it."

Something rattled and finally gave way inside the fridge, allowing the bowl to slide into place at last. She smiled and adjusted the plastic wrap on top, smoothing it down, making sure it stayed. "I'm thinking about it, yes."

"What about his family? What about Alyson? Did he go to Belgium to meet her?"

"Didn't have to. His mother flew her over the day after the party. The family stayed on and she stayed with them. I've seen her helping out at the bistro now and then. Alyson really is cute. Blond and slim, very haute couture, just like his mother and sisters. She probably is perfect for him, but she left last week. Told him she'd like to continue seeing him, but only if he goes home. Took him a while, but he finally decided he wants to stay here, and he wants me to come back."

I shook my head. "Come on, Eva. Do you honestly believe you can just walk across the road and pick up where you left off? Act like nothing ever happened?"

"We can work it out."

"Why would you want to?"

"Because he's my husband." She slammed the fridge shut and stood staring at her reflection in the glass. "And because I'm lonely, okay. A lonely, pathetic bald bitch."

I went to stand behind her. "It's not pathetic to be lonely."

"Isn't it?" She turned abruptly. "I'm the one who talks about being strong and independent, but the truth is, I miss him. I miss being married." Tears glistened in her eyes, and she sniffed loudly. "I hate going to bed alone and waking up alone. I hate having no one to talk to until I get here. And then it's all just menus and shopping lists, and Johnny's stupid roses."

"I think the roses are sweet."

"Me too." Tears slid down her cheek. "That's the most pathetic thing of all."

I didn't know what to do. Some small, distant voice said, *To hell with professional distance. Put an arm around her.* But survival hollered, *Back off! You don't know what could happen.*

She wiped her nose and started to laugh. "Now I feel like a goof too. Are you happy?"

Oddly I was, so I took a chance. Put my arms around her, hugged her, and she didn't hit me. In fact, she hugged me back. Sniffed loudly and held me harder while she cried. And I wanted to smack Leo for being a jerk. For throwing her away so easily. And for thinking he could have her back when he was ready.

Johnny burst through the swinging door. "You forgot the garlic croutons." He stopped when he spotted us and jammed his fists into his hips. "All right, that's it. What is going on in here?"

"It's a girl thing," Eva said, surprising me again.

But things quickly returned to normal when she pushed me

away, picked up a bowl of croutons from the counter, and walked it over to him. "Do you need anything else?" Johnny shook his head. "Then get out of here."

He backed out the door, and Eva turned to me. "You know what the really dumb part is in all of this? I knew going into it that the relationship wasn't going to work out."

I followed her back to the grill. "Don't be ridiculous. No one can know that in advance."

"I told you before, my mother is a psychic. That's why I believed you about Rosie right away." Eva turned down the grill and scraped crumbs off the cutting board. "Spirits talk to my mother all the time."

Realizing she was not going to tell me anything else about Leo, I followed her lead and took an empty pot to the sink. "Your mother sees ghosts?"

"No, but she said she heard voices every time she told a fortune. The cards, the palms, all that shit was just props, things people expect. She got the real dirt from the voices. She just didn't talk about it much."

"Because people would think she's crazy."

"Her own mother had her committed. That's where she met my dad, in a nuthouse in Donegal. He was a cleaner, and every night she'd talk to him through her door. Tell him something about himself, something she couldn't possibly have known. She scared the crap out of him, if you want the truth, but when she offered to go into business with him, split the profits fifty-fifty if he got her out of there, he took her out the back way and they kept on running. Left the country and set up shop in Cape Breton, but she never told anyone how it really works."

"Except you."

"She had to tell me something, didn't she? I mean, how weird is it when your mother comes running into your room in the middle of the night, crying because she knows the woman next door has just turned on her gas stove without lighting a match?"

"You figure someone was whispering in her ear."

She dumped the dregs of the basting sauce into the sink and carried the bowl over to the dish pit. "She never knew the specifics of how the voices worked, but after what you've seen, it's pretty clear."

"Does she still hear them?"

"I have no idea. I haven't talked to her in a while."

"Why not?"

"Because you can't talk to a woman who knows every goddamn move you're about to make and can't resist telling you exactly how you're going to screw up your life."

"Like Leo?"

"And plenty more before him. When I first met Leo, I told her I didn't want to know anything, but she couldn't keep her mouth shut. She had to tell me that one day, I'd hear for myself that he wasn't the man I thought he was. So I blocked her number on my phone and haven't talked to her since." Eva glanced over at me. "The good news is that everything from the moment I left the bistro has been a surprise."

I collected cutlery and prep dishes and loaded them into the dishwasher. "Including me?"

"And Rosie."

Johnny peeked through the door with an armload of dirty dishes. "Is it safe to come in?"

Eva scowled at him. "Why wouldn't it be?"

"No reason," he said and walked with the same mincing steps to the dish pit.

"How's everything out there?" I asked.

"Good. In fact, I think we're about done. Everyone is working on dessert and coffee, and no one new is stopping by."

Derek came through the door with an armload of dirty dishes.

"You don't have to do that," I said, reaching for them, the hairnet forgotten until I watched his smile broaden.

"That's an interesting look," he said, sidestepping me and carrying the stack to the dishwasher. "Neat. Compact. Oddly sexy."

I patted the net and pouted at him over my shoulder. "Wait till I pull on my rubber gloves."

"Tease," he said, loading the racks with an efficiency that came only from experience.

"You're pretty good at that," I said.

"Years of practice." He closed the door and snapped the lock to start the machine. "Table three's looking for their bill," he said to Johnny, then leaned close to me. "What color are the gloves?" he whispered.

"Baby pink," I whispered back.

He sucked in a low, hissing breath. "I'm going to lose sleep," he said on his way to the door.

"Can we keep him?" Johnny asked when he was gone.

"We'll see," I said, pushing him out the door again and wincing myself at his tiny, painful steps.

"His feet must be killing him," I said to Eva.

"It's his own fault. I told him a couple of match heads ground up really fine would be enough. But you know our Johnny. Had to go for a whole box instead. Wooden ones at that."

"Will they keep ghosts away?"

She went back to the grill for more pots. "Absolutely, although sometimes they do attract demons. The sulfur reminds them of hell. It's a risk you take."

I stared at her back. "You're kidding, right?"

She laughed. "Always remember that half of what you hear about the paranormal is bullshit."

"And the other half?"

"That's the part you have to memorize." She dumped the pots

into the sink and handed me the hose. "Speaking of which, did you see Rosie at the park?"

I nodded, and because she obviously wasn't going to tell me anything else about Leo, I figured it must be my turn to share again and told her about the cat.

Her brow furrowed as she sprayed the pots. "I've never heard of anything like that."

"Me neither." I rolled my shirt sleeves up a little higher, pulled on the rubber gloves, and promised myself I'd put an ad in the paper for a dishwasher tomorrow. "By the way, Michael is coming over after closing."

"You're not washing those right," she said, using a hip to bump me out of the way. "And for what it's worth, I still think you should back off on this Michael thing. At least until we know more about the cat."

I handed her the gloves. "Thanks, but I'm not worried. It hasn't hurt Julie, so why would it hurt me?"

"Because you're not supposed to see it. You're a whole new ball game for the animal. What if Rosie drops it off here and it decides to stay? Starts hanging around you instead of Julie? Climbing into *your* bed at night?"

I stared at her. "Can it do that?"

"I don't know, and neither do you. And we don't know enough about Rosie to be safe, either." She picked up a pot and started to scrub. "You ask me, you shouldn't have anything more to do with that bitch or the cat without getting some professional advice first."

"But I don't have a lot of time. I know she's over there right now, trying to get Michael to go back to Huntsville sooner than planned, working on him through the kid. If I don't get rid of Rosie before he leaves, he might never come back."

She held out a clean pot to me. "How do you know you want him to come back?"

I snatched the pot out of her hand and hung it on the rack above the sink. "Because we made a connection in the park this afternoon."

She didn't say anything, just laughed and pushed another pot under the spray.

"We did," I insisted. "And I'll be damned if I'll let go until I find out where it can lead. Rosie is not going to win this time."

"Fine, but how exactly are you planning to get rid of her? I don't know how much experience you've got with this sort of thing, but you're going to need more than holy water and a medallion."

She had a point. I hadn't thought of anything beyond getting Michael alone more, keeping him and Rosie apart as much as possible. I couldn't even say why I thought I'd be able to give her the slip again. Chances were good that Rosie would show up here tonight *with* Michael. I'd end up serving nightcaps to both of them. And then what?

"You're right," I said. "I need help. Can you call your mother?"

"Not a chance."

"Then can *I* call your mother?"

"Sam, you don't need a psychic. You need . . . I don't know . . . something else."

"A ghostbuster, perhaps?"

She carried the pot to the rack herself. "Not the kind you're thinking about, but yes, something like that."

"Fine."

I left the kitchen and headed for my office, a windowless box that used to be a supply closet, but has the advantage of being conveniently located by the back door and directly across from the bathroom/locker room. I laid claim to the room when I was renovating and so far have managed to squeeze in a small table, a chair, and a two-drawer credenza where I keep a cleanup kit, makeup, and what is left of a secret stock of underwear I came to rely on when I was renovating and would camp out on the drop sheets. I even hung a mirror on the wall and screwed in a couple of coat hooks on the back of the door, where I now maintain a supply of fresh shirts and skirts for days when I can't get home between shifts. Like today.

I took the phone book out of the credenza and flipped it open on my desk.

Eva filled the doorway, rubber gloves dripping on the floor. "What are you doing?"

"Looking for help." I pulled off the hairnet and shook out my ponytail while I flipped through the Yellow Pages. I paused at Parachutes and ran a finger down the page. "There must be something here. Paranormal whatevers."

She spun the book around and opened it to a new page. "Right there. Under Astrologers."

She was right. Witches, psychics, people willing to cleanse my home of unwanted spirits. Everything I could ask for under one simple heading.

"Only problem now," Eva said, "is separating the cranks from the real thing. You could be in deeper trouble if you pick the wrong name."

"Then let me call your mother."

She closed the phone book and headed for the door. "You do not want to use my mother."

I dashed after her. "But she's perfect. Spirits talk to her all the time, you said so yourself, so we know she's not a crank."

Eva bent over the pots at the sink again. "Trust me, you don't want to use my mother."

I pushed in front of her and hoped she wouldn't punch me. "Then why don't *you* help me get rid of Rosie? I already know you believe in her, and you must have picked up something from your mother."

"I went out of my way *not* to pick up anything from my mother." She didn't hit me, but didn't back up either, didn't give me an inch. For the first time, I fully appreciated just how tall she was.

"Then I'll just go back in there and call a number, any number." I squeezed back out the way I'd come in, strolled down to my office, and flipped open the phone book again. Started reading ads out loud. "I could call The Cozy Tea Room, that sounds safe enough. Or how about Ikbal Nepal, Indian Spiritualist, guaranteed results. You can't beat a guarantee." I peeked into the hall. No sign of Eva heading my way. I turned the page and called louder. "Then there's the Hollow Hill Group. They come complete with machines. That should drive Rosie crazy." I paused, reread the next name in the list and couldn't stop a smile from spreading across my face. Mary Margaret McRae. Kensington Market. What were the odds that she was Eva's mother?

"Or how about Mary Margaret MacRae?" I called. "Celtic Fortune Teller. Maybe I'll start with her."

That brought Eva to the door. "Dial that number and I'll make sure my mother finds out you're an undercover cop. A member of the fraud squad."

"She'll know I'm not. She's a psychic."

"One who never knows anything about herself. It's a common problem. Why do you think they're not all rich?" Eva said it with such sincerity, such a straight face, it was hard to know if this was truth or just more of the paranormal bullshit she'd warned me about.

I closed the phone book. "Then help me out yourself. You admitted I could be in more trouble if I pick a crank."

She opened her mouth to argue, then sighed and gave her head a weary shake. "All right, I'll help you. But you have to do exactly as I say. No improvisation. No running off whenever you feel like it. We have to stay in constant contact."

"Constant contact, got it." I sniffed my shirt. "I am in desperate need of a washcloth."

"Are you listening to me?"

"Absolutely." I took the cleanup kit from the credenza and

checked it for toothbrush, deodorant, razor, everything I'd need to prep for my date with Michael. Satisfied that I had enough to make myself presentable, I pulled the drawstring closed and looked over at her. "When do we start?"

"Tomorrow, but not too early. I like to sleep in on my day off. But if you're going to see Michael tonight, you might as well do some groundwork." She snatched the bag out of my hand and gave me a pen and a scrap of paper instead. "Write this down. First, find out as much as you can about the days before Rosie's death. How was the marriage? Were they fighting? Maybe thinking of separating? Definitely find out if he was having an affair." She looked taken aback when I glanced over. "What? You think that's impossible? The man was engaged to you when he was screwing her, wasn't he?"

"Please don't worry about my feelings. Just speak your mind."

"I always do."

And I liked her honesty. In small doses. Very small.

"Okay, what next?" I asked as I scribbled.

"Find out more about the accident. Exactly where and when it happened. The kind of car she was driving and what she was doing immediately prior to getting *into* the car. Where she was, who she was with, and where she was heading next."

I jotted down the questions, then went to the door and took a change of clothes from the hangers. "How can any of this help get rid of her?"

"I have no idea. It just makes sense to have as much information as possible. We'll have time tomorrow to sit down and figure out what to do. But if you see Rosie again between now and then, promise me you'll back off. Try to avoid her as much as possible until we have a plan, understood?"

I glanced over. Saw concern in the furrowed brow, understanding in the fists jammed into her waist, and I decided it couldn't hurt to keep professional distance on hold a while longer. "I'll avoid Rosie if you promise to avoid Leo. Give yourself time to really think about what you want."

Her jaw worked as she stared at me, and I wondered if my life would flash before me when I died. Then she nodded, and said, "That's probably a good idea," and I understood the joy in taking another breath.

"I also promise to do my best with these," I said, laying her page of questions on the desk and holding out my hand for the cleanup bag. "And just so you know, I really do appreciate your help."

"You're welcome," she said, handing the paper back, along with the bag. "And just so *you* know, this does not make us friends."

"Thank God," I said, and went into the bathroom to change.

TWELVE

There was no real reason for me to believe that things were looking up. Nothing concrete to explain the growing lightness in my chest or the smile on my face. Eva had no clear plan for getting rid of Rosie, and nothing I'd tried so far had come close to working. But just as the brush of Loretta's useless medallion against my skin gave me an odd sort of comfort, simply knowing that Eva was going to help made winning seem possible for the first time.

I stuck her list of questions into the frame of the mirror above the sink, committing them to memory while I changed and flossed and tried to make myself beautiful for Michael. Exactly where and when had Rosie died? Were they fighting prior to the death? Was either of them having an affair?

The name Kirsten Clancy suddenly popped into my mind. Kirsten Clancy, the neighbor who cooked for Julie and Michael after Rosie's death. She really should be on the list, now that I thought about it. Not that I was worried. Derek had said it was only a few dinners. Probably casseroles at that. Tuna and potato chips, macaroni and hot dogs, mushroom soup and anything. Poor Michael, it must have been hell. Rosie on one side and KitchenAid Kirsten on the other. No wonder he was going under.

I zipped up my makeup bag and checked my progress in the mirror. Even with shiny lips and curled eyelashes, I still looked pretty much the same—neat and efficient—not at all what I wanted for my first official date with Michael. Hot was more what I had in mind. Maybe if I opened another button on my blouse, gave my hair a shake, pouted a little. I sighed into the mirror. The look was perfect if I was trying out for a part in *Naughty Waitresses—Table 69*.

Deciding I'd get him to take me home so I could change, I tied up my hair and refastened that third button, making a mental note to keep civilian clothes on hand at all times as I snatched the list from the mirror.

Dashing across the hall to my office, I scribbled *Kirsten Clancy* on the bottom of the page and shoved the list into the drawer. I didn't need to have it with me. I knew those questions better than Eva did, I was sure of it. The only thing I didn't know was how to actually *ask* them.

Even if I thought Rosie would answer me honestly, which she wouldn't, I wasn't supposed to talk to her, and I wasn't about to confront Michael directly. Why make him think about her when he was with me? The man clearly needed to change his focus, to stop living in the past and start thinking about the future. Our future, right here at the Swan. I could already picture him helping out in the dining room, tending bar and delivering orders the way Derek had.

It would be the two of us together again, working hand in hand, building a name for ourselves. The Silver Swan, home of great food and great times. Home of Michael and Sam, Sam and Michael. And Julie too, of course, who wouldn't be any more help with those answers than her mother would be, I was sure of that. Which left me with only one possible source. Derek, my ace in the hole.

Who could say how much Michael had told his brother over the past two years? Maybe he had even confided an affair, which would explain a lot, but still left me with that one pressing question: How do you lead someone into a conversation of such a personal nature without appearing pushy and nosy, even disrespectful? And what if Derek was good at keeping secrets? What if he'd promised Michael he'd take those confidences to his own grave? Worse still, what if he'd already left the Swan?

I swung around the corner into the kitchen, coming to a sliding stop by the prep counter.

The floor in front of me was wet, and Eva was finishing up with the mop by the dish pit. "You have the worst timing," she said without looking over.

"Sorry," I said, tiptoeing across the wet floor to the swinging door. "Is Derek still here?"

"Might be." She leaned on the mop and frowned at my footprints. "You want anything to eat before I'm done?"

I shook my head, aware of the rumbling in my stomach for the first time. "I'll eat with Michael later."

She plunged the mop into the bucket and dragged it over my guilty footprints on her way to the office. "Then I'm out of here. I'll leave the garbage for you."

"I'll take care of it later. Right now I need to talk to Derek. With a little luck, I'll have the answers you need tonight."

"What kind of answers are you looking for?" he asked.

I snapped my head around, saw him standing in the doorway with two empty beer cases.

"Because whatever you need," he continued, "I'm here to help. Especially if it will get rid of the ghosts in the dining room."

My breath caught, making a dismissive laugh difficult. But I managed a smile and a wag of my finger. "You've been talking to Johnny."

Derek walked past me with the empties and stacked them by the fridge. "Listening mostly. From what I hear, you've got a real problem in there."

"I thought you weren't a believer."

He came back to where I stood, gave me that grin I was coming to like. "He's very convincing."

"What do you expect? He's an actor."

I turned and headed into the dining room, taking up my usual spot behind the bar. Needing a moment to regroup, to plan, to think about what box you tick when you fire someone for having a big mouth.

The former-employee-known-as-Johnny was busy escorting the last of our customers to the door—a sleek blonde, two carefully tousled brunettes, and one meticulously spiked redhead. He looked over at me, an apology already on his face, but I ignored him and picked up the blender, getting ready to break it down to start the nightly cleanup, when it dawned on me that the blender was already clean. In fact everything was clean. The counters shone, the fridges were stocked, even the glass washer was empty. Derek had been busy.

What a nice guy. If he'd just let the ghost issue drop, he'd be almost perfect.

With nothing to clean, I lifted the lid on the condiment tray and popped a handful of maraschino cherries into my mouth, treating them like tiny tasteless appetizers while I tried to come up with some way to get Derek off ghosts and onto Rosie.

"You ladies have a fabulous night," Johnny said, holding the door open and slipping halfway out of his shoes, a sure sign that he'd finally had enough of those match heads. Any other time, I would have felt sorry for him, might even have helped him get things moving over there. But not tonight. As far as I was concerned, he deserved to stand there forever.

Johnny urged the ladies forward. "Be sure to come again."

"Count on it," the blonde said, then stopped and pointed past me. "Especially if *he's* going to be making martinis. They were unbelievable."

"Glad you liked them," Derek said, joining me behind the bar.

She gave a low throaty laugh. "Liked them? We positively *loved* them."

"That's nice." Johnny herded them forward again. "Good night now."

"How was the meal?" I asked.

The ladies stopped again, and I thought Johnny might cry. "The meal was amazing," the spiky redhead said. "Especially the prawns."

"But the martinis." The blonde lowered her chin and smiled at Derek. "Fabulous."

He laughed. "I'll tell you the secret next time."

"I'll hold you to it," she said, moving out to the street at last.

"That must have been one hell of a martini," I said, watching the women file past the window and catching a last glimpse of the blonde catching a last glimpse of Derek. "You should have asked for her number."

"Already have it." He fished a card out from under the condiment tray. "Amber Freihaut, mortgage broker." He smiled when she waved, waited until she was out of sight, then dropped her card into the wastebasket. It fluttered down, coming to rest face up among the crumpled napkins, the lemon rinds, the used swizzle sticks.

"Not your type?" I asked.

"Never was."

I glanced down at the card, wondering what his type might be and realizing for the first time how attractive he must be to some women. Plenty of women, now that I looked at him more closely.

"Do me a favor?" Johnny said, already locking the door and hanging up the Closed sign. "Tell Eva to wait for me."

"Tell her yourself," I said, still refusing to feel sorry for him when he hobbled past me to the kitchen.

"Do they work?" Derek asked when Johnny was out of sight.

"Do what work?"

"The match heads. He offered me some, but I passed, and I'd hate to think I was wrong. That there might be ghosts whispering in my ear right now."

A nice guy, yes, but sadly not perfect. "Did Johnny tell you that?"

"Right after he told me there was no heaven or hell, no white light and no granny. He seemed especially upset about that. Seems he'd been counting on there being a granny."

"That's because it wouldn't have been Loretta." I fished an olive out of the condiment tray and popped it into my mouth. "This whole thing is her fault. She must have spooked him with her prayer group and her holy water. I'll talk to him later."

"Then you honestly don't believe there are ghosts in here."

"In here? Definitely not." Consciously resisting the urge to check the windows for signs of Rosie, I picked up the blender instead. "You want a drink or something?"

He didn't answer, just stood watching me. I was afraid he wasn't going to let the ghost issue go this time, which would have been fine if I'd known how he would react to the truth. Telling him about Rosie might even be the perfect lead-in to Eva's questions, but I still couldn't read him well enough to take the chance, to risk having him turn his back on the crazy woman.

"I guess not," I said and was surprised when he said, "Then you'd be wrong."

He reached past me, taking two glasses from the rack above my head and nestling them in the last of the ice. "Do you like martinis?" he asked, making the change in subject subtle yet official.

"Absolutely. Especially when I don't have to make them." Relaxing again, I set the blender back on the base and handed him the shaker. "You'd better not keep the secret from me, or I'll have no choice but to call Amber and give her your number."

"You're a hard woman." He plunked the bottle of Tanqueray gin and a pen in front of me. "Write this down. No gin but this one."

I pulled over a paper coaster and jotted down *Tanqueray only*. "What about vodka?"

"If you want vodka, you drink gimlets. Not martinis."

I laughed and scribbled *No vodka unless pressured.* "I would never have figured you for a martini snob."

"There are no snobs. Just the enlightened and those still waiting."

He put the shaker back and took a small glass pitcher from the shelf instead.

"Stirred, not shaken?" I shook my head. "James Bond would be appalled."

"James Bond was a brute. Now watch closely."

He dropped a handful of ice into the pitcher, then poured in two ounces of gin and an equal amount of Noilly Prat vermouth.

I hesitated before writing. "You sure you want that much?"

"People are always afraid of the vermouth."

"I'm not afraid. Just leery."

He leaned close. "Then prepare to be amazed," he said, his breath tickling my ear.

I laughed and sat back, already amazed. "Where did you learn to make martinis?"

"I worked at a little piano bar on St. Denis in Montreal. Every weekend it was the Rat Pack, sidecars, and martinis. You either loved it or left it. I stayed for four years, hence the change in music. I hope you don't mind."

I hadn't noticed there was music at all, let alone that it had changed, but now that I listened, I heard the voice of Old Blue Eyes, daring luck to be a lady.

"I can plug in something else if you like," Derek said.

"No, don't. To be honest, I like Sinatra. But if you tell Loretta, I'll deny we ever spoke."

"Deal." He gave his concoction a gentle stir, then strained the mixture into the two chilled glasses and added a twist to each. He held out one to me. "Taste," he said and waited while I sipped, and sipped again. "Well?"

"Okay, you win. More vermouth is better."

He smiled and clicked his glass with mine. "You think that's good, you should taste my gimlets."

I was about to grab another coaster when Eva came into the dining room, helmet in one hand, leather jacket in the other.

"I'm out of here," she said and looked at me expectantly.

I shook my head behind Derek's back. No answers yet.

Disappointment showed in the set of her jaw. "I'll be at home if you need me. If not, I'll see you tomorrow —"

"Don't go yet." The kitchen door banged open and Johnny held up a hand. "Let me get my backpack, and I'll leave with you."

Eva stared at him. "Why would I want that?"

"Because I know how much you like bluegrass, and there's a new act at the Toad and Tree, down the street."

"Big Mountain Blue," Derek said. "They're really good."

Johnny pointed a finger at him. "That's exactly what I heard. Which got me thinking, hey, why not stop in on our way home and check them out?"

Eva looked at Johnny the way I look whenever someone suggests I try camping. "You're not serious."

"Of course I am." He stepped back into the kitchen, but his voice carried into the dining room. "You'll really like them."

"Forget it," Eva called. "I'm going home."

He poked his head out again. "That works too. Just give me one minute."

The door swung shut and she turned to me. "What's happening here?"

"I think you're taking Johnny home with you."

"You really should stop at the Toad on the way," Derek said. "They're worth hearing."

Eva frowned and glanced out the window at the bistro across the street.

Dusk was slowly settling over the Danforth, but unfortunately there was still enough light to clearly see that jerk Leo coming out of the bistro for a smoke. Eva spotted him right away, of course, and I couldn't look away either, wondering if anyone else would make an appearance with him. A well-meaning brother. A caring sister. Someone who would do their best to take him home again. Sadly, no one else came out. It was just Leo and his cigarette, all alone by the door. He kept his eyes on the ground, his hands in his pockets. A man preoccupied with something other than the business at hand. Perhaps his wife?

I jammed more cherries into my mouth so I wouldn't say anything, but I had the strangest feeling the scene had been staged for Eva's benefit. And unfortunately it worked, because she turned from the window and looked straight at me. "I don't want to hear the singer," she said. "I want to go home."

"Then we'll go to your place." Johnny shuffled into the dining room with his backpack dangling from one shoulder and a brand-new motorcycle helmet in his hands. All black and shiny and jack-boot macho. Not at all what I would have chosen for him.

"You can invite me up for coffee when we get there." He held up the helmet. "What do you think?"

"I think it's obnoxious, but even if I liked it, you are not coming home with me." She opened the door and glanced back at me. "Call me," she said and stepped outside.

Johnny hurried after her as best he could. "Is it okay to take these match heads out of my shoes now?"

Eva's answer was lost in the slamming of the door behind them.

"He doesn't stand a chance with her, does he?" Derek asked.

I wandered closer to the window. "Not as long as she's married."

They argued on the front step for another minute or two, voices rising, attracting the attention of passersby, but Leo had gone inside by then, missing his chance to play the white knight to the damsel in distress. As impossible as I knew his chances were, I found myself rooting for Johnny anyway, hoping Eva would just once look seriously at the poor guy, see that there were alternatives to Leo.

She finally threw her hands up and walked away, leaving our Johnny alone with his shiny new helmet and his shoes full of match heads.

"Does he know she's married?" Derek asked.

"Not unless she told him."

Johnny sat down on the front step. Shook out first one shoe, then the other. As he walked away, I wished I'd been less hard on him. "I only found out myself a little while ago." I went back to the bar and my martini. "Her husband owns the bistro across the street."

Derek peered through the glass. "Why isn't she going home with him?"

"Because they're separated. It's complicated. Better we concentrate on the gimlet recipe instead."

Derek sat on the stool next to me and pulled his martini closer. "It's too bad they didn't go to the Toad. I would have asked them to save me a table."

I dipped into the condiments again, going for an orange slice this time. "Sounds like you're a real bluegrass fan."

"More a fan of the lead singer, Amanda Jeffries. I've known her a long time and I'm not kidding when I say she's good."

I dropped the peel on a napkin and went for another olive, suddenly curious about this Amanda. Wondering what she looked like, what she sang, whether *she* was his type.

"The Toad is an important venue," he continued. "She's a little nervous, so I promised I'd drop by, make sure there's at least one pair of hands clapping."

My own hand froze on the way to the cherries. "You're going there tonight?"

"As soon as I leave here." He picked up the pitcher and topped up our glasses. "Why don't you come with me? She's worth hearing, even if you're not a fan, and we could get you some real food."

I felt my face warm. Why hadn't it occurred to me that Derek might have a life of his own? That Michael and I weren't always the first thing on his mind? "Thanks for asking, but I'm supposed to be going out with Michael tonight. And I think he's counting on you to stay with Julie," I said, feeling more the fool when he set the pitcher down and looked at me. "I'm sorry, I just assumed he'd already asked."

"He probably did, but I've had my cell turned off." Derek pulled the phone from his pocket and flipped it open. "He's called twice," he said, punching in Michael's number.

I finished my drink, my stomach tightening around those damn condiments while he waited for Michael to answer. If he told Derek he wasn't coming, if that bloody Rosie had changed his mind again—

"Mike," Derek said. "I know. I'm sorry. I'll be there shortly."

"Good news," Derek said when he hung up. "Julie's already asleep."

"No cat," I said, picturing Rosie with that orange cooler and wondering where she'd taken the thing.

"I was betting on the afternoon Frisbee tournament, but you might be right." Derek closed the phone and set it on the bar. "Either way, it makes things easier for all of us."

"But what about Amanda?"

"I'll run down to the Toad now, stay for a few songs, then head over to Mike's. She'll understand."

I carried the pitcher and the glasses to the sink. "You're a very sweet guy."

"That's what Amanda tells me." He pulled another coaster toward him. "I'll write down that gimlet recipe before I go. You can try it with Mike."

I sat down next to him, watching him scribble a list of ingredients and thinking that Michael and I should drop by the Toad later. Check out the menu, the music. Amanda, who thought Derek was sweet.

He slid the recipe toward me. "I'll call you the moment Michael leaves."

He started to get up. I laid a hand on his arm, stopping him. "I really appreciate your help in all of this. If you ever need a job, you know where to come."

He laughed and covered my hand with his, squeezing just a little. "I had a good time. Reminded me why I used to push Michael to make good on all his talk about opening his own place one day."

"He still wanted to do that?"

Derek nodded and took his hand away. "He talked about it a lot when we were alone, but it was never going to happen. Rosie wasn't about to let him do anything that reminded him of you. Can't say I blame her. You were a tough act to follow."

I smiled, realized my hand was still on his arm, and reached for the gimlet recipe instead. "As flattering as that is, I find it hard to believe."

"You shouldn't. We only met a few times when you were dating Mike, but I always thought he was a lucky guy."

I lifted my eyes, snappy comeback at the ready, but he was already on his feet and heading for the door. "I should be going. Too bad we didn't get a chance to talk about the patio."

"Michael and I already discussed it, at the park."

He looked surprised. "You're clear about what you want, then?"

I nodded. "Red pickets."

He laughed. "To match your grandmother's door. Good choice. I'll fax in an order for the wood tonight. That way I can pick up everything he needs first thing tomorrow."

"Will you be back in the morning?" I asked.

Derek shook his head. "Mike can handle it."

A twinge of disappointment had me on my feet, following him to the door. I'd have to try to get those answers, after all.

"Is there anything I should have ready for the morning?" I asked.

"Nope. He'll bring what he needs. I'll take Julie to the lumberyard, keep her out of his hair. She loves it there for some reason. Knows all the different kinds of wood and what they're best suited for. And she can't wait to use the power tools."

"She comes by that naturally enough," I said and realized I'd just been handed the perfect way into the questions. The trick now would be to walk through it smoothly. "Her mother loved to build things," I said. "I imagine Rosie was a big help to Michael when he went into the contracting business."

Derek fished his keys out of his pocket. "She taught him everything he knows."

"I'll bet she did." I smiled, trying to keep my tone light, casual.

"But running a business together can be a real strain on a relationship. Did it hurt them at all?"

"They seemed okay."

"Would you call them a happy couple?"

"As happy as any."

"Did they fight?"

"Everyone fights."

"But were theirs worse than normal?"

"Why does it matter? She's dead, it's over."

I shrugged and warned myself to slow down, take a breath. *For God's sake, don't scare him away.*

"I just wonder, that's all. I mean, if Michael can't move on, perhaps guilt has something to do with it. Maybe they had a horrible fight before she was killed. Or maybe he was thinking of leaving. Or even having an affair."

"Mike have an affair?" Derek shook his head. "Not possible. The guy is so straight it hurts. But now that you mention it, he did say something once about them having a fight before she left the house that morning."

Bingo, I thought, but said, "That's too bad," with as much sincerity as I could muster. "Must have played on his mind for a while."

"He doesn't talk about that day or the accident much at all. In fact, he used to tighten up if I even mentioned it, so I started letting it go."

He turned the knob and started to open the door. I took a deep breath. It was time to press harder or back away.

"Did Michael ever say what they were fighting about that morning?"

Derek shrugged. "Something about her working too many hours, never being home on the weekends."

"Why was that?"

"Because she sold real estate."

"No one told me that. Why didn't anyone tell me that?"

"Because it doesn't matter."

"But it does. In fact, it explains a lot. Real estate is a demanding field, with late hours and weekend work." *And plenty of opportunities to fool around.* "Was she any good at it? Real estate, I mean. Was she good at it?"

"She was okay. But I think she spent more time sitting in open houses than she did selling them."

"Then she wasn't rolling in commissions."

"What are you getting at?"

"Nothing. Just wondering if Michael might have been jealous of her commissions. Felt emasculated, perhaps." I smiled. "Lord knows she wouldn't have let him off easily if she was the main breadwinner."

"She wasn't. Mike's business kept them afloat."

"He told you that?"

"He told me money was no problem."

"Who did she work for?"

"A broker in Huntsville."

"Do you know the name?"

Derek stared at me. "Why are you asking me all this?"

"Like I said, I'm just curious." I reached past him and straightened the Closed sign on the door. "So do you know the name?"

"No, I don't." He checked his watch again. "I should be going."

I had the feeling he knew not only the name of the broker, but a whole lot more he wasn't telling me. A man with integrity. Just my luck. Now I'd have no choice but to get the answers from Michael himself.

"Will you be okay alone until Mike gets here?"

I had to laugh. "Are you kidding? I spend more time alone here than I do at my house."

He nodded and opened the door. "Working too hard because there's no reason to go home. I understand that."

"That's not the case," I said. "The pub just takes up a lot of time."

"So does home building, if you let it."

"And you let it?"

He shrugged. "Beats watching TV by myself. Do you still have my cell phone number, just in case?"

"I do," I said, feeling bad about Amanda again and wondering how a man like Derek ended up spending his nights alone anyway.

"Be sure to call if you need anything," he said. "And I'll let you know as soon as Mike leaves."

He stepped outside, and I joined him on the front step. Day had finally given way to night, but the air was still warm and the Danforth was hopping, living up to its reputation as the up and coming place to be on a Saturday night. Patio tables were full and the sidewalks pleasantly crowded with people laughing, talking, making their way to a club or a café, or simply out for a stroll, hand in hand, just as Michael and I would be soon. Just as Amanda and Derek should have been.

"I won't be long at the Toad," he said. "Which should put me at Mike's in about forty-five minutes."

I smiled and leaned a shoulder against the door frame. "Thanks again, Derek. I really appreciate your help in this. And I'm sorry for ruining your date with Amanda."

He didn't deny it was a date, just shrugged and said he'd find a way to make it up to her. I didn't promise that Michael and I would drop by the Toad later, but watching Derek walk away, on his way to catch the mysterious Amanda's show, the idea felt more and more like a good one.

THIRTEEN

With Derek gone and Michael not due for a while, I had enough time to make myself something to eat. It was either that or refill the condiment tray again.

I was almost through the door when I heard a voice call, "Samantha, how nice to see you again. How is business?"

I sighed and turned, watching Leo come toward me, walking slowly, smoking a cigarette, a wide smile on his handsome face. I forced my shoulders to relax and smiled back, matching his level of self-assurance, or at least pretending to.

"Hi, Leo. Taking a break?"

He chuckled and joined me on the step. "Even the boss has to do that sometimes."

"I suppose." I gestured across the street. "Nice crowd you've got there."

"Not bad," he said and shrugged in that way that is supposed to say *It's nothing* but really means *Eat your heart out*

"I should get back to work," I said and turned to go inside. He shifted slightly to the right. Not enough to block the way, but enough to make a point, to let me know he wasn't finished, and if I was smart, I'd step back and listen. Not always being smart, I stayed where I was, crowding him, almost touching him, still the master of my own front door.

He smiled again, indulging me, patronizing me. "Samantha, just because she's coming back does not mean we should be enemies."

"Are you sure that's what she's doing?"

"I know my wife."

"Perhaps," I said, and we stood like that a moment longer, two cats claiming the same territory, waiting for one to give.

Leo smiled and stepped aside. Took another drag on his cigarette, and dropped the butt, crushing it on my step. His way of pissing on my shoes, letting me know he wasn't backing down, just changing tack.

"Since you are already finished for the night," he said, "why not come over for a drink? Meet my family and friends."

"Too bad Alyson's already gone. It would have been fun to meet her."

He didn't look as surprised as I'd hoped, merely amused. "Eva has told you, then."

"Everyone talks to someone." I folded my arms and tried to stand the way Eva might, to be the proud bald bitch. "Tell me, Leo, was Alyson worth it? Was she as lovely as promised?"

"I will not discuss this with you."

"I'm kind of busy right now anyway," I said and smiled in the way that is supposed to say *No problem* but really means *Get out of my face, you bloody weak bastard*.

I turned to leave.

He stepped forward, openly blocking my way this time. "Samantha, you must understand. Things happen within a marriage.

Things that are sometimes hard to understand, harder still to justify. But I am her husband, and I need her to come back."

"Really, Leo? Or is it the bistro that needs her?"

He sighed and gave me another patronizing smile, as though he really were a bloody royal. "Let me ask you one thing. Have you ever been married?" I shook my head. "I am not surprised, and I do not expect you to understand the bond between a man and his wife. A bond that can transcend not only mistakes, but time itself."

I laughed. "My God, you've been talking to Rosie."

"I do not know any Rosie."

"It doesn't matter." I took a quick look up and down the street, knowing she was out there somewhere, using every device she could think of to hold on to Michael, including Leo.

"It's been nice talking to you," I started, but he held up a hand.

"Samantha, let me put this simply. You need to butt out."

"Now that is classic Rosie," I said and smiled when his brow furrowed. "You have a good night, Leo. And say hello to Alyson."

I closed the door once and for all and switched out the light, leaving him in darkness on my step. We both knew I'd have to turn it on again for insurance purposes, but for now I was proud of the stand I'd taken for myself, for Eva, for the right of marriages everywhere to end.

I busied myself in the dining room, straightening perfectly aligned silverware and smoothing already smooth tablecloths until Leo was safely back on the other side of the street. Then I switched on the front light again and went behind the bar to turn off the CD player. I did the same thing every night after Eva and Johnny left, and usually I enjoyed the quiet. Found calm in the hum of the coolers, the thud of the pipes, even the creak of the old wooden floorboards. But not tonight. Tonight the quiet felt thin and twitchy, like a breath held too long. And every creak of those floorboards made the hairs on my arms stand straight up.

"You're being ridiculous," I muttered but switched the CD back on nonetheless. Even cranked it up a notch and joined Dino in the chorus of "That's Amore" on my way to the kitchen with the garbage. But I didn't realize Johnny had already turned out the lights back there. I froze in the doorway, the song dying in my throat while I groped for the light switch and watched the pots sway gently on the rack above the prep stand. Back and forth, back and forth like a sign, a warning set in motion by unseen hands. Rosie's hands?

"Get a grip, Marcello," I said and flicked on the lights. But as determined as I was to be reasonable, to tell myself she wasn't in my kitchen, I couldn't make my feet move until I scanned the room, satisfying myself that the bitch wasn't lurking in a corner. "Happy now?" I muttered and picked up a second bag on my way to the back door, stopping long enough to grab a key from the hook in my office before carrying the bags out into the night.

The alley was deserted. No kids behind the fruit market, no one taking a cigarette break, not even a fellow restaurateur rolling out a garbage bin. It was just me out there, alone with the shadows and their small, skittering sounds. Mice, raccoons, rats if I was honest. They all found their way to my alley eventually.

It certainly wasn't the first time I'd been alone out there, and never once had I felt spooked taking out the garbage. But tonight I found myself hesitating when the door swung shut behind me, holding the bags tighter and jumping at the sound of footsteps approaching. I felt like a fool when Mario walked out of the shadows, tipping an imaginary hat and wishing me luck with the patio.

"Thanks," I said, making my fingers lighten up on the bags.

I carried them over to the plastic shed where we store the bags. It's not a Dumpster by any means, just a plastic box about three feet high and four feet wide with doors that open in front and a top that lifts like a lid. It keeps the recycling dry and the bags intact until garbage day. While Johnny calls the padlock overkill, I call it practical, ensuring that nothing ends up living inside.

I set the bags down in front of the shed and stuck the key in the lock as I do every night without incident, without worry, without sweat running down my back. I glanced back at the door. Where was Michael? And why couldn't I get the stupid lock to open?

I jiggled the key in the padlock, swore once, and jumped for the second time when I heard footsteps behind me again. Probably Luigi this time. I put a smile on my face and turned, and was glad the storage shed gave me something to hold on to when Rosie stepped out of the shadows.

"Marcello, I have had the best night," she said. "You won't believe who I saw."

She was still in her jeans and Wild Rose T-shirt, but her hair was tied back in a ponytail and she'd exchanged the stilettos for a pair of running shoes. Instead of the orange cooler, she was carrying a slice of baklava in one hand, an unlit joint in the other, and she had tucked a bottle of Evian under her arm. Trying to have everything at once, as usual.

"Hold this," she said, pushing the water and the baklava into my hands before hoisting herself up onto my garbage shed. She wiggled backward until she could lean against the wall, then patted the spot beside her. "Take a load off. You look beat."

"I've been working," I said, dumping her stuff in her lap. Funny, but now that I knew where she was, I wasn't afraid anymore. In fact, I was relieved. Better the devil you know, and all that.

"What are you doing here anyway?" I asked and jiggled the padlock again, trying to pull the key out or push it back in, anything so I could get away from her. Avoid all communication, as Eva had said. But the key was stuck, refusing to budge. I dropped the lock and frowned at her. "And where's the bloody cat?"

"Pickering probably. Or maybe Oakville. Who knows?"

I shook my head. "I don't follow."

Rosie smiled and pulled a lighter out of her pocket. "I put the bag on a GO train. I'm hoping someone calls it in as a suspicious package and they blow the thing up. But even if they just put it in the lost and found, the little bastard is out of my life at last." She held up the joint. "Smoke?"

"No. And what makes you think the cat won't find its way back?"

"Because it's not that smart. The way I see it, the thing will finally realize it's licked and start following some other lucky soul." She lit the joint and put it to her lips, barely touching the end while she drew air in around it, a technique I never could master. Then she leaned back and closed her eyes, holding the smoke for a count of ten before letting it out on a sigh. A slow smile curved her lips. "I can't remember the last time I got high. Michael grew the stuff for a while, did you know that?"

"How would I know that? Besides, I don't believe a word you say. And you can't smoke that here." I tried to snatch the joint away, but her arms were longer and she held it out of reach. "Where did you get it anyway?" I asked.

"Some kid outside the Gospel Hall. She was doing a good business, so I didn't think she'd miss a couple."

"A couple?"

She laughed. "Okay, three. But this is definitely my last." She set the joint down on my shed and peeled back the waxed paper on the baklava. "You know, it was really fun walking through the old neighborhood, seeing all the old haunts. You ever get down there? The old neighborhood, I mean?"

"Only when I visit Loretta. Now get off my shed."

"In a minute. Anyway, I always wanted to go back, but something always came up so I never did. But once I was rid of the fucking cat, I figured, what the hell? The weather's good and since I was halfway there anyway, I might as well take a stroll down memory lane. Especially since we'll be leaving for Huntsville soon and chances are good we won't be coming back. Ever." She held out the baklava. "You should try this. It's the best I've ever tasted."

"Maybe later," I said and jiggled the key in the lock again.

She lifted a shoulder in the same offhand way Julie was perfecting. "Suit yourself. Anyway, I went to my Aunt Barb's, and you won't believe who I saw."

I dropped the lock and stepped back. "I don't care. Get off my shed."

"Are you always such a grouch?"

"I'm not a grouch, you're stoned. How does a ghost get stoned anyway?"

"Very carefully," she said and giggled. "Do you want to know who I saw or not?"

"Not," I said, and headed for the doors with the garbage bags. They could camp out in the kitchen for one night.

"It was Fred Skerry," Rosie called after me.

I stopped and looked back. "Not *the* Fred Skerry?"

"In the flesh. Can you believe it?"

No, I couldn't. Fred was in his fifties when we were kids. Which meant he had to be—

"Over seventy," Rosie said. "Still lives next door to my Aunt Barb, still lifts weights every day in that back room of his."

I tossed the bags inside the door and came back a step. "Naked?"

"Totally."

We both screwed up our faces. "Ewww."

Fred Skerry was the first man I had ever seen totally naked. Sure, I'd had glimpses of my father and brother from time to time, but Fred Skerry was more than a glimpse, more than a peek. He was a full-fledged study in male anatomy.

Everybody in the neighborhood knew he lifted weights in the room he built onto the back of his house. He had windows all around, air conditioning, and special blinds that came up from the bottom, letting natural light in while keeping nosy neighbors out. But what nobody knew, including Fred, was that Rosie and I had a perfect view into that room through the peephole in the bottom of our tree house. A peephole normally covered by old magazines and just large enough to accommodate a pair of binoculars. There had been rumors that Fred pumped iron in the nude, but we were the only ones who knew for sure.

We watched him every day at precisely four P.M., passing the binoculars back and forth between sets and reps. Upper body workout on even days. Lower body on odd. Fred was good looking for an older man, but when he was lifting weights, the veins stood out on his arms and legs and his skin got all shiny and sweaty. We didn't know it back then, but as steely manroots went, Fred Skerry's was one of the best.

Rosie smiled. "He still doesn't know we can see him from the tree house."

I walked back to the shed. "It's still up there?"

"Every board. That's why we used pressure treat." She held out the joint to me. "You should see the place, Sam. Nothing's changed in all this time. Even the books we hid in the wall are still there. Remember those? Rosemary Rogers, Fern Michaels, Kathleen Woodiwiss."

"Kathleen Woodiwiss," I repeated.

"*The Wolf and the Dove*," Rosie whispered.

I sighed and took the joint from her. "I loved *The Wolf and the Dove*. To this day, I have a thing for dark and stormy knights." I put the joint to my lips, tried to suck air around it. Gave up and pulled on it like a cigarette. I held the smoke to a count of one and coughed it out. "It's been a while." I gasped.

"Don't worry." Rosie opened the water and held it out to me. "It's like riding a bike. You never really forget."

I took a quick swallow and handed the bottle back. "What's Fred look like now? No, wait. Do I want to know?"

She shook her head. "Ignorance is better. Keeps the memories intact." She took a swig from the bottle herself and smiled. "Remember the pact we made? That we'd never let any boy touch us . . ."

"Down there," we said in unison and started to laugh, the kind of deep belly laugh that only comes when you're smoking pot.

I hoisted myself up on the shed beside her and leaned back against the wall, letting the high settle around me until the edges of the alley softened and Eva's warning seemed far away. I took another pull on the joint and counted to three before the choking started. Rosie held out the water. I nodded my thanks. "I have to tell you," I said between swallows. "I really like your T-shirt."

"Thanks." She pulled the shirt out in front of her, stretching the letters and smiling down at them. "I know it's tacky, but I couldn't resist."

"Did they bury you in that?"

"Are you kidding? I was wearing this horrible navy blue thing with a lace collar. I bought it years ago, for another funeral, so of course he put me in it for my own."

We looked at each other and burst out laughing, great rolling guffaws that had us leaning into each other and holding our stomachs and shouting, "Stop! Stop!" which only made us start all over again.

"Men can be such assholes," I said, gasping for air.

"Damn right." She raised the baklava high. "To assholes everywhere."

I sat up straighter, watching that cake move slowly toward her mouth. It was just a triangle of nuts, honey, and phyllo pastry, but to me it was the most beautiful sight in the world. Keep your truffles and your cheesecake. All I needed was that slice of baklava.

"Give me that," I said and snatched it out of her hand, making her laugh all over again. She took the joint in exchange, but I didn't care. I was focused on dessert now. I hadn't eaten all day.

Nothing but cherries and olives and one sad slice of orange. Now Michael was late, and screw him anyway. Life was too short to spend it waiting for an asshole.

I bit into the pastry and moaned. It was that good. Sweet enough to make your teeth ache, yet crunchy enough to make it seem like real food. "You're right," I said. "This is the best I've ever had."

Or maybe it was just the pot. I didn't know and I didn't care. I was having a great time.

"To baklava," I said.

"To pot," Rosie countered and gave me a high five.

Her hand was cold, but what had I expected? She was dead, after all.

I smiled and went back to the pastry, taking a smaller bite this time and wishing the piece were bigger and wondering if there was an all-night Greek bakery in the neighborhood.

"Honestly, Sam." Rosie said. "You'd have loved it."

I glanced over. She was smiling and looking at me expectantly. I smiled back. "I'm sorry. What were we talking about?"

"The funeral, what else?" She snatched back the last of her baklava and popped the morsel into her mouth. "You really would have loved it. No organ, no priest, no empty goddamn prayers. Just friends and family warming the seats and Kurt Cobain on the boombox."

"Sounds loud."

"And obnoxious. I know for a fact that they still talk about it at the funeral home." She crumpled the waxed paper into a ball, tossed it neatly over the fence into the yard on the other side of the alley, and smiled, obviously satisfied that her throwing arm was still good. She took another hit, offered the joint to me, and laughed when I shook my head. "I'd forgotten what a cheap date you are."

"I'm not cheap, just pacing myself."

She laughed again and sat back, eyes on the smoldering joint, a smile still on her lips. "Listen," she whispered. "I can hear Roy Orbison."

She started humming "Pretty Woman" and I finally heard it, faint but unmistakable, the familiar tune drifting down to us on a breeze from somewhere up the street. We sat there with our eyes closed, humming along and keeping the beat with our toes, moving them from side to side, side to side. I hadn't felt so relaxed in years. Then again, I hadn't smoked up in years either. I was starting to wonder if I should get to know the girl down at the Gospel Hall when Rosie turned to me again.

"It really was a great day," she said. "Open bar, fantastic food, everything exactly the way I would have wanted it."

It took me a moment to catch up, to realize she wasn't talking about today. She was back at the funeral again. But she didn't seem to notice my lapse, just kept talking and talking, her voice soothing in the quiet of the alley.

"The best part was watching my Aunt Barb's jaw drop when Michael wouldn't let her see me."

"See you?"

"It was a closed casket. Michael and I always agreed on that, but Barb insisted he open it so she could say good-bye. Can you believe that? The bitch threw me out when I was pregnant, then turns up all snotty-nosed and teary-eyed six years later, begging for one last moment together. A fucking hypocrite right to the end."

"I didn't know she threw you out," I said.

"You didn't know a lot of things. But I was better off without her poking around in my life, always trying to save my soul. I don't know how she found out I was dead, but I was pleased Michael didn't give in to her." Rosie glanced over at me. "Did I mention that she looked like shit?"

I nodded in case she had, and she sighed and put the joint to her lips again. "I tell you, Sammy, it was a perfect day. I just wish it had come forty years later."

"You were definitely too young," I said, thinking I should go in and make us some sandwiches. Wild boar with a little mustard would really hit the spot about now. But Rosie held the joint out to me again and I took it, figuring it would be rude to walk away when she obviously needed to talk.

"Damn right I was too young." She uncapped the water and put the bottle into my hands with the joint. I whispered my thanks and she sat back, watching me cough and drink. "But you know what the really shit part is?" she said. "I shouldn't even have died that day. I'd still be alive if that bastard hadn't run off and left me there."

"What bastard?" I said between gasps. "Who ran off and left you?"

"I don't know his name, but he's the one who caused the accident."

Without warning, Eva's list of questions drifted up through the haze and smacked me in the face. Told me to wake up, to pay attention, goddamn it. I had a job to do, and if I'd smarten up, I might just get all the answers I needed right here, right now. I sucked in a deep breath and handed her back the joint. "But Michael said yours was the only car on the road, that you lost control in the storm."

"That's the conclusion everyone came to, but someone else was there."

"Someone with you?"

Her lip curled. "No stupid, in another vehicle. A black pickup. He was behind me, but he was all over the road, almost in the ditch one minute, bouncing off the snowbank on the other side the next."

"Sounds like he was drunk."

"Nope, just stoned." She held the joint in front of her, examining it closely as though only now realizing it was there. "And not only did I have an idiot behind me, the goddamn cat was all over the inside of the car, howling as if it knew exactly what was coming."

"What was the cat doing there anyway?"

"Drying out, mostly." Rosie sighed. "The thing got caught in the storm and by the time I spotted it on the side of the road, it was covered in snow and obviously lost. There isn't a day goes by that I don't wish I'd hit the bastard. But I didn't. I stopped. The guy in the pickup stopped too, but he wouldn't take it, of course. Might make his truck messy. So I tossed the animal into the passenger seat, thinking it could live in the barn with the others. More barn cats means less mice, which is fine by me."

She stopped there, took a pull on the joint, then sat back and closed her eyes. "You know, Marcello, if I'd been smart I'd have ignored both that cat and the idiot in the pickup and concentrated on the road in front of me. But how could I do that when the fucking cat was screaming and the asshole kept coming up on my bumper and dropping back, coming up and dropping back. I could see him in the rearview mirror, smiling and laughing, playing his little-boy games as though he was the cutest thing on this earth."

"Was he?"

"Without a doubt. Which meant I was on the S curve before I knew it. I made the first turn, skidded on the second, and did three complete doughnuts before slamming into a power pole on the third. The cat was killed instantly, lucky bugger. But I was pinned behind the steering wheel, still alive and losing blood through some internal injury I didn't even know I had. The idiot in the pickup came to the window all wide-eyed and panicky. I told him to calm down, told him I was trapped and he needed to open the door, get my cell phone out of my purse and call 911."

"They didn't get there in time?"

"The bastard wouldn't make the call. 'I can't be connected to this,' he said. 'I'll lose everything,' he said. Then he started to cry. Kept saying, 'I'm so sorry, I'm so sorry,' like that made it all right. Then he got in his truck and he drove away."

My stomach clenched around the baklava. "Who would do such a thing?"

"A fucking coward, that's who." She slid off the shed and stood with her back to me. "I'll never forget the way he looked on the other side of the glass, blond hair falling across his forehead, green eyes all watery and sad. A good-looking shit with no heart at all." She took another drag on the joint. "Apparently he did call for help from the pay phone in town, but it took him a while to get there in that weather and meanwhile the snow kept falling and falling, covering his tracks and piling up on the windshield until I couldn't see out anymore. I don't know how long I was there, lying in the dark, thinking about Michael and Julie and willing that goddamn coward to call someone before I froze to death. By the time they found me, it was too late. I was already dead."

I stared at the straight, unwavering line of her back, unable to think fast enough, to make sense of what she was saying or the horror of those last moments. I slid off the shed and went to stand beside her, put a hand on her shoulder. She tensed but didn't look at me. "Does Michael know about this?" I asked.

"I mentioned it at the funeral, but he wasn't listening."

"Have you tried again?"

"Nope." She shook me off and flicked the joint into the darkness. It sizzled in a puddle while she bent to pick up a rock. "We both got caught up taking care of Julie, and after a while it didn't seem important. Just a lot of bother for nothing."

"How can you say that?" I walked around in front of her, waited until she finally looked at me. "Rosie, what happened on that road was murder. Let me put a bug in Michael's ear for you, make him think about it. They could reopen the investigation, find this guy and put him in jail."

"It's too late."

"It's never too late."

"Just leave it alone, okay?" She bounced the rock in her hand, took up a pitcher's stance, and squinted down the length of the alley. "Ten bucks says I can hit that sign on the first throw."

There was a No Parking sign under a light about two hundred feet away, a stretch even when she'd been in top pitching form.

She cocked a brow, waiting for an answer. I couldn't understand why she was trying to change the subject, why she wasn't determined to see the coward prosecuted or at least found and questioned. But my brain was still fuzzy from the pot, so what did I know? Maybe she had a point, and maybe I'd figure out what it was later. "What would you do with ten bucks?" I asked.

She scuffed her sneakers on the asphalt and lined up the sign. "Nothing. I'd just enjoy taking it from you."

"And if you lose?"

She looked hurt. "I'm good for it."

I walked back to the garbage shed and hoisted myself back up on the lid. "Go ahead and try."

I watched her wind up for the pitch. Saw the muscles in her arms tense and flex, the graceful column of her neck arch back as she gauged the distance to the sign. Like a dancer, she lifted one leg off the ground, leaned back, and then sent the rock soaring far down the alley. Glass shattered. An alarm went off. Rosie glanced over at me. "You win."

I had to laugh even as a door opened and a woman hollered, "Who's out there?"

I slid off the shed and pressed myself into the shadows. I couldn't think whose window it might have been. I only knew that she'd be down here in a matter of minutes, asking what I'd seen, and I was still too high to lie effectively.

Rosie strutted over to the shed. "I'll get you that ten later," she said, and I couldn't help thinking about the coward who'd let her die. Imagining how different things would have been if he'd only picked up her cell phone and punched in 911 before running away. She'd be alive now, breaking windows somewhere else.

The alarm shut off and a light flicked on farther down the alley. "I know there's someone out there," my neighbor hollered.

I crouched down beside the shed, hoping she wouldn't see me if she came this far.

Rosie crouched beside me. "What are we doing?"

"Hiding. So how come you aren't haunting the blond guy instead of Michael?"

"I'm not haunting Michael. Besides, I don't know where the guy is. It's not like you get some kind of all-knowing, all-seeing power when you die. You're just out here on your own, wandering around, trying to figure out what's going on and where you belong."

"Isn't there someone who could help you?"

She leaned forward and peeked into the alley, watching the commotion farther down. "Sure, lots of people, but everyone on this side of the fence just talks at you, not to you. *Rosie, there's a great adventure waiting. Rosie, you need to take that first step. Rosie, what are you waiting for*? No one ever just wants to go for coffee or a smoke. They're all so fucking earnest it drives me nuts. It's not like talking to you at all." She sat back and looked at me. "I've missed you, Sammy."

"I've missed you too," I said, surprising myself as much as her.

"Bastards," my neighbor hollered, and the echo of a slamming door floated down the alley.

"I thought she'd never go inside." Rosie got to her feet and held a hand out to me. "You got anything decent to eat in that kitchen of yours?"

I let her pull me up. "I have everything."

"Which is exactly what I want." She raised a hand high in the air. "To girlfriends," she said, and I laughed and slapped her palm again.

"Sam?" It was Michael, calling from inside the Swan.

Rosie and I stilled, our hands locked in that high five.

"Sam?" he called again. "Are you here? The front door was open so I . . ."

The front door open? How could I have forgotten? And why hadn't Derek called to tell me Michael was on his way?

"I'm double parked," he called. "Are you ready to go? Sam?"

Rosie's fingers closed around mine. "Promise me you'll do the right thing, Marcello. Promise me."

I wrenched my hand away, held it close to my body. "I'm in the alley," I called back, and tried to shake off my high on the way to the door.

FOURTEEN

Michael was already at the back door, grinning at me through the screen. He wore jeans and a leather jacket the color of cognac, and in his hand he held a single red rose.

He held up the rose and gave me a silly, sheepish smile. "Tell me honestly. Is it corny or romantic?"

I laughed. "Definitely corny. But in a romantic way."

"I was afraid of that." He lifted his head, sniffed the air. "Are you smoking up back there?"

"Of course not." I came inside and quickly closed the door. "Just putting the garbage out."

He pointed to his feet. "But the bags are sitting here."

"That's because I can't open the shed."

"Let me help." He reached past me, started to open the door.

"No," I shouted and smiled brightly when he looked confused. "What I mean is that you should go and park the car. I'm not nearly ready and you don't want to get towed."

"In that case, I'll be right back." He got as far as the prep counter, set the rose down, and turned back to look at me. "I'm embarrassed to admit how much I've been looking forward to this."

"Same here." But right now, I just needed him to go, to give me time to do something about Rosie. "You should probably hurry."

"Okay, but first I want to honor our first official date with a little silence."

I watched him unclip the BlackBerry from his belt, turn it off, and lay it down beside the rose. "If anyone wants me, they'll have to come and get me." He headed for the swinging door. "Don't go away," he said and went out into the dining room.

When I heard the front door close, I strolled over to the prep counter, picked up the rose, and inhaled the sweet scent of corny romance. I couldn't help smiling. He really hadn't changed at all.

Setting the rose down, I slid the BlackBerry closer. Spun it around. Accidentally turned it on and jumped when the thing started to vibrate. Michael had mail.

The BlackBerry fell silent again and lay there, harmless, waiting. I picked it up, put it down, picked it up again, and quickly thumbed through the icons until I reached E-mail.

He had two new messages. An update from Universal Currency and a note from kirsten54@heybob.ca. Why was she sending him messages? What exactly was going on between her and Michael?

I drummed my fingers on the BlackBerry. If I read his mail, would it qualify as invasion of privacy or merely fact finding?

Loud pounding on the back door made me jump again. "Marcello?" Rosie hollered. "Do not make me come in there and get you."

The last thing I wanted was Rosie in my kitchen. So I turned off the BlackBerry, set it down exactly where Michael had left it, and hurried to the back door, opening it enough so I could see her. "What do you want?" I demanded.

She grabbed me by the shirt and yanked me outside. "Is Michael still in there?"

I shook my head. "He went to park the car."

"Tell me you're not going through with this date crap," she muttered. I didn't answer right away and she shoved me backward into the alley. "Jesus Christ, Marcello. After everything I've told you, you're still going to screw me?"

I stumbled but kept my balance, stayed on my feet. "How can I screw you? You're dead."

"Exactly my point. I was robbed that afternoon, Marcello. Cheated out of everything that was important to me, and I'll be damned if I'll let it happen again."

"Ever think it was karma, Rosie? Payback for stealing him from me in the first place?"

She laughed. "I didn't steal him, Marcello. That boy was ripe for the taking."

"And you couldn't find a way to resist?"

"Not when he was the only interesting thing going on." She bent to pick up a rock. "Life may have been good for you back then, sweetcheeks, but it was hell for the rest of us. I wasn't serious about him at first. Just having a little fun, keeping him warm till you got home. But when I found out I was pregnant, I was not about to let him go."

"You bitch."

"I'm not a bitch, Marcello. I just needed him more than you did."

"You used him."

"You'd like that to be true, wouldn't you, but the truth is I loved Michael. I still do. He was the best thing that ever happened to me. I can only imagine where Julie and I would be now if he'd chosen you instead."

I caught a glimpse of two people coming our way, an angry woman in a white lab coat and a police officer trying to keep up with her. "You there," the woman called. "Did you see anyone out here throwing rocks?"

"Please, ma'am," the cop said. "Let me handle this."

I recognized the woman from the spa and cosmetics shop half a dozen doors down. She'd been open only a few weeks, a new addition to the block and somewhat out of touch with the neighborhood if the prices of her creams were any indication. "Someone broke my window," she said.

"Did you see anything?" the officer asked me.

Rosie stood behind him, bouncing the rock in her hand.

"Sorry, officer," I said. "I just came out here now."

"I heard you talking to someone." The woman sniffed the air. "And it smells like marijuana out here." She narrowed her eyes at me. "Are you sure you weren't out here with someone?"

"Positive." I turned back to the cop. "And I always talk to myself when I'm out here. It keeps me from being scared."

"Well, I'm not scared," my neighbor said and looked slowly around, scanning the shadows for suspects. Rosie kissed her on the cheek and blew in her ear. The woman frowned but turned her head slightly to the side. Rosie kissed her again, then looked over at me. "I think she likes it," she said. "Now that is definitely scary."

The woman touched her fingertips lightly to her cheek, and I had to look away before I laughed out loud.

"You think this is funny?" She shoved a finger in my face. "Let me tell you something right now, if I get my hands on whoever threw that rock, it will not be pretty."

"Stupid cow," Rosie said and bit that finger hard.

The woman leaped back, holding her hand to her chest. "What did you do to me? Officer, she just did something to me."

"Ma'am, she didn't do anything and you need to calm down." The cop looked over at me. "Let me know if you see or hear anything suspicious."

"Absolutely," I assured him and smiled as he led my neighbor back along the alley to her shop.

"That was close," I said and turned in time to see Rosie holding another rock in her hand and lining up my bathroom window. "For God's sake, you can't be serious."

She glanced over at me. "You think not?"

I stepped in front of her, standing close enough to feel the chill of her skin on mine. "Why are you doing this?"

"Because you're too stubborn to be believed. I pour out a story that could melt the coldest heart and you still don't budge. Obviously it's time to change tactics."

"What do mean, a story?"

She took a step to the side. "Even you can figure that one out."

I moved with her, staying between her and my window. "Are you saying you made the whole thing up?"

"As I went along."

"Then there wasn't a black pickup?"

"Not that I saw."

"No blond-haired guy either?"

She looked past me, sizing up the window again. "I thought you'd like that detail."

"You lying bitch."

She grinned and pitched the rock over my shoulder. My breath caught and held until I heard the rock land on the ground behind me with a dull thud. Rosie laughed and headed for my door. "You really are predictable, Marcello."

I hurried ahead, blocking the way. "It's time for you to leave."

"As soon as I have a word with Michael. Let's wait inside, shall we?"

"Leave him alone."

She gave me a sympathetic smile. "As pissed as I am at you, I honestly can't blame you for trying. He looked great, didn't he? I helped him pick out that leather jacket. He only wears it on dates. I think it's become a sort of good-luck charm. Worked especially well with Kirsten. Have you asked him about her yet?"

What was left to ask? I already knew the woman was keeping herself in the running. But I wasn't about to share that with Rosie.

"I don't care about Kirsten or anyone else. Michael is here to see me."

"True. And I admire the fact that you didn't rush home and change. Most women would have gone for something sexy on a first date, something guaranteed to make a man sit up and take notice, but not you. You stayed true to form, and by God, you look perfectly presentable. Just promise me you're not wearing granny underwear." I didn't answer, and she laughed. "Shit, Marcello, you are, aren't you?"

"Not anymore." The pot must have still been working because I didn't stop to think, just hiked up my skirt and pushed that granny underwear down to my ankles, plucked it up in one smooth motion, and dangled it in front of her. "Satisfied?"

Her mouth rounded to a soft O. "Now I am impressed. And the dirty schoolmarm is such a great look for you. But you might want to brush those crumbs off your shirt before he gets back."

I gave my shirt a quick brush and tried not to think about the cool air drifting up my skirt while Rosie bent to pick up another rock.

"While I'm sure you can use the sex," she said, "I wouldn't read too much into any of it if I were you." She straightened and stood with her back to me, bouncing the rock in her hand while she eyed my bathroom window again. "You need to understand that Michael and I are a couple. We're bound by—"

"A bond that transcends time?" I smiled and stuffed the underwear into my pocket. "I heard the sermon from Leo earlier."

She smiled back. "Nice guy, that Leo. Very receptive."

"I'm not surprised you like him. You two have so much in common, after all."

She set the rock on the shed, then bent down to pick up two more. "What are you talking about?"

"Isn't it obvious? You both had a good marriage, and you both managed to screw it up."

"I didn't screw up anything." She laid the larger of the two rocks beside the first on the shed, then glanced over at me. "You have two picture windows out front, right?"

I folded my arms, refusing to be distracted. "If you didn't screw it up, then why were you and Michael fighting the day you died?"

If it was possible for a ghost to grow pale, I swear she did it right then. "Who told you that?"

"Derek."

She laughed. "I told you before, Derek doesn't know everything."

"But he knows about this. Michael told him the two of you were fighting before you went out that day. From what I understand, it was the same topic as always. Something about you working too much, never being home on the weekends. Any of this ringing a bell?" I tilted my head to the side, studying her face, her hands, the subtle shift in her posture that told me I'd hit on something good, something painful. "It was a bad one, wasn't it."

"I had no choice and Michael knew it. I was showing a cottage that day."

"What cottage? Where was it?"

"What difference does it make?"

"It might help me understand why you wouldn't simply change the appointment, spend a snow day with your family—"

"My client was only in town that weekend, okay?" She turned away. "Selling rural property in the winter is hard enough. I was not about to blow him off."

"Who was he?"

"No one you'd know."

"But important enough to make you go out with a major snowstorm in the forecast."

"Will you get off that? We live in the north, Marcello. Northerners drive through snowstorms all the time."

"Really? Then how come no one found you in that ditch? How come none of those hearty northern drivers were out there when you needed them?" I walked slowly toward her. "You want to know what I think? I think there's something about that day that you're not telling me. Something big, something important."

She laughed and took a few steps into the center of the alley, keeping to the shadows so I couldn't see her face. "You're really reaching, Marcello."

"Am I? Then why won't you tell me the name of the client or the address of the property? And why won't you let me tell Michael about the pickup truck on the road?"

"I made that up, remember?"

"I don't think you did. I think the black pickup and the blond guy are both real. I just don't know why you're protecting him."

Rosie threw up her hands. "This is nuts."

"No, covering up a murder is nuts."

"It wasn't murder."

"He left you to die."

"He called for help."

"Just not when you needed it." I walked around in front of her and moved to block the way when she tried to escape. "Come on, Rosie, you can tell me. What happened that day?"

"I died," she said and went around me to the door. "Why don't we wait for Michael inside? I'd love to see your little pub." She turned the knob, but just like the lock on the garbage shed, the screen door wouldn't budge. She rattled it a few more times, then looked over at me. "Your door is broken."

I pushed her aside and opened it. "It's all in the wrist."

"Wrist nothing. There's a trick and you know it."

She tried to follow me inside, but it was as though an invisible wall had gone up where the door used to be, and she couldn't get through.

I thrust my arm outside and touched her, yet she couldn't do the same. Couldn't get as much as a finger inside my kitchen.

I stepped back and watched her keep on trying. She looked like a mime out there, testing the edges of that invisible wall, trying to find where it ended, where she could get through. She banged her shoulder against it, kicked it a few times, even hurled her entire body against it, but whatever the barrier was, it was there to stay, and so was she. Safely on the other side.

"This is good," she said, rubbing her shoulder and backing away. "It's new, but it's good. After two years, things were starting to get a little tired, but this adds a whole new twist. Something for me to really sink my teeth into."

"You have fun out there." I pulled the underwear from my pocket and waved it like a hanky while I closed the door. "Because I know I'll be having fun in here."

"You don't have the balls, Marcello," she called and hit the door again.

"We'll see," I said and slammed the door. Stood watching the knob rattle and the wood tremble when she kicked the door.

"Bitch," she hollered, and then everything went quiet. Too quiet. Any minute I expected a rock to come sailing through the bathroom window. I waited by the door, barely breathing, hoping to hear her, get a hint of what she was up to, but there was nothing.

I stepped back from the door. Maybe she left. Went around the front to take out my picture windows.

I kicked the garbage bags into my office and went into the kitchen, intending to guard the dining room from attack. But there on the prep counter sat the rose and the BlackBerry, exactly as Michael had left them.

Leaving the picture windows to their fate, I laid the underwear beside the rose and picked up the BlackBerry. Kirsten54 was still in there. What kind of message was she sending anyway?

I glanced over at the swinging door. Michael would be back soon. Invasion of privacy be damned. If I was going to finish my fact finding tonight, it had to be now.

I switched the phone on and rolled the dial on the side, thumbing through the icons again until I reached Messages. I moistened my lips, took a deep breath, and pressed Open. There she was. Kirsten54, begging to be read.

Hi there, she wrote. A nice, noncommittal opening that led to a few rambling lines about the weather and hoping he was having fun. She got to the point around line three, telling him that some kids had wrecked that stretch of fence by the road again, and the cows had wandered into Al's field, which had made the old man none too happy LOL. But she'd rounded them up and brought them back, so he wasn't to worry. She was looking forward to seeing him again soon, and what did he think about coming for dinner the night he arrived home? Save him cooking after a long drive. She signed off with an affectionate but nonthreatening *Hugs, Kirsten.*

I thumbed through the rest of the e-mails, most of them also from Kirsten. Reports on the cows, updates on the weather, and the latest local gossip. She sounded the same in each one, bubbly and capable, with just the right blend of encouragement and distance, and I knew Rosie had been right about her all along. Kirsten54 was definitely in the running, but so far, I was sure I was in the lead.

"Sam?" Michael's voice again. He was back.

"Be right there," I called while I thumbed through the icons again, trying to get to Off before he came through the door.

I hit the button and nearly cried when the screen said Shutting Handheld Down but stayed on anyway. I hadn't realized how long these suckers took to shut down.

I heard the front door close. Footsteps coming closer.

"Sorry I was so long," Michael said. "I had to park a mile away."

"Come on, come on," I muttered and breathed again when the screen finally went black.

Then I saw the underwear.

Michael pushed open the swinging door. "You ready?"

"Almost." I bunched that damn underwear up in my fist and shoved it behind my back.

He came toward me. "Anything I can do to help?"

"Not that I can think of."

I couldn't move. Just stood there, smiling and gripping my underwear, my face growing hotter with every step he took. Greeting a man half naked was not my usual approach on a first date, or any date, for that matter. What would Michael think when he discovered my stupid secret? Worse still, what if he never discovered it at all?

"I drove all the way to Logan before I found a spot," he said. "It's a bit of a hike, I'm afraid."

"It's a nice night for it." I smiled and started walking backward toward the bathroom. "Will you excuse me a minute?"

I was closing the bathroom door, halfway to a clean escape, when I heard the knob on the back door rattle softly. I froze and peeked into the hall. Watched the knob turn first to the left, then the right. Didn't she ever give up?

"Is everything all right?" Michael called.

"Everything's perfect. Did you lock the front door?"

"The moment I stepped inside. Didn't want to risk someone coming in looking for a table."

"Or worse." I stepped out into the hall, snapped the lock on the back door, and slid the chain into place. Whatever was keeping Rosie out seemed to be holding, but it was only prudent to take every precaution possible.

"Are you sure you're okay?" he asked.

"Couldn't be better," I said and turned back to the bathroom, fully expecting one of her rocks to come flying through the window, just to prove she could ruin my evening without being in the room.

"Sam, what's going on?"

He was still standing by the prep counter, rose in hand again, waiting to take me out, to start our date. That was when I realized we wouldn't be going anywhere. We'd be staying right here, the one place where Rosie couldn't touch us.

"Let me show you," I said, and I did what I should have done the moment I saw him. I tossed that granny underwear into the bathroom, switched off the light, and closed the door. Then I took a deep breath and closed the gap between us, feeling very naughty, very sexy as I strolled toward him.

He held out the rose. "To corny romantic gestures."

"May they never end," I whispered, laying the rose back on the counter and reaching for him instead.

He groaned and wrapped his arms around me, his eyes on my mouth, his hands moving over my back, pulling me closer, molding me to him. "I have been thinking about this all day," he said. "But I didn't want to rush things, didn't want to risk scaring you off."

"I don't scare easily."

I pushed my fingers into his hair and drew his mouth down to mine, almost wishing Rosie would go ahead and throw one of her damn rocks, just so she could find out how little I cared.

Michael kissed me, gently at first, his lips touching and retreating, touching and retreating, until my knees softened and my lips parted. When at last he deepened the kiss, I held him harder, letting my hands roam over his back and down to his ass, brushing off skills I hadn't used in a while and smiling with satisfaction when he suddenly picked me up and sat me on the prep counter.

"This isn't what I planned," he said, still kissing my face, my throat, the tender lobe of my ear while his fingers deftly flipped open the buttons on my shirt. "I thought we'd have dinner first. And I bought a bottle of wine for after."

"After is highly overrated. I much prefer here and now."

"Damn right," he said, tugging shirt from skirt in a matter of seconds.

I wished I'd worn a prettier bra, or at least one that was newer, less laundered, but the thought was gone as quickly as it came, fading on a sigh when he freed my breasts from lace and wire that were obviously of no interest to him whatsoever. And I couldn't think at all with his mouth on my breasts and his hands slowly sliding my skirt up my thighs. He slipped a hand between my legs, his touch strong, his fingers sure until he realized there was nothing in his way, no barrier at all. He raised his head and looked at me, his breath as quick and ragged as my own. And he stopped breathing all together when I spread my legs wider and guided his hand the rest of the way.

How long had it been since I'd been this daring, this wanton, this openly sexual? I couldn't remember and I didn't care. Everything I wanted right now was standing in front of me, wanting me too.

"Look at me," he said, his breath hot against my skin while his hand moved between my legs, expertly taking me to the edge again and again, but not yet taking me over. The instinct to hold still, to be a lady was kept in check only by the look on his face. "Don't stop now," he whispered, cupping my sex and putting me in control. I moved my hips, riding his palm and watching his eyes darken and his lips part; realizing he liked it when I was bold and demanding and vulnerable all at the same time.

"You are so beautiful," he said, sliding my hips to the edge of the counter and unzipping his pants. He positioned himself between my thighs and it occurred to me that Eva would kill me if she knew what I was about to do in her kitchen. But what she didn't know couldn't hurt me, so I took him in my hands, learning all over again what made him gasp and what stopped his breath. He dropped his head back, his fingers tightening on my ass, holding me firmly in place, positioned to take him inside when he couldn't take any more.

"Jesus Christ, Rosie," he moaned, and in one swift motion he was deep inside me and holding perfectly still.

We stared at each other, both breathing hard.

He was the first to break the silence. "I'm sorry, Sam. I don't know why I said that."

I felt him slipping away, leaving me for her again.

"I'm so sorry," he whispered again and had the grace to step back, to turn around so I could close my legs and my shirt. Scrape together a little dignity while he shook his head and kept repeating, "I'm so very sorry," over and over like it was some kind of goddamn mantra.

I can't say why, but for some reason, I thought of Rosie trapped in the car on that back road, dying slowly while some asshole told her over and over again how sorry he was.

"Forget it," I said, and slid off the counter, tugged down my skirt. Fumbled with the buttons on my shirt and refused to give in to the sting behind my eyes, the ache in my throat. I would not cry. Not here, not now. "You need to go."

Michael turned to me and held out a hand. "Sam, please—"

"Michael, I swear if you tell me one more time how sorry you are, I will hit you." I moved away, needing to put some space between us. I opened the fridge. Eva's mango salad was on its side, the plastic wrap losing the battle against the dressing.

"I just want you to talk to me."

"And I just want to eat something," I said, needing a little help to swallow the lump in my throat, ease the gnawing, hollow feeling in my stomach. Leaving Eva's toppled bowl to its fate, I grabbed the carton of eggs from the shelf above, picked up a block of cheddar, and carried both to the grill, keeping my eyes down as I passed him.

Of course he followed me and stood right behind me while I took a pan from the rack and slammed it down on the burner, turning the gas on high enough that the flames licked up around the sides of the pan. "Sam, look at me," he said.

His voice was soft, his hands gentle on my shoulders, and my eyes started to sting all over again. So I focused on the food. Jammed four slices of bread into the toaster and pushed the button down hard. Picked up two eggs and cracked them into the pan, remembering too late that the oil should have gone in first.

"We have got to talk about this," he insisted.

I switched off the gas, dumped the pan in the sink, and turned the water on hard. "What's to talk about? It's obvious Rosie's still on your mind. While that may have come as a shock to you, it doesn't surprise me in the least. In fact, the only surprising thing is that you're still here when I've asked you to leave."

"Not yet." He turned off the water and tried to take my hands in his but I backed away, knowing tenderness would only break me down, lay me open again, and I wasn't nearly ready for that. I walked over to the fridge again, searching the shelves for jam I knew we didn't have, shuffling mayonnaise, moving mustard, rearranging that damn mango salad. Anything to keep from looking at him.

"If you really want me to go, then I will," he said.

I closed the fridge and walked back to the grill. "Thank God."

The toast popped. Michael beat me to it, grabbed up the slices, and refused to hand them over when I held out a plate. "Please come with me. We can go somewhere else, have a drink, eat something besides toast."

"There's no point."

"Why the hell not?"

"Because we're screwed, Michael. No matter what we do, or where we go, or how hard we try, you and I don't stand a chance in hell of making this work."

"You can't know that."

"You'd be surprised what I know."

"Then share it with me."

"I can't." I slid four more slices of bread into the toaster and pushed the button down. "It'll be better for everyone if you just go home."

Michael popped the button up and unplugged the toaster. "I'm not going anywhere until you tell me what makes you so sure about everything, because frankly I'm confused as hell right now, and I could really use a little enlightenment from the expert."

I turned on him. "You want enlightenment? Okay, how's this? Your future is Rosie."

"Rosie's dead."

"True, but that doesn't mean she's gone. The woman couldn't be more present if she was standing here right now."

"What the hell are you talking about?"

"I'm talking about Rosie being with you all the time. In your head, your heart, your goddamn soul for all I know, and I can't compete with that, Michael. I don't know *how* to compete with that. And I'm not sure I want to try anymore." I jammed the plug back into the socket. "Touch that again and I might just kill you."

"Do your worst." He snapped the plug out of the wall, dropped it on the counter, and turned to leave. "I'm done here."

"No one is surprised," I shouted after him. "Rosie wouldn't have it any other way."

He was on me before I knew it, jerking the cord from my hand and backing me up against the counter. "I don't know why you're saying these things, why you want to push me away, but it's not what I want at all. I don't know what happened here tonight, and I don't know whether we can make it as a couple or not, but I'm standing here right now, trying my damnedest to get through to you, because I want to give it a try."

"Sure, you feel that way now," I said. "But the moment you walk out that door you'll change your mind. You'll start doubting yourself before you even reach your car."

"That's not true."

"Michael, it happens all the time. Think about yesterday afternoon when you wanted to call and cancel our date."

"Come on, Sam, I was nervous. I hadn't seen you in years."

"It wasn't nerves."

"Whatever you say. All I know is that I've felt more in these past two days than I have in the past two years, and I don't want it to end. Tell me what I have to do to convince you that I'm serious. Tell me how to change your mind."

As much as I wanted to think the worst of him, I had to admit that he looked sincere. And confused and frustrated and sad—everything I was feeling written clearly in the lines around his eyes and the slump of his shoulders. I'm not sure what it says about me, but his misery gave me a quick jolt of pleasure, a smug satisfaction in knowing I wasn't the only one Rosie would hurt this time.

I laid my hands on his chest and pushed him back. Started walking toward the swinging door. "If you're so sure, then call my cell the moment you get to Derek's. If you do, we'll go back to my place, continue our date. If you don't, then we'll both know we're finished."

He followed me through to the pub. "This is silly. Of course I'll call you."

"We'll see." I went straight to the front door and turned the lock. "Either way, you need to leave now."

I swung the door back and wasn't at all surprised to see Rosie sitting on my step reading a book. *Twenty-Five Twisted Tales of Revenge*. How fitting.

As soon as Michael stepped outside, Rosie snapped the book shut and got to her feet. "What gives, Marcello? You couldn't keep him entertained for even an hour? I should have given you some pointers."

I ignored her and tried to close the door, but Michael put up a hand and held it open. "I'll call you."

"Pay no attention," Rosie said. "He says the same thing to all his first dates."

Michael frowned and kept the door open when I tried again to close it. "Sam, I'm serious."

Rosie looked from me to Michael, then back at me. "What happened in there, Marcello? You didn't do it with him, did you?" She smiled slowly. "Holy shit, you did. And now you honestly think he'll call you." She started to laugh. "Oh, Marcello, this is too funny."

She was right. It was hysterically funny. To think I'd truly believed I could win. That Samantha Marcello could beat Rosie Fisk at anything. I'd have laughed too if that damn lump in my throat hadn't come back.

"Just shut the hell up and leave me alone," I whispered and forced the door closed. Locked it so neither of them could come inside.

Michael banged a fist on the door. "Sam, don't leave it like this." I turned my back and started walking to the kitchen. He banged again. "Sam, please open the door."

I didn't turn around and I didn't look back. How could I when all I'd see was Rosie whispering in his ear, twisting his thoughts, making him dance to whatever tune she decided to call.

I pulled the cell phone from my pocket, checked to make sure it was on and that the battery had plenty of life, and then slapped it down on the bar as I passed. "Here's to us," I said and went through the swinging door into the kitchen.

I stood with my back against the frame and closed my eyes. Tried not to think about the silence that surrounded me. The fact that Michael wasn't knocking anymore. That he'd already left with her. And my phone was not going to ring.

Hot tears slid down my cheeks. I wiped them with my sleeve and pushed away from the wall. "I will not cry," I said out loud and grabbed a plate from the shelf. Smashed it against the dishwasher. "I will not fucking cry."

I had two more in my hands when I heard the familiar ring of my cell phone in the dining room.

My heart all but stopped. I laid the plates down gently and crept to the swinging door. Waited.

The phone rang again.

I banged back that door and ran into the pub. Skidded to a stop in front of the bar, and snatched up my phone. Took one long breath before putting it to my ear, but couldn't keep from smiling when I answered, "That was quick."

"Quick nothing. Now get out here and pay the cab driver."

My smile froze. "Loretta?"

It couldn't be, of course. Angie was keeping her for three days. Three days. Still, there was no mistaking Loretta's voice on the other end telling me to hurry up and not to forget my purse. And that was definitely her outside the pub, standing beside a cab, talking into someone's cell phone.

"What are you doing here?" I asked. And why hadn't Angie warned me?

"We'll talk later," Loretta said. "Just get out here before he turns the meter back on."

She didn't say good-bye, just hung up on me and handed the phone to the driver. She reached into the cab for her purse, then looked back at my window and threw her hands in the air. “Will you get out here?” she hollered loudly enough to be heard not only inside the pub, but across town as well.

Yes indeed. Loretta was back. And Angie had a lot of explaining to do.

FIFTEEN

I smoothed back my hair and wiped my palms across my cheeks before fishing my purse out from under the bar and running to the front door. Loretta was still waiting for me beside the taxi, back rigid, chin jutting out farther than usual. I hadn't seen that stance in years, yet part of me fully expected her to point a finger and holler *You're grounded* the moment I set foot on the sidewalk.

"Why aren't you at Angie's?" I asked when I reached her.

"Just pay the man," she said, her lips pinched so tightly she could barely make words. "We'll talk later."

It wasn't exactly *You're grounded*, but the meaning was the same. *Do as you're told, and don't argue*. On any other night I would have been happy to jolly her along, follow orders, and wait for an explanation. But this was not any other night, and I was in no mood to play games with my grandmother.

"You bet we'll talk," I said and leaned down to talk to the driver. "How much?"

He looked up from the clipboard on his lap. "Sixty dollars."

"Sixty dollars from Union Station to the Danforth? Nice try. How much is it really?"

He didn't smile. "Sixty dollars flat rate from Oakville. She was real upset, so I cut her a deal."

"She took a cab from Oakville? Who takes a cab from Oakville?" I turned to Loretta. "Who takes a cab from Oakville?"

She glared at me. "I don't ride the train at night."

"Then why didn't you wait until morning?"

"I said we'll talk later. Give the man his money."

"No," I said and stiffened my own spine, stuck out my own chin. Even raised it a notch when she glared at me. "Not until you tell me why you're here."

"You want to know why I'm here? Okay, I'm here because I'm a pain in the ass."

"What has that got to do with anything?"

"It's true, then. That's how you see me." She turned her back. "Don't bother to argue. Angie told me everything."

My mouth went dry. Surely "everything" didn't include telling Loretta the real reason she had been summoned to Oakville. Surely that was too low, even for my sister.

"What exactly did Angie say?"

"Take a guess."

I didn't have to guess. The answer was written in that rigid spine, those white knuckles. My sister had screwed me again and stuck me with the bill, as usual.

"God damn you, Angie," I said.

"He may do that," the driver said, "but right now I need my money."

I dug through my wallet and came up with forty-two dollars and eighty-five cents. "I don't have enough." I turned to Loretta. "Do you have any cash?"

"Yes," she said, but made no move to part with it.

"Great." I poked my head back into the cab. "Do you take charge cards?"

He pointed to a sign. "Cash only, lady."

I shoved the wallet back in my purse. None of this was fair. Not the bill, not Angie's screwup, not even Loretta's anger. And to top it all off, Michael hadn't called.

"I'll be right back," I said to the driver and grabbed Loretta's arm, dragging her with me to the front step of the pub. "Did you know how much it would cost to take a cab to Toronto?"

"Of course."

"Then why did you do it?"

"Because you owe me this." She shook herself loose but followed me inside. "And I don't accept your apology."

"I didn't give you one," I said, going ahead of her to the bar.

"*Porca miseria*." She went around to the other side and uncorked the bottle of red. "When are you going to get some decent wine in this place?"

"When are you going to accept that the best wines are not always Italian?"

She muttered another curse, grabbed a small rocks glass, put it back, and went for something bigger. She filled it and glowered at me over the rim as she chugged. Loretta can hold a grudge for weeks, months, years if necessary. While the prospect of years passing without my grandmother poking her nose into my life held an undeniable appeal, I couldn't let it end this way. I wasn't Angie, and she was still my Nona.

I grabbed a handful of bills from the till, slammed the drawer shut, and made the first move. "Loretta, I can only imagine what Angie told you, and how she said it. But you could have called me before you left, let me tell you my side."

"She told me everybody's side just fine." Loretta knocked back the rest of her wine, refilled the glass, and snatched the bills from my hand. "You got enough here for the tip?"

"Yes." I snatched the bills back and headed for the door. "I know you're ticked, but I still don't understand why you didn't wait till the morning."

She was right behind me, wine bottle and glass in hand. "And spend the night on that witch's porch? No, *grazie*."

I thrust the bills at the driver, shook my head when he started to make change.

"Good luck," he whispered, and I turned back to Loretta as he pulled away.

"Why would you spend the night on Angie's porch?" I asked. "She has a beautiful guest room."

Loretta shrugged, took a long pull on the wine bottle, and made a rude gesture to a passing couple who made the mistake of looking at her. "That room's not so beautiful," she said, holding the gesture until the couple hurried on. "The wallpaper's peeling. She went cheap, as usual."

I took the bottle away, leaving her with only the glass. "Loretta, stop this. Tell me what Angie said to you."

"She said you hate me."

I watched her knock back the rest of the wine, wipe her mouth with the back of her hand, and giggle when she belched loudly. I'd never seen her like this. The warrior, the runner, the head of our family, slowly losing control in public. "Nona," I said gently. "I don't hate you."

"But you complain about me behind my back. You say I come around your pub too much, and I play Dean Martin too much. And today, I was so bad you had to lie to get rid of me."

I sighed and looked away. "I wish I'd never called her."

"Angie said the same thing right before she pushed me out the front door and locked it."

"Come on, Loretta. Even she wouldn't do that."

"Call Andy Barber, her next-door neighbor. He saw the whole thing, including the part where she threw my purse out a bedroom window. He's a nice man. Sat with me till the cab came. I should send him something nice. And Angie something with fleas."

She started walking back to the pub. I had to jog to keep up with her. "Why would Angie do this to you? What did you do out there?"

"Nothing. I just talked to Maria, like you told me to."

She didn't pause to hold the door for me, just went straight to the bar and started opening another bottle of my horrible wine.

I took that bottle from her too and filled her glass with water instead. "Tell me what you said to the kid."

She eyed the water, pushed it away, and went back around to the civilian side of the bar. "I said she should be nicer to her sister."

"And?"

She slumped into a chair, put her elbows on the bar. "And she rolled her eyes and said, 'Are you done yet?' So I told her no, I'd only started. Then I told her she was growing up to be a horrible girl and soon it would start to show in her face. Slowly but surely, she'd become as ugly on the outside as she was on the inside, and no one would ever want to marry her, and she would die alone and go straight to hell and burn forever. Then I told her to have a look in the mirror. See where the first pimple had already taken root."

I winced. "Loretta, that's horrible."

"True, but it worked. She started to cry, which meant she was listening. I thought we were getting somewhere until Angie came roaring in, screaming and cursing, and telling me to go to my room."

"Oh, God."

Loretta nodded. "So I let her have it, too. Told her the kids are holy terrors and no one likes them and it's all her fault, and the next time she has trouble, she shouldn't call me. That's when she told me there was no trouble. Just a phone call from you begging her to get me out of your pub."

"I didn't beg."

"But you did call her." She rose and walked over to the window. "You know, *bella*, you could have lied. Denied everything Angie said, and I swear I would have believed you."

I could see she was doing her best to hold on to the anger, but the way she kept her back turned and the slow controlled way she was breathing told me I'd hurt her more than she was willing to admit. She could probably cry if she let herself; she would just rather die first, something I understood all too well.

"Nona, I'm sorry," I said. "I didn't know how else to stop the prayer circle. And when you said you were going for the priest, I panicked."

"You only had to ask me to stop."

"I did."

"But not like you meant it." She sighed and came back to the bar, sat down heavily, and reached for the glass of water I'd poured for her. "I was scared for you, *bella*. All that talk about ghosts. I just wanted to help. That's all I ever want to do."

"I know."

"Yet it makes me a pain in the ass?" She shrugged and stared into the glass. "I don't understand, Sammy. I just don't understand."

For the first time in her life, my grandmother looked like an old woman—tired and confused, unsure of her ability to help herself let alone anyone else—and I wanted to kick myself for being thoughtless and ungrateful, unable to bear the weight of her love a while longer. But Angie had forced open a door that had been closed all of our lives, and there was no way to start over, to pretend nothing had changed. All I could do was move forward and hope Loretta came with me.

I eyed what was left in her bottle of wine, emptied it into a glass of my own, and took a breath. "The helping is not the problem," I said. "It's the way you do it."

I took a swallow of wine, giving her time to cut in, to argue with me the way she normally did. But she held her tongue and kept staring into her glass, waiting for me to finish breaking her heart.

"I love you, Loretta. How could I not? You were my best friend when I was little, my champion when I was older. Who else could have come up with such a creative way to return that engagement ring?"

She smiled a little. "It was my best moment."

"Definitely one of them. But the truth is that no one understood me the way you did back then, and it hurts that you don't understand me now. That you can't see why I need you to give me the kind of help I need, not the kind you want me to have."

She lifted her head and again I waited for the blast, but it didn't come. Instead she said, "Go on," as though she were truly hearing what I had to say at last.

"My pub is everything to me," I continued. "And I'm not going to change it simply to please you, to measure up to some standard of Italianness that I don't understand. If you want to help me, if you want to be part of my life, then you have to do things my way. You can't come in here and undermine my choices, my decisions."

"I don't do that."

I held up my glass. "You like the wines I serve?"

She had the grace to look away, to concede the point, if only with silence.

I took another gulp and opened another door. "And you have to leave the music alone. I like Celtic harps and reed flutes, not because they remind me of Michael, but because the music is beautiful and haunting, and it touches something inside me. It makes me happy. Dean Martin just makes me want to drink."

She nodded at my nearly empty glass. "Me too. Okay we agree, no more Dino. Anything else?"

"You have to stop fighting with Eva. I respect the work she

does, and more important, I like her and I won't let you, or anyone else, insult her."

I was surprised that the admission had come so quickly, so easily, but now that the words were out, I realized it was true. I did like Eva MacRae, and if she went back to the bistro, I'd miss more than her cooking.

"Okay, okay," Loretta said. "The bald girl stays. What else?"

I hesitated, then pushed ahead, hoping I didn't hate myself in the morning. "Just this. If you genuinely want to help out at the Swan, then I'd love to have you around. I'm desperate for someone in the kitchen, but you're only welcome if you follow Eva's orders. No more olives, no more recipes, and no more threats in Italian. You do what she says or you go home, that's the rule, understand?"

Loretta laughed. "How can I not? Finally, you're saying it like you mean it. Tell me something else."

I felt my shoulders relax, felt myself smile. "Okay. No more prayer groups and no more holy water."

She looked around. "You're sure there's no ghosts in here?"

"Not a one."

"So it already worked. And so did this." She kissed her fingertip and touched it to the medallion at my throat. "*Grazie, Maria, grazie.*"

"It didn't work," I started, but stopped myself. I'd already won. I didn't need to pound home every small point. "All right, it worked, but we don't need anything more. Which means you have to call off the priest. I don't want him here tomorrow, understand?"

She smiled and laid a hand softly against my cheek. "Don't worry, *bella,* I get it. Just because you don't have a husband or even a car, you're still a grown woman. And if you want to screw up your life, I have to let you."

It wasn't the interpretation I'd hoped for, but it was a start. And it was more than either of us had an hour ago.

"We're agreed, then? No more cannoli on my doorstep?"

"You want cannoli, you come to my house and get it."

"And you'll start work Monday morning. You'll clock your hours and I'll pay you, like everyone else."

"I don't need your money."

"I'll pay you, or forget about it. When you're here, you're not my Nona, you're an employee. And Eva can fire you if you tick her off."

"The bald girl can fire me?" I nodded, and she shrugged. "Okay, she can fire me and you'll pay me. With time and a half for overtime."

I held up my glass. "Deal."

She clinked her water glass against it, and we drank to our deal. Then she rose and came around the bar, pulled me into a hug. "Things will be different, *bella*. You'll see."

"I'll remind you when they aren't."

"Good. That way, we don't fight." She broke away, tipped her head to the side, and studied me closely. "You've been crying. Why? What happened?"

I held up my bandaged finger. "I cut myself in the kitchen."

She didn't believe me, I could tell. But she didn't pursue it, didn't hound me with a million questions. She simply shrugged and pulled the phone toward her. Tapped a finger on the sticker on the receiver and asked, "This cab company any good?"

I nodded, and she dialed the number. True to her word, she was going to let me screw up my life, and I couldn't have been more grateful.

"Hello?" she said. "Yeah, I need a cab."

She told them the address and hung up. "They'll be here soon. What time you want me here on Monday? Never mind. I'll come at eight o'clock."

"I'll get a key made," I said.

"Don't worry. I already got one." She gave me a peck on the

cheek and headed for the door, each step filled with purpose again.

"Loretta, wait. Do you need cab fare?"

"Are you kidding? When Angie saw her neighbor sitting on the curb with me, she sent her husband out with a hundred dollars to help me get home. Not bad for a girl who hates to part with a dollar." She paused before stepping outside. "I didn't think. You want to share the cab? My treat."

I shook my head. "I have things to do in the kitchen."

And Michael still hadn't called, but that was another bit of news best added to the list of small points that could be pounded home later. "You go ahead."

"See you Monday, *bella*," she said and went outside to wait.

I watched her walk to the curb, check the street for the cab, and throw up her hands in frustration when it wasn't there. I was glad she was coming to work for me. Really, I was. We needed help, after all, and Loretta was punctual, hardworking, and experienced. What more could I ask? All I had to do was find a way to break the news to Eva and hope she didn't quit.

I finished what was left in my glass as Loretta's cab pulled up to the curb. Once she was settled inside, I opened the bottle I'd denied her, took out my cell phone, and checked to make sure I hadn't somehow missed Michael's call. The screen was clear and there were no messages in my voice mail, but I was feeling lighter now than I had when he left. Optimistic even. Open to the idea that people could change, that things could indeed work out the way you wanted them to, and I asked myself: What does that blank screen really mean?

I refilled my glass and took a quick sip, realizing that a million things could have happened after he left the Swan. Julie could be giving him a hard time. Or Kirsten54 could have him on the phone, going on and on about cows and fences and God only knew what else. Or he could have been in an accident. He could be lying in a hospital at this very minute, whispering my name and begging for a phone. Or Rosie could simply be doing what she did best, and he was never going to make that call.

Which left me wondering how long I should wait before turning the phone off. Another hour? Two? At what point did hopeful become pitiful? And if I called him instead, would I be admitting defeat, or merely cheating myself?

Probably both if I was honest, but was keeping the phone on all night necessarily pitiful? Perhaps it was simply being practical, giving the poor man time to deal with whatever was in his way at the moment, be it kids or cows or a packed emergency room. Imagine how devastating it would be to finally conquer all obstacles, to finally push those buttons, to make that call only to be greeted by *Hi, this is Sam. I can't take your call at the moment.* How could I do that to the man I once loved?

I laid the cell phone down on the bar to avoid any accidental button pushing in my pocket, polished off that glass of wine, and turned my attention to the one call I had to make. I pulled the Swan's phone around to face me. My finger hovered above the speed dial button with Eva's name on it. Maybe I was being hasty. Maybe I should tell Johnny first. Get his reaction to Loretta's employment. Let *him* tell Eva. Now there was a much better plan.

I pushed Johnny's button, listened while the phone dialed the numbers for me, but hung up before the first ring.

Maybe I should call Derek first. Talking to Michael's brother wouldn't qualify as either admitting defeat or cheating myself. It would merely be more fact finding, more information gathering in order to determine a course of action. Perfectly logical, perfectly sensible. And I could avoid confessing my deal with Loretta to anyone for a while yet.

I took out Derek's card, dialed the number, and told myself to breathe normally when the line started to ring. And ring. And ring.

Hi, this is Derek. I can't take your call at the moment.

I hung up again and reached for the bottle. Of course he couldn't take the call. He probably left the house the moment Michael walked through the door. Went back to the Toad to catch another set of his good buddy Amanda, live and in concert and switched off his phone. It all made perfect sense when I wasn't thinking only of myself.

Why would a good-looking single man spend Saturday night at home with Michael if he didn't have to? Why wouldn't he go to a bar and spend the night with a bluegrass singer instead? Let her put on a private show for him later, and sing him to sleep after a few encores. It would definitely be better than sitting around watching Michael do whatever the hell he was doing right now. And I was pretty sure Derek wouldn't blow it all by calling some other woman's name at an inappropriate moment.

I topped off my glass and checked my watch. The singer wouldn't be finished for a while yet. I could go over there and look for Derek. Make him buy me a drink, cry on his shoulder about his brother the jerk, and ruin his evening too. If I didn't like Derek so much, I might have done it. Then again, the Toad would be noisy, and I might not hear the phone, and Michael might think I was punishing him by not answering, and Rosie would use it against me, and I'd get his message too late, and it would all end badly.

The best thing I could do right now would be to take my phone and go home. Do some paperwork while I waited. Or even some laundry. Wash the sheets so they'd be ready if he called, because if he called, he'd want to come over, and I'd want everything to be perfect. And that was where things fell apart again. If he came to my house, Rosie would come with him, and if she could get past my front door, we'd be right back where we started.

The Swan, on the other hand, had already proven itself to be a safe place, a place Rosie couldn't enter. Maybe that meant there was something positive at work here. Maybe if I stayed here with the phone, it would ring. And when Michael came, we could start all over again. The theory sounded as good as any, even made sense if I didn't think about it too hard, if I took it on faith.

I picked up the cell phone and turned it over in my hand. How hard could it be to just sit tight and think happy thoughts until the goddamn thing rang? I could call it a vigil. Light a few candles. Drink a little more wine. And wasn't grilled cheese the perfect food for a vigil?

Agreeing that it was, I fixed myself two and carried them back to the dining room, picking up the rose Michael had given me along the way. I took another sip from my glass and lit two of Loretta's candles. Placed them on either side of the phone and positioned the rose in front, creating an altar and trying not to think of St. Jude, the patron saint of lost causes. Then I plugged Dean Martin into the CD player, picked up the bottle of wine, and made myself comfortable in front of the flickering candles. Refilled my glass and leaned back, listening to Dean tell me I was nobody till somebody loved me, and willing that phone to ring.

SIXTEEN

My vigil came to an abrupt end at precisely six fifteen A.M. the next morning, not with a phone call, but with a fist pounding on the door. I'd fallen asleep with my head on the table sometime during Dean's third rendition of "Ain't That a Kick in the Head." That damned song was playing again and I looked around, realizing the candles were out, the rose had wilted, and there was a good possibility my neck would be turned to the right for the rest of my life. And still no call from Michael. So much for happy thoughts.

"Sam, open the door," Derek called. "I need to talk to you."

"Forget it," I called back, closing my eyes and gingerly rubbing my neck. "Your brother's a jerk. Leave me alone."

"Yeah, he's a jerk, but he's in trouble, and I have to talk to you. Now open the door."

"Sunday is my day off," I said, turning my head slightly to the left and wincing at the pain. "Go away."

"Sam, please."

It was the *please* that got me on my feet. That and the fact I knew he wasn't the type to give up easily. I stood with a hand on the bar a moment, kicked a couple of wine bottles out of the way, and walked in a more or less straight line to the door. "Go ahead and talk," I said, resting my head against the frame and hoping there weren't more wine bottles rolling around somewhere. Two was more than enough.

"You have to open the door."

"Picky, picky." I turned the lock.

The door swung back, and Derek scowled at me. "What the hell did you do to my brother last night? And how much have you had to drink?"

This was not the Derek I had come to expect. Where was the smile I liked so much? The easygoing manner that made him fun to have around? My Derek was gone, replaced by one that seemed somehow larger, darker, and just a little scary. "I don't remember." I blinked at the bottles on the floor. "But probably that much."

"I don't believe this." He walked to the bar and came back with a large glass of water. "Sit down, drink this, then tell me what happened between you and Mike."

I sat, and I drank while Derek picked up my empties and carried them to the bar.

"It's all Dean Martin's fault," I said between gulps. "I should never play Dean Martin."

"I'll try to remember that." He switched Dino off and came back to my table. "Keep drinking. And try to remember what you did to my brother."

"I didn't do anything to him," I said, and that's when I noticed the bruise on his cheek. "What happened to your face?"

"I took a punch."

I nodded sagely. "I've heard the Toad can be rough. Especially on bluegrass night."

"It didn't happen there." He nudged the water toward me again. "Drink."

I raised the glass and downed the rest to make him happy. If I'd known it would be his cue to get me another, I'd have shown more restraint.

"Now tell me what happened here last night," he said when I'd finished off half of the second one. "And don't play dumb with me this time. I let it go yesterday, but now I want answers."

I rose and walked toward the swinging door, on a hunt for aspirin. "That's a little personal, don't you think? Let's just say things didn't go as planned, and leave it at that, okay?"

"Not a chance." He followed me into the kitchen, paused by the broken plate, then joined me at the grill. "I want to know what happened."

"I can't believe you're this interested." I took the first-aid kit down from the shelf, popped it open, and fished out the bottle of aspirin. Tried turning the cap, pushing it, pulling it, putting it between my teeth and tugging.

Derek took the bottle from me, popped off the cap, and handed me two pills. "It's not idle curiosity. It's important that I know."

I swallowed the pills without water, hoping they were the quick-acting kind. "Okay, here's the breakdown. We didn't have dinner, we argued more than we talked, and he left. Not half as exciting as the evening you must have had. Does the other guy look worse?"

He set the aspirin back in the box and put the kit up on the shelf. "You know it's funny, but I never figured you for a liar. Care to try again?"

I cocked my head to the side, thought better of it, and looked him straight in the eye instead. "We had sex. Is that what you wanted to hear?"

"No, and you didn't. He tried, but it didn't happen."

I felt my mouth drop open. "He told you that?"

"Right before he punched me in the face."

"Serves you right. I don't know how any of this is your business anyway. Now if you'll excuse me, I need to use the ladies' room."

I turned to leave, but Derek took hold of my wrist, drew me back. "It's my business because my brother spent the night locked in a room with my laptop, talking to himself and searching the Net for grief counselors."

"Grief counselors?" I pulled away and headed to the bathroom. "Did he try to call me?"

"He dialed your number a hundred times. Then he finally said you were right and threw his cell phone against the wall. What does he mean by that? What are you right about?"

"Everything. And I need to brush my teeth."

I closed the door, leaned heavily on the sink, and told myself to straighten up. If Michael had tried to call me half that many times, then Rosie must be feeling the pressure. And if Rosie was feeling pressured, then I needed to be able to think.

Even after two bottles of wine, I could picture her clearly. Following him around, endlessly nagging, endlessly accusing, feeding his guilt and driving the poor guy slowly out of his mind. It's a terrible thing to admit, but I couldn't have been happier. It meant I was still in the running, and I gave a point to St. Jude.

I opened the door and jumped when I saw Derek standing there. The man was too quiet by half. "Is he okay?" I asked.

"Of course he's not okay. He was pacing back and forth, talking to himself—"

"He wasn't talking to himself. And he doesn't need a grief counselor."

"Then what does he need?"

"I wish I knew." I walked past him to my office across the hall. "I need to change."

"Fine," he said, and I closed the door. "But if you can't tell me what he needs, at least tell me what led to this. Maybe I can figure it out."

"I doubt that." I stripped the plastic off a shirt, grabbed another black skirt from the hanger, and went to the credenza, hoping to find one pair of fresh underwear. It was then that I remembered I wasn't presently wearing underwear. I shook my head and dug through the drawer. Who'd have thought you could grow accustomed to the all-natural feel of things so quickly?

Grabbing the last pair from the bottom of the credenza and the cleanup kit from the top, I opened the door and walked back across the hall into the bathroom.

"Sam, believe me," Derek said on my way by, "I don't want to know what went wrong when you guys were trying to . . ."

I paused and looked back at him. "Have sex?"

He didn't look away as I'd expected, just nodded and said, "That would be it. I don't want details, I only want to know what you said to him before he left."

"I told him we might as well call it quits because we weren't going to make it as a couple."

"You told him it was over because you didn't have sex?"

I was the one to break eye contact, to turn away. "Of course not. Who do you think I am?"

"I don't know anymore. You might be the cruelest woman I've ever met, the worst thing to happen to me in years. But I'd rather believe you're holding something back the way you were yesterday. And if you would just come clean, maybe it would help Michael."

If only it were that easy. He was already thinking the worst of me; how could telling him I see ghosts possibly make anything better? I hadn't even risked telling Michael the truth, merely alluded to Rosie being a presence in his life, and look at what had happened. Telling Derek, a self-confessed nonbeliever, that she was more than just a memory, and much more than any grief counselor could handle, wouldn't help my case at all. He'd either think I was an honest crazy woman who should be kept away from his family, or he'd go on thinking I was a lying bitch who should be kept away from his family. Either way, I'd lose, and that would be a shame because I'd really miss having him around. And Rosie would win by default.

"It's complicated." I started to close the door. "You wouldn't understand."

"Try me," Derek said, his voice softer, gentler. More like the one I was used to. "You might be surprised."

I hesitated a moment, watching him through the crack, and thinking how nice it would be to be surprised. So I took a breath and a chance. Kicked the tangled grannies at my feet into a corner and hung my clothes on the hook. "You asked for this," I said and opened the door, sat down on the toilet, and told him all about seeing Rosie in the back of Michael's car on Friday morning, and again at the house that afternoon.

"Go on," he said, sitting on the floor with his back against the door frame, listening without comment while I explained in detail how she whispered to Michael and Julie in order to get them to do what she wanted, and how she moved things around for fun.

"You ever lose something?" I asked. "Yet know exactly where you last had it?"

"All the time."

"That's Rosie amusing herself. She doesn't like you much, you know."

"She never did."

"Her loss." I looked down at my hands. "Do you believe any of this?"

"Not really, but let me make sure I've got it straight. Rosie has been dead for two years, but hasn't left because she feels she has a duty to protect her family."

He might not believe me, but he wasn't running out the door either, and right now, that was all the encouragement I needed. Plus, I had learned years ago how to wash and talk at the same time.

I rose and put the plug in the sink, turned on the taps, and tested the water while I continued. "She not only wants to protect them, she wants to be an active part of their day-to-day lives. She believes she was cheated out of her life, and she's not about to leave without a fight. That's why Michael can't call me, even if he wants to. You said yourself that he was excited about seeing me when you left here the other day, but before you reached the house, he was already waffling, doubting his decision." I started to close the door again. "Now, if you'll excuse me, I really do need to use the ladies' room."

Derek rose and stepped back, but he didn't leave. Just kept talking to me from the other side of the door. "You're telling me that his second thoughts really came from Rosie?"

"Exactly." I eyed the lock, decided I could trust him, and shucked off my clothes. "She was sitting in the backseat of the car, blathering on from the moment he took the wheel."

"If what you're saying is true, then this has been going on for two years. Why the sudden change in him tonight? What was different tonight?"

I lathered up the soap and raised my voice as I washed. "Tonight before he left, I told him we had no future because Rosie is always there, in his heart and his mind. I didn't come right out and tell him the truth, but I made it clear she was still a presence in his life. He didn't believe me, of course, so I told him to phone me when he got home. If he could do it, then I'd agree to see him again. If he couldn't, then he'd know I was right, and we were finished."

"You gave him an ultimatum. And when he couldn't call, he panicked."

"Looks like," I said, toweling off quickly and reaching for my clothes.

"No wonder he's acting this way. Losing you over a phone call would make any man crazy. But your solution was a little harsh, don't you think?"

"I had to do something. If I didn't, then nothing would change. He'd be stuck in the same rut forever."

"And you? Where would you be?"

I looked into the mirror and smiled at the white shirt, the schoolmarm ponytail, and the circles under my eyes. "I'd be right here, feeling bad for him, but knowing it's where I belong and what he wants. What he chose."

"It's not, though. That's why he's fighting it."

I opened the door and carried my dirty clothes past him to the office. "So it appears."

"You don't seem thrilled."

I shrugged and dumped the clothes on the desk. "I'm just being practical. Rosie's there, and I'm not. She's a strong influence, and he's been marching to her tune for a long time now. She may be too hard for him to resist."

I came out into the hall and closed the office door.

He smiled. "Feeling better?"

"Much. And I don't always dress this way, you know. I do have other clothes."

"I like those ones. They're kind of sexy."

"You don't get out much, do you?" I said, and he laughed as we walked back into the pub together.

"What about Julie?" he asked. "Rosie tells her what to do, too?"

I nodded and went around behind the bar to pour another glass of water. "Whose idea do you think it was to play Barbie in the frigging Slime Pit?"

"Rosie's?'

"Good call."

He shook his head and sat down opposite me. "I don't know, Sam. This is all a little hard to swallow."

"There's more." I finished the water, set the glass down gently, and played my final card. "I see the cat too," I said, and waited, certain this would be the part that either made him take me seriously or sent him on his way.

He stared at me a moment, then sat back, obviously considering. "Then Julie's not crazy. Because the cat is real."

"As real as a dead animal can be. And it's every bit as horrific as the sketches she draws. To be honest, I don't know why the kid hasn't cracked completely before now."

"She's close," he said quietly. "So, is Rosie battered up too? Since she was in the same accident?"

"No, and that's the one thing I don't understand."

"The one thing?"

"I know it all sounds ridiculous, but it's the truth. I don't know why the cat's battered, and I don't know why it's there. All I know is that it was in the car because it was caught in the storm and Rosie stopped to pick it up. She rescued it."

"Then she killed it."

"Unintentionally, yes."

Derek rose and walked to the window. "Julie's been through hell over the last two years, and I can't even think about what might be next on the list of therapies without getting pissed off at everyone. Mike, the doctors, even Julie herself. Now you tell me it's all Rosie's doing." He sighed and looked back at me. "She always was one helluva strange mother."

"The cat's not there because Rosie wants it around, believe me. She keeps trying to get rid of the thing, but it keeps coming back. No one can figure out why it haunts Julie."

"No one? Who else knows about this?"

"Just Eva and Johnny. And my grandmother."

His smile was small and bitter. "Hence the match heads and the holy water, leaving Mike and me as the only ones who were still in the dark."

"It's not the easiest thing to tell people."

"I guess not." He came back and sat down at the bar. "Which brings me to the only question that matters. Now that we know she's there, how do we get rid of her? How do we keep that bitch away from my family?"

I had to smile. Even after my story, I wasn't the one he wanted to keep away from his family. That had to count for something.

"Then you believe me now?"

"No, but since I have no other explanation for what's happening to Mike, I'm willing to go along. What do we do first?"

Even though he didn't believe, I could use all the help I could get in this battle with Rosie. So I told him about Eva's list of questions and Rosie's explanation about what had happened on the day of the accident. The black pickup, the blond coward, everything.

"He left her there?" Derek asked.

"She denied it later, but I think it's true. I think she told me too much and then tried to backtrack. I just don't know why."

"Sounds like she's protecting him."

"He killed her. Why would she care what happened to him?" I came out from behind the bar and sat down beside him. "None of it makes sense, but I'm seeing Eva later. Maybe she'll come up with something."

"I'm not sure Mike will be here later. He was sleeping when I left, but before that he'd been yelling something about going home and staying put once and for all. Which makes no sense, because Julie's supposed to see that therapist on Monday, and it's not like him to blow off an appointment with a specialist."

"That's Rosie talking. She's been wanting him to leave for Huntsville ever since she first saw me. He must be scaring the hell out of her right now, so she's putting the pressure on."

"Why would it matter?"

"Probably because she's safe there. Everything's familiar. Everything's hers."

He got to his feet. "Or maybe that's where she's strongest. Maybe it's like a center of power or something."

It was my turn to smile. "For a guy who doesn't believe, you're giving this a lot of thought."

"I just want to help my brother, and I think we need to get to Huntsville before he does. I think we should go there now."

"Now? Like, right this minute?"

"We can be there in less than three hours, but we need a plan. It won't do us any good to get there and have no idea what to do next. Any suggestions?"

"None. That's why I need to talk to Eva. She went home to do some research, and we were going to talk about it later today."

He held out his cell phone. "Call her now. Tell her what's going on. Maybe she's already come up with something we can use."

"But it's still so early."

"If we wait much longer, he'll be gone."

I took the phone and followed him to the door. "Where are you going?"

"To figure out a way to keep Mike from leaving. I'll call to find out what Eva said. Leave your phone turned on."

"It's been on for quite a while now."

"Don't worry," he called on his way through the door. "No one can change my mind. I'll definitely call."

SEVENTEEN

It was a little after seven thirty when I called. Eva was still in bed and not happy about Derek's suggestion that we go to Huntsville. "Are you nuts? Get over here now."

She lived three blocks from the Swan in a two-story house I'd only heard about in passing. While the magazines she left lying around the kitchen did suggest a penchant for country kitsch, I wasn't prepared for a wildflower garden, a white picket fence, and enough straw hats, wreaths, and birdhouses to stock a small shop. But it wasn't until I stepped through her front door that I understood the true depth of Eva's romantic side.

Every table was covered with lace doilies, every chair boasted at least two embroidered pillows, and there wasn't a knickknack-free zone anywhere: dancing ladies on the end tables, slender nuns on the mantel, a family of bunnies run amok in a cabinet that was obviously losing the containment battle.

"Breathe a word to anyone about this," she said softly, "and I will take you out."

"It goes with me to the grave," I said and managed to contain a smile until she turned her back.

"I'm not surprised Rosie couldn't get into the pub," she said, leading me past the living room to the kitchen. "I don't know why I didn't think of it before."

"Think of what?" I asked, taking in the rogues' gallery of portraits lining the hall. The collection was nothing special, just the usual shots of children and old people, but what caught my eye was a sixteen-by-twenty portrait of Eva and Leo on their wedding day, positioned at eye level for better viewing.

I couldn't help myself. I stopped and gaped at the image of Eva with hair. Lots of it, just as she'd said, flowing from beneath a dainty headpiece of crystals and pearls. They stood on a boat at sunset, Eva looking fabulous in a white dress with an empire waist and lots of cleavage, and Leo resplendent in deck shoes and a tux. They were looking into each other's eyes, smiling and happy, leading me to believe there had indeed been good times.

"Did you hear a word I just said?" Eva called from the kitchen.

Any other woman would have come back into the hall, flushed and beaming, only too happy to tell me all about the picture, the wedding, the funny incident she could laugh about now, but that had almost ruined everything that day. Going on and on until I wanted to smack myself for even glancing at the picture let alone stopping and staring. But not Eva. She stayed in the kitchen, arms crossed, waiting for me to get back to my business and leave hers alone.

"I got distracted," I said, giving the portrait one last look before continuing along the hall to the kitchen, a room of white cupboards, floral paper, and matching ruffled chair cushions. "What did you say?"

"I said I know why Rosie can't get into the pub." She smiled and pulled out a chair. "She can't get in because she's not welcome."

As though that explained everything, Eva motioned me to sit and went to the stove to deal with a bubbling kettle.

The walk over from the Swan had only taken me fifteen minutes, yet the table was laid with matching cups and plates, and Eva was making tea and setting out warm cinnamon rolls. I didn't ask how she'd managed it, and I didn't wait to be invited, just helped myself to a cinnamon roll. It was the breakfast hour, after all, and those rolls weren't going to stay warm forever.

She set the teapot on the table and sat down across from me. "A ghost can only enter a place that's welcoming. You were obviously not welcoming, so she couldn't get past the door. Michael, on the other hand, is welcoming as hell, so she hasn't had trouble hanging on to her own house, or entering Derek's at will."

I nodded and took a bite of the cinnamon bun, knowing instantly that they could become habit forming. "How do we change that?"

"That's what I've been working on, but my research time has been cut short because you had to talk to Rosie, after I explicitly told you not to."

"It wasn't like I went looking for her. She was just there in the alley."

"Doesn't matter where you ran into her. None of this would have happened if you'd ignored her."

"I didn't have much choice," I said between bites.

"There's always a choice." Eva stirred the tea, then tucked a cozy around the pot and sat back with her knees tucked up under her. Sitting there in her robe and slippers, she looked cute, if that was a word you could use for a six-foot bald woman with tattoos, and I made a note to take a closer look at the other pictures in the hall, certain I'd find one of a younger Eva among them.

"Rosie can be very persuasive," I said and went on to tell her about sharing a joint and baklava, and ended with the story about the pickup truck and the man on the road who left her to die. "She said later that she'd made it up, but I don't believe her, and neither does Derek. We think she's covering something up."

"It's quite possible, dear," a woman said. "Ghosts usually have secrets."

Eva rolled her eyes, and I turned around to see an older woman coming into the kitchen from the hall. She was short, barely five feet tall, with spiky blond hair, slim blue jeans, and a fitted black jacket I would have liked to get my hands on. Her eyes were brilliant blue and nestled in a bed of crow's feet that must have come from a lifetime of smiling just the way she was now. Her face was delicately boned like her hands, and her nails were painted dusty rose to match her lipstick.

She lowered a backpack to the floor, kicked off her shoes, and looked over at Eva. "The door was open, so I let myself in. I hope you don't mind."

"You could have at least made some noise," Eva said. "Let me know you were there. But of course you didn't because you like to appear from out of nowhere, poof, and take everyone by surprise." She took another cup and saucer from the cupboard and sat down again. "It's her favorite party trick."

"Evie, don't be like that," the woman said.

"Like what? Honest?" Eva gestured toward me. "Mom, this is Sam. Sam, my mother."

I rose and offered a hand. "It's nice to meet you, Mrs. MacRae."

"Call me Mary Margaret." She took my hand in both of hers, didn't so much shake it as hold it firmly in place. "You must be Sam with the ghost. Eva told me all about it when she called. Interesting situation indeed, but don't you worry, dear, we'll do everything we can to help." She released my hand, sat down in front of the third cup, and helped herself to a cinnamon roll. "These look wonderful, Evie. Did you use Granny G's recipe?"

"It still needs updating," Eva said, dropping one on her own plate. "No one should eat that much butter."

I heard her mother sigh as she unfolded her napkin, and I made a point of smiling at her when I reached for another bun, letting her know at least one of us was glad to see her. "This is indeed an unexpected pleasure," I said. "When I suggested Eva call you yesterday, she seemed a little reluctant."

"Reluctant?" Mary Margaret laughed. "Oh my dear, you're lucky she didn't take your head off for even thinking about it."

"She almost did," I said and smiled at Eva. "But everyone can have a change of heart."

"Change nothing." She stuffed half a roll into her mouth and frowned at me while she chewed. "If I'd had more time I could have figured this out for myself. But then you pushed everything ahead this morning, and I knew I was going to need help. Unfortunately, my mother's was the only number I could come up with in a hurry."

"Oh, Evie, don't feel badly," Mary Margaret said. "You haven't devoted yourself to the paranormal the way I have. If you had, you wouldn't need anyone's help, I'm sure of it." She turned to me. "Now, Sam, I know you're in a rush to get this situation cleared up, so let's not waste time. Tell me why you want to go to Huntsville."

"Michael is talking about going home today. I'm afraid that once Rosie gets him there, he'll never come back."

"Why do you feel that way?" Mary Margaret asked.

"There's no concrete reason, but Rosie has been anxious to get him back there ever since I met him. She never says, *Let's go to Disneyworld or the south of France or even over to the Island.* It's always *Let's go home, let's go to Huntsville*. I can't help feeling there's a connection. Derek thinks the house might be a power source or something, the place where she's strongest."

"He's absolutely right," Mary Margaret said. "A ghost can

travel at will, but is always connected to one place more than any other. Rosie has likely set down deep roots in Huntsville, both psychically and physically. If you can stop her from getting into the house, Michael might have a chance of breaking free of her."

"Might?" I asked.

Mary Margaret looked down at the roll on her plate. "Rosie has been a big part of his life for the past two years, maybe bigger than she was in life because now she has no distractions. She can spend twenty-four hours a day working on him, influencing his decisions, charting his future, doing whatever she likes, and he doesn't even know it. The fact that your ultimatum made him realize something is wrong is good. But if he lets go of her, he'll need something else to grab on to right away."

"What are you saying?" I asked.

Mary Margaret smiled. "I'm saying that if he doesn't have something to fill the void, Rosie will likely weasel her way back into his life, and then she'd be twice as difficult to get rid of. But we don't have to worry about that, do we, dear? You're in love with this man, are you not?"

I smiled. "Actually, it's only been a couple of days—"

"But you do want him in your life," Mary Margaret insisted. "That's why you're doing all this. So you can have Michael in your life."

The correct answer was *Yes, I want Michael in my life*. But the idea of him grabbing on like I was some kind of lifeline was a little scary. And didn't people die every year trying to save someone else who was drowning?

"Sam, are you certain you want to do this?" Mary Margaret asked. "Because there's a possibility he'll get rid of her on his own one day. A slim one to be sure, but it is there."

Eva picked up the pot and poured three cups of tea. "What she's trying to say in her annoying roundabout way is that you don't have to do this. You can call Derek and tell him you're done."

"And let Rosie win?" I shook my head. "Absolutely not. I'm going to Huntsville. I just need to know what to do when I get there."

Mary Margaret studied me for a long, silent minute, and when things were more than a little uncomfortable she finally said, "Then let's get started," and pulled the sugar bowl toward her. "The first thing you need to do is to turn Rosie's house against her."

She paused and spooned three heaping helpings into her cup, stirred the tea precisely three times, slowly, in a clockwise motion, tapped the spoon three times, and set it in her saucer. "Because the house is not naturally uncomfortable for her, you have to make it uncomfortable. Make it impossible for her to get inside, just as she couldn't get into your pub."

"If you were staying there, it wouldn't be a problem," Eva said. "She probably wouldn't be able to get in, just like she couldn't get into the pub."

"But I'm not staying there," I said. "I have to be here, at the Swan."

"Exactly," Eva said. "Which is why we need to get in there, plant some psychic bombs, and get out again, before she comes back."

"We?"

Eva scowled and pulled the sugar bowl toward her. "I'm not letting you go there without me. It won't be safe."

"How do you know?"

"I don't know. I just have this feeling."

"And haven't I always told you to go with your gut?" Mary Margaret said.

Eva groaned and spooned three sugars into her cup, stirred it slowly three times, clockwise, tapped the spoon three times, and set it in her saucer. I looked down at my cup, trying to remember which way I usually stirred and how many times, and wishing I knew why it mattered.

Her mother shook her head. "Evie doesn't like to think she's inherited my gift, but I honestly believe she has."

"Not possible," Eva said. "The gift always skips a generation."

Her mother's laughter rippled across the table. "That's just an old wives' tale. These gifts have a mind of their own. But she's quite right about the dangers involved in this sort of mission. The lion's den is never a good place to be, especially when you're trying to oust the lion." She held out the basket of cinnamon buns to me. "I can't eat more than one. Please have another for me."

After I took a third cinnamon bun, Mary Margaret picked up her cup and started sipping the bubbles from around the edges. "Now that you know it can be dangerous," she said between sips, "are you still certain you want to go to Huntsville?"

"More than ever," I said, watching her turn the cup to the right and sip, turn the cup to the right and sip, making sure she didn't miss a bubble before finally taking a real drink of her tea.

"Then it sounds like you're ready." She set the cup back in the saucer and folded her hands on the table, obviously getting down to business. "Before we start, I need to ask if there's anything you haven't told us about last night. Anything that happened that we should know about."

I focused on my own tea. "I can't think of anything."

"Liar," Eva said.

"Evie, really," her mother said.

"Well, she is, and Sunday is my day to sleep in and I have no patience for her crap." Eva kept her eyes fixed on me even as she chased the bubbles in her own tea, turning the cup, taking a sip, turning the cup, taking a sip. She stopped before she got the last few. "I cannot believe I just did that."

"Why wouldn't you? It's good luck," Mary Margaret said, then turned to me. "But she's right, dear. All this beating around the bush isn't helping a thing. Why don't you tell us the rest of it?"

No one needed to know the rest of it. It was enough that I knew myself. What possible good could it do to share that kind of humiliation with anyone else? But they were both looking at me expectantly, and I knew I wasn't going to get out of this without giving them something

"It's a little embarrassing to admit," I said, focusing on the cinnamon bun on my plate so I wouldn't have to look at either one of them. "I went snooping in Michael's e-mail. Who could resist when his BlackBerry was right there? I found out Rosie was right about that Kirsten woman. Reading those e-mails made it pretty clear that she's determined to be The One."

"I don't care about Kirsten," Eva said, "I need to know what happened between you and Michael. Why you issued him an ultimatum."

"It was nothing. I just got frustrated." I scooped the topping off the bun with my finger and shoved it into my mouth. "These are really good. You should make them at the Swan."

Eva smacked her hands on the table and got to her feet. "If you're not going to tell me the truth, then I'm not going to waste any more of my time. Let yourself out."

Having the gift might make Eva interesting, but it did nothing to improve her social skills.

I chased her into the hallway. "He called me Rosie while we were having sex. Is that what you wanted to hear?"

She stopped at the bottom of the stairs. "I only wanted to hear the truth. And I suppose you think it was your fault in some way."

"How can I not?" I turned my back on her. "You have the most incredible talent for making me feel like a goof."

Face red, I went back to the table. Mary Margaret kept her eyes averted, feigning fascination with her tea and showing more grace than I'd seen in a long time. I sat down and stared at the bubbles in my teacup, wondering if I should chase after them too. Turn my cup round and round until I got every last one, just in case Eva and her mother were on to something. Instead, I wiped my sticky fingers on a napkin and dropped it on the naked cinnamon bun, my appetite for sweet suddenly gone.

Eva came back to the table, picked up the plates, and carried them to the sink. "You issued this ultimatum because you think it's a big deal, him saying her name that way?"

"And you don't?"

"Of course not. Knowing Rosie, she's been making love to him every night since she died. Whose name did you expect him to say?"

It had never occurred to me that Rosie would do something like that. Probably because she was dead, and weren't you supposed to assume a certain dignity about the dead? But remembering the way Loretta had shivered when Rosie whispered in her ear, the way the woman from the spa had turned her head for another kiss, it made sense that she could make her touch felt if she wanted to. And if both of them could feel her, then what chance did Michael have?

Mary Margaret lifted her eyes and smiled at me with such empathy that I felt as if I'd known this woman all of my life. "Evie's right, dear. Your Michael probably assumes he's dreaming when she touches him, and from what I've heard about Rosie, she's likely made sure these dreams have come to him every night since she died. No living couple I've ever known has that much sex. How can he possibly equate those same sensations with anyone but her?"

It made sense when she put it that way, but even if she was making it up as she went along, I was feeling a whole lot better about my role in the whole thing. Which might have been Eva's point, now that I thought about it.

"Based on what you've told me," Mary Margaret continued, "I'd say you're going to need every weapon available in order to get the better of Rosie."

"Do you honestly think it's possible to beat her?" I asked.

"That depends on what you mean by beating her. You can't use force to exorcise a ghost the way you can a demon. They can't be banished to hell, or locked in a box, or any of those other things you see in movies. All you can do is make it difficult for her to stay where she is and encourage her to move along. Get her to look forward to a new adventure so she stops looking back at what she's lost."

"And if she won't go voluntarily?"

Mary Margaret smiled. "Then we use a little persuasion." She rose and unzipped her backpack, took out a locked wooden box, and set it on the table. "This is your basic ghostbusting kit. Usually we only use one or two items for the desired effect, but with Rosie, I suggest you give it everything we have."

She took a small gold key from her pocket and opened the box. Reached inside and came out with a bundle of dried twigs. "First, we have dried sage for smudging. Open all the windows, then light this and go into every room, all the while telling the ghost you want her to leave."

"I've already told her to leave," I said.

"Not with burning sage in your hand."

"Sage is good," Eva said quietly, so I shrugged and sat back. I obviously had a lot to learn.

Next, Mary Margaret took a bud of garlic from the box and laid it on the table. "Garlic is always part of your front-line defense. You hang a clove in each doorway, not a whole bud, just a clove."

"Do we peel it first?" I asked.

"Not unless you want the place to stink." Reaching into the box again, she withdrew a small bouquet of dried flowers and handed it to me. "This is commonly known as a posy, a simple but effective combination of five-finger grass, cinnamon, and echinacea. Keep it in your pocket. It's not meant to drive a ghost away, simply to keep you safe."

Like Johnny's match heads and Loretta's medallion, I wondered how anything as simple as a posy could have any effect on Rosie, but I shoved it into my back pocket anyway. Covering my ass, so to speak.

Mary Margaret then produced a small silver bell, letting it tinkle merrily in her hand. "You ring this in every doorway, then sprinkle sea salt across the threshold because a ghost can't cross a line of blessed sea salt."

I took the bag from her. "You had it blessed?"

"On my way over. I was lucky to catch Father Reynolds before the morning service. What good would it do you otherwise?"

She was sincere, I had to give her that, and her earnestness humbled me. I set the salt down beside the bell.

"One last thing, dear," Mary Margaret said. "You're worried about a decision you've made, and you needn't be. You will be well pleased with her help in the morning."

"Help?" Eva sat up straighter, looked from her mother to me. "Whose help?"

"A charming woman who knows more about food than you've had time to learn, my girl," her mother said before turning to me. "You're worried about having your grandmother around, aren't you?"

"Your grandmother?" Eva sputtered. "Damn right she should be worried about having her around. When did this happen?"

"Very recently," her mother said. "But neither of you needs to worry." She reached out and covered my hand with hers again. "Your grandmother loves you very much, and she won't do anything to push you away." She glanced over at Eva. "Contrary to popular belief, people can change. Even the most stubborn, pigheaded know-it-alls can learn to keep their mouths shut if they want to." She looked back at me. "And your grandmother definitely wants to, dear."

I had to consciously keep my jaw from dropping open. "How do you know this?"

She smiled. "A little birdie told me."

My eyes widened. "You mean a ghost?"

She laughed and motioned to her kit. "With all this in the room? Not a chance."

I turned to Eva, who only shrugged and reached for another bun. "I warned you. My mother will drive you crazy if you let her. But we definitely need to talk about your grandmother."

"Let's not worry about that now," Mary Margaret said. "Let's just get you equipped for your trip to Huntsville. Evie, do you have a container I can put these things in? With a tight-fitting lid, of course."

Eva found a cookie tin with a lid, then excused herself to go upstairs and change. I stayed in the kitchen with Mary Margaret, jotting down notes about the order in which things were to be done and listening to the last of her instructions.

"You can try a séance while you're there if you like. Those are always fun, and Evie used to be very good at them. Then again, you're already talking to Rosie, so perhaps there's not much point." She pushed the lid down on the cookie tin and held it out to me. "You'll need to turn all the shoes in the house around so that one faces forward and one faces back. That always confuses a ghost. And you should take some rice as well. Pour a little in the corners of the high-traffic areas. Ghosts can't resist counting things for some reason, so it slows them down."

I looked down at the tin. "Makes ghosts sound pretty dumb."

"And you're worried because Rosie is anything but dumb."

I nodded and set the cookie tin on the table in front of me. "I don't mean to be ungrateful, but I'm having a hard time believing that any of this stuff will work."

"It probably won't, but there isn't a soldier in the world who would go into battle without his armor, even when he knows he's outgunned, because you never know when a miracle will happen." She took hold of my hands and looked at me with those earnest blue eyes. "You're fortunate to have Evie and Derek on your side. The collective will of three people who truly want to save this man and his child can make all the difference between success and failure in this sort of action. Each room you enter, each order you give for her to leave must be done with conviction. You need to be positive going into that house, show confidence to the point of being cocky, otherwise Rosie will walk all over you."

"I have the feeling you already know the outcome, don't you."

"Honestly, no I don't, but I do know that every spirit has its weak spot, its Achilles' heel. Find Rosie's and you'll be on your way to getting rid of her."

"What about the cat? Can we get rid of it too?"

Mary Margaret got to her feet. "Sadly, no. The only one who can do that is Rosie."

I stood up, taking the cookie tin with me. "But she's tried, I've watched her."

"She's tried to dispose of it, yes. But she hasn't done the one thing that will truly help."

"Which is?"

"She has to claim the poor little thing as her own. Animals can't cross over by themselves. They need a human to take them. She killed it; now she's stuck with it. All she needs to do is admit it." Mary Margaret rose up on her toes and kissed me on the cheek. "I should be going. Let you get on your way."

"I wish you were coming with us."

She laughed and zipped the wooden box into her backpack. "With Evie there? Not a chance. She'd hate us both before the day was out, and that would be a shame for the two of you." She hoisted the backpack onto her shoulders. "Walk with me to the door." We paused in front of the rogues' gallery in the hall, and she smiled at the wedding portrait. "It was a beautiful day," she said. "Beautiful boat, beautiful weather, beautiful bride too." She smiled at me. "But I guess I'm biased."

"No, you're right. She is beautiful."

"She's bald." Mary Margaret cast a quick glance up the stairs, then leaned closer and lowered her voice. "This is the first time I've seen her this way, and it was all I could do to keep from commenting when I walked into the kitchen. How long has she been that way?"

"A few months. Did she tell you he left?"

She looked back at the picture. "No, she's too proud. But I knew as soon as I heard her voice. I can't say a word, of course, but she's better off without him. She just doesn't know it yet."

"I think she's figuring it out."

She reached out and touched the portrait lightly. "I hope so, because just as some people can and do change, others will always be incapable of it because they never see themselves as wrong."

I thought about Leo in the alley with Eva, seducing her, playing her, using her own weakness, her Achilles' heel, to win her back. He was the one Mary Margaret was talking about, the one who was incapable of change, and I could see she was as worried as I was that Eva's need to make her house a home again would override her common sense. The only difference was that I didn't already know which way things would go.

"I'm sure it will work out," I said.

Mary Margaret gave me a small, sad smile. "I hope so, because if she lets him come back, I'm finished for good. And I don't think I could take it if she didn't speak to me again."

The cell phone in my purse chirped. "I'm sorry, but I have to take this. Maybe it'll be Derek with good news. Maybe we won't be going to Huntsville after all."

Eva's mother held up a hand. "Fingers are crossed."

Walking into the kitchen to take the call, I had to wonder how difficult it must be to have to pretend like that all the time.

"Derek? What's going on? Is he any better?"

"He seems to be. He's still locked in the room, and I could hear him punching keys on the laptop and talking to someone, but at least he's not pacing anymore."

"Has he given up trying to call me?"

Derek hesitated and, like Mary Margaret, I knew the answer before he spoke.

"I don't think it's a question of giving up as much as it is postponing. The only thing he would say is that he'll be talking to you soon, so that has to be a good sign."

"I'll take your word for it. What about Julie?"

"She's holed up with a movie and a bowl of cereal. Mrs. Moore from across the road came over to stay with her until Michael comes out of that room."

"What if he decides to leave, then? Makes it to Huntsville at the same time we do?"

"He can't." Derek lowered his voice. "I stole the keys to his Lexus."

I laughed, liking him more and more. "Then let's roll."

I gave him directions to Eva's house and went back out to the hall. Mary Margaret was still there, waiting for me.

"Michael's brother is a nice man," she said. "But he's had his heart broken too."

I screwed up my nose. "You mean Derek? When was this?"

"A while ago, but it holds him back, makes him cautious."

I glanced down at the phone. "With everything he knows about Michael and me, you'd think he'd have said something."

"That's not his way. He doesn't talk much about himself, past or future. But you could ask him about Amanda. See what happens."

"Amanda? The bluegrass singer? Is she his future?" I jammed my fists into my waist. "Damn it. She is, isn't she?"

Eva's mother looked at me curiously. "Why do you care?"

"I don't. I just don't think a singer is the right kind of woman for him. Singers travel too much. How can you have a family with a woman who's always traveling?"

"Maybe he doesn't want a family."

"Of course he does."

"How can you be so sure? Did you ever talk about it?"

"No. I just have a feeling."

"A gut feeling?" She laughed merrily. "Then I guess he wants kids after all." She stepped out onto the porch and held the door open for me. "One other thing. Kirsten54 is not your rival. Remember that when the time comes." She rose up on her toes again and looked past me into the house. "Good-bye, Evie."

Footsteps on the stairs. Eva's voice calling, "You're leaving?"

"I have clients to see," her mother called back.

Eva hurried to the door, stopped at the threshold, and instantly turned awkward. "Thanks for coming," she said, looking down at the floor, back at her mother, then down at the floor again. "I appreciate it."

"I know you do." Mary Margaret took her daughter's hand and smiled up at her. "You be careful, you hear? Even though Rosie's not there right now, it doesn't mean she won't show up while you're in the middle of your work. And if she does, there's no telling what she'll do to protect her home."

More cheap tricks, no doubt. And knowing Rosie, she'd have saved the best till last.

"Call me if you need anything at all," Mary Margaret said.

Eva sighed heavily. "I'll be fine."

"I never doubted that for a moment." She let go of Eva's hand, waved to me, and went down the stairs to the winding flagstone walkway. She was almost at the street when Derek's truck pulled into the driveway. "You must be the brother," she called to him and trotted over to the truck to chat while Eva and I pulled on our shoes.

"While we have a minute," Eva said. "Please tell me your grandmother isn't really going to be working with us. Tell me you didn't hire her without even talking to me."

"I know I should have run it by you first, but it just happened."

"Like Rosie just happened?"

"Yes, exactly like that. But I told Loretta she could only stay if she followed your orders. One word from you and she's gone, so I know she'll be good. I'll tell you everything that happened in Oakville later, but for now you have to trust me. My grandmother will be an asset, I promise. It's like your mother said, people can change."

"Not everyone." Eva dug her keys out of her purse. "Look at her. She's still out there yammering on and on. We'd better hurry before she drives him away."

I followed her out to the porch. "I don't care what you say. I like your mother."

"I'm not surprised."

"And she's missed you."

"I know." Eva locked the door and swung her purse over her shoulder. "The hard part is, I've missed her too. But if Leo comes back, I don't know what will happen."

EIGHTEEN

I blame my father for my love of road trips. A serious man by nature, made more so by living with Loretta, he became a different person when spring arrived. For a few weeks each year, he'd whistle while loading his tools into the truck, wave to the dog walkers instead of scowling as they went by, and sometimes before he left for another day of fixing toilets or installing bathtubs, he would turn and wave to me as well, the only one up and standing by the window at sunrise. The only one still young enough to hope that this would be the day he'd smile and call out, "Do I have to make this trip alone?"

Derek's truck was like my dad's. A working vehicle with tools in the back, a single bench seat in the front, and country music on the radio. While Derek was nothing like my father physically or emotionally, when he waved from behind the wheel and called out, "Do I have to make this trip alone?" those two wonderful words came to mind. *Road trip.*

"Hurry up, you two," Mary Margaret called. "You've got a long drive ahead of you and a nice-looking man to take you there."

Derek laughed and cranked the radio up another notch. Shania Twain was feeling like a woman, Mary Margaret and Derek were singing along, and even Eva was smiling by the time we piled into the truck. Mary Margaret blew us a two-handed kiss, and on Derek's count of three, we returned it as a group.

It was midmorning on a Sunday and the street was still quiet. Everyone else was sleeping in, or reading the paper, or sitting in church receiving a blessing, and we were setting off to battle a ghost, armed with nothing more than old wives' tales and superstition. Yet the atmosphere inside the truck couldn't have been more lighthearted, more filled with confidence and laughter.

As Derek pulled away from the curb, Johnny Cash fell into a ring of fire and even Eva couldn't keep still. She hung her arm out the window and kept time on the side of the truck. I kicked off my shoes and sang along. Derek joined in on the chorus. We turned onto the Danforth, waved to people in other cars, and sang all the louder when some of them applauded. We looked like fools and sounded worse, but who cared? We were on a Road Trip for Right, and if we needed to crank the tunes a little louder, then so be it. Anything to keep the doubts and the demons at bay.

Traffic through Toronto was light, but it wasn't until we hit the 400 North that Derek put his foot down and drove like the devil was at his back, which he may have been for all I knew. But we weren't thinking about that as the towns clicked past. We were too busy laughing and talking and planning our strategy. By the time we hit Wonderland, we'd agreed that Eva would smudge, Derek would turn shoes, and I would ring the bell and sprinkle salt. The garlic would be left until the end, and whoever drew the short straw got the job.

Just past Barrie, both Derek's and Eva's cell phones rang, with

Michael looking for his keys, and Mary Margaret looking for an update.

"Sorry, buddy, didn't see them," Derek said.

"We're fine, Mom," Eva muttered.

And I laughed at them both.

Derek turned off his phone as soon as he hung up. I did the same, in case Michael tried mine, and Eva followed suit, certain her mother would call for another update before long.

No one could reach us now, and that suited our mood just fine.

By the time we reached Orillia, the motion to hold a séance had been formally nixed, with Derek being defeated in a vote of two to one. Naturally, he was disappointed, but Eva promised to hold one in the pub some evening so he could see for himself that such events are not all about floating tables.

It wasn't until we passed Rama that the mood inside the truck slowly shifted, grew sober and quiet. Derek turned down the radio. Eva announced that she was going to sleep, and I put my shoes back on. We'd be in Huntsville in just over an hour.

"Don't wake me till we get there," Eva said, wrapping her arms around herself and huddling close to the door. Within minutes, she was breathing deeply and evenly. Loretta always says that the ability to fall asleep quickly is a sign of a clear conscience. I try not to think about that every time I take a sleeping pill.

Derek held to a speed and the trees and rock faces raced by, broken here and there by campgrounds, motels, and burger joints. I sat up straighter. Drummed my fingers on the goody box. Checked the clock, then the odometer. "Not much farther now," I said.

"Not much," Derek agreed.

I nodded and drummed. "You nervous at all?"

"Nope. How about you?"

"Nope. I'm good." I drummed and checked the clock. "Is that time right?"

"To the minute." He laid a hand on my fingers, stilling them. "Tell me what's on your mind."

I sighed and left my fingers where they were, glad for the warmth of his touch. "It's just strange, that's all. I haven't been afraid of Rosie all this time, yet now I keep thinking about Mary Margaret's warning. Wondering if Rosie is already there waiting for us, and what cheap trick she's got up her sleeve this time."

"Cheap trick?"

"That's how she refers to her ghostly abilities. Like walking through walls and appearing from out of nowhere. Those are pretty benign, but I'm worried she might have something bigger in her own goody box."

"Like slime on the ceiling or swarms of bees under the bed?"

"You're thinking of demons."

"I do that all the time."

"Common mistake." I looked over at him. "Why aren't you nervous?"

"I guess because the way I see it, if Rosie was on to us, she wouldn't waste time going to Huntsville. She'd be in the truck right now, trying to get me to drive off the road." He started fighting with the wheel, veering slightly to the right. "Oh my God. It's happening. She's here. Help me. Help meeee!!"

"Not funny," I said and punched him in the arm. But it was, and it made me smile. Made me glad he was there beside me.

"Honestly, Sam, I think we're pretty safe. Nobody knows where we're going except the three of us and Eva's mother, and I can't see her ratting us out to Rosie."

"True." I consciously relaxed my shoulders and laid my hands on the cookie tin again, no drumming this time. "In fact she's probably doing everything she can to protect us."

"I wouldn't be surprised. She's quite a character. Even believes her own patter."

"You don't, I suppose."

"If I don't believe in Rosie, why would I believe in Mary Margaret?"

"Because she's the genuine article." I tucked my feet up under me and wrapped my arms around myself the way Eva had. "What did she tell you?"

"Something about a trip over water and a tall, dark stranger coming into my life."

"She did *not* tell you that."

He smiled at me. "Okay, she didn't say that. Although I would have liked a trip over water."

Another road sign came into view. FORTY MINUTES TO JERRY'S—BEST BURGERS IN HUNTSVILLE. The chill was back. I rubbed my hands up and down my arms and focused on Derek instead. "What did she really tell you?"

"She said I was understandably worried about my brother, but it's time to start thinking about what I want too."

"A little generic, but usually a good idea."

"Unless what you want isn't available."

I waited, hoping for an explanation, a brief anecdote, even an oblique hint. But as Mary Margaret said, Derek was not a man to talk about himself, which only made me want to know more. "Did she say anything else?"

"That's it." He glanced over. "What did she tell you?"

"She told me to ask you about Amanda. Why would she do that?"

"I have no idea. Amanda and I were married for a while, but it was a long time ago."

I drew my head back. "You were married to her? Why didn't you say something earlier?"

"Because it's water under the bridge. What difference does it make now? She's remarried and has two kids, but we keep in touch. You really should go and see her show. She was always good."

Another road sign. What luck. Jerry's was only twenty minutes away now.

I shivered and hunched my shoulders. Told myself it was a coincidence. I could not be cold. I must be tired. "Is that why you broke up? Because of the performing?"

"No, we broke up because she was sleeping with her manager. That's the guy she's married to now." He looked over at me. "Are you cold?"

I shook my head. "Just tired." He raised a single brow. "All right, yes, I'm cold. If Jerry had fewer signs, I'm sure I'd be fine." I sighed. "There's another one. Ten minutes to go. Somebody should tell him about the dangers of overkill."

Derek smiled. "Or maybe you just need to stop looking for them. Come here," he said and put his arm around me, pulling me gently to him.

I let myself be persuaded, let him hold me closer and tuck my head into his shoulder. "Is that okay?" he asked.

It shouldn't have been. I was supposed to be spoken for. A woman on her way to free the man she might love from a dark fate. But I was cold and he was there, and what harm could it do to share a little warmth with a man even Mary Margaret approved of? Besides, only Derek and I ever had to know, and there would be plenty of time for awkwardness later.

"It's perfect," I said, finding the right spot for my head. "Thanks."

"No problem," he whispered, and I would have sworn he added, "It's exactly what I want."

We drove in silence the rest of the way, the motion of the truck and the weight of his hand on my arm finally lulling me into something close to sleep. My mind floated, drifting from Rosie out on that road in a storm, to Leo who had decided Eva would do, finally coming to rest on Amanda Jeffries, the bluegrass singer who had broken Derek's heart. Arriving at the conclusion only a moment before he woke me that there was simply no accounting for fools.

"You should wake Eva," Derek said, taking his arm away. "We're almost there."

If I'd expected awkwardness, there wasn't any, at least not on Derek's part. As we drove, he pointed out a home that Michael had built and another he had helped restore to its turn-of-the-century glory, talking to me as easily as he always had, as though nothing had happened between us. Maybe he was right. Maybe nothing had happened after all.

We'd made good time, reaching the turnoff for downtown Huntsville in two and a half hours. I hadn't seen the town since the summer Rosie and I were sent home from camp in disgrace, and I wasn't ready for the changes. Chichi boutiques, coffee bars, and a new playhouse now graced the main street of what had once been a plain and aging lumber town.

We stopped at a light and I noticed three real estate brokers nestled like snakes among the decorating shops, the bakeries, and the chocolatiers. Only one stood out as an independent: J. E. Maxwell and Associates—Carriage Trade Homes. Perhaps that was where Rosie had worked.

Eva was awake now, stretching and rubbing the top of her head and looking at me with the oddest smile on her face.

"What?" I asked.

"Nothing," she said, and turned her attention to Derek. "How much longer?"

"About ten minutes," he said and turned onto a side road, taking us out of town.

After two more turns he finally stopped the truck at the end of a driveway. "This is it. The Hughes family farm."

I leaned across Eva for a better look. It was just like Julie's picture. Blue sky, green grass, and a two-story farmhouse with a barn in the distance. Everything was there: the swings, the trees, even the garden. Yet with all the blinds drawn and no one about, the place looked deserted, forbidding. A haunted house if ever there was one.

"Let's get this over with," Derek said and drove on, taking us closer to the house, to Rosie's den.

The driveway was circular, passing close to the house, and as we swung around, I saw window boxes on the porch railing and a fire pit surrounded by three Muskoka chairs about ten feet from the front of the house. I couldn't see cows anywhere, but I knew they had to be lurking nearby. Kirsten54 would have seen to that.

"Mike usually leaves a key under the mat," Derek said as he shut off the truck. "Let's hope he's a creature of habit, or one of us will be squeezing through that window up there." He pointed to a small, round window on the second floor. "The lock has been broken since the day they moved in."

Derek climbed out one side, Eva climbed out the other, and I sat in the middle, staring up at the house, unable to move. Wondering if we were making a mistake.

Derek jogged up the front steps, lifted the corner of the mat, and held up the key. "We're in luck. Give me a minute to open the door."

Eva walked to the stairs but I stayed in the truck, my skin crawling with gooseflesh and my mouth suddenly dry. The rational half of my brain reminded me that we had already been over this, patiently explaining how silly it was to be scared. After all, if Rosie was in there, she wasn't the type to wait and surprise us. She'd be out here already, stampeding the cows or toppling trees, making it clear we were the ones who were not welcome. The irrational side of my brain, however, the one that was holding me still and making me have to pee at the same time, kept screaming, *Repent ye sinners and get the hell out of here.*

Had Derek taken any longer to get that door open, I might

have run headlong down that driveway to the road. But the moment he threw open the curtains in the living room and Eva stood on the porch hollering, "Will you get your ass out here?" the place no longer seemed haunted, just empty. And maybe a little lonely, stuck out here by itself. But wasn't that what people loved about the country? The privacy, the isolation. The fact that no one could hear you scream.

I slid across the truck seat and leapt out before I could scare myself anew. "Let's do this thing," I called and jogged to the steps, the goody box rattling, ready to get to work.

"No sign of Rosie yet," Eva said when I arrived, "but we need to stay close at all times. There's safety in numbers and we're fortunate our number is three. Three is always lucky."

Three musketeers. Three blind mice. Three on a match. I sighed. Not *that* lucky.

She held out her hand for the goody box. "We move through the house systematically, starting at the top and working our way down. We touch nothing unless it has to be moved in order to complete the task. And we put it back exactly as we found it."

"But if the music begins to build," Derek said, "run."

"If the music begins to build," Eva said dryly, "I'll beat you to the door." She turned to me. "You ready?" I nodded, and she took a deep breath. "Here we go."

Clearly taking the idea of a mission to heart, Eva burst through the front door like a commando and headed straight for the stairs, not pausing to check out a picture or a knickknack or anything else along the way. Our goal was the top floor and that was where we were heading. No deviation, no tangents. Is that clear, soldier? Sir, yes, sir!

Derek was not in as much of a hurry. He closed the door behind us, laid the key on a table, and bent down to rearrange the two pairs of shoes on the mat. One for papa bear, one for baby bear. Only mama was missing. When he straightened, they were lined up neatly according to Mary Margaret's instructions: one forward, one back, one forward, one back. Michael was sure to notice that if he came home, but I supposed it could be blamed on vandals. Weird, cultish vandals.

Derek smiled at me. "You don't have to do this. You can wait in the truck if you want."

"And be out there by myself? Not on your life. I know the rules of horror. She who stays alone dies." I pointed up the stairs. "I'm with Eva."

To be honest, I wasn't scared anymore. I had been worried that being inside Rosie's house would make me more nervous, but now that I was here, I was oddly calm, and curious. It wasn't a big house. Living room, dining room, kitchen on this floor, bedrooms presumably upstairs. White walls throughout with blue checkered sofas, a woodstove on a raised tile platform, and everywhere, framed posters and programs of plays they might have attended, black-and-white photographs of places they might have been, and artwork that could only have been done by Julie. I realized then that the white walls were not meant to be trendy or sophisticated; they were simply a backdrop for their collectibles.

"We don't have all day," Eva called, and I hurried on, wondering when they had visited the Eiffel Tower and why it smelled so bad upstairs.

"It's the sage grass," Eva said when she saw my face. She held the smoking bundle of grass away from her and fanned the air between us with her hand. "It's okay once you get used to it, and this wouldn't be a proper cleansing without it."

Derek moved along the landing, putting distance between himself and the smoke. "Is that the technical term for what we're doing? A cleansing?"

"Yes it is. And the technical word for nonbelievers is bait." Eva handed him the container of rice and pointed him toward a corner. "Go sprinkle. Just a small, subtle pile in as many corners as you can. Make sure it's behind something else so it doesn't get vacuumed up right away. And don't forget to check the closets for shoes. We don't want to lose by default."

The second floor was no more impressive than the first. A narrow landing with windows and a silk ficus at each end, and four closed doors. Assuming one was a bathroom, that meant the other three were bedrooms. One of which was Michael's. But which one?

"Open all the windows," Eva ordered.

I opened the window at one end of the hall while Derek opened the window at the other. Then he bent down to pour an anthill of rice behind one of the ficus trees while Eva took the silver bell and the salt from the goody box and held them out to me. "The bell is an important step. You have to stand in every doorway after I smudge, ring it a few times, then sprinkle the salt in a line across the threshold. Got that?"

"Ring and sprinkle. Got it."

"And touch nothing." She walked to the door at the other end of the hall and threw it open. Pink walls and white furniture. Julie's room.

Eva thrust the sage grass into the room ahead of her. "All spirits leave this place," she said in the voice that always made Johnny move faster. How it would work on Rosie remained to be seen.

She went boldly forward, smudging under the bed, behind the curtains, inside the closet, not missing a spot, just as her mother had instructed, but not leaving anything looking disturbed either. If Mary Margaret was right about confidence being the key, then we were guaranteed success in that room at least.

I checked on Derek's progress. He was on his knees by the second ficus, pouring another anthill in another corner.

He caught sight of me watching and sat back on his heels. "You want to trade? Rice for bell? Shoes for salt?" He held out the rice. "It's more fun than you think."

"I'll stick with the bell. But thanks for thinking of me."

He shrugged and went back to his corner, taking such pains with his anthill that I honestly hoped the vacuum cleaner steered clear for a while. And that Michael knew how lucky he was to have a brother like Derek.

I carried my tools to door number two. Drew in a breath. Turned the handle, and pushed. Floral print paper, two single beds, and matching chenille spreads. A guest room. Damn.

Eva's voice echoed in the hall. "All spirits leave this place."

"None of that stuff is going to work," a woman's voice said.

I gasped, Eva came running, and Derek said, "Hi, Kirsten. How's it going?"

Kirsten54 stood at the top of the stairs, an average-looking woman about my age with a slightly long face, expressive brown eyes, and a shotgun at her side. She wore jeans and a T-shirt and her hair was flat and uncombed. Too preoccupied to brush her hair, but not preoccupied enough to forget the gun. An interesting woman, I decided. Intense, but interesting.

"I was driving by and I saw the truck in the driveway," she said, propping the gun against the wall. "There aren't supposed to be trucks, so I got the gun and came back. And I can tell you now that what you're doing won't work. I've tried it all, but she's still here."

I took a step forward. "You see her?"

"No, thank God. I just know there's something wrong in this house. Has been ever since Rosie died, so I figured it has to be her." She jerked her chin at the goody box. "If you'd like a hand with that, I'm a pro with the garlic. Should be, considering I've been stashing some here every week for the last six months."

Six months of garlic and nothing. I was starting to hold out less and less hope for our own mission.

Eva, on the other hand, was holding out the cookie tin to our guest. "Help yourself," she said, then introduced herself and me.

Kirsten54 shook Eva's hand. "Kirsten Clancy. Nice to meet you." She turned to me and extended a hand. "You must be the Sam Mike told me about in an e-mail the other day. Said he'd known you for years and couldn't believe his luck in running into you again."

She wasn't glaring at me. In fact, she was smiling. A big wonky grin that took up half her face and made me smile back. Mary Margaret was right. Kirsten54 had felt like a threat. Kirsten Clancy was not.

"I've heard about you too," I said. "You're looking after the place while Michael and Julie are gone. It's very good of you, considering the trouble those cows have been."

She laughed. "I swear Michael's cows are the orneriest in the province. But I think we've got the problem with the fence solved now." She held up the garlic. "You're sure you want to do this?"

"Absolutely," Eva said. "With four of us working on it, the odds of us keeping Rosie out are even better."

Four seasons. Four winds. Four horsemen of the Apocalypse. Is nothing guaranteed lucky?

"I'm game to try," Kirsten said and cracked open the garlic.

Eva joined me at the doorway of the guest room. "All spirits leave this place," she commanded and went in to open the window.

Derek slid past me. "Excuse me. Some of us have rice to spill."

While Eva smudged and Derek made his anthill in the corner behind a dresser, I went back to Julie's doorway, took an authoritative stance, and shook the silver bell, wondering if we wouldn't be better off with something that sounded less merry. A cowbell, for example. Or a gong. Or better yet, one of those nasty brass bells the nuns used to ring in the schoolyard right over your head if you were doing something wrong. But Mary Margaret had given us this one, Eva had deemed it appropriate, so who was I to judge?

Bell work completed, I opened the salt, sprinkled a fine line across the threshold, and left them to finish while I took on door number three.

This had to be it. I turned the handle and pushed gently. Bathroom. Which left door number four.

I turned the knob and pushed the door open wide. King-size mahogany bed, plaid spread with matching drapes, and only a handful of throw pillows for decoration. Bingo. The master suite. A tasteful blend of masculine and feminine, meant to make both husband and wife feel at home. Rosie had done her decorating homework.

I took my authoritative stance, rang the bell, and was about to sprinkle the salt when something caught my eye. On one of the dressers sat a pink makeup bag and a white, padded jewelry box. The kind that probably had a ballerina inside. Makeup and a ballerina in Michael's bedroom. Definitely odd.

I crossed the room slowly, the tiny hairs on my arms standing up straighter with each step. I picked up the makeup bag, slid back the zipper. Took out a new bottle of foundation, an untouched compact of pressed powder, pink blush that had never seen the stroke of a brush. I dumped the bag on the dresser. Every container was the same. Eye shadow, eyeliner, mascara, lipstick, all in Rosie's colors, all untouched. What was going on here?

I dropped the mascara and lifted the lid on the jewelry box. No ballerina, but it did have two tiers and velvet lining. Inside, a woman's watch and rings in the upper tray, delicate silver chains hanging from tiny hooks, a few pins laid end to end in the bottom, and earrings neatly matched into pairs and poked into the appropriate spot. Every piece in that box had been placed with care, as though the owner would be back shortly to claim it. As though she had only stepped out for the evening. Or left to show a house.

I closed the lid and surveyed the rest of the room. Her slippers waited at the side of the bed, her robe was draped over a chair in the corner. I opened a closet. Her suits, her dresses, her nightgowns, all lined up and clean.

I opened a dresser drawer. Bikinis and thongs.

I opened another. Pantyhose, stockings, and bras.

A third. Sweaters.

A fourth. T-shirts.

Every drawer was the same, each one filled with Rosie's clothes. Clothes that had been fashionable two years ago and had sat here neatly folded and untouched since the day she died.

I touched the medallion at my throat and backed away from the dresser. Banged into the vanity, jostling jars of cream, a tin of mousse, a comb and brush, a bottle of perfume. *L'Air du Temps* in a Lalique crystal bottle with two doves on top. *A classic design for a classic scent,* Rosie always said. I'd never known her to use any other.

Unlike everything else on the vanity, however, the perfume was only half full. On a hunch, I walked over to the bed, pulled back the spread, and picked up a pillow. Sniffed it. *L'Air du Temps.* The fucking bitch was scenting the sheets.

Moving faster now, I opened the second closet, expecting to find Michael's things, but again, it was Rosie. Evening wear, cruise wear, swimwear. It was like she was holding her own pageant in there. I checked the armoire, the other dresser, even the nightstands. Nothing there but real estate textbooks and course notes. Everything belonged to Rosie. Not a sign of Michael anywhere. Only his robe tossed across a chair and his slippers by the bed.

I gripped the bell and backed to the door. This room was not the master suite. It was a shrine. A shrine to Rosie where Michael was surrounded by her things, enveloped in her scent, and seduced by her memory night after night. No wonder she wanted him back in Huntsville.

"All spirits leave this place," I muttered and rang the damn bell again and again, but the happy tinkling sound only mocked me, mocked all of us. Rosie was too strong, too firmly entrenched. All the bells and salt in the world weren't going to do a thing.

I raced to the guest room and opened the closet. Sure enough, Michael's shirts, pants, and sport jackets were all there. In the dresser, his underwear and socks, T-shirts and jeans. She made him keep his stuff in the guest room. What kind of wife does that?

"What are you doing?" Eva asked. "I told you, don't touch anything."

"I'm not touching, I'm fact finding." I grabbed her arm. "Come with me," I said and shouted over my shoulder, calling to Derek and Kirsten. "Everybody, come with me."

They emerged from Julie's room, staring at me blankly. "Move it, now!" I shouted, which got their feet moving.

I dragged Eva along the hall to Rosie's room with Derek and Kirsten right behind. "This room needs smudging," I said. "And rice, and garlic, and anything else you can think of." I went to the bed and yanked off the comforter, started pulling up sheets. Eva took hold of me and Kirsten took hold of the sheets.

"What are you doing?" Eva demanded. "You touch nothing, disturb nothing—"

"Bullshit," I said, breaking free of her grasp and yanking the sheets out of Kirsten's hands. "Smell this," I said, shoving the sheets at Eva. "Smell this and tell me we should leave them there."

She sniffed the sheets and shrugged. "They have a scent. Could be detergent, fabric softener."

"Or this." I snatched the bottle of perfume from the vanity, unscrewed the cap, and handed it to her. "*L'Air du Temps*. I was there when the pastor's nephew slipped her a gift on the bus out of camp. It was this brand, this kind of bottle. A shiny new testament to her sexuality, and it's been her signature ever since. I don't know why I couldn't smell it on her these past few days, but she's obviously using it here, on Michael. God only knows where else she's left her mark." I gripped the sheets harder and turned to

Kirsten. "Where's the washing machine? I can't put these back on unless they're clean."

She looked from me to Eva and back again. "I've always been told that you're not supposed to change anything during a cleansing. You'll mess up the psychic energy, put things out of balance."

I went to work on the pillowcases. "And that method's been working well for you so far, hasn't it?"

"Point taken." She headed for the door. "I think there's detergent in the kitchen. If not, I'll zip over to my place and get some."

When she was on the stairs, I pitched the sheets into the hall and turned to Eva. "This room needs the most attention. It's the one that maintains her hold over Michael, I'm sure of it. Take a look in the closets, the drawers. Rosie is everywhere."

Derek moved slowly between the dressers and the closets. "I had no idea this was going on," he said quietly. "I helped him get rid of this stuff over a year ago. We packed it all up in boxes and took everything out to the barn."

"And as soon as you were gone, he brought it all back in," Eva said.

"That might explain the clothes, but what about this?" He picked up the makeup bag. "Everything in here is new. So are all the creams, the lotions, even the tin of mousse." He dropped the bag as though it had burned him. "I cleared out these things myself. Put all of her shit into a garbage bag and took it to the landfill site in my truck. I know I tossed that goddamn bag on the pile, so how do you explain this?"

"Michael bought it," I said. "Rosie would have been there in the store with him, whispering which brands to buy."

"Michael would have assumed it was his own memory telling him what to get," Eva said. "More proof of his undying love for his wife."

"A bond that transcends time," I muttered.

"What?" Eva asked.

"Nothing," I said and went to join Derek by the dresser.

He shook his head at the array of cosmetics. "I feel like an idiot."

"Don't," I said. "Rosie wouldn't have allowed Michael to do anything else. She was accustomed to getting her way when she was alive; why would it be any different just because she's dead?"

"Is there anything else we can use against her?" he asked, and for the first time since I told him about Rosie, I knew he was ready to start taking me seriously.

"A few more herbs," Eva said. "Maybe some incantations, but we already have the most powerful weapons available. The important thing is to use them effectively." She walked gingerly through the room, closing drawers and shutting closets. Righting bottles of cream and dropping makeup back into the bag. "You're right about this room being the center of her hold on Michael," she said when she was finished. "We need to focus our attention here, but we need to leave things exactly as they were. We need to arouse as little suspicion in Michael as possible."

"Won't the shoes be a bit of a clue?" I asked.

"The ones in the hall, yes. I'm just hoping the ones in the closet don't register for a while." She picked up the comforter and spread it on the bed, set the pillows in place, and then smiled at me. "In case the sheets aren't dry before we have to leave."

Eva opened the windows, preparing to smudge the room, and Derek was already busy turning all of Rosie's shoes around. I touched his arm and waited until he turned to look at me. "We're not finished yet," I told him. "Everything's going to work out just fine."

He laid a hand against my cheek, stroked his thumb lightly across my skin. "Mike's a lucky guy," he said softly. "I'll make sure he never forgets that."

"I found detergent," Kirsten called up the stairs. "You coming or not?"

"Coming," I called back, but couldn't leave him this way. I took his hand and squeezed it tight. "I like you, Derek. If nothing else comes from this, I'm glad I got to know you."

He looked as though he wanted to say something, but there was no time for talking. Kirsten was calling, Eva was smudging, and time was not on our side. "Good luck with those shoes," I said, then turned to Eva. "Smoke the bitch out of here. Smoke her like a goddamn Sunday ham."

Picking up the sheets again, I hurried down the stairs, meeting Kirsten at the bottom. "Do we have main-floor laundry, or are we looking at the basement?"

"Basement is too nice a word for these old farmhouses. Cellar is more like it." She smiled that big wonky grin and preceded me out to the kitchen and around a corner, hit a light switch, then opened another door.

She wasn't kidding about the cellar. The stairs were steep and narrow, the stone walls sweating and dank, and the floor made of dirt. She pulled a string on our way to the laundry room. Three bare lightbulbs came to life, adding a pale yellow glow to the gloom around us.

"Why didn't Michael ever change this?" I asked as I picked my way across the floor to a bright and shining front-end loader washing machine with matching dryer. "Especially with machines like these."

"Rosie always said no," Kirsten said. "He talked a lot about putting in cement blocks and pouring a proper floor, but Rosie never wanted the cellar improved. She said it was bad enough they put drywall upstairs, but the cellar was sacred. The only truly historic part of the house."

I screwed up my nose and Kirsten laughed. "I know. She was seriously nuts, that one."

I stuffed the sheets into the machine. "Did you know her well?"

"Only as neighbors." She poured detergent into the cup and locked the door. "Rosie wasn't interested in having friends. Not women friends, at any rate."

"But men were okay?"

Kirsten shrugged. "There were a lot of rumors, but she was a beautiful woman with a career, a great husband, and a lovely little girl. Lots of people were jealous of her, and jealousy breeds rumors."

"Were any of them true?"

Kirsten bowed her head and kicked at the dirt. "I don't like to speak ill of the dead."

I could see she was holding something back, struggling with her conscience. On any other day I would have appreciated her integrity, but not today. Today, I needed dirt.

"Kirsten, we're talking about Rosie here. You know how firm her hold is on this house and on Michael, so if you know anything about the last months of her life, anything at all that could help us get rid of her, you need to spill it now."

She considered a moment, then cocked a finger and motioned me to follow her deeper into the cellar. "I'll show you something. You draw your own conclusion once you've seen it."

If it was possible, this part of the cellar was even worse, with ceilings low enough that both Kirsten and I had to stoop, and an old cistern big enough to drown in.

She brushed cobwebs aside, took me past the cistern, and stopped. Waved a hand in the air, and grabbed hold of another string. "I've never told Michael about this," she said, still holding that string, still keeping me in the dark. "Maybe he knows, maybe he doesn't, but I wasn't going to be the one to bring it up. The poor guy has already been through enough."

"Sounds like you know him well."

"As well as anyone these days." Her face was half in shadow, yet I could see a small, shy smile turning up the corners of her mouth, and her voice took on a wistful tone. "We've seen more of each other since Rosie's death, of course. Dinner a few times a month, some afternoons in town, and I try to come by at least once a week to make sure he's got everything he needs."

"You're really looking after him," I said, not sure what that meant. Or whether I liked it.

"Someone has to. The way that poor man was grieving after she died would break your heart. He'd smile and look fine on the outside, but he wasn't. He's still not."

"So you just let yourself in now?"

"He always asked me to look after the animals whenever he had to go into the city for one of Julie's appointments, and eventually he gave me my own key. That's when I started ringing the bells and planting the garlic."

"A secret cleansing."

"It had to be that way. I tried a few times to talk to him about the possibility of Rosie being here, but he wasn't receptive, which left me on my own." Kirsten looked around, her shoulders drawing up protectively, instinctively. "I'll tell you honestly, this house scares me when I'm alone. It's like she's here, watching me. Gives me the shivers just to talk about it. Since nothing I did ever worked anyway, eventually I gave up. Almost gave up on Michael too, but I couldn't. I really like him. He's different from anyone I've ever met. Hates hunting and fishing, and as an added bonus he likes kids and traveling to places other than Florida. You don't find that kind of man up here too often, believe me. But it's been hopeless, until now. Until you."

She gave me another of those wonky grins, and that's when it hit me. Kirsten Clancy was hoping I'd help her get rid of Rosie so she could move in on Michael. She didn't see me as a rival at all. She had obviously misinterpreted his e-mail. And when she smiled at me that way I couldn't help feeling a twinge of guilt, knowing I was the one he wanted. But honesty wasn't necessarily the best policy right now, so I kept it to myself and figured a sleeping pill would get me through the night.

"Here's to saving Michael," I said.

"Amen," she said and pulled the string. A single bulb came to life, revealing a set of shelves directly in front of us, stacked with boxes, old appliances, and not-so-gently-used toys—a fine example of the common household burial ground, where things one cannot live without go to die.

Kirsten stepped closer, batting at cobwebs as she went. I made sure I stayed right behind her, riding her wake to avoid the spiders.

"What are we looking for?" I asked when she started pushing boxes to the side and groping in the back for something.

"Rosie's mementos," she whispered as she slowly slid a shoebox out to the edge of the shelf. "I found this last year when I was helping Michael bring down the Christmas decorations. Judging by the dust that was on it then, I'd say no one had touched it in over a year."

The box was not unique in any way. I didn't even recognize the brand name of the shoes on the front. But the cardboard was thick and it was a one-piece construction with a spring-back lid, making it ideal for storing mementos. Across the top, Rosie had written in tight neat script, *Tax Receipts.*

Kirsten dusted the top and handed it to me. "Have a look. See what you think."

NINETEEN

The box was heavier than I'd expected and the tape was barely holding down the lid, as though whatever was inside was pushing its way out, trying to break free. I slit the tape with a fingernail. The lid sprang back, revealing stacks of letters bound together with elastic bands. I picked one up and tried to read the return address in the dim light. "You want me to read all these?"

"Only if you want to. They're mostly from her mother, telling Rosie why she couldn't come home. A few from her Aunt Barb and one from a guy she met at camp." She sighed when I lifted my eyes to hers. "Okay, so I read a few. How could I not? She was the one who wrote *Tax Receipts* on the top. I knew right away it was a lie. Michael has a filing cabinet for that stuff, and he's meticulous with his records. This was like a red flag saying *Open me up. See what's really here.*" She gestured to the stacks of letters. "Reading those made me so angry at that mother of hers. Thank goodness she had her Aunt Barb. She at least seemed to care."

I looked down at the box. "You got all that from these?"

"I had to open the ones that were still sealed, of course, but I figured what the heck. In for a nickel, in for a dime."

I smiled at her. "You are my kind of woman, Kirsten."

She smiled back. "I'll take that as a compliment. Anyway, the truly interesting stuff is at the bottom of the box."

"We're not worried about disturbing psychic energy, then?"

"Not here. I drew a circle in the dirt when I found the box. See? It runs all around us, keeps us safe. Whatever we do in here, stays in here."

"Kind of like going to Vegas," I said, liking her more and more.

I lifted out the letters, set them on the shelf, then turned the box upside down, emptying out ticket stubs, dried corsages, and a strip of pictures of the two of us, taken at one of those machines that gave you four for a dollar.

We were huddled together, mugging for the camera and laughing harder in each shot. As soon as I saw the strip, I remembered why. That was the day we discovered we could see Fred Skerry from the tree house, and we'd gone to the mall to celebrate. Hot dogs and orange drinks all around.

"Here's what you're looking for," Kirsten said, picking up a flat, square tin that had once held some sort of bandage. She opened it up. Inside was a small spiral notebook. "This is it," she said and held the notebook out to me.

I laid the strip of pictures back in the box and took the book from her. Turned back the cover and recognized Rosie's handwriting right away.

January 2. Blahs are setting in already. Can't wait to get away. Michael is talking about Bermuda. Pink sand. Blue water. Does it get better?

I flipped through a few more pages. January 5. Detailed plans for the trip. January 7. Shopping she did. Outfits she bought, all of which were probably still in the closets upstairs. Page after page of mundane details, nothing juicy at all. I looked over at Kirsten. "This looks like a journal, but why would she put it in this box? Why wouldn't she have kept it upstairs?"

"She probably thought no one would look in here. She started this one two months before she died, so I figure she wrote in it when she did laundry. It's the only notebook I found, but as you read on, you'll see that she makes references to things she's entered before, so she probably started a new one each year and destroyed the old one."

"Or maybe she's got other boxes down here." I glanced around. "Maybe that's why she never wanted Michael to fix up the basement. Maybe this is where all of her guilty secrets are hidden."

"Could be, but I've been through just about everything and I didn't find anything else." My eyes widened and she smiled. "That's why you need to be friends with women, so they don't go snooping around in your stuff after you're dead."

I laughed and flipped open the book again. "What exactly should I be looking at?"

"The last few entries."

I turned the pages, scanned them quickly, and stopped at the last line of the last entry.

March 3. Seeing J. tomorrow. Michael thinks I have a showing. Will tell all soon.

I read the words over again. "She was having an affair with J?"

"That's the conclusion I came to."

"Any idea who J is?"

"I'm thinking J. J. Maxwell."

"The real estate broker?"

Kirsten laughed. "No, that's J. E. Maxwell, the old man. John James is his son, but everyone calls him J. J. Blond hair, green eyes. Great body. He's not into real estate like his dad. Prefers to be outside, teaching skiing in the winter and sailing in the summer. Everyone knows Rosie took sailing lessons from him the summer before she died. After seeing her journal, it seems logical that he was her J."

I glanced down at the book in my hand. I couldn't believe my luck. I'd found Rosie's Achilles' heel. The one thing that could bring her down in Michael's eyes. An affair with J. J. the sailor man.

Kirsten started piling things back into the box. "I always thought he was such a nice guy. Clean cut, hardworking. Even came back from college to marry his childhood sweetheart. They've got two kids now, five and one, which means that two years ago his wife would have been pregnant with the youngest."

"He was sleeping with Rosie while his wife was pregnant?"

"Not such a nice guy after all, I guess."

I held up the journal. "Do you mind if I keep this?"

She hesitated a moment, then shrugged and went back to filling the box. "Sure, why not? What could it hurt?"

"Nothing at all," I said. And it could definitely help me prove to Michael that his wife was not the saint he imagined her to be.

I tucked the notebook into my back pocket. Remembering the posy still in there, I smiled and patted them both. Maybe there was something to be said for these things after all.

Kirsten closed the flaps and pulled the tape gun across the lid, sealing up what was left of Rosie's secrets before sliding the box to the back of the shelf. "Washer's done. I'll put the sheets in the dryer. They won't take long. You go on upstairs."

Eva was still smudging the shrine when I reached the second floor. While the effect on Rosie remained to be seen, the smell of burning sage grass was definitely enough to keep me out of the room. "Where's Derek?" I asked from the doorway.

"He took the truck and went out to the barn. Rice would only make the mice happy, but he wanted to make sure any shoes or boots out there were turned as well." She came into the hall with the smoldering grass. "The poor guy is really taking the state of this room badly. Like he should have known, somehow Or been paying more attention."

"He *was* paying attention, he just didn't do an inventory every time he came over, and I don't think anyone will fault him for that. But I have something that should make him feel a whole lot better." I waved away the smoke and held up the notebook. "Rosie's journal, and the last entry was written the day before she died. Judging from what I've seen in here, she was definitely having an affair, and the guy on the road was her lover."

"Her lover left her to die?"

"Looks that way." I flipped to the last page. "Right here, she wrote that she was planning to meet someone named J the next day, but had told Michael she'd be showing a house."

I went on to explain what Kirsten had said about J. J. being Rosie's sailing instructor the summer before her death, and the fact that he was married with two children, and had blond hair.

"Kirsten thinks it's likely that he's the J in the journal, which could also make him the coward in the pickup." I slapped the notebook against my hand. "This is exactly what we've been looking for. If Michael finds out Rosie was having an affair, he'll stop thinking she was some kind of saint, turn the shrine into a tool room, and our work here will be done."

I held the notebook out for Eva's inspection. She shook her head. Waved the sage grass at it instead. "I assume you're going to tell Michael about J. J. leaving her to die? See that justice is done?"

I drew the book back and waved it at the smoke. "I'd like to, but how can I when it was Rosie who told me? No, I think J. J.'s going to continue to get away with this one."

"So you're only using it to make Michael hate Rosie?"

"That's the idea, yes." I slid the notebook back into my pocket. "I thought you'd be pleased about this."

"I'd be more pleased if you showed it to Rosie and threatened to tell Michael if she didn't leave."

"Why?"

"Because she's dead. If you're not going to pursue the blond coward, what good does it do to reveal this kind of thing now?"

"It lets Michael know that his wife was a slut?"

"To what end? So he'll go out and spit on her grave? Have nothing good to say to Julie about her mother?"

"That's a bit harsh, but I do like the part about spitting on the grave. Especially after seeing that room."

"Sam, the point of all this is not to leave him with nothing. It's to make her move forward so the family can move forward as well. Ruining his memories of her isn't necessary. It's only vengeful. Is that what you're really after? Revenge?"

"Of course not," I said quickly. "I only want what's best for Michael."

"I hope so, because revealing this information to him now could turn him against you in the future. Part of him will come to hate you for destroying what he believed in, for making a lie of his whole life with her."

I shook my head. "Hating me would not be good."

"Then leave well enough alone. Threaten Rosie with the notebook and hope it's enough to send her on her way."

"And if it's not?"

"Then it's your call," Eva said, heading down the stairs with the sage grass. "I'm going to start smudging the main floor."

"Sheets will only be a little while longer," Kirsten called from the bottom of the stairs. "You have to love a front-end loader."

"I'll take your word for it," I said as Derek came into the front hall from the kitchen.

"Barn's ready for bells and salt." He looked up at me. "Tell me I didn't just say that."

I laughed. "And destroy this moment of bonding?"

"I'm going to need some serious help when this is over," he said and came up to the landing with Kirsten. "In the meantime, you might as well give me the bell and the salt. I can take care of the barn while you and Kirsten finish in the bedroom."

"That would be great." I looked around. "If I could remember what I did with the bell."

"He's here," Eva called, taking the stairs two at a time. "Michael's here."

"That can't be," Derek said. "I have his keys."

"I'm telling you, I saw him." She ran past us into the bathroom and doused the sage grass under the tap. "He must have rented a car." She picked up the cookie tin and dropped the soggy sage grass inside. "We have to get out of here. Gather everything up, but be quiet. And don't forget to close the windows."

Derek and Kirsten helped Eva close the windows while I gave the shrine a cursory once-over, checking for the bell. When I couldn't find it I gave up and went to the window, intending to close it, but discovered that it overlooked the porch. Outside, a small red car was still running. Michael was behind the wheel, checking something on his BlackBerry, and Rosie was beside him, jabbing a finger in the air and talking, talking, talking. I couldn't hear what was being said, but I had no trouble hearing the *thump, thump, thump* of a bass speaker. He must have had the radio cranked up as high as it would go. Probably trying to drown her out, make it impossible to hear his own thoughts by filling the car with noise, and that had to be driving Rosie crazy.

I smiled and leaned a shoulder against the window frame. Maybe Mary Margaret was on to something after all. Maybe the collective will of three people was already having an effect. Or it could simply be the ultimatum I'd given him. Either way, it was clear that Rosie's control was slipping away.

I ran out into the hall. "Rosie's with him. They're in the car, but he's not listening to her."

Derek came out of the guest room. "That's good news, right?"

"Hopefully," Eva said. "Did anyone find that bell?"

"Hold everything," Kirsten said and pointed a finger at me. "You can see her?" I nodded. "Then she really has been haunting Michael all this time?" I nodded again. "I knew it," she said and grabbed my arm, leading me back into the shrine and straight to the window. "Where is she now?"

"Beside him in the car."

"What's she doing?"

"Talking," I said. "As usual."

With Kirsten on my right, Derek took up a position to my left. "What's happening?"

"Nothing's changed."

They were still seated side by side, Michael playing with his BlackBerry and Rosie talking. The only difference was that Michael's lips were moving now too. He might have been using the hands-free unit to talk on the phone, but it didn't look that way. It looked more like he was singing along with the music, making doubly sure he couldn't hear her.

"We don't have time for this," Eva said as she squeezed in beside Kirsten. "Bring me up to speed quick."

I found myself smiling, feeling more and more optimistic about Rosie's fate while I briefed Eva on what Rosie was up to and then explained to everyone my theory about Michael using the music to drown out the sound of her voice inside his head.

"Do you think he's figured out that she's talking to him?" Derek asked.

"Not likely," Eva said. "He probably just thinks he's nuts. And he's looking for a cure."

"Makes sense," I said, "but where's Julie?"

"He wouldn't leave her in Toronto," Derek said. "Maybe she's sleeping in the back"

Eva screwed up her nose. "With the music that loud?"

Kirsten shrugged. "She grew up with Rosie. Whenever Michael wasn't home, you could hear the house thumping from the end of the driveway, like a heartbeat. Naturally, that girl can sleep through anything, but I don't think she's in the car. Michael probably dropped her off at a friend's down the road. I imagine she'd like that after being away for a while."

"And it gives him time to do whatever he's come to do," Eva said.

Kirsten gasped. "He's getting out of the car."

"We should go," Eva whispered, but no one moved. "Fine, we'll stay. But whatever happens, we don't interfere. We've done what we can. Whatever is going on now is between the two of them, understood?"

I knew she was talking to me, referring to the notebook in my pocket, worried about what I might do with it. Judging by the determined look on Michael's face when he climbed out of that car, I might not have to use it at all. I glanced over at her. "Understood," I said, but reserved the right to change my mind, if necessary.

The music inside the car was still playing—the unmistakable sound of Weird Al Yankovic urging us all to just *eat it, eat it, eat it* loud enough to wake the nearest neighbor had she not been standing beside me. Weird Al had been our guilty pleasure when we were dating, the CD we used to sing along to on our own road trips. The one that Rosie couldn't stand.

Michael turned to the house and spread his arms. "Hello, house," he yelled. "Hello, tree. Hello, you wonderful old swing set."

My stomach tightened. No one else knew what he was doing, but I recognized it immediately. He didn't know I was there, yet Michael was mimicking Jimmy Stewart. Reworking my favorite scene from my favorite Christmas movie. One more thing that Rosie had always hated.

"What's he doing?" Kirsten asked.

I could have told her the truth. I could have said, *Kirsten, let's be frank. You've been wasting your time, chasing cows for nothing*. But when I looked into those round brown eyes, the words wouldn't come. I couldn't bring myself to say out loud that Michael was in love with me, and we were going to be together. What was the point in breaking her heart now? Better to let Michael take care of it later.

"He's just making noise," I said.

Kirsten nodded. "Listening to his own voice instead of hers. I get it."

She seemed satisfied. She didn't ask more questions at any rate, which was a relief. But it might only have been because Michael had started River Dancing on the driveway. He wasn't doing a bad job, either, considering how long ago it was that we had seen the show together. The one Rosie refused to sit through.

"Michael, stop it," she shouted. "You're acting like a madman."

"A madman?" He laughed and dropped his head back, addressing the heavens in a loud, clear voice. "Of course I'm a madman. Who but a madman would be River Dancing in running shoes? But all that is about to change." He took a folded piece of paper from his pocket, opened it up, and waved it at the sky like a white flag. "See this? This is the answer to all my problems, the ticket to perfect sanity."

"Don't be ridiculous." Rosie tried to snatch the page out of his hand. "This is crap and you know it."

"Yes, it's crap," he told the sky. "Pop psychology psychobabble designed to make money off the vulnerable. And I am ready to believe."

Rosie folded her arms in disgust. "I thought you were smarter than this."

"I *am* smarter than this." He smiled at the page, and lowered it slowly to eye level. "Four Surefire Steps to Recovery by Dr. Bob.

Available online, twenty-four hours a day. Payable by credit card only. Don't you love technology?"

Rosie grabbed for it again. The page fluttered from his hand, but he caught it midflight and stuffed it back into his pocket. "And as Dr. Bob says, there is no more time to waste. I've been stuck in Step Three long enough. Let Step Four begin."

"What's he talking about?" Kirsten asked. "What's Step Four?"

"I have no idea," I said. "But if Rosie doesn't like Dr. Bob, then he must be okay."

He reached into the car and shut off the radio. The sudden silence unnerved me, made me shrink back from the window, as though the noise had somehow blocked us out as well, made us invisible to them, to Rosie. I held my breath but she didn't look this way, didn't look at the house at all in fact. The only things on her mind right now were Michael and that page in his pocket.

He faced the house and threw out his arms. "Let the process begin," he shouted and started up the walkway to the house.

"They're coming in," I said.

"We should have left," Eva whispered.

"Too late now," Derek said. "Just keep quiet and we'll be fine."

"What if he comes up here?" I asked.

"Then we hide."

Heavy footsteps on the stairs.

Eva tensed. Kirsten breathed slowly, self-consciously, and Derek whispered, "I still can't believe this is happening."

"Me neither." I leaned closer and put my lips to his ear. "But I can't wait for Step Four, whatever it is."

Footsteps still climbing. Michael's voice, singing another Weird Al song, and through it all, Rosie talking, talking, talking. "I can't believe you dumped your daughter like that. Poor little thing. She just wanted to come home."

"She wanted to play," Michael yelled. The footsteps reached the upstairs landing and stopped. Someone sniffed the air. "What the hell is that smell?" he asked.

"Shit," Eva muttered.

"Sage grass," Rosie said.

"Incense," Kirsten called and stepped into the hall to greet him.

The three of us left behind exchanged incredulous glances. There is a fine line between initiative and foolhardiness, and there was no way of knowing which side Kirsten was now on. Hoping for the best, we crept to the door and peered through the crack.

"The place was lousy with mosquitoes when I came over," she said. "Must have gotten into the cistern. Anyway, I hear they hate incense so I was burning some, and as you can see, it worked. But you're back early. I didn't expect you for days."

"Obviously," Rosie said.

Michael stood at the top of the stairs looking flushed, distracted, and utterly exhausted. Rosie, on the other hand, just looked pale and irritated as she strolled toward Kirsten.

"Back again, I see." She smiled and stood close enough that Kirsten shivered from the touch of that cold skin against her arm. "What are you up to this time? More salt in the doorways? A little rice in the corners? Shall I have him get the vacuum now? Save some time later."

I could tell by the way her shoulders tightened that Kirsten could sense Rosie in some way, yet she didn't back away or run for the door. In fact, she raised her chin and clenched her fists at her sides, ready for the fight. I couldn't help smiling. Kirsten Clancy was one of the tough girls. Who'd have guessed?

"Kirsten?" Michael asked, as though finally figuring out who she was. "Is something wrong with the cows?"

She laughed and walked toward him. "The cows are fine. I just thought I saw something odd and came over to check. Even brought my gun." She laughed and moved it away from the top of the stairs. "Do you need help with anything?"

"I need help all right. Just not the kind that you can give."

Rosie came up behind her and whispered in her ear, "You heard the man. Now bugger off."

Kirsten ignored her. "Do you have luggage? I could bring it up."

Rosie stepped in front of her. "I said go home, Kirsten."

Michael held up a hand. "If you really want to help, you can go over to the Bottomley's and check on Julie. We spotted little Amy in the yard when we were driving in, and Julie asked if she could stop and play for a while. I'm sure she'll be fine, but I have something I need to take care of right now, and I need to know she's okay."

Rosie threw up her hands. "You can't be serious. Julie hates Kirsten and you know it."

"No, she doesn't," he said to Kirsten. "Julie doesn't hate you. She just doesn't know you well."

Kirsten smiled. "That's certainly a relief. And of course I'll go. What are you taking care of?"

"Nothing," Rosie said.

"Step Four," Michael told her.

"Not this again." Rosie sidled up to him and cupped his cheek in her hand. "It's been a long day, sweetheart. What you really should do is go and lie down on our bed for a while. You're tired and confused right now, but if you lie down for a while, you'll be back to normal in no time at all."

Michael shook his head and backed up a step. "I don't want that to be normal," he said to Kirsten. "And I don't want to lie down."

"Then you don't have to," she said softly. "In fact, it's probably better if you don't."

"Stay out of this," Rosie warned.

"She doesn't know we're here, does she," Derek said.

"She's preoccupied," I told him. "I've seen it happen before when she was concentrating on something and completely lost track of what was going on around her."

"Thank God for that," Eva said. "Who knows what she'll do when he gets to Step Four."

"Thanks, Kirsten," Michael said and went back downstairs.

"Don't get any ideas about him," Rosie whispered to Kirsten. "He only lets you look after the cows because he thinks you are one."

Kirsten sucked in a deep breath and walked to the edge of the landing. "I'll go and see Julie now," she called after Michael.

The front door opened in reply, then closed with a solid *thud*. Rosie leaned close to her. "See what I mean? He's not interested. Go home before you get hurt."

She jostled Kirsten, but Kirsten caught herself with a hand on the railing and stepped back, away from the edge.

"See you soon," Rosie said lightly and was gone, her best cheap trick yet.

"You okay?" Eva asked when Kirsten joined us at the bedroom door.

"I'm fine, but I'm worried about Michael. He looks terrible." She turned to me. "Rosie was there, wasn't she?"

I nodded. "The whole time."

"I don't know how Mike stands it," Derek said, and the four of us went back to the window.

"Where are they now?" Eva asked.

"Rosie's sitting on the car and Michael's over by the swing set." I turned to Derek. "What's over there?"

"The woodpile. Michael must be getting logs for the woodstove."

But Michael didn't bring the logs inside. Instead, he dropped them by the fire pit, returned to the woodpile, and came back with an armload of twigs for kindling.

"He's going to build a fire," I said.

"Why?" Eva asked.

Rosie was on her feet, asking the same thing, only louder. "Why are you doing this? What are you hoping to accomplish?"

"Step Four," he said aloud. "Action."

He went to the car, took a newspaper from the front seat, and carried it back to the fire pit.

Rosie closed her eyes, drew in a long calming breath, and gave the soft approach another try. "Sweetheart, please. Think before you do something we'll all regret. Nothing good can come of this. You're just going to hurt everyone, including yourself."

"Step One," he said and knelt down by the stones. "Shock and sadness."

Rosie gave up on soft and started to pace instead. "I can't believe you're falling for this."

He crumpled sheets of newspaper and arranged them in the center of the pit. "Step Two. Emptiness and yearning."

She threw up her hands. "For God's sake, stop and think."

He mounded twigs on top of the paper. "Step Three. Immobility and decline."

She got down on her knees beside him. "Michael, listen to me. Let's pack up Julie and go somewhere. We won't tell anyone. We won't even tell ourselves. We'll just get in the car and head north the way we used to. What do you say?"

"Step Four. Action and reconstruction."

Gone was his earlier euphoria, madness, call it what you like. He was serious now, intense in a way that I had never seen. Stacking the logs, unstacking them and stacking them again, placing each one precisely and carefully. When he was satisfied, he took the folded page from his pocket once again and held it high in the air.

"To Dr. Bob," he said, and crumpled the page, then stuffed it beneath the logs with the rest of the papers.

"Who is this Dr. Bob?" Kirsten asked.

Derek shrugged. "Mike was surfing for grief counseling earlier. Dr. Bob is probaby the one who was available online, twenty-four hours a day."

"I don't care where he found him," I said. "As long as Rosie's *that* nervous, the good doctor has told him something right."

"Michael, please," Rosie said. "I'm begging you."

He drew a package of matches from his pocket. Broke one off. Struck it against the pack. Cupped the tiny flame in his hand and held it next to the crumpled newspaper. Waited while the flame caught and held.

"You can't do this," Rosie wailed.

"Yes," he said. "I can."

The paper roared and the flames rose up, devouring the twigs and licking the logs.

Michael got to his feet and walked back into the house, leaving Rosie staring at the flames.

We looked at each other. He could be heading anywhere. There was a good chance he wasn't coming up here.

Footsteps on the stairs again.

Then again, there was an even better chance that he was coming straight at us.

"Hide," Eva whispered.

"I'll try to slow him down," Kirsten said and ran out the door.

The footsteps stopped. "That certainly was quick," Kirsten said. "Would you like something before I leave? A cup of coffee? A drink? You look like you could use a drink."

"Later," he said. "Right now, I need to get by."

"But—"

"I said later."

He was coming down the hall.

"Quick," Eva whispered and opened the evening gown closet. "In here."

I was doubtful, but she shoved the gowns aside, stepped in, and held the tide back with her body. "Hurry."

I slid in beside her, Derek fit himself in beside me, and I thought we might be okay until she closed the door and the space decreased significantly. But the louvers on the doors gave us some air and a fairly good view of the room. Things could definitely have been worse.

Kirsten preceded Michael into the shrine. "It's still a little smoky in here. That incense lasts longer than I expected. You sure you don't want to go downstairs for a bit? Let it clear up in here a little more?"

"Positive." He went to the other closet and yanked open the door.

Rosie appeared in front of him, standing almost nose-to-nose, blocking the way. "If you do this, Julie will hate you forever. I guarantee it."

He hesitated long enough for me to realize I wasn't breathing. I exhaled silently. *Come on, Dr. Bob.*

"I'll take the chance," Michael said, and suddenly he was reaching past her, through her. Hauling out a cream-colored suit. A pair of black trousers. A red blouse.

Rosie stepped back and folded her arms. "That's Julie's favorite dress-up blouse."

He closed his eyes, inhaled deeply through his nose, and took out a green dress. A white shirt. A beautiful black jacket.

Rosie laughed. "You can't be serious. Do you know how much that jacket cost?"

"A fortune," Kirsten said, her eyes wide as Michael dumped the clothes on the bed.

"I told you to stay out of this," Rosie shouted and shoved Kirsten out of the way, landing her hard against the dresser.

I expected Michael to say something, to question what had just happened, to at least help her up, but he was focused solely on those clothes. Wrapping them up in the jacket and tying the bundle tightly with the sleeves, completely oblivious to what was going on around him.

Kirsten got herself up, shook her hair out of her face, and joined him by the bed. "Can I help you take anything else downstairs?"

I almost laughed. The woman had guts, you had to give her that. Kind of like Rosie with class, although wasn't that an oxymoron?

Michael looked up, clearly surprised to see her standing beside him. "Did you say something?"

Rosie laughed, but Kirsten kept on smiling. "I asked if you need help getting anything else downstairs."

Michael shook his head. "Last time I tried this I had help, and it didn't work. This time, I'm doing it alone."

"Is that Dr. Bob's advice?" Kirsten asked.

"No. That's something I realized all by myself." He threw the bundle over his shoulder like Santa's sack and faced the door. "Step Four," he said, like it was his new mantra, and started walking.

"Michael Hughes," Rosie shouted. "Those are my things. You have no right to do this."

He didn't pause and he didn't look back, just kept right on going. Into the hall, down the stairs, and out the front door. Derek grinned at me, I grinned at him, and instead of cheering we low-fived it down by our sides.

"Bastard," Rosie muttered, then sidled up beside Kirsten. "Do not be here when I get back," she said softly, and gooseflesh rose on my arms when she ran a fingertip down Kirsten's cheek.

TWENTY

As soon as Rosie was gone, I pushed open the closet door and pointed at Kirsten. "You need to get out of this house. For some reason, Rosie doesn't know we're here, but she's gunning for you."

"Let her come," she said and headed over to the window. "Julie will be fine awhile longer. I'm not going anywhere yet."

Eva pushed in front of her, blocking the way. "Don't be a fool. She's already shoved you once. Who knows what else she's capable of?"

"I'll take my chances." Kirsten walked around her and parked herself in front of the window. "I'm not leaving."

Eva turned her around, held on to her shoulders when Kirsten tried to shake her off. "Listen to me. The best thing you can do for Michael right now is go and look in on his daughter. Rosie's filling him with guilt about leaving her there, and knowing that someone he trusts is looking out for her will give him comfort. Might even make him better able to carry out Step Four, whatever it is."

I could tell Kirsten was thinking about it when her fists unclenched and her shoulders relaxed. "Will you call and tell me if anything bad happens?"

Eva recognized the window of opportunity and used it to get Kirsten moving toward the door. "I promise we'll keep you informed. But the important thing now is to keep you safe."

Kirsten dug her feet in at the door and held on to the frame with both hands. "You'll need my cell phone number."

Derek handed her a pen and a business card. "Write it down for me."

She scribbled a number on the card, handed it back, and looked over at me. "You'll watch out for Michael?"

"Count on it," I said, and gave her a thumbs-up when she finally headed out to the stairs.

With Kirsten safely on her way, Eva, Derek, and I returned to the window. The fire in the pit was burning well, white fingers of flames reaching two feet above the circle of stones. Michael had dropped the bundle of clothes beside the pit and was getting more logs from the woodpile. Rosie was standing beside the bundle, arms crossed, foot tapping, feigning indifference as she looked out over the lawn.

He came back to the fire, slid another log into the flames, and rolled the rest to one side. Kneeling down, he untied the sleeves of the jacket and folded it back. The clothes, each piece beautiful on its own, were now just a jumble of colors.

He made no effort to separate them, simply picked up the bundle and dropped it on the fire. Rosie yawned and kept looking out over the lawn, paying no attention whatsoever as the pile smoldered, creating a thick cloud of smoke that made Michael turn away and rub his eyes. I found it interesting that nothing ignited immediately, not even the delicate red silk, as though giving him time to change his mind, to rescue her things before it was too late. If it was a test, then he passed the moment the flames burst through the cloth like Dr. Bob's avenging angel, destroying everything in its path.

It wasn't until the fire settled down again that Rosie turned and looked at Michael. "Have you got it out of your system now? Do you feel better? Different somehow?"

He stared at the fire. Shook his head.

"Are you really surprised?" She looped an arm through his and leaned her head against his shoulder. "Dr. Bob doesn't know you the way I do. He's just another asshole with another theory that means nothing to you and me. What say we forget all this nonsense and go lie down?"

"I'm not done yet," he shouted, leaving Rosie behind as he went back to the house for another load.

"We can keep this up all night if you want to," she called after him. "But nothing is going to change. You know that as well as I do."

He was inside the house again, coming up the stairs.

"Positions," Eva whispered.

I hurried into the closet with her and Derek, hoping Michael didn't decide to change course and go with evening wear this time.

Fortunately, he has always been the kind who appreciates order, so I should have known he would return to the first closet before starting the second. Still, I breathed a little easier when he hauled out an armload of clothes, hangers and all this time, and threw them on the bed. I expected Rosie to make an entrance any second and launch a counterattack against both Michael and Dr. Bob, but he was back at the closet, clearing out a two-foot swath and piling it on the bed with the first bunch, and still no sign of her.

"She's not with him," I whispered.

"What do you think she's up to?" Derek asked.

"Nothing good," Eva muttered.

Michael left the clothes and pulled the plastic bag out of the wastebasket. Held it up to the vanity and started scooping in the hairbrush, the creams, the tin of mousse. He had his hand on the half bottle of *L'Air du Temps* when Rosie appeared at the window, hovering there like Dracula.

"She can't get in," I whispered.

"Who?" Derek asked.

"Rosie. She's at the window."

Funny how people will look even when they know they won't see anything.

"What do you think did it?" he asked. "Sage grass or Dr. Bob?"

"A bit of both," Eva said. "The important thing now is to keep her on that side of the window, because if she gets back in, it'll be twice as hard to get her out again."

"And she hasn't given up yet," I said, watching her tap on the glass and call to Michael.

"Michael, listen to me," she said. "Just stop for one second and look at what you have in your hand."

He stilled and looked down at the bottle in his hands.

"Do you remember when you gave that to me?"

"Our first Christmas," he said. "A special limited edition."

"You searched for it for weeks, didn't you?"

He smiled and stroked the tip of a dove's wing. "You never said anything, but I knew you wanted it."

"You're the only one who ever knew exactly what I wanted."

"You were so excited when you opened it."

"Oh shit," Eva said. "He's talking directly to her now, isn't he?" I nodded, and she pursed her lips. "That can't be good."

"Open the bottle, baby," Rosie said.

He closed his eyes, still owning himself, still in charge, and she laughed lightly. "Oh, come on. What can it hurt to open one little bottle?"

I closed my own eyes. "Don't do it, don't do it."

"Just this once, baby," Rosie said softly. "For old times' sake."

I opened one eye. Michael had put down the bag. He was holding the bottle at arm's length.

"What's he doing?" Derek asked.

"Trying not to open the perfume," I said.

"What happens if he does?"

"Then we lose," Eva said and took my hand. "Collective will. Everybody concentrate."

I took Derek's hand and shrugged when he looked dubious. "Think happy thoughts," I whispered, and couldn't help wondering what those thoughts might be when he closed his eyes too.

"Step Four," Michael said softly.

I squeezed the hands in mine and started mouthing my own mantra. *Don't open it, Don't open it. Don't goddamn open it.*

So far, he was holding on. Looking at that bottle and thinking.

"That's it, Michael," I whispered. "Put the damn thing down and walk away. Walk away."

"Baby, please," Rosie said. "Open it for me. Let me know you haven't forgotten already."

I shook my head. "Don't fall for it. Step Four. Remember Step Four."

"How can I forget you?" Michael said and drew the bottle closer. Took hold of those bloody doves. And pulled.

The stopper was out. The bottle was open, and like a genie released, the room quickly filled with the sweet scent of *L'Air du Temps.* Before I could blink, there was Rosie, standing at the foot of the bed.

"She's inside," I whispered.

"Not good," Eva said.

Derek sighed. "He never could say no to her."

Rosie moved toward him, cupped his hand in both of hers, and helped him raise the bottle to his nose. "Everything's going to be all right, baby," she whispered. "All you have to do is breathe."

Inside the closet, no one was breathing, our money still riding on Collective Will. *Hold your breath, hold your breath.*

But Derek was right. Michael couldn't say no to her. He closed his eyes again and inhaled. I felt the air leave my body in a rush. We'd never get rid of her now.

"That's it, baby," she said. "Now take those things out of the bag and let's forget all of this nonsense." Michael opened his eyes. Looked over at the bag. Started to laugh. "Step Five. Go back to Step Three."

"Don't be so hard on yourself," she cooed. "Come and lie down. Everything will be better in a little while."

Michael set the bottle and the stopper on the nightstand, then sat on the bed and pulled back the edge of the comforter.

"She's going to win," Eva whispered.

"Not bloody likely," I shouted and shoved the door open, revealing the three of us standing there like stooges.

Rosie spun around. "What the hell is this?"

Michael stood up. "Sam? I was going to call you. Derek? What are you doing here? And I don't believe we've met," he said to Eva.

Derek stepped forward, his hands raised in a gesture of surrender. "Michael, listen. I can explain."

I pushed past him. "No, he needs to see this first." I barely had the notebook out of my pocket and Rosie was in front of me, trying to snatch it out of my hand.

"Where did you get that?" she demanded.

"In the basement," I said.

Michael shook his head, confused. "You want me to see the basement?"

"No, I want you to see this."

"Sam, don't do it," Eva said.

"Do what?" Derek asked. "What is that?"

"It's nothing," Rosie said and went to stand with Michael. "Tell them to leave. They have no business here, any of them."

His shoulders slumped, as though it were becoming an effort to simply stay on his feet. "Perhaps you should leave," he said and sat on the bed. "I can't think anymore."

"You don't need to think," I said. "All you need to do is listen." I held up the notebook. "This is Rosie's journal, written in the months before she died. In here is proof that she was having an affair with J. J. Maxwell."

Michael raised his head. "John James?"

I nodded vigorously. "That's the one. The blond guy who taught her sailing."

"This is all lies," Rosie said. "She'd say anything to blacken my name. Don't pay any attention to her, Michael."

"It's the truth," I said and flipped through the pages. "Look at the handwriting. It's Rosie's. She was planning to meet him the day she died. She lied and told you she had a showing, but she was going to see J. J. She left you to be with him."

"You fucking bitch," Rosie roared and leapt at me, knocking me flat and sending the book flying. Eva caught it and stuffed it down her shirt, which must have suited Rosie just fine because she came at me again. "How dare you come into my house and say these things about me. How dare you."

"Because it's all true," I shouted. "Every word."

Derek helped me to my feet and tried to stand between Rosie and me, which was sweet but ultimately useless because she shoved an arm straight through him and punched me in the jaw. "Get out of my house."

Derek caught me before I crumpled, then helped me over to the bed. "What the hell just happened?"

That silly tinkling bell sounded in the corner. "All spirits leave this place," Eva said in a voice that God himself would envy and rang the bell again.

"Tell her to stop before I throw her out the window," Rosie said.

"Don't you lay a finger on her, you goddamn bitch," I said.

"All spirits—"

"Eva, stop." I motioned to the window. "She's going to throw you out otherwise."

Eva eyed the window, then my jaw. "I'll get some ice," she said and tossed the bell on the bed.

I waved a hand. "Don't bother. Just give me the damn book."

I thought she might challenge me at first, but something changed her mind. She fished the book out of her shirt and gave it to Derek. "Just be careful," she said and took up a position far away from the window.

"Michael," I said. "I hate to be the one to break it to you, but your wife was definitely cheating on you."

"Hate to be the one? That's good, Marcello." Rosie knelt down in front of him. "Don't listen to her, Michael. I wouldn't do that and you know it. I love you. I've always loved you."

"Oh, for God's sake." I snatched the book from Derek's hand and threw it in Michael's lap. "Page seventeen. Read it for yourself."

Rosie snapped the book up, and for everyone but me, it was gone. Sucked up into thin air, just like that. "Where'd it go?" Derek asked.

"Rosie has it," I said and shrugged when Michael looked over at me. "She's here, okay? Has been since the day she died. She's got the journal now, so you can't see it anymore. But it doesn't change what's written on the pages. I've seen them, and so have Kirsten and Eva—"

"How come I haven't seen them?" Derek asked.

"You were busy in the barn. The point is that I'm telling the truth. Rosie was having an affair. She was screwing the sailor."

"You are so dead, Marcello," Rosie whispered.

"No," I said. "You're dead. And you need to get the fuck out of everybody's life." I sat down beside Michael. "You have to listen to me. Rosie was not a saint and you know it. She wasn't even in the running. The girl was a slut from the time she turned fifteen and she didn't change for you. I just wish you could see that damn journal."

"I don't have to," he said quietly. "I know it's true."

"What?" Rosie and I asked at the same time.

"I knew she was having an affair with John James from the day it started. Before that it was Greg Robinson, and before that it was Noah McMillan, and before that it was some guy who called himself Blue. I never understand what makes people call themselves by a single name, but Rosie must have liked it because she was showing him houses within a few hours of meeting him. Usually it took a little longer than that."

"He was a musician," she said by way of explanation. "He was only in town for a few days." She hung her head "That sounds really bad, doesn't it?'

I couldn't argue with her. I couldn't say anything at all. I was too busy coming to terms with the fact that Michael not only knew about the affairs, he had names and dates to go with them. What kind of man keeps information like that to himself?

Derek must have wondered the same thing because he was still shaking his head when he sat down on the other side of his brother. "Let me make sure I have this right. You knew your wife was screwing around and you were okay with that?"

"Of course not. I hated it, but I also understood why she did it."

Rosie closed her eyes and ran her hands over her face. "Michael, I am so sorry. I had no idea you knew."

"That's all that bothers you?" I asked. "The fact that he knew?"

She grabbed my shirt and yanked me to my feet. "Stay out of this, Marcello. It's none of your business."

Derek leapt up and pulled me to him. "Leave her alone," he

said, and even though he was looking over her head instead of at her, the effect was the same. It pissed her off, which only made me like him more.

"It's none of your business either, asshole," she snarled. "Michael, tell your brother and his friends to bugger off. We need to talk."

I expected him to follow orders, to throw us out then and there, but there must have been a little of Dr. Bob's message still floating around in his head somewhere because he didn't parrot what she'd said. He merely sighed and continued to explain.

"I didn't like what she was doing, but I didn't confront her with it either because I knew that once I did, we'd be finished. She would have left or would have made me feel ridiculous if I stayed. What kind of man stays with a woman who cheats on him, over and over and over again?"

"Oh Michael, sweetheart," she started, but he wasn't listening. He was doing the talking now, something I was sure he hadn't done in a very long time.

"She would have lied to protect herself anyway," he went on, "because that was how she survived. She protected herself, and those affairs were just another way of making sure she didn't get hurt. Cheating on me before I could do it to her."

Derek sat down beside him. "But you would never cheat."

"She didn't know that. Correction, she wouldn't *allow* herself to know that. She wouldn't ever let herself believe that I genuinely loved her. That I wasn't always thinking of Sam, and that I wasn't going to leave her one day."

I looked over at Rosie. "You really were worried about me?"

"What do you think? You were the golden couple, for Chrissake. Sam and Michael, Michael and Sam." She turned to the nightstand and put the stopper back in the perfume bottle. "Like my Aunt Barb loved to say, *He's only marrying you because you tricked him.*"

"Rosie always put on a good front," Michael said. "But she

didn't like herself much. Her family made sure of that." He pushed himself to his feet. Went to the dresser and opened the plastic bag. Put back the hairbrush, the creams, the tin of mousse. "It didn't matter what I did or even what she said; in her heart she never trusted me to love her, never trusted anyone for that matter. She always figured it would only be a matter of time before I walked out, just like everyone else in her life."

He fit the empty bag back into the wastepaper basket, then picked up a sapphire-blue dress from the pile on the bed and took it back to the closet. Hung it up and ran a hand over the skirt, smoothing out the creases he'd made, the damage he'd done. "She never knew how much I needed her, never understood that I was nothing without her. It tore me apart every time she was with another man, and I kept hoping each one would be the last. That one day she'd realize she didn't have to protect herself from me. She could let go and love me, the way I loved her."

Rosie opened her mouth to speak, then closed it again. Opened it, closed it. For the first time in her existence, she had no words. Michael had rendered her speechless.

He walked back to the bed and picked up a black dress and a tweed jacket. Carried both back to the closet. "I know it sounds corny, but Rosie really was my better half. She brought fun and noise into my life, and since her death, there's been none of that. Everything is dull and colorless, and nothing matters anymore. I plant flowers I don't see, feed cows I don't care about."

"Fix fences you'd rather leave alone," I said.

"Exactly." Michael walked back to the bed, picked up a hot-pink jacket, and ran a hand over the fabric. "It's like I'm on automatic pilot, like someone is thinking for me, which is good because I can't think straight most of the time anyway. I smile and nod, and I fool most of the people most of the time, but inside I'm numb. Julie's the only reason I keep going. The only reason I don't lock myself in the barn and let the car run."

"Michael, stop it," Derek said. "That's crazy talk."

"You think I don't know that?" He carried the pink jacket to the closet, hung it up, and pushed it in next to the tweed one. "That's the reason why I go to your place, and into town. It's why I keep working, for Chrissake. No one has to tell me it's time to move forward, to get on with it. Why else would I have tried so hard to believe in *Dr. Bob and his Four Surefire Steps to Recovery*? The sad thing is, I honestly wanted it to work, but when it came down to the crunch, I couldn't get rid of her stuff. I couldn't do it because every time I close my eyes, it's like she's right there beside me, and all my best intentions come crashing down. I can't go forward because there's nothing there that I want. All I want is what I had." He shoved the pile of clothes off the bed onto the floor. "All I want is my goddamn life back."

"I want our life back too," Rosie said softly and knelt down among her things. Gathered an emerald-green shirt into her lap and straightened the collar, fastened a button that had come undone. "That's all I've wanted from the beginning. A chance to start over, to get it right this time."

Michael ran a hand over his face, then sat down beside his brother. "But I can't have what I want, can I? Rosie's dead and I'm stuck in Step Three, idling here for the rest of my life."

"Immobility and decline," Eva said from the doorway. "Messing up the life you have now because you're too busy looking back at what you've lost to notice the good things sitting right in front of you."

"That's it exactly," Michael said. "And I don't want to do that anymore."

I had only seen Rosie cry once before, the day her sister Marcie told her it would be better if she stayed away, if she didn't run home anymore because it only made the boyfriend crazy, and then she and their mom paid too. I remember Rosie cried all that night, a river of silent tears that made her Aunt Barb wring her hands and pray that Jesus would take pity on this difficult little girl. "Make her an easy child, Lord," she prayed, yet years later that was the very thing she threw in Rosie's face. Embarrassed because that difficult little girl had turned into the easiest thing in the neighborhood.

She was crying in that same way now. Silent tears falling on her pale, cold cheeks, and breaking my heart when all I wanted to do was keep on hating her.

She laid the shirt down carefully and got to her feet. Wiped her tears with the heels of her hands and went to where Michael sat. Touched his hair lightly, almost timidly, before turning to me. "You told him once that I'm here. Tell him again, and tell him to listen. I have something to say."

I took Michael's hand and waited until he looked up at me. "Remember I told you that Rosie's here? It's true, whether you believe me or not. She wants to tell you something and she needs you to listen and understand that it's her voice you're hearing."

He nodded and looked around. "Where is she?"

"I'm right here," she said and sat down on the pillows beside him. He turned toward her and she smiled. "I've always been right here."

He smiled and blinked back tears. "I love you, Rosie."

"I love you too, and this is all my fault. I was stupid and thoughtless and I did this to us because I loved you more than you can imagine, and it scared the shit out of me. There was no one I wanted to be with more, and nowhere I ever wanted to be but here in this house with you, because this is the one place in the world where everything is about you and me. Michael and Rosie, Rosie and Michael. It's always been my piece of heaven, the one place where I feel safe. But I threw it away because every time things were going fine, that stupid voice inside my head would tell me that it was all a sham. Remind me that everyone leaves. My mother, my sister, even Sam."

"I didn't leave," I said.

She rounded on me. "You fucking left. You could have gone to school in Toronto or Hamilton, even Guelph, and still lived at home, but you didn't. You went to Kingston, which is a four-hour drive on a good day. It wasn't like I had other girlfriends, Sam. You were it, my whole life. And then I didn't even have you. I was lonely, just like Michael, and how many times did you ask either one of us to come down and see you?"

"Rosie, I'm sorry," I said. "I never thought about it like that."

She sniffed back fresh tears. "I know you didn't, and that hurt too. But in the end it was the best thing you could have done. It was only because the two of us were missing you that we found each other. It's funny when you think about it."

"What's going on?" Derek whispered.

"Tell him to shut up and wait," Rosie said.

"I'll tell you later," I told him. "She's a little testy right now."

"Testy? Damn right I'm testy. I was never happier in my life than when I was married to his brother, and then I'd get these stupid notions that he was going to leave and I'd go looking for someone else to tell me I'm beautiful. To reassure myself that I wouldn't be alone when he left. I'd even think that maybe I'd leave him first if I found someone better, but they never were. They never cared how I took my coffee or what kind of perfume I used. They didn't want to know what I thought about the Middle East or the presidential race or anything else. They only wanted to fuck me, just like every other man I'd ever met, until Michael. He was the first man who ever wanted to know me. And he remembered everything about me. He made life good for me, for all of us, and that's why I'm going to make things right for him now."

"How?" I asked. "How are you going to make things right?"

She sighed and touched a hand to his cheek. "I'm going to leave him alone."

"You're leaving?" I asked, then turned to Derek and Eva. "She's leaving."

"That's great," Derek said and slapped his brother on the knee. "Michael, did you hear that?"

Michael nodded. "And it scares the hell out of me."

"No," Rosie said. "Everything will be great, you'll see. You and Julie will be better without me here poking my nose into things and acting like I own the place." When he didn't smile, she sighed and grew serious again. "Michael, it's time to move on, and there are wonderful people around to help you do it."

"I know," Michael said. "I've felt it ever since I saw Sam on Friday."

"That's not who I meant," Rosie said, but it was too late.

Michael had already turned to me, even managed a smile. "Each time I've been with you I've felt lighter than I have since the accident. I'd find myself looking at you and thinking about the future. I know we had our difficulties, and I didn't believe it when you said I wouldn't be able to call you last night, but you were right, and it shook me up, made me see that I had to do something and quick. I realize now that Dr. Bob can't help me. Only you can do that."

"Michael, hold on," Rosie said.

"Let the man talk," I said and smiled at him. "You were saying?"

"I was saying that when I'm with you, I can move forward, I can do anything. But when you're not around, I'm immobilized again, unable to dial a simple telephone number." He rose and took my hand, twined his fingers with mine. "I want a new life, Sam, but I can't do it without you. I need you beside me, the way we used to be. I can come to the pub or you can come to the farm; whatever you want is fine with me because I don't care where I work or where I live. All that matters is that I'll be with you. I need you to help me move forward, to help me let go of Rosie. What do you say? Can we give it a try?"

A try? Was he serious? Here was exactly what I'd been hoping for—the life I should have had with Michael returned to me on a platter, laid out like a Thanksgiving turkey with all the trimmings. House, child, successful business—everything Rosie had taken from me eight years ago. Looking into his handsome face with the hopeful smile and the pleading blue eyes, I remembered Mary Margaret's words. If he lets go of Rosie, he'll need something else to grab on to. He'd need me.

I wanted to return his smile. Wanted to say, *Oh yes, Michael, I'll be your rock, your lifeline, your hero. I'll be the one to save you from yourself.* But suddenly his hand felt like a dead weight on mine, holding me still and making me want to run at the same time. I felt smothered, unable to breathe under the burden of his expectations, his affection, his need to be together every waking minute. This was why I'd gone away to school, I realized. This was why I hadn't wanted him in the Dominican. He was a good man, a real catch. Just not the one for me.

I looked over at Rosie. She'd been right all along. She didn't steal him. I'd given him away. And I didn't want him back. But how could I tell him that now, when everyone was watching me, waiting for the answer that would make his world right again while utterly destroying mine.

Kirsten skidded around the corner and into the room, distracting him and giving me time to think. "It's Julie," she said. "I had to bring her home. She saw the cat again."

"That fucking bastard," Rosie said.

"Where is she?" Michael asked.

"In her room," Kirsten said.

Michael and Rosie raced past Kirsten and down the hall into Julie's room. The rest of us followed and watched from the doorway. The cat was there all right, sitting on Julie's bed, watching her cower in the corner where Derek had neatly piled the rice.

Michael sat down on the floor beside her, took her in his arms, and rocked her. "It's okay, sweetie. Just close your eyes. Don't look at it."

The girl closed her eyes tightly and buried her face in his chest. "Make it go away, Daddy. Make it go away."

Michael looked at me. "Everything's going to be fine, sweetie. You wait and see."

Eva leaned close and whispered in my ear. "He's really counting on you, isn't he?"

He winked at me.

I had to look away. "Thanks for the hot tip," I said to Eva.

"What are you going to do about it?" she asked.

"I have absolutely no idea."

"Here kitty, kitty," Rosie said. She held out a hand. "Come on kitty, kitty. I don't have a bag this time. It's okay."

The cat moved back a few steps and tried to meow, but no sound came out. Rosie sighed and dropped her hand. "Poor little bugger," she said at last. "I did this to you, didn't I?"

"Tell her the cat needs someone to take her over," Eva told me.

"Tell her I can hear her just fine," Rosie said. "And I've been told that before, but because I wasn't planning on going anywhere, I didn't figure it was up to me to help the nasty thing."

"And now?" I asked.

She shrugged a shoulder in that offhand way, trying to brush off the choice she had to make as insignificant, just part of another busy day. But the deep breath she took when she looked over at Julie told the truth. "And now I'm going," she said softly, then held out her hands to the cat. "Come on, ugly. Let's go."

The cat stood up, but it wasn't the same cat. This one was whole. Sleek and beautiful, as she must have been when she was alive.

Julie stopped crying. She scrambled out of Michael's arms and walked toward the bed.

"The cat's fine now," I said. "Just like in your pictures."

"She's perfect," Julie said, her eyes wide and her smile broad. "She's just perfect."

The cat walked to the end of the bed, and Rosie picked her up.

Julie looked up at me, then back at the bed. "It's gone. The cat's gone."

I smiled at Rosie. "And this time it really won't be back."

Julie must have believed me because she started to laugh and she hugged her dad. "It's not coming back," she said. "I know it this time." She turned to Kirsten. "The fucking thing is gone!"

"The horrible thing is gone," Kirsten corrected. "Which calls for a celebration. Who's for hot chocolate?"

"With marshmallows," Julie said, then snapped her fingers. "There's a bonfire outside! Can we roast the marshmallows?"

Kirsten shrugged. "I don't see why not, but let's clear it with your dad first." She held out a hand and helped Michael to his feet. "What do you think, Daddy? Is it too early for marshmallows?"

"It's never too early for marshmallows."

Julie whooped and raced down the stairs to the kitchen. Michael gave the three of us standing in the door a quick smile. "Anyone else up for marshmallows?"

"I'm fine, thanks," Derek said. "The question is, how are you?"

"I'm okay." Michael beamed at me. "I'll be better once Sam gives me an answer."

"What answer?" Kirsten asked. "What's going on?"

All eyes were on me again, and I knew my face was turning a bright, hot, guilty red.

"I think we've been standing around here long enough," Derek said, smoothly switching the attention back to his brother by clapping him on the shoulder. "We should get a move on, do something constructive. Do you want me to start clearing out some of Rosie's things?"

Michael nodded slowly. "That would be great, thanks."

"Do you want me to burn them?" Derek asked.

"No, take them back to the city and put them in one of those Goodwill boxes. Let someone else look like a million bucks in them. Just leave the evening gowns. Those are Julie's favorites."

"No problem," Derek said and pulled his brother into a hug. "It's good to have you back, Mike."

"I'll get some garbage bags," Eva said.

"Under the sink in the kitchen," Kirsten whispered. "I stocked him up with some extra-large ones a while back."

"Bitch," Rosie muttered, but quickly held up a hand. "Just a slipup. I'm not saying anything else. Lips are sealed. Honest."

"Daddy, come for marshmallows," Julie called up the stairs.

"I'll get her started," Kirsten said. "But hurry."

Derek and Eva went downstairs to fetch garbage bags, and Kirsten followed them down, leaving Michael and me alone in the room.

He smiled and took both my hands in his. "It's just you and me now. You can answer my question. Are you ready to give it a try?"

Rosie put the cat down and popped up between us, forcing me to step back and let go of his hands. "I'm sorry," she said. "I know I gave my word and all that, but it never counted for much anyway, and I cannot let him do this to you."

She took hold of his shirt and leaned close to his ear one more time. "Michael, you're being ridiculous. Sam is not the one. The woman you need is outside by the fire with your daughter." She frowned when he looked past me into the hall and started to shake his head. "Michael Hughes, you listen to me, because this is the last time I'm going to talk to you. The one you want is Kirsten."

Michael tipped his head to one side, confused. "But Sam's right here."

Rosie groaned and put her hands on either side of his face, looked directly into his eyes. "Sam's here now, but Kirsten will be here tomorrow and the next day and the next. Kirsten cares about you. She's the one who wants to be with you."

Michael brought his eyes back to me. "You don't want to be with me?"

I couldn't look at him. I lowered my eyes and studied the floorboards beneath my feet. "It's not that I don't care for you, Michael. I only wish I could see a way to make it work. We've both changed since we were kids. We want different things now."

"You don't want to be with me," he repeated, but this time it wasn't a question. It was the dawning of the truth.

I looked up, ready for an argument, at the very least a long and painful discussion. What I wasn't ready for was a small, rueful smile on that handsome face. Or the gentle touch of his fingers on my cheek. "When I told you earlier that I felt more with you today than I have in the past two years, I meant it. You were always so full of life, always brimming with plans and talk about where we could go and what we could do. I loved being in love with you, Sam. That holiday in Ireland still stands out as one of the best times of my life. But even then, deep inside, I knew I couldn't hold on to you. It hurt like hell to let you go once, and it hurts this time too, but you're right. We have always wanted different things, I just never admitted it."

I covered his hand with mine. "Oh, Michael."

"It's okay," he said. "It really is."

He took my hand and kissed my palm, and I knew he wasn't simply making this easy for me. He was seeing me, seeing us, as we really were for the first time.

"Even though things aren't going to work out the way I hoped they might," he said, "I can't tell you how great it has been seeing you again. And how much I appreciate everything you've done."

I threw my arms around his neck and hugged him. "It's been my pleasure." I said, kissing him on the cheek and deftly stepping back when he started to hold on a bit too long. "Kirsten's waiting. And I think you two have a lot of catching up to do."

"I guess we do, although I'm still not sure why."

"You'll get it soon enough."

Rosie smiled as he went past me and down the stairs. "Michael never really thought Kirsten was a cow. I just did my best to make him think he did." She turned to me again. "I've been a shit, haven't I?"

"For years," I said, and she laughed.

"I really have missed you, Marcello."

"I've really missed you too."

I saw Eva coming back up the stairs with Derek and a box of Kirsten's garbage bags. She gave me a thumbs-up on her way to the shrine, and Derek couldn't stop smiling.

"That man is so hot," Rosie said quietly. "Too bad he was never my type." She picked up the cat and snuggled it in her arms like a baby. "Can you believe this thing?" She stroked its ears and rubbed her chin across the top of its head. "Who knew she'd clean up this nice?" She put the cat's nose next to hers. "You ready to go?" she asked it, then laid her over her shoulder and smiled at me. "We should be on our way. You know how impatient cats get."

We went down the stairs and out to the porch. The door closed behind us and Rosie couldn't resist. She tried the handle, but couldn't get back inside. "How about that. He really is moving on."

I reached out and stroked a hand down the cat's back. "You want to hitch a ride back with us?"

"No, it's a nice night. I think I'll walk for a while."

We went down the stairs and paused on the walkway. Michael had brought the fire back to life again. He and Kirsten were relaxing in the Muskoka chairs, watching Julie roast marshmallows on a stick. She looked happy out there. In fact, they all did, and Rosie lingered a moment, her face soft, her voice a little huskier than usual when she spoke. "They'll be fine. Kirsten's strong and loving, but pushy, which is what he needs, what the business needs." She glanced over at me. "He's a good man, but hopeless when it comes to organization. He needs a woman who will keep on top of things, a woman he can count on to take care of the details, and take care of him."

"A woman like you," I said.

"Yeah." She turned back to the scene on the lawn and smiled at her daughter kneeling by the fire with Kirsten. "A woman like me."

The cat lifted her head and nudged Rosie's cheek. She noogied the top of its head, and we walked on quietly down the driveway, neither of us wanting to disturb them.

"You know it's odd," Rosie said when we reached the road. "My Aunt Barb always said I made it impossible for her to love me. I see now that I must have. She tried, but I wouldn't let her near me, I wouldn't let anyone near me. Just you, and then Michael. Even Julie I kept at a distance, can you believe that? I was so sure she'd love her dad more than me that I kept her at arm's length and guess what? She did."

"You're wrong," I said quietly. "That little girl will always love you."

Rosie grinned and held up the notebook. "And she'll only ever hear good things too."

I laughed. "Guaranteed."

We walked a little way along the dirt road and looked back at the house. With the fire burning and Julie playing on the swings, now there was nothing forbidding or lonely about the house anymore. On the contrary, it looked warm and inviting. A real family home.

"You did a good job with Julie," I said. "She's going to be all right."

"If she stops swearing."

"Kirsten will make sure of that."

"I hope so." She bent her head over the cat and closed her eyes. "I just wish I had stayed home that day. I wish I hadn't been on the goddamn road with that fucking coward. But I can't change that." She opened her eyes and glanced over at me. "J. J. was a good lover. Better than Michael, if you want the truth. But he wasn't Michael, and I got tired of him, the same way I got tired of them all. That afternoon, I told him we couldn't see each other anymore. That's why he was following me, why he kept coming up on my bumper, trying to get me to pull over, to talk to him again. But the roads were bad and I wanted to get home, which only ticked him off more. When I stopped to pick up the cat, he got out of his truck and I thought he was going to hit me. But he didn't. He just kept screaming at me, calling me a slut who wasn't worth his time."

"Why didn't he just leave you alone?"

"He said he wasn't done with me yet, and no goddamn slut was going to tell him no." She sighed and walked a few more steps along the dirt road. "When the accident happened, he was truly sorry. He even cried when he said he couldn't make the call. Told me his wife was pregnant and he couldn't be associated with this."

"He could have used your cell phone and still placed the call anonymously."

"I said he was a good lover, not bright. He panicked and left me there and I hate him for that, but I won't hurt his wife by dredging it up. I won't do that to her."

"So he gets away with it?"

She nodded. "Looks like."

Turned out I'd been right all along. She was protecting someone. Another woman.

I watched her lower her head, scratch the cat's ears again, and bury her nose in its thick, soft fur.

"No more allergies?" I asked.

She lifted her head, sniffed a little, then smiled at the cat. "How do you like that? A genuine miracle." The cat started to purr, and she laughed. "Can you hear that? This thing sounds like a bloody motorboat."

"What are you going to call it?"

"Motorboat."

"You're not serious."

"Let's try it out. Hey, Motorboat." The cat lifted her head and blinked sleepy green eyes. "See, she likes it."

We walked along the road for a few more minutes, stopped when we reached the fence that marked the boundary of the Hughes property. "I should be getting back," I said. "You sure you don't want to come back to the city with us?"

"I'm sure." She looked along the road ahead. "I'm thinking of paying a call on J. J."

"He certainly deserves it."

She grinned again. "Bet your ass." She stroked the cat's ears, then put it down on the road beside her and crouched down to pat it. "There's one more thing I need to tell you. That doughnut Michael brought for you the other night? It wasn't my idea."

I stared at her. "You mean he really did remember?"

She didn't look at me. "I don't think he ever forgot anything about you. But I couldn't let you know that, could I?"

I smiled. "I guess not."

She raised her head and smiled back. "He really did love you, Sam."

"But he loved you better."

"Damn right." She rose and squared her shoulders. "Come on, Motorboat, we're leaving. Take care of yourself, Marcello."

"You too, Rosie."

They walked off down the road, Rosie and the cat. Just as she'd said, there was no white light, no granny, and no crossing over. Just the two of them disappearing around a bend, starting off on a journey that could take them to Hong Kong, Sydney, even Venus if they felt like it, with maybe one quick stop at the home of John James Maxwell first. I was still smiling when I got back to the house.

Kirsten and Julie were both standing by the fire waving flaming marshmallows, and Michael was snapping pictures. Something new for the walls. Something fresh and good.

They didn't see me and I knew I didn't belong, so I climbed the stairs to the porch instead, reaching the door in time to see Derek coming down the stairs with two bags stuffed full of clothes. I stepped back and he came outside.

"What's up?" he said, then noticed the fireside three, set the bags down, and walked over to the stairs. "I don't understand. What's Kirsten doing with Michael?"

I leaned against the railing. "I'd say she's falling in love."

Derek shook his head. "Am I missing something? Last I heard you and Michael were making future plans."

"Michael was making plans. I was searching for an exit route."

"But I thought you wanted to be with him."

I watched Julie hug her dad's neck and couldn't help smiling. You don't have to want something to be able to appreciate its value.

I turned back to Derek. "I thought so too, but I was wrong. Michael said himself I was running away when I left for school, and he was right. Just like I wanted to run away tonight. I don't love him. I don't think I can. He's perfect for someone like Rosie or Kirsten, but he's not the kind of man I need."

"I see," he said and sat on the railing beside me, his eyes on the scene by the fire. "What kind do you need?"

"I haven't thought about it much, but I'd have to say the independent kind. The kind who doesn't need to live in my pocket and doesn't need me to live in his."

We were still avoiding eye contact, still watching the three by the fire knock back marshmallows and sing camp songs. It wasn't what I wanted at all, not now anyway. What I wanted was back in the city, and I needed a man who understood that. A man who loved the city, and pubs, and martinis. And me?

I swallowed my own fears, moistened my dry, dry lips, and decided it was time to move myself forward. Climb out on a limb and throw out a line. Not a lifeline. Just one a man could take hold of if he wanted to, and keep me from falling off that limb.

I turned my head, realized what a great profile Derek had, and took a chance. "I think I'm looking for someone who's been single for a while, but has been involved in a long-term relationship at least once so he won't be stuck in his ways. He'll know how to compromise, meet a woman halfway on things."

Derek nodded. "A guy who's handy would probably be good too. Someone who knows his way around a power tool, but is also in touch with his feelings."

I laughed. "You're catching on. But I'd have to know if that kind of guy had the same thing in mind. I'd have to know what he's thinking about right now."

He turned his head. Looked into my eyes. "Right now, I'd say he's thinking about kissing you. The same thing he's been thinking about for quite a while."

My heart started to race. "Yet he hasn't done anything about it."

"The time wasn't right."

"Is the time right now?"

"The time is perfect, but he's discovering he's nervous. And he's not usually the nervous type."

I smiled. "Maybe he just needs a little encouragement." I looped my arms around his neck and let him close the gap between us. "Do you think this will be weird for Michael?"

Derek wrapped his arms around me, drew me closer still.

"After what he's been through, I don't see how he could find anything weird. And frankly, I don't care. Like Mary Margaret said, it's time to think about what I want."

We were awkward. Both of us reaching forward, retreating, reaching forward again, reminding me more of pigeons than lovebirds. Then he laughed and I laughed and we both relaxed, and the kiss was wonderful. Memorable even. Hot and sweet at the same time. Making me rise up on my toes, for God's sake, and I can't remember the last time that happened. When he lifted his head we were both breathless and smiling and staring into each other's eyes like we'd just found a gold mine.

"This could be good," he said softly.

"Very good," I murmured and was planning to go for round two when the door opened again and Eva stepped onto the porch.

"This is the last of it," she said, dropping two more bags at the top of the stairs. "You two want to go upstairs for a while, or shall we take this home?"

Kirsten, Julie, and Michael came to the truck to say good-bye. Julie was polite but distant, which was understandable. I'd always be a reminder of the cat, and the sooner both of us were forgotten, the better. But when Kirsten put an arm around both her and Michael, Julie relaxed, and I knew she would be fine. They all would be.

I smiled and hugged Michael one last time. "It really was great to see you again."

"You too," he said softly and held me close. "You too."

"We'll always have Ireland," I whispered.

He laughed and stepped back, letting me go one more time. "You take care."

"Come by the pub next time you're in the city," I said. "All of you."

"We'll do that," Kirsten said and hugged me too.

We said our last good-byes and piled into the truck as the

afternoon slipped slowly into evening. We stopped for some of Jerry's best burgers as we passed through Huntsville. Then I told Derek I needed to drop by the Swan before going home, and I slept the rest of the way back, my head on his shoulder and Eva's on mine. When Derek woke me, it was nine fifteen P.M. The sun was setting, the white lights were twinkling in the trees, and he had his pick of the parking spots outside the Swan.

Derek helped us out of the truck, and we stood by the bike rack, stretching and waking up. Sunday night is usually quiet on the Danforth, but tomorrow morning the cars would be back, the old man at the fruit market would hose down the sidewalk, and the girls at the hardware store would load up their bargain bins for the day. Up and down the block, everything would be back to normal. Nothing new except my red front door.

"That was quite a day," Derek said, but before I could answer, that red door opened and Johnny came running out to meet us.

"What is going on?" he called. "I have been calling your cell phones all day, worried sick."

"I'll explain everything," I said.

"No time for that right now," he said. "You won't believe what's happened. I came over to drop something off, and the phone started ringing as soon as I unlocked the front door. I answered it of course, and took a lunch reservation for thirty for tomorrow afternoon."

"We're expecting a group of thirty?" I asked.

Johnny nodded. "It's some kind of meeting for some group I can't remember the name of, but the place where they usually meet had an electrical problem and can't open up, and apparently someone mentioned us as a great alternative. Then Loretta arrived, and we started arranging tables, and we can fit thirty people beautifully. Aren't you pleased?"

"We're ecstatic," Eva said, and turned to me. "Why is your grandmother here already?"

"She was dropping something off too," Johnny said. "She's inside. You can ask her about it."

"You bet I will," Eva said, and headed for the door.

"Eva," a man called. "Eva, wait."

We all turned to see Leo coming across the road, his smile broad, his steps quick and light. Eva grew still, immobilized again by this dark and handsome man who had sworn to love, honor, and not say nasty things about his wife. The same one who had spent three months with another woman, flaunting her right here on the street where Eva worked, yet assumed he could snap his fingers and have her walk back into his life as easily as he'd made her walk out. Judging by the look on her face, he might just be right.

He drew up in front of us, smiled at me, then turned to his wife. "I know it is bold of me, but I could not reach you by phone. I have told everyone you are coming back today. We have planned a party of sorts, with cake and that coffee you like so much." He offered his arm. "Shall we go?"

"Step Four," I said softly. "Remember Step Four."

Eva nodded, but looked over at the bistro, her expression soft, almost wistful. Leo saw the opening and reached for her hand, and I knew if she walked across that road, we would never get her back.

I opened my mouth, fully prepared to put my foot into it and damn the consequences, when Johnny stepped in for me. Positioned himself between her and the bistro, which wasn't the smartest place to be, but I had to give him points for bravery. And possibly the name of a good chiropractor if this didn't go well.

"I don't know anything about Step Four," Johnny said. "But I know you can't leave. Not now. Not with him, at any rate. You said yourself that he's a shit to work for. Why would you want to go back there? Why would you want to leave us?"

Eva brought her gaze back from the bistro to our Johnny and

studied him for a long, frightening moment. To his credit, he didn't waver, and didn't seem to be sweating too much either. But when Eva said, "You're right. I don't want to go anywhere," I thought the poor guy might faint on the spot. Again, he surprised me.

"Then come inside," he said softly. "We've got coffee that you sort of like. And three kinds of cake, including one of those strawberry ones with whipped cream in the middle. I know you like those."

"Who is this person?" Leo asked in that royal tone that made me want to smack him.

"This is Johnny," Eva said and smiled at the kid in a way she never had before, a way that made him blush and start to stammer before turning her attention to Leo. "He's right about you. You're a shit, and I'm not going anywhere with you."

"Eva, you're being hasty," Leo said.

"Hardly hasty, Leo. It's been twelve weeks, after all. Plenty of time for both of us to do some serious thinking." She turned back to Johnny. "Did you say something about coffee?"

He grinned and saluted her. "Coming right up."

He dashed back into the Swan and Eva turned to Leo again. "You should be going. Plenty to do at the bistro, I'm sure."

He threw up his hands and started back across the road. "I cannot believe I even entertained the idea of having you back."

"Trust me, Leo. I was not entertained." But her smile faded when he disappeared into the bistro.

"Are you okay?" I asked.

"Not yet, but I hope to be." She looked at me, her eyes threatening to tear up and make both of us awkward. "Did I do the right thing?"

"Absolutely." I smiled up at her. "Plus, you can go for half the bistro in the settlement."

She laughed and swiped at needless tears. "I knew there was a reason I like you."

"You're back," Loretta called from the doorway. "I thought you'd abandoned us for sure."

She came over to where we stood by the bicycle rack, gave me a hug, and pointed a finger at Eva. "I see that look, but don't you worry. I only came over to bring some new music. Celtic harps and other silly things. Then I saw a broken plate and figured I'd clean it up. Then there was all this yellow fruit dripping in the fridge, so I cleaned that too. And then Johnny came and he put a rose in the fridge for some reason I don't understand, and he told me about the big lunch. I asked what we could do, and he showed me your prep list. We did everything on it, just the way you like." She looked back at me and smiled. "So, you girls had some fun today? I hope so, because, *bella*, you look like crap."

"I know, and thanks for noticing." I took off the miraculous medallion she had given me on Friday and fastened it around her neck. "Thanks for the loan. She did her part."

"She always does." Loretta kissed her fingertips and touched them to the Virgin Mary, welcoming her home. "I'll see you girls inside. Lots to do before the big lunch."

"Sounds like you have another rose waiting," I said when Loretta was gone.

Eva smiled. "Sounds like. Who knows? I might even keep this one."

Loretta appeared in the doorway again. "What's going on? You want me to make up tomorrow's menu for you?"

"Definitely not," Eva said and scowled at me. "I'm telling you right now—"

"Don't worry," I said. "This is going to be okay. Even your mom said so."

"Then it's pointless to argue." She pointed to Loretta. "I'll be there in a minute. Touch nothing." Loretta nodded and wandered off. Eva reached into her purse for her phone. "Speaking of annoying women, I should call my mother. Let her know everything's okay before we get started."

She walked away with the phone, and I turned to see Derek still standing by his truck, looking tired but happy.

He gave me that smile I already liked too much. "Definitely an interesting day."

"Yup," I said, looking him up and down, pleased all over again that Amanda had been a fool.

He closed the space between us and looped his arms around my neck. "You still want a patio?"

I rested my hands on his hips and smiled up at him. "Only if you'll build it."

"That was the plan." His gaze dropped to my lips. "I'll get started in the morning."

"I was hoping you would."

"And I was hoping you'd have dinner with me tonight." He bent and kissed me, lightly, tenderly. The kind of kiss that leaves you wanting more, and soon.

Instead I sighed and gave my head a shake. "I have a lunch to plan. But we can go tomorrow night."

"Tomorrow it is." He touched his lips to mine again. And once more after that. And a third time because I was holding onto his belt and not yet ready to let go. "I'll be back in the morning," he whispered.

"I'll count on it," I said, and was still smiling when he finally walked back to his truck.

Eva stuffed the cell phone into her pocket and joined me by the bike rack. "Seems like you're already over Michael."

I waved when Derek pulled away. "I was over Michael a long time ago. It was Rosie I was still missing."

"She must have been something."

"She was indeed."

Eva nodded and motioned to the Swan. "We should get started on tomorrow's menu."

We strolled back to the pub. Me and the six-foot bald girl who spoke her mind, rode a Harley, and filled her house with dried flowers and ceramic bunnies. She looked as tired as I felt, and I'm sure the last thing she wanted to do right now was start planning a lunch for thirty. Yet here she was, on her way through my red front door, ready to work.

"This won't take long," I said. "Then you can go home and get some sleep."

She shrugged as we crossed the pub. "I'm not that tired."

Oddly, neither was I anymore.

I stopped her when we reached the swinging door. "Do you want to go see a movie when we're done? Make it a girl's night out?"

She looked down at me, that familiar scowl on her face. "You serious?"

I smiled. "Yeah, I guess I am."

Eva laughed and propelled me through the swinging door. "Good God, Marcello, I thought you'd never ask."